Praise for *The Cousins' War* series:

'Gregory creates feisty, attractive heroines . . . Fast-paced, convincing, vivid and engrossing' *Daily Express*

'A terrific story, told with Gregory's customary confidence and zest' *The Sunday Times*

'[I] became thoroughly hooked by a fascinating tale told with energy, insight and passion' Catherine Dunne, *Sunday Express*

'Riveting' *Woman*

'This is yet another fabulous book from *The Cousins' War* series, and Gregory's painstaking historical research has certainly paid off. It's a brilliant read' *Manchester Evening News*

'Of Woodville herself, Gregory makes a fascinating heroine; strong, ambitious, vengeful, beautiful and tinged with more than a hint of witchcraft. Popular history at its best' *Daily Mail*

'As with *The Other Boleyn Girl*, Gregory's clever blend of fact and fiction is a lot racier than the average historical biography . . . her tale of Elizabeth Woodville's tenacious fight for her family's position during the Wars of the Roses oozes sex appeal and suspense' *Glamour*

'Whips along with lashings of historical intrigue' *Company*

'Entrancing' *Telegraph*

'Passion, mystery and superb research make this a truly top-drawer historical novel' *Sun*

The Cousins' War

THE KINGMAKER'S DAUGHTER

PHILIPPA GREGORY

SIMON & SCHUSTER

London · New York · Sydney · Toronto · New Delhi

A CBS COMPANY

First published in Great Britain by Simon & Schuster UK Ltd, 2012
This edition published by Simon & Schuster UK Ltd, 2013
A CBS COMPANY

3 5 7 9 10 8 6 4 2

Simon & Schuster UK Ltd
1st Floor
222 Gray's Inn Road
London WC1X 8HB

Simon & Schuster Australia, Sydney
Simon & Schuster India, New Delhi

www.simonandschuster.co.uk

A CIP catalogue record for this book is available from the British Library

B Format ISBN 978-1-47116-103-2
A Format ISBN 978-0-85720-749-4
Ebook ISBN 978-0-85720-750-0

Typeset by M Rules
Printed and bound by CPI Group (UK) Ltd, Croydon, CR0 4YY

For Anthony

ANNE NEVILLE'S FAMILY TREE
in summer 1465

Richard Duke of York 1411–1460 m Cecily Neville 1415–

Richard Earl of Warwick 1428– m Anne Beauchamp 1426–

Margaret of Anjou 1429– m Henry VI 1421–

Elizabeth Woodville 1437– m Edward IV 1442–

George Duke of Clarence 1449– m Isabel 1451–

Richard (2) Duke of Gloucester 1452–

Anne 1456– m Edward (1) 1453–

My Lady Mother goes first, a great heiress in her own right, and the wife of the greatest subject in the kingdom. Isabel follows, because she is the oldest. Then me: I come last, I always come last. I can't see much as we walk into the great throne room of the Tower of London, and my mother leads my sister to curtsey to the throne and steps aside. Isabel sinks down low, as we have been taught, for a king is a king even if he is a young man put on the throne by my father. His wife will be crowned queen, whatever we may think of her. Then as I step forwards to make my curtsey I get my first good view of the woman that we have come to court to honour.

She is breathtaking: the most beautiful woman I have ever seen in my life. At once I understand why the king stopped his army at the first sight of her, and married her within weeks. She has a smile that grows slowly and then shines, like an angel's smile. I have seen statues that would look stodgy beside her, I have seen painted Madonnas whose features would be coarse beside her pale luminous loveliness. I rise up from my curtsey to stare at her as if she were an exquisite icon; I cannot look away. Under my scrutiny her face warms, she blushes, she smiles at me, and I cannot help but beam in reply. She laughs at that, as if she finds my open adoration amusing, and then I see my mother's furious glance and I scuttle to her side where my sister Isabel is scowling. 'You were staring like an idiot,' she hisses. 'Embarrassing us all. What would Father say?'

The king steps forwards and kisses my mother warmly on both cheeks. 'Have you heard from my dear friend, your lord?' he asks her.

'Working well in your service,' she says promptly, for Father is missing tonight's banquet and all the celebrations, as he is meeting with the King of France himself and the Duke of Burgundy, meeting with them as an equal, to make peace with these mighty men of Christendom now that the sleeping king has been defeated and we are the new rulers of England. My father is a great man; he is representing this new king and all of England.

The king, the new king – our king – does a funny mock-bow to Isabel and pats my cheek. He has known us since we were little girls too small to come to such banquets and he was a boy in our father's keeping. Meanwhile my mother looks about her as if we were at home in Calais Castle, seeking to find fault with something the servants have done. I know that she is longing to see anything that she can report later to my father as evidence that this most beautiful queen is unfit for her position. By the sour expression on her face I guess that she has found nothing.

Nobody likes this queen; I should not admire her. It shouldn't matter to us that she smiles warmly at Isabel and me, that she rises from her great chair to come forwards and clasp my mother's hands. We are all determined not to like her. My father had a good marriage planned for this king, a great match with a princess of France. My father worked at this, prepared the ground, drafted the marriage contract, persuaded people who hate the French that this would be a good thing for the country, would safeguard Calais, might even get Bordeaux back into our keeping, but then Edward, the new king, the heart-stoppingly handsome and glamorous new king, our darling Edward – like a younger brother to my father and a glorious uncle to us – said as simply as if he was ordering his dinner that he was married already and nothing could be done about it. Married already? Yes, and to Her.

He did very wrong to act without my father's advice; everyone knows that. It is the first time he has done so in the long triumphant campaign that took the House of York from shame, when they had to beg the forgiveness of the sleeping king and the bad queen, to victory and the throne of England. My father has been at Edward's side, advising and guiding him, dictating his every move. My father has always judged what is best for him. The king, even though he is king now, is a young man who owes my father everything. He would not have his throne if it were not for my father taking up his cause, teaching him how to lead an army, fighting his battles for him. My father risked his own life, first for Edward's father, and then for Edward himself, and then, just when the sleeping king and the bad queen had run away, and Edward was crowned king, and everything should have been wonderful forever, he went off and secretly married Her.

She is to lead us into dinner, and the ladies arrange themselves carefully behind her; there is a set order and it is extremely important that you make sure to be in the right place. I am very nearly nine years old, quite old enough to understand this, and I have been taught the orders of precedence since I was a little girl in the schoolroom. Since She is to be crowned tomorrow, she goes first. From now on she will always be first in England. She will walk in front of my mother for the rest of her life, and that's another thing that my mother doesn't much like. Next should come the king's mother but she is not here. She has declared her absolute enmity to the beautiful Elizabeth Woodville, and sworn that she will not witness the coronation of a commoner. Everyone knows of this rift in the royal family and the king's sisters fall into line without the supervision of their mother. They look quite lost without the beautiful Duchess Cecily leading the way, and the king loses his confident smile for just a moment when he sees the space where his mother should be. I don't know how he dares to go against the duchess. She is just as terrifying as my mother, she is my father's aunt, and nobody disobeys either of them. All I can think is that the king must be very much in love with the new queen to defy his mother. He must really, really love her.

The queen's mother is here though; no chance that she would miss such a moment of triumph. She steps into her place with her army of sons and daughters behind her, her handsome husband, Sir Richard Woodville, at her side. He is Baron Rivers, and everyone whispers the joke that the rivers are rising. Truly, there are an unbelievable number of them. Elizabeth is the oldest daughter and behind her mother come the seven sisters and five brothers. I stare at the handsome young man John Woodville, beside his new wife, looking like a boy escorting his grandmother. He has been bundled into marriage with the Dowager Duchess of Norfolk, my great-aunt Catherine Neville. This is an outrage; my father himself says so. My lady great-aunt Catherine is ancient, a priceless ruin, nearly seventy years old; few people have ever seen a living woman so old, and John Woodville is a young man of twenty. My mother says this is how it is going to be from now on: if you put the daughter of a woman little more than a witch on the throne of England you will see some dark doings. If you crown a gannet then she will gobble up everything.

I tear my eyes from the weary crinkled face of my great-aunt and concentrate on my own task. My job is to make sure that I stand beside Isabel, behind my mother and do not step on her train, absolutely do not step on her train. I am only eight, and I have to make sure that I do this right. Isabel, who is thirteen, sighs as she sees me look down and shuffle my feet so that my toes are under the rich brocade to make sure that there is no possibility of mistake. And then Jacquetta, the queen's mother, the mother of a gannet, peeps backwards around her own children to see that I am in the right place, that there is no mistake. She looks around as if she cares for my comfort and when she sees me, behind my mother, beside Isabel, she gives me a smile as beautiful as her daughter's, a smile just for me, and then turns back and takes the arm of her handsome husband and follows her daughter in this, the moment of her utter triumph.

When we have walked along the centre of the great hall through the hundreds of people who stand and cheer at the sight of the beautiful new queen-to-be and everyone is seated, I can look again at the adults at the high table. I am not the only one staring at the new queen. She attracts everyone's attention. She has the most beautiful slanty eyes of grey and when she smiles she looks down as if she is laughing to herself about some delicious secret. Edward the king has placed her beside him, on his right hand, and when he whispers in her ear, she leans towards him as close as if they were about to kiss. It's very shocking and wrong but when I look at the new queen's mother I see that she is smiling at her daughter, as if she is happy that they are young and in love. She doesn't seem to be ashamed of it at all.

They are a terribly handsome family. Nobody can deny that they are as beautiful as if they had the bluest blood in their veins. And so many of them! Six of the Rivers family and the two sons from the new queen's first marriage are children, and they are seated at our table as if they were young people of royal blood and had a right to be with us, the daughters of a countess. I see Isabel look sourly at the four beautiful Rivers girls from the youngest, Katherine Woodville, who is only seven years old, to the oldest at our table, Martha, who is fifteen. These girls, four of them, will have to be given husbands, dowries, fortunes, and there are not so very many husbands, dowries, fortunes to be had in England these days – not after a war between the rival houses of Lancaster and York, which has gone on now for ten years and killed so many men. These girls will be compared with us; they will be our rivals. It feels as if the court is flooded with new clear profiles, skin as bright as a new-minted coin, laughing voices and exquisite manners. It's as if we have been invaded by some beautiful tribe of young strangers, as if statues have come warmly to life and are dancing among us, like birds flown down from the sky to sing, or fish leapt from the sea. I look at my mother and see her flushed with irritation, as hot and cross as a baker's wife. Beside her, the queen glows like a playful angel, her head always tipped towards her young husband, her lips slightly parted as if she would breathe him in like cool air.

The grand dinner is an exciting time for me, for we have the king's brother George at one end of our table and his youngest brother Richard at the foot. The queen's mother, Jacquetta, gives the whole table of young people a warm smile and I guess that she planned this, thinking it would be fun for us children to be together, and an honour to have George at the head of our table. Isabel is wriggling like a sheared sheep at having two royal dukes beside her at once. She doesn't know which way to look, she is so anxious to impress. And – what is so much worse – the two oldest Rivers girls, Martha and Eleanor Woodville, outshine her without effort. They have the exquisite looks of this beautiful family and they are confident and assured and smiling. Isabel is trying too hard, and I am in my usual state of anxiety with my mother's critical gaze on me. But the Rivers girls act as if they are here to celebrate a happy event, anticipating enjoyment, not a scolding. They are girls confident of themselves and disposed for amusement. Of course the royal dukes will prefer them to us. George has known us for all his life, we are not strange beauties to him. Richard is still in my father's keeping as his ward; when we are in England he is among the half-dozen boys who live with us. Richard sees us three times a day. Of course he is bound to look at Martha Woodville who is all dressed up, new to court, and a beauty like her sister, the new queen. But it is irritating that he totally ignores me.

George at fifteen is as handsome as his older brother the king, fair-headed and tall. He says: 'This must be the first time you have dined in the Tower, Anne, isn't it?' I am thrilled and appalled that he should take notice of me, and my face burns with a blush; but I say 'yes' clearly enough.

Richard, at the other end of the table, is a year younger than Isabel, and no taller than her, but now that his brother is King of

England he seems much taller and far more handsome. He has always had the merriest smile and the kindest eyes but now, on his best behaviour at his sister-in-law's coronation dinner, he is formal and quiet. Isabel, trying to make conversation with him, turns the talk to riding horses and asks him does he remember our little pony at Middleham Castle? She smiles and asks him wasn't it funny when Pepper bolted with him and he fell off? Richard, who has always been as prickly in his pride as a game-cock, turns to Martha Woodville and says he doesn't recall. Isabel is trying to make out that we are friends, the very best of friends; but really, he was one of Father's half-dozen wards that we hunted with and ate with at dinner in the old days when we were in England and at peace. Isabel wants to persuade the Rivers girls that we are one happy family and they are unwanted intruders, but in truth, we were the Warwick girls in the care of our mother and the York boys rode out with Father.

Isabel can gurn all she wants, but I won't be made to feel awkward. We have a better right to be seated at this table than anyone else, far better than the beautiful Rivers girls. We are the richest heiresses in England, and my father commands the narrow seas between Calais and the English coast. We are of the great Neville family, guardians of the North of England; we have royal blood in our veins. My father has been a guardian to Richard, and a mentor and advisor to the king himself, and we are as good as anybody in the hall, richer than anyone in this hall, richer even than the king and a great deal better born than the new queen. I can talk as an equal to any royal duke of the House of York because without my father, their house would have lost the wars, Lancaster would still rule, and George, handsome and princely as he is, would now be brother to a nobody, and the son of a traitor.

It is a long dinner, though the queen's coronation dinner tomorrow will be even longer. Tonight they serve thirty-two courses, and the queen sends some special dishes to our table, to honour us with her attention. George stands up and bows his thanks to her, and then serves all of us from the silver dish. He sees me watching him and he gives me an extra spoonful of sauce with a wink. Now and then my mother glances over at me like a watch-tower beacon flaring out over a dark sea. Each time that I sense her hard gaze on me, I raise my head and smile at her. I am certain that she cannot fault me. I have one of the new forks in my hand and I have a napkin in my sleeve, as if I were a French lady, familiar with these new fashions. I have watered wine in the glass on my right, and I am eating as I have been taught: daintily and without haste. If George, a royal duke, chooses to single me out for his attention then I don't see why he should not, nor why anyone should be surprised by it. Certainly, it comes as no surprise to me.

I share a bed with Isabel while we are guests of the king at the Tower on the night before the queen's coronation as I do in our home at Calais, as I have done every night of my life. I am sent to bed an hour before her, though I am too excited to sleep. I say my prayers and then lie in my bed and listen to the music drifting up from the hall below. They are still dancing; the king and his wife love to dance. When he takes her hand you can see that he has to stop himself from drawing her closer. She glances down, and when she looks up he is still gazing at her with his hot look and she gives him a little smile that is full of promise.

I can't help but wonder if the old king, the sleeping king, is awake tonight, somewhere in the wild lands of the North of England. It is rather horrible to think of him, fast asleep but knowing in his very dreams that they are dancing and that a new king and queen have crowned themselves and put themselves in his place, and tomorrow a new queen will wear his wife's crown. Father says I have nothing to fear, the bad queen has run away to France and will get no help from her French friends. Father is meeting with the King of France himself to make sure that he becomes our friend and the bad queen will get no help from him.

She is our enemy, she is the enemy of the peace of England. Father will make sure that there is no home for her in France, as there is no throne for her in England. Meanwhile, the sleeping king without his wife, without his son, will be wrapped up warm in some little castle, somewhere near Scotland, dozing his life away like a bee in a curtain all winter. My father says that he will sleep and she will burn with rage until they both grow old and die, and there is nothing for me to fear at all. It was my father who bravely drove the sleeping king off the throne and put his crown on the head of King Edward, so it must be right. It was my father who faced the terror that was the bad queen, a she-wolf worse than the wolves of France, and defeated her. But I don't like to think of the old king Henry, with the moonlight shining on his closed eyelids while the men who drove him away are dancing in what was once his great hall. I don't like to think of the bad queen, far away in France, swearing that she will have revenge on us, cursing our happiness and saying that she will come back here, calling it her home.

By the time that Isabel finally comes in I am kneeling up at the narrow window to look at the moonlight shining on the river, thinking of the king dreaming in its glow. 'You should be asleep,' she says bossily.

'She can't come for us, can she?'

'The bad queen?' Isabel knows at once the horror of Queen Margaret of Anjou, who has haunted both our childhoods. 'No. She's defeated, she was utterly defeated by Father at Towton. She ran away. She can't come back.'

'You're sure?'

Isabel puts her arm around my thin shoulders. 'You know I am sure. You know we are safe. The mad king is asleep and the bad queen is defeated. This is just an excuse for you to stay awake when you should be asleep.'

Obediently, I turn around and sit up in bed, pulling the sheets up to my chin. 'I'm going to sleep. Wasn't it wonderful?'

'Not particularly.'

'Don't you think she is beautiful?'

'Who?' she says; as if she really doesn't know, as if it is not blindingly obvious who is the most beautiful woman in England tonight.

'The new queen, Queen Elizabeth.'

'Well, I don't think she's very queenly,' she says, trying to sound like our mother at her most disdainful. 'I don't know how she will manage at her coronation and at the joust and the tournament – she was just the wife of a country squire, and the daughter of a nobody. How will she ever know how to behave?'

'Why? How would you behave?' I ask, trying to prolong the conversation. Isabel always knows so much more than me, she is five years older than me, our parents' favourite, a brilliant marriage ahead of her, almost a woman while I am still nothing but a child. She even looks down on the queen!

'I would carry myself with much more dignity than her. I wouldn't whisper with the king and demean myself as she did. I wouldn't send out dishes and wave to people like she did. I wouldn't trail all my brothers and sisters into court like she did. I would be much more reserved and cold. I wouldn't smile at anyone, I wouldn't bow to anyone. I would be a true queen, a queen of ice, without family or friends.'

I am so attracted by this picture that I am halfway out of my bed again. I pull off the fur cover from our bed and hold it up to her. 'Like what? How would you be? Show me, Izzy!'

She arranges it like a cape around her shoulders, throws her head back, draws herself up to her four feet six inches and strides around the little chamber with her head very high, nodding distantly to imaginary courtiers. 'Like this,' she says. '*Comme ça*, elegant, and unfriendly.'

I jump out of bed and snatch up a shawl, throw it over my head, and follow her, mirroring her nod to right and left, looking as regal as Isabel. 'How do you do?' I say to an empty chair. I pause as if listening to a request for some favour. 'No, not at all. I won't be able to help you, I am so sorry, I have already given that post to my sister.'

'To my father, Lord Rivers,' Izzy adds.

'To my brother Anthony – he's so handsome.'

'To my brother John, and a fortune to my sisters. There is nothing left for you at all. I have a large family,' Isabel says, being the new queen in her haughty drawl. 'And they all must be accommodated. Richly accommodated.'

'All of them,' I supplement. 'Dozens of them. Did you see how many of them came into the great hall behind me? Where am I to find titles and land for all of them?'

We walk in grand circles, and pass each other as we go by, inclining our heads with magnificent indifference. 'And who are you?' I inquire coldly.

'I am the Queen of England,' Isabel says, changing the game without warning. 'I am Queen Isabel of England and France, newly married to King Edward. He fell in love with me for my beauty. He is mad for me. He has run completely mad for me and forgotten his friends and his duty. We married in secret, and now I am to be crowned queen.'

'No, no, *I* was being the Queen of England,' I say, dropping the shawl and turning on her. 'I am Queen Anne of England. I am the Queen of England. King Edward chose me.'

'He never would, you're the youngest.'

'He did! He did!' I can feel the rise of my temper, and I know that I will spoil our play but I cannot bear to give her precedence once again, even in a game in our own chamber.

'We can't both be Queen of England,' she says reasonably enough. 'You be the Queen of France, you can be the Queen of France. France is nice enough.'

'England! I am the Queen of England. I hate France!'

'Well you can't be,' she says flatly. 'I am the oldest. I chose first, I am the Queen of England and Edward is in love with me.'

I am wordless with rage at her claiming of everything, her sudden enforcing of seniority, our sudden plunge from happy play to rivalry. I stamp my foot, my face flushes with temper, and I can feel hot tears in my eyes. 'England! I am queen!'

'You always spoil everything because you are such a baby,' she declares, turning away as the door behind us opens and Margaret comes into the room and says: 'Time you were both asleep, my ladies. Gracious! What have you done to your bedspread?'

'Isabel won't let me . . .' I start. 'She is being mean . . .'

'Never mind that,' Margaret says briskly. 'Into bed. You can share whatever it is tomorrow.'

'She won't share!' I gulp down salt tears. 'She never does. We were playing but then . . .'

Isabel laughs shortly as if my grief is comical and she exchanges a look with Margaret as if to say that the baby is having a temper tantrum again. This is too much for me. I let out a wail and I throw myself face down on the bed. No-one cares for me, no-one will see that we were playing together, as equals, as sisters, until Isabel claimed something that was not hers to take. She should know that she should share. It is not right that I should come last, that I always come last. 'It's not right!' I say brokenly. 'It's not fair on me!'

Isabel turns her back to Margaret, who unlaces the fastening of her gown and holds it low so that she can step out of it, disdainfully, like the queen she was pretending to be. Margaret spreads the gown over a chair, ready for powdering and brushing tomorrow, and Isabel pulls a nightgown over her head and lets Margaret brush her hair and plait it up.

I lift my flushed face from the pillow to watch the two of them and Isabel glances across at my big tragic eyes and says shortly: 'You should be asleep anyway. You always cry when you're tired. You're such a baby. You shouldn't have been allowed to come to dinner.' She looks at Margaret, a grown woman of twenty, and says: 'Margaret, tell her.'

'Go to sleep, Lady Anne,' Margaret says gently. 'There's nothing to carry on about,' and I roll on my side and turn my face to the wall. Margaret should not speak to me like this, she is my mother's lady in waiting and our half-sister, and she should treat me more kindly. But nobody treats me with any respect, and my own sister hates me. I hear the ropes of the bed creak as Isabel gets in beside me. Nobody makes her say her prayers, though she will certainly go to hell. Margaret says: 'Goodnight, sleep well, God bless,' and then blows out the candles and goes out of the room.

We are alone together in the firelight. I feel Isabel heave the covers over to her side, and I lie still. She whispers, sharp with malice: 'You can cry all night if you want, but I shall still be Queen of England and you will not.'

'I am a Neville!' I squeak.

'Margaret is a Neville.' Isabel proves her point. 'But illegitimate, Father's acknowledged bastard. So she serves as our lady in waiting, and she will marry some respectable man while I will marry a wealthy duke at the very least. And now I come to think of it, you are probably illegitimate too, and you will have to be my lady in waiting.'

I feel a sob rising up in my throat, but I put both my hands over my mouth. I will not give her the satisfaction of hearing me cry. I will stifle my sobs. If I could stop my own breath I would; and then they would write to my father and say that I was quite cold and dead, and then she would be sorry that I was suffocated because of her unkindness, and my father – far away tonight – would blame her for the loss of his little girl that he loved above any other. At any rate, he ought to love me above any other. At any rate, I wish he did.

L'ERBER, LONDON, JULY 1465

I know that something extraordinary is going to happen for Father, back in England in our great house in London, is mustering his guard in the yard and his standard bearer and the gentlemen of his household are bringing their horses out from the stables and lining up. Our home is as grand as any royal palace; my father keeps more than three hundred men at arms in his livery and we have more servants under our command than anyone but the king. There are many who say that our men are better drilled and better disciplined than the king's own; they are certainly better fed and better equipped.

I am waiting by the door to the yard, for Father will come out this way, and perhaps he will see me and tell me what is happening. Isabel is in the upstairs room where she takes her lessons, and I am not going to go and find her. Isabel can miss all the excitement for once. I hear my father's riding boots ring on the stone stairs and I turn and sink down into my curtsey for his blessing but see, to my annoyance, that my mother is with him and her ladies behind her, and Isabel with them. She sticks out her tongue at me and grins.

'And here is my little girl. Are you waiting to see me ride out?' My father puts his hand gently on my head in blessing and then bends down to look into my face. He is as grand and as big as always; when I was a little girl I thought his chest was made of

14

metal, because I always saw him in armour. Now he smiles at me with dark brown eyes shining from beneath his brightly polished helmet, his thick brown beard neatly trimmed, like a picture of a bold soldier, a military god.

'Yes, my lord,' I say. 'Are you going away again?'

'I have great work to do today,' he says solemnly. 'Do you know what it is?'

I shake my head.

'Who is our greatest enemy?'

This is easy. 'The bad queen.'

'You are right, and I wish I had her in my power. But who is our next worst enemy, and her husband?'

'The sleeping king,' I say.

He laughs. 'Is that what you call them? The bad queen and the sleeping king? Well enough. You are a young lady of great wit.' I glance at Isabel to see how she – who calls me stupid – likes this? My father goes on: 'And who do you think has been betrayed to us, caught, just as I said he would be, and brought as a prisoner to London?'

'Is it the sleeping king?'

'It is,' he says. 'And I am riding out with my men to bring him through the streets of London to the Tower and he will stay there, our prisoner forever.'

I look up at him as he looms above me, but I dare not speak. 'What is it?'

'Can I come too?'

He laughs. 'You are as brave as a little squire, you should have been a boy. No, you can't come too. But when I have him captive in the Tower you can look through the doorway sometime and then you will see that there is nothing for you to fear from him any more. I have the king in my keeping, and without him the queen his wife can do nothing.'

'But there will be two kings in London.' Isabel comes forwards, trying to be interesting, with her intelligent face on.

He shakes his head. 'No. Just one. Just Edward. Just the king that I put on the throne. He has the true right, and anyway, we won the victory.'

'How will you bring him in?' my mother asks. 'There will be many wanting to see him go by.'

'Tied,' my father says shortly. 'Sitting on his horse but with his feet tied by the ankles under its belly. He is a criminal against the new King of England and against me. They can see him like that.'

My mother gives a little gasp at the disrespect. This makes my father laugh. 'He has been sleeping rough in the hills of the north,' he says. 'He's not going to look kingly. He has not been living like a great lord, he has been living like an outlaw. This is the end of his shame.'

'And they will see that it is you, bringing him in, as grand as a king yourself,' my mother observes.

My father laughs again, looks towards the yard where his men are as smartly dressed and as powerfully armed as a royal guard, and nods in approval at the unfurling of his standard of the bear and ragged staff. I look up at him, dazzled by his size and his aura of utter power.

'Yes, it is me that brings the King of England into prison,' he acknowledges. He taps me on the cheek, smiles at my mother, and strides out into the yard. His horse, his favourite horse called Midnight for its dark shiny flanks, is held by his groom at the mounting block. My father swings into the saddle and turns to look at his men, raising his hand to give the order to march out. Midnight paws the ground as if he is eager to go; my father has him on a tight rein and his other hand strokes his neck. 'Good boy,' he says. 'This is great work that we do today, this finishes the work that we left half-done at Towton, and that was a great day for you and me, for sure.'

And then he shouts, 'March!' and leads his men out of the yard under the stone arch and into the streets of London to ride to Islington to meet the guard that has the sleepy king under arrest, so that he will never trouble the country with his bad dreams ever again.

BARNARD CASTLE, COUNTY DURHAM, AUTUMN 1465

We are both summoned, Isabel and me, to my father's private rooms in one of our houses in the north: Barnard Castle. This is one of my favourite homes, perched on cliffs over the River Tees, and from my bedroom window I can drop a stone into the foaming water a long, long way below. It is a little high-walled castle, surrounded by a moat and beyond that a grey stone outer wall, and behind that, clustered around the wall for safety, is the little town of Barnard Castle where they fall to their knees when we ride by. Mother says that our family, the Nevilles, are like gods to the people of the North, bound to them by oaths which go back to the very beginning of time when there were devils and sea serpents, and a great worm, and we swore to protect the people from all of these and the Scots as well.

My father is here to dispense justice, and while he sits in the great hall, settling quarrels and hearing petitions, Isabel and I and my father's wards including Richard, the king's brother, are allowed to go out riding every afternoon. We go hunting for pheasant and grouse with our falcons on the great moors that stretch for miles, all the way to Scotland. Richard and the other boys have to work with their tutors every morning but they are allowed to be with us after dinner. The boys are the sons of noblemen, like Francis Lovell, some the sons of great men of the

North who are glad of a place in my father's household, some cousins and kin to us who will stay with us for a year or two to learn how to rule and how to lead. Robert Brackenbury, our neighbour, is a constant companion to Richard, like a little squire to a knight. Richard is my favourite, of course, as he is now brother to the King of England. He is no taller than Isabel but furiously brave, and secretly I admire him. He is slight and dark-haired, utterly determined to become a great knight, and he knows all the stories of Camelot and chivalry which he some-times reads to me as if they were accounts of real people.

He says to me then, so seriously that I cannot doubt him: 'Lady Anne, there is nothing more important in the world than a knight's honour. I would rather die than be dishonoured.'

He rides his moorland pony as if he were heading for a cavalry charge; he is desperate to be as big and strong as his two older brothers, desperate to be the best of my father's wards. I under-stand this, as I know what it is like to always come last in a rivalrous family. But I never say that I understand – he has a fierce touchy northern pride and he would hate for me to say that I understand him, as much as I would hate it if he sympathised with me for being younger than Isabel, for being plain where she is pretty, and for being a girl when everyone needed a son and heir. Some things are better never spoken: Richard and I know that we dream of great things, and know also that nobody must ever know that we dream of greatness.

We are with the boys in the schoolroom, listening to them taking their lessons in Greek, when Margaret comes with a mes-sage that we are to go to our father, at once. Isabel and I are alarmed. Father never sends for us.

'Not me?' Richard asks Margaret.

'Not you, Your Grace,' she replies.

Richard grins at Isabel. 'Just you then,' he says, assuming, as we do, that we have been caught doing something wrong. 'Perhaps you'll be whipped.'

Usually when we are in the North we are left alone, seeing

Father and Mother only at dinner. My father has much to do. Until a year ago he had to fight for the remaining northern castles that held out for the sleeping king. My mother comes to her northern homes determined to put right everything that has gone wrong in her absence. If my Lord Father wants to see us, then we are likely to be in trouble; but I cannot think what we have done wrong.

My father is seated before his table in his great chair, grand as a throne, when we come in. His clerk puts one paper after another in front of him and my father has a quill in his hand and marks each one W – for Warwick, the best of his many titles. Another clerk at his side leans forwards, with candle in one hand and sealing wax in another, and drips red wax in a neat puddle on the document and my father presses his ring to make a seal. It is like magic, turning his wishes into fact. We wait by the door for him to notice us and I think how wonderful it must be to be a man and put your initial on a command and know that at once, such a thing is done. I would send out commands all day just for the pleasure of it.

He looks up and sees us as the clerk takes the papers away, and Father makes a little beckoning gesture. We go forwards and curtsey as we should, while my father raises his hand in blessing, and then he pushes back his chair and calls us around the table so that we can stand before him. He puts out his hand to me and I go close and he pats my head, like he pats Midnight, his horse. This is not a particularly nice feeling for he has a heavy hand, and I am wearing a cap of stiff golden net that he crushes down with each pat, but he does not summon Isabel any closer. She has to stand rather awkwardly, looking at the two of us, so I turn to her and smile because our father's hand is on me, and it is me who is leaning against the arm of his chair as if I am comfortable to be here, rather than alarmed at these signs of his favour.

'You are good girls, keeping up with your studies?' he asks abruptly.

We both nod. Undeniably we are good girls and we study every morning with our own tutor, learning Logic on Mondays, Grammar on Tuesdays, Rhetoric on Wednesdays, French and Latin on Thursdays, and Music and Dance on Fridays. Friday is the best day of the week, of course. The boys have their tutor for Greek, and work with a weapons master as well, jousting and learning how to handle a broadsword. Richard is a good student and works hard at weapon practice. Isabel is far ahead of me in her studies, and she will only have our tutor for another year until she is fifteen. She says that girls' heads cannot take in Rhetoric and that when she is free of the schoolroom I will be left there all alone and they won't let me out until I get to the end of the book of examples. The prospect of the schoolroom without her is so dreary that I wonder if I dare mention it to my father, and ask to be released, while his hand rests so heavily on my shoulder and he seems to be feeling kindly towards me. I look into his grave face and think: better not.

'I sent for you to tell you that the queen has asked for you both to join her household,' he says.

Isabel lets out a little gasp of excitement and her round face goes pink as a ripe raspberry.

'Us?' I ask, amazed.

'It is an honour due to you because of your place in the world as my daughters; but also because she has seen your behaviour at court. She said that you, Anne, were particularly charming at her coronation.'

I hear the word 'charming', and for a moment I can think of nothing else. The Queen of England, even though she is Queen Elizabeth who was only Elizabeth Woodville, who was then little more than a nobody, thinks that I am charming. And she told my father that she thinks I am charming. I can feel myself swell with pride and I turn to my overwhelming father and give him what I hope is a charming smile.

'She thinks, rightly, that you would be an ornament to her rooms,' he says.

I fix on the word 'ornament' and wonder exactly what the queen means. Does she mean that we would decorate her rooms, making them look pretty like tapestries hung over badly washed walls? Would we have to stand very still in the same place all the time? Am I to be some kind of vase? My father laughs at my bewildered face and nods to Isabel. 'Tell your little sister what she is to do.'

'She means a maid in waiting,' she hisses at me.

'Oh.'

'What do you think?' my father asks.

He can see what Isabel thinks, since she is panting with excitement, her blue eyes sparkling. 'I should be delighted,' she says, fumbling for words. 'It is an honour. An honour I had not looked for ... I accept.'

He looks at me. 'And you, little one? My little mouse? Are you thrilled like your sister? Are you also rushing to serve the new queen? Do you want to dance around the new light?'

Something in the way that he speaks warns me that this would be the wrong answer, though I remember the queen as a dazzled acolyte might remember the sight of a feast-day icon. I can think of nothing more wonderful than to serve this beauty as her maid in waiting. And she likes me. Her mother smiled at me, she herself thought I was charming. I could burst for pride that she likes me and joy that she has singled me out. But I am cautious. 'Whatever you think best, Father,' I say. I look down at my feet, and then up into his dark eyes. 'Do we like her now?'

He laughs shortly. 'God save us! What gossip have you been hearing? Of course we love and honour her; she is our queen, the wife of our king. She is his first choice of all the princesses in the world. Just imagine! Of all the high-born ladies in Christendom that he could have married – and yet he chose her.' There is something hard and mocking about his tone. I hear the loyal words that he speaks; but I hear something behind them: a note like Isabel's when she is bullying me. 'You are a silly child to ask,' he says. 'We have all sworn fealty to her. You yourself swore fealty at her coronation.'

Isabel nods at me, as if to confirm my father's condemnation. 'She's too young to understand,' she assures him over my head. 'She understands nothing.'

My quick temper flares up. 'I understand that the king didn't do what my father advised! When Father had put him on the throne! When Father could have died fighting the bad queen and the sleeping king for Edward!'

This makes him laugh again. 'Out of the mouths of babes indeed!' Then he shrugs. 'Anyway, you're not going. Neither of you will go to court to serve under this queen. You are going with your mother to Warwick Castle, and you can learn all you need to know about running a great palace from her. I don't think Her Grace the queen can teach you anything that your mother has not known from childhood. We were royal kinsmen when this queen was picking apples in the orchard of Groby Hall. Your mother was born a Beauchamp, she married into the Nevilles, so I doubt that she has much to learn about being a great lady of England – certainly not from Elizabeth Woodville,' he adds quietly.

'But Father—' Isabel is so distressed that she cannot stop herself speaking out. 'Should we not serve the queen if she has asked for us? Or at any rate shouldn't I go? Anne is too young, but shouldn't I go to court?'

He looks at her as if he despises her longing to be in the centre of things, at the court of the queen, at the heart of the kingdom, seeing the king every day, living in the royal palaces, beautifully dressed, in a court newly come to power, the rooms filled with music, the walls bright with tapestries, the court at play, celebrating their triumph.

'Anne may be young, but she judges better than you,' he says coldly. 'Do you question me?'

She drops into a curtsey and lowers her head. 'No, my lord. Never. Of course not.'

'You can go,' he says, as if he is tired of both of us. We scurry from the room like mice that have felt the breath of a cat on their little furry backs. When we are safely outside in his presence chamber and the door is shut behind us I nod to Isabel and say: 'There! I was right. We don't like the queen.'

We don't like the queen. In the early years of her marriage she encourages her husband the king to turn against my father: his earliest and best friend, the man who made him king and gave him a kingdom. They take the great seal of estate from my uncle George, and dismiss him from his great office of Lord Chancellor, they send my father as an envoy to France and then play him false by making a private treaty with the rival Burgundy behind his back. My father is furious with the king and blames the queen and her family for advising him against his true interests but in favour of her Burgundy kinsman. Worst of all, King Edward sends his sister Margaret to marry the Duke of Burgundy. All my father's work with the great power of France is spoiled by this sudden friendliness with the enemy. Edward will make an enemy of France and all my father's work in making friends with them will be for nothing.

And the weddings that the queen forges to bring her family into greatness! The moment she is crowned she captures almost every well-born wealthy young man in England for her hundreds of sisters. Young Henry Stafford the Duke of Buckingham, who my parents had picked out for me, she bundles into marriage with her sister Katherine – the little girl who sat on our table at the coronation dinner. The child born and raised in a country house at Grafton becomes a duchess. Though the two of them are no older than me, the queen marries them to each other anyway, and brings them up in her household, as her wards, guarding the Stafford fortune for her own profit. My mother says that the Staffords, who are as proud as anyone in England, will never forgive her for this, and neither will we. Little Henry looks as sick as if someone had poisoned him. He can trace his parentage back to the Kings of England and he is married to little Katherine Woodville and has a man who was nothing more than a squire as his father-in-law.

Her brothers she marries off to anyone with a fortune or a title. Her handsome brother Anthony gets a wife whose title makes him Baron Scales; but the queen makes no proposal for us. It is as if the moment that Father said that we would not go to her court we ceased to exist for her. She makes no offer for either Isabel or me. My mother remarks to my father that we would never have stooped to one of the Rivers – however high they might try to fling themselves upwards – but it means that I have no marriage arranged for me though I will be twelve in June, and it is even worse for Isabel, stuck in my mother's train as her maid in waiting, and no husband in sight though she is sixteen. Since my mother was betrothed when she was just out of the cradle, and was wedded and bedded by the age of fourteen, Isabel feels more and more impatient, more and more as if she will be left behind in this race to the altar. We seem to have disappeared, like girls under a spell in a fairytale, while Queen Elizabeth marries all her sisters and her cousins to every wealthy young nobleman in England.

'Perhaps you'll marry a foreign prince,' I say, trying to console Isabel. 'When we go back home to Calais, Father will find you a prince of France. They must be planning something like that for us.'

We are in the ladies' chamber at Warwick Castle, supposed to be drawing. Isabel has a fine sketch of the landscape from the window before her and I have a scrawl which is supposed to be a bunch of primroses, newly picked from the banks of the Avon, beside Richard's lute.

'You're such a fool,' she says crushingly. 'What good would a prince of France do us? We need a connection to the throne of England. There's the new king on the throne, there's his wife who gives him nothing but girls. We need to be in the line of succession. We need to get closer. You are as stupid as a goose girl.'

I don't even flare up at the insult. 'Why do we need a connection to the throne of England?'

'Our father did not put the York house on the throne of England to oblige *them*,' she explains. 'Our father put the Yorks on the throne so that he might command them. Father was going to rule England from behind the York throne. Edward was like a younger brother to him, Father was going to be his master. Everyone knows that.'

Not me. I had thought that my father had fought for the Yorks because they were the rightful heirs, because the queen Margaret of Anjou was a bad woman and because the king had fallen asleep.

'But now that King Edward is advised by no-one but his wife and her family then we will have to join that family circle to rule him,' she says. 'You and I will marry his brothers the royal dukes, if Mother can possibly get them for us.'

I feel myself flush. 'You mean that I would marry Richard?'

'You can't like him!' She bursts into laughter. 'He's so dark-haired and olive-skinned and awkward . . .'

'He's strong,' I say at random. 'He can ride anything. And he's brave, and . . .'

'If you want a horseman for a husband why not marry John the groom?'

'But are you sure they are going to arrange it? When will we marry?'

'Father is determined on it,' she says, dropping her voice to a whisper. 'But She is certain to try to stop it. She won't want the king's brothers married to anyone but her family and friends. She won't want us all at court, showing her up, showing everyone how a truly great English family behaves. She spends all her time trying to take the king away from Father because she knows Father tells him the truth and gives him good advice, because she knows Father advises the king against her.'

'Has Father asked the king for permission? For us to marry?'

'He's going to do it while he is at court,' she says. 'He could be asking him now: today, right this moment. And then we two will be betrothed – both of us – and to the brothers of the King of England. We will be royal duchesses. We will outrank the queen's mother, Jacquetta, we will outrank the king's mother, Duchess Cecily. We will be the first ladies of England after the queen herself.'

I gape at her.

'Who else should we be?' she demands. 'When you think who our father is? Of course we should be the first ladies of England.'

'And if King Edward has no son,' I say slowly, thinking aloud, 'then his brother George will be king when he dies.'

Isabel hugs me in her delight. 'Yes! Exactly! George Duke of Clarence.' She is laughing with joy. 'He will be King of England and I will be queen.'

I pause, quite awestruck at the thought of my sister becoming queen. 'Queen Isabel,' I say.

She nods. 'I've always thought it sounded well.'

'Izzy, you will be so grand!'

'I know,' she says. 'And you will be a duchess beside me always. You will be the first lady of my household. We shall have such clothes!'

'But if you live a long time, and have no sons either, and then George dies, then Richard will be the next heir and the next queen will be me: Queen Anne.'

At once her smile fades. 'No, that's not very likely at all.'

My father comes back from the court in stony silence. Dinner is served in the great hall of Warwick Castle, where hundreds of our men sit down to eat. The hall buzzes with the clatter of plates and the clash of mugs and the scrape of knife on trencher, but at the top table where my father sits and glowers, we eat in total silence. My mother sits on his right-hand side, her eyes on the table of the ladies in waiting, alert to any misbehaviour. Richard sits on his left, watchful and quiet. Isabel sits next to my mother, frightened into silence, and I come last as usual. I don't know what has happened. I have to find someone to tell me.

I get hold of our half-sister Margaret. She may be Father's bastard but he has recognised her from her birth and Mother paid for her upbringing and keeps her among her ladies in waiting, a trusted confidante. She is now married to one of Father's tenants, Sir Richard Huddlestone, and though she is a grown woman of twenty-three and always knows everything, she – unlike everyone else – will tell me.

'Margaret, what's happening?'

'The king refused our father,' she says grimly, as I catch her in our bedroom, watching the maid sliding a warming pan in the cold bed, and the groom of the bedchamber thrusting a sword between the mattresses for our safety. 'Shame on him. He has forgotten all that he owes, he has forgotten where he has come from and who helped him to the throne. They say that the king told your father to his face that he would never allow his brothers to marry the two of you.'

'For what reason? Father will be so angry.'

'He said he wanted other matches for them, alliances perhaps in France or the Low Countries, Flanders again, or Germany. Who knows? He wants princesses for them. But the queen will be looking out for her kinswomen in Burgundy, no doubt she will have some suggestions, and your father feels himself to be insulted.'

'We are insulted,' I assert. Then I am uncertain: 'Aren't we?'

Emphatically she nods, waving the servants from the room. 'We are. They won't find two more beautiful girls for the royal dukes, not if they go to Jerusalem itself. The king, God bless him, is ill-advised. Ill-advised to look elsewhere than the Neville girls. Ill-advised to slight your father who put him where he is today.'

'Who tells him to look elsewhere?' I ask, though I know the answer. 'Who advises him ill?'

She turns her head and spits in the fire. 'She does,' she replies. We all know who 'She' is.

When I go back to the hall I see Richard, the king's brother, in close conversation with his tutor, and I guess he is asking him for the news, just as I spoke to Margaret. He glances over to me and I am certain that they are speaking of me and that his tutor has told him that we will not be betrothed, that the queen, though she herself married the man of her choice, will make loveless matches for the rest of us. For Richard there will be a princess or a foreign duchess. I see with a little surge of irrita-tion that he does not look in the least upset. He looks as if he does not mind at all that he will not be commanded to marry a short, brown-haired, fair-skinned thin girl who has neither height nor blonde hair and no sign whatsoever of breasts, being persistently as lean as a lathe. I toss my head as if I don't care either. I would not have married him, even if they had all begged me. And if I suddenly grow into beauty, he will be sorry that he lost me.

'Have you heard?' he asks, walking over to me with his diffi-dent smile. 'My brother the king has said that we are not to marry. He has other plans for me.'

'I never wanted to marry you,' I say, instantly offended. 'So don't think that I did.'

'Your father proposed it himself,' he replies.

'Well, the king will have someone in mind for you,' I say crossly. 'One of the queen's sisters, without a doubt. Or one of her cousins, or perhaps a great-aunt, some old lady with a hook nose and no teeth. She married her little brother John to my great-aunt, you take care she doesn't match you with some noble old crone. They called it the diabolical match – you'll probably have one too.'

He shakes his head. 'My brother will have a princess picked out for me,' he says confidently. 'He is a good brother to me, and he knows I am loyal heart and soul to him. Besides, I am of an age to marry and you are still only a little girl.'

'I am eleven,' I say with dignity. 'But you York boys all think you're so wonderful. You think you were born grown-up, and high as lords. You'd better remember that you would be nowhere without my father.'

'I do remember it,' he says. He puts his hand on his heart as if he was a knight in a fairytale and he does an odd little bow to me as if I was a grown-up lady. 'And I am sorry that we won't be married, little Anne, I am sure you would have made an excellent duchess. I hope you get a great prince, or some king from somewhere.'

'All right,' I say, suddenly awkward. 'I hope you don't get an old lady then.'

That night Isabel comes to bed shaking with excitement. She kneels to pray at the foot of the bed and I hear her whisper: 'Let it be, lord. Oh lord, let it happen.' I wait in silence as she sheds her gown and creeps under the sheets and lies first one way, and then another, too restless to sleep.

'What's happening?' I whisper.

'I'm going to marry him.'

'No!'

'Yes. My Lord Father told me. We are to go to Calais and the duke will join us secretly there.'

'The king has changed his mind?'

'The king won't even know.'

I gasp. 'You'll never marry the king's brother without his permission?'

She gives a little gasping giggle and we lie silent.

'I shall have such gowns,' she says. 'And furs. And jewels.'

'And does Richard come too?' I ask in a very small voice. 'Because he thinks he is to marry someone else.'

In the darkness, she puts her arm around my shoulder and draws me to her. 'No,' she says. 'He's not coming. They will find someone else for you. But not Richard.'

'It's not that I like him especially . . .'

'I know. It is that you expected to marry him. It's my fault, I put the idea in your head. I shouldn't have told you.'

'And since you are to marry George . . .'

'I know,' she says kindly. 'We should have been married together to the brothers. But I shan't leave you. I'll ask Father if you can come and live with us when I am a duchess and living at court. You can be my maid in waiting.'

'It's just that I rather wanted to be a duchess myself.'

'Yes; but you can't,' she says.

CALAIS CASTLE, 11 JULY 1469

Isabel wears a gown of brilliant white silk with cloth-of-gold sleeves. I walk behind her carrying her ermine cloak, wearing white and silver. She has a high headdress draped with a white veil of priceless lace that makes her look six feet tall, a goddess, a giantess. George, the bridegroom, is in deep purple velvet, the colour of emperors. Almost everyone from the English court is here. If the king did not know of the secret wedding he will have realised it when he woke this morning to find half his court is missing. His own mother, Duchess Cecily, waved off the wedding party from Sandwich, blessing the plans of her best-loved son George over the plans of her disobedient son Edward.

Richard was left behind with his tutor and friends at Warwick Castle; Father didn't tell him where we were going, he didn't even know we were coming here to celebrate a grand wedding. I wonder if he is sorry that he has been left out. I hope very much that he thinks he has missed a great chance and been played as a fool. Isabel may be the oldest Neville girl, and the most beautiful, she may be the one that everyone says is so graceful and well-bred – but I have an inheritance as great as Isabel's and I may very well grow into looks. Then Richard will have missed a beautiful wealthy wife and some shabby Spanish princess will not be half such a treasure as I might have been. I think with some pleasure of him being filled with regret when I grow rounded and curvy and my hair goes fair like the queen's, and I get a secret smile like hers and he sees me married to a wealthy prince, dripping in furs, and he knows that I am lost to him, just like Guinevere.

This is not just a wedding; it is a celebration of my father's power. Nobody seeing the court assembled here at my father's invitation, bowing as low to him as if he were a king when he walks through the beautiful galleries of Calais Castle, set in the fortress town that he has held for England for years, can doubt for a moment that here is a power equal to the King of England, perhaps even greater than the King of England. If Edward chooses to ignore my father's advice he can consider that there are many who think that my father is the better man; certainly he is a richer man with a bigger army. And now here is the king's brother, forbidden to marry, but freely taking my sister's hand in his own, smiling at her with his blond easy charm, and pledging himself.

The wedding feast goes on for all the afternoon, long into the night: dish after dish comes from the kitchen trumpeted by our musicians, meats and fruits, breads and sweetmeats, thick English puddings and French delicacies. It makes the queen's coronation feast seem like nothing. Father has outdone the King of England in a great demonstration of his wealth and power. This is a rival court that outshines Edward and his commoner wife. My father is as grand as the wealthy Duke of Burgundy, grander than the French king. Isabel sits in state in the middle of the top table and waves dish after dish down the hall to the tables that must be honoured. George, handsome as a prince, puts little cuts of meat on Isabel's plate, leans towards her, whispers in her ear, and smiles over at me, as if he would have me in his keeping too. I cannot help but smile back: there is something thrilling about George in his wedding suit, as handsome and as confident as a king himself.

'Don't fear, little one, there will be a grand wedding for you too,' my father whispers to me as he walks behind my table where I am seated at the head of the ladies in waiting.

'I thought—'

'I know you did,' he says, cutting me short. 'But Richard is heart and soul for his brother the king, he would never do anything against Edward. I could not even ask him. But George here,' he glances back at the top table where George is helping himself to another goblet of malmsey wine, 'George loves himself before any other, George will take the best route for George, and besides, I have great plans for him.'

I wait in case he will say more, but instead he gently pats my shoulder. 'You will have to take your sister to her bedroom and get her ready,' he says. 'Your mother will give you the word.'

I look up at my mother who is eyeing the hall, judging the servants, watching the guests. She nods at me and I rise to my feet, and Isabel suddenly pales as she realises that the wedding feast is over and the bedding must start.

There is a noisy and joyful parade that takes George to my sister's new big bedroom; the respect for my mother prevents it being too bawdy, but the men of the garrison bellow their encouragement and all the wedding guests throw flowers under her feet and call out blessings. My sister and her new husband are put to bed by an archbishop, twenty maids in waiting and five knights of the garter, in a cloud of incense wafted by half a dozen priests, to the stentorian bellow of my father's shouted good wishes. My mother and I are the last to leave the room, and as I glance back Izzy is sitting up in bed, looking very pale as if she is afraid. George leans back on the pillows beside her, naked to the waist, his blond hair glinting on his chest, his broad smile very confident.

I hesitate. This will be the first night in all our lives that we have slept apart. I don't think I want to sleep alone, I don't think I can sleep without my sister's peaceful warmth in my bed, and I doubt that Izzy wants George, so loud, so blond, so drunk, as a bed-mate. Izzy looks at me as if she would say something. My mother, sensing the bond between us, puts a hand on my shoulder and starts to lead me from the room.

'Annie, don't go,' Izzy says quietly. I turn back and see that she is shaking with fear. She stretches out a hand to me as if she would keep me with her, for just a moment longer. 'Annie!' she whispers. I can't resist the alarm in her voice. I turn to go back into the room as my mother takes me firmly by the arm, and closes the bedroom door behind us.

That night I sleep alone, refusing the company of one of the maids; if I cannot be with my sister then I don't want any bed-fellow at all. I lie in the cold sheets and there is no-one to exchange a whispered account of the day, no-one to tease, no-one to torment me. Even when we fought like cats in a basket, there was always the comfort of having Izzy there to fight with. Like the very walls of Calais Castle she is part of the scenery of my life. I was born and bred to be secondary to her: the beauty of the family. I have always followed behind an ambitious, deter-mined, vocal older sister. Now suddenly I am alone. I lie awake for a long time, staring into the darkness, wondering what my life will be, now I no longer have an older sister to tell me what to do. I think that in the morning everything will be utterly different.

CALAIS CASTLE, 12 JULY 1469

In the morning things are even more different than I had dreamed in my solitary night. The whole place is wide-awake at dawn. The rumble of cartwheels from the kitchen yard to the quayside, the shouting from the armoury, and the scramble and haste in the basin of the port show that far from celebrating a wedding, Father is preparing to go to sea.

'Is it pirates?' I ask my tutor, catching his hand as he goes past me with a writing desk towards my father's rooms. 'Please, sir, is it a raid of pirates?'

'No,' he says, his face pale and frightened. 'Worse. Go to your mother, Lady Anne. I cannot stop and talk now. I have to go to your father and take down his orders.'

Worse than pirates must mean that the French are about to attack. If so, then we are at war and half the English court has been caught in a castle under siege. This is the worst thing that has ever happened. I go to my mother's rooms at the run but find everything unnaturally quiet. Mother is seated beside Isabel. Isabel is in her new gown but there is no excited chatter of bridal joy. Isabel looks furious, the women, sewing shirts in a circle, are silent with a sort of feverish anticipation. I curtsey low to my mother: 'Please, Lady Mother,' I say. 'What's happening?'

'You may tell her,' my mother says coolly to Isabel, and I scurry to my sister and pull up a stool beside her chair.

'Are you all right?' I mutter.

'Yes,' she replies. 'It wasn't too bad.'

'Did it hurt?'

She nods. 'Horrible. And disgusting. First horrible, then disgusting.'

'What's happening?'

'Father's making war on the king.'

'No!' I speak too loudly and my mother shoots a sharp look at me. I clap my hand over my mouth and I know that over the top of my gagging palm my eyes are huge with shock. 'Isabel – no!'

'It was planned,' she whispers fiercely. 'Planned all along, and I was part of it. He said he had a great plan. I thought he meant my wedding. I didn't know it was this.'

I roll my eyes towards the stony face of my mother who simply glares at me as if my sister is married to a treasonous royal every day of the week and it is vulgar of me to show any surprise.

'Did our Lady Mother know?' I whisper. 'When did she find out?'

'She knew all along,' Isabel says bitterly. 'They all knew. Everyone knew but us.'

I am stunned into silence. I look around the ladies of my mother's chamber, who are all stitching shirts for the poor as if this were an ordinary day, as if we were not going to war with the very King of England that we put on the throne only eight years ago.

'He's arming the fleet. They're sailing at once.'

I give a little whimper of shock and bite my palm to silence myself.

'Oh come on, we can't talk here,' Isabel says, jumping to her feet and bobbing a curtsey to our mother. Isabel drags me into an anteroom and up the winding stone stairs to the leads of the castle where we can look down at the frantic hurry on the quayside as the ships are loaded with weapons and the men carry their armour and tug their horses on board. I can see Midnight, my father's great black horse, with a hood over his head so that he will walk up the gangplank. He goes with a great bound, frightened of the echo of the wood under his metal-shod hooves. If Midnight is anxious then I know there is danger.

'He's really doing it,' I say disbelievingly. 'He's really setting sail for England. But what about the king's mother? Duchess Cecily? She knew. She saw us all leave from Sandwich. Won't she warn her son?'

'She knows,' Isabel says grimly. 'She has known for ages. I should think just about everyone knows but the king . . . and me and you. Duchess Cecily has hated the queen from the moment they first told her that Edward was married in secret. Now she turns against queen and king together. They have had it planned for months. Father's been paying men to rise up against the king in the North and the Midlands. My wedding was their signal to rise. Think of it – he told them the very day that I was going to take my vows, so they could rise at the right time. Now they are up, looking like a rebellion of their own making. They've fooled the king into thinking it is a local grievance – he is marching north out of London to settle what he thinks is a small uprising. He will be away from London when Father lands. He doesn't know that my wedding was not a wedding but a muster. He doesn't know that the wedding guests are sailing to march against him. Father has thrown my bridal veil over an invasion.'

'The king? King Edward?' I say stupidly, as if our old enemy the sleeping King Henry might have woken and risen up from his bed in the Tower.

'Of course King Edward.'

'But Father loves him.'

'Loved,' Isabel corrects me. 'George told me this morning. It's all changed. Father can't forgive the king for favouring the Rivers. Nobody can earn a penny, nobody can get a yard of land, everything that can be taken, they have taken, and everything that is decided in England is done by them. Especially Her.'

'She's queen . . .' I say tentatively. 'She's a most wonderful queen . . .'

'She has no right to everything,' Isabel says.

'But to challenge the king?' I lower my voice. 'Isn't that treason?'

'Father won't challenge the king directly. He'll demand that he surrenders his bad advisors – he means Her family, the Rivers family. He will demand that the king restore the councillors who have guided him wisely – that's us. He'll get the chancellorship back for our uncle George Neville. He'll make the king consult him on everything, Father will decide on foreign alliances again. We'll get it all back again, we'll be where we were before, the advisors and the rulers behind the king. But one thing I don't know . . .' Her voice quavers in the middle of these firm predictions, as if she has suddenly lost her nerve: 'One thing I really don't know . . .' She takes a breath. 'I don't know . . .'

I watch as they swing a great cannon on a sling and lower it into the hold of a ship. 'What? What don't you know?'

Her face is aghast, like when we left her in her marriage bed last night, and she whispered: 'Annie, don't go.'

'What if it's a trick?' she asks in a voice so quiet that I have to put my head against hers to hear her. 'What if it is a trick like they played on the sleeping king and the bad queen? You're too young to remember but King Edward's father and our father never challenged the sleeping king. They were never open rebels against him. They always said only that he should be better advised. And they led out the armies of England against him, always saying that he should be better advised. It's what Father always says.'

'And when they beat him in battle . . .'

'Then they put him in the Tower and said that they would hold him forever,' she finishes. 'They took his crown from him although they always said they just wanted to help him rule. What if Father and George are planning to do that to King Edward? Just as Father and Edward did it to the sleeping king? What if Father has turned traitor to Edward and is going to put him in the Tower along with Henry?'

I think of the beautiful queen, so confident and smiling at her coronation feast, and imagine her imprisoned in the Tower instead of being the mistress of it, and dancing till dawn. 'He can't do that, they swore fealty,' I say numbly. 'We all did. We all said that Edward was the true king, the anointed king. We all kissed the queen's hand. We said King Edward had a better claim to the throne than the sleeping king. We said he was the flower of York, and we would all walk in the sweet garden of England. And we danced at her coronation when she looked so beautiful and they were so happy. Edward is the King of England: there can't be another. She's queen.'

Isabel shakes her head impatiently. 'You think everything is so easy! You think everything is straightforward like that? We swore fealty when Father thought that he would rule through King Edward. What if he now thinks he will rule through George? Through George and me?'

'He will put you on the throne of England?' I say incredulously. 'You're going to wear Her crown? You're going to take Her place? Not waiting for Edward to die? Just taking everything?'

She does not look excited as she did when we used to play at queens. She looks aghast. She looks afraid. 'Yes.'

CALAIS CASTLE, SUMMER 1469

Isabel's new husband George, my father, and all the men that assembled as wedding guests, turn out to be a recruited force, sworn to loyalty to each other, ready to invade England, and they set sail, land in Kent, and march on the Midlands. Men pour out of the cities to join them, throw down their spades in the fields and run after Father's army. He is still remembered by the people of England as the leader who freed the country from the curse of the sleeping king, he is beloved as the captain who holds the narrow seas and keeps both pirates and the French from our shores. And everyone believes him when he says that all he wants is to teach the young king how to rule, and free him from the command of his wife: another strong-minded woman, another bad queen that will curse England if the men give way to another female ruler.

The people of England learned to hate the bad queen, Margaret of Anjou. At the first mention of another woman, a strong-willed determined woman who is presuming on her position as the king's wife to try to rule the kingdom, they turn out in a frenzy of offended male pride. My uncle George, whose post of Lord Chancellor was taken off him by the king and his wife, catches Edward on the road as he is riding to join his army, captures him and sends him under guard to our home: Warwick Castle. Father captures the queen's own father and her brother as they ride away into Wales. He sends a special force to Grafton in Northampton and snatches the queen's mother from her home. Events tumble after one another too fast for the king. Father hunts down the Rivers family before they realise they are prey. This is the end of the king's power, this is the end of the bad councillors for the king. For certain, it is the end of the Rivers family. Of the queen's extensive family, Father holds in his power three of them: her father, mother and brother.

Only slowly, with a growing dread, do we realise that this is not a threat from Father, to teach them a lesson. These are not kinsmen who have been taken for ransom in the ordinary way: this is a declaration of war on the Rivers. Father accuses the queen's own father and her handsome young brother John of treason and orders their execution. Without rule of law, without a proper trial, he has them brought from Chepstow to our stronghold, Coventry, and executed without chance of appeal, without a chance of a pardon, outside the hard grey walls. The handsome young man, married to a woman old enough to be his grandmother, dies before his ancient bride, his head on a block, his dark curls gripped by the executioner. Lord Rivers puts his head down in his son's blood. The queen, stricken with grief, in terror for herself, separated from her husband, fearing that she will be an orphan, barricades herself and her little girls into the Tower of London and sends for her mother.

She can't reach her. The queen's mother, who planned the table for the children at the coronation dinner and smiled at me, is in my father's power at Warwick Castle. Father creates a courtroom to have her tried and brings witnesses against her. One after another they come with reports of lights burning in her stillroom at night, of her whispering to the river which runs near her home, of rumours that she could hear voices and that when one of her family was going to die she was warned by singing, spectral singing from the night sky.

Finally they search her home at Grafton and bring in the tools of necromancy: two little figures made of lead, bound together in a devilish union with wire of gold. Clearly one is meant to be the king, the other Jacquetta's daughter, Elizabeth Woodville. Their secret marriage was brought about by witchcraft, and King Edward, who has acted like a madman since he first set eyes on the Northampton widow, was all this time under an enchantment. The queen's mother is a witch who brought about the marriage by magic, and the queen herself is the daughter of a witch and half-witch herself. Clearly, Father will obey the injunction in the Bible that says *Thou shalt not suffer a witch to live*, and put her to death, doing God's work and his own.

He writes all this to Mother, as we wait in Calais, and she reads it in her measured voice as the ladies sit around and forget to sew, open-mouthed with shock. Of course, I want Midnight to ride with his high-stepping stride over all the kingdom; but I cannot rejoice at the thought of that young man John putting his handsome head on the block. I remember how he looked like a lamb going to the slaughter at the coronation feast when they made him go handfast with his elderly bride – but now he is a slaughtered lamb indeed and he has died before the old lady. My father rebels against the rules of nature as well as those of kingship. The queen's mother, Jacquetta, who smiled at me so kindly on the night of the coronation feast, has been widowed by my father's executioner. I remember her walking into dinner with her hand in her husband's arm, their pride and joy shining from them like candlelight. Yet my father has killed her boy, and her husband too. The queen herself is fatherless; is she to lose her mother as well? Is Father going to burn Jacquetta, Lady Rivers?

'She is our enemy,' Isabel says reasonably. 'I know that the queen is beautiful and she seemed very pleasant, but her family are grasping and bad advisors, and Father will have to destroy them. They are our enemy now. You must think of them as the enemy now.'

'I do,' I say; but I think of her in her white gown and her high headdress and her veil of lace, and I know that I don't.

For most of the summer we are in a state of constant excitement as the reports come from England that Edward, the one-time king, is living as our forced guest at Warwick Castle, that Father is ruling the realm through him, and the reputations of all of the Rivers are being destroyed. Father tells everyone that the evidence from the trial of the queen's mother shows clearly that the royal marriage was brought about by sorcery, and the king has been under an evil spell. Father has saved him, he is keeping him safe and he will kill the witch and break the spell.

My mother has waited in Calais for news before; we waited here when my father fought one brilliant battle after another to defeat the sleeping king. It is as if we are re-enacting those days of victory and Father is once again unstoppable. Now he has a second king in his keeping and he is going to put a new puppet on the throne. The French servants who come into the city of Calais tell us that the French call my father 'the kingmaker' and say that no-one can hold the throne of England without his permission.

'The kingmaker,' my mother murmurs, savouring the word. She smiles at her ladies, she even smiles at me. 'Lord, what foolish things people do say,' she remarks.

Then a ship from England brings us a packet of letters and the captain comes to the castle, to see my mother in private, and tell her that the news is all over London that King Edward was born a bastard, not his father's son but the misbegotten child of an English archer. Edward was never the heir of the House of York. He is base-born. He should never have been on the throne at all.

'Are people really saying that Duchess Cecily lay with an archer?' I ask out loud as one of the ladies whispers the gossip. The king's mother, our great-aunt, is one of the most formidable ladies of the realm, and no-one but a fool would believe such a thing of her. 'Duchess Cecily? With an archer?'

In one swift angry move, my mother rounds on me and boxes my ears with a ringing blow that sends my headdress flying across the room.

'Out of my sight!' she shouts in a rage. 'And think before you dare to speak ill of your betters! Never say such a thing in my hearing again.'

I have to scuttle across the room to get my headdress. 'My Lady Mother . . .' I start to apologise.

'Go to your room!' she orders. 'And then go to the priest for a penance for gossiping.'

I scurry out, clutching my headdress, and find Isabel in our bedroom.

'What is it?' she asks, seeing a red handprint across my cheek.

'Lady Mother,' I say shortly.

Isabel reaches into her sleeve and lends me her special wedding handkerchief to dry my eyes. 'Here,' she says gently. 'Why did she box your ears? Come and sit here and I'll comb your hair.'

I stifle my sobs and take my seat before the little silvered mirror, and Isabel takes the pins out of my hair and combs out the tangles with the ivory comb that her husband gave her after their one night of marriage.

'What happened?'

'I only said that I couldn't believe that King Edward was a bastard foisted on his father by the duchess,' I say defensively. 'And even if I am beaten to death for saying it, I still can't believe it. Our great-aunt? Duchess Cecily? Who would dare to say such a thing of her? She is such a great lady. Who would say such a thing against her? Won't they get their tongue slit? What d'you think?'

'I think it's a lie,' she says drily, as she twists my hair into a plait and pins it up on my head. 'And that's why you got your ears boxed. Mother was angry with you because it's a lie that we are not to question. We are not to repeat it, but we're not to challenge it either. It's a lie that our men will be telling all over London, Calais too, and we are not to contradict it.'

I am utterly confused. 'Why would our men say it? Why would we not forbid them to speak, as I am forbidden? Why would we allow such a lie? Why would anyone say that Duchess Cecily betrayed her own husband? Shamed herself?'

'You think,' she advises.

I sit staring at my own reflection, my brown hair shining with bronze lights where it is elegantly plaited by Isabel, my young face creased in a frown. Isabel waits for me to follow the tortuous path of my father's plotting. 'Father is allowing the men to repeat this lie?'

'Yes,' she says.

'Because if Edward is illegitimate, then George is the true heir,' I say eventually.

'And so the true King of England,' she says. 'All roads lead to George taking the throne and me at his side and Father ruling us both forever. They call him the kingmaker. He made Edward, now he unmakes him. Next, he makes George.' Her face in the mirror is grave.

'I would have thought you would be pleased to be queen,' I say tentatively. 'And to have Father win the throne for you.'

'When we were little girls playing at being queens we didn't know the price that women pay. We know now. The queen before Elizabeth, the bad queen, Margaret of Anjou, is on her knees like a beggar asking for help from the King of France, her husband in the Tower, her son a prince with no principality. The present queen is hiding in the Tower, her father and brother dead on a scaffold, beheaded like common criminals, her mother awaits death by burning for witchcraft.'

'Iz, please tell me that Father wouldn't burn Jacquetta Woodville!' I whisper.

'He will,' my sister says, her face grim. 'Why else arrest and try her? When I wanted to be a queen I thought it was a story, like the legends, I thought it was all about beautiful dresses and handsome knights. Now I see that it is pitiless. It is a game of chess and Father has me as one of his pieces. Now he uses me on the board, next I may fall to one side and he won't even think of me, as he brings another piece into play.'

'Are you afraid?' I whisper. 'Are you afraid of falling off to one side?'

'Yes,' she says.

ENGLAND, AUTUMN 1469

My father has England in his grip. Victorious, he sends for us to share his triumph. My mother, Isabel and I take ship from Calais in the best vessel of my father's great fleet, and arrive in London in great state as the women of the new royal house. The former queen Elizabeth skulks in the Tower, my father transfers the former King of England to our castle at Middleham and holds him there. In the absence of any other court we suddenly become the centre for London, for the kingdom. My mother and the king's mother, Duchess Cecily, are seen everywhere together, with Isabel following behind them, the two great women of the realm and the bride who will be made queen at the next parliament.

This is our moment of triumph: the kingmaker deposing the king who has wearied him to install another, his son-in-law. It is my father who decides who will rule England. It is my father who makes and unmakes the Kings of England. And Isabel is with child, she too is doing just what Father requires, she too is being a kingmaker; she is making a King of England in her belly. Mother prays every morning before a statue of Our Lady that Isabel has a boy, who will be Prince of Wales, heir to the throne. We are a triumphant family blessed by God with fertility. The former king, Edward, has only three daughters, he has no son and heir, there is no prince in his nursery, there is no-one to bar

George from the throne. His beautiful queen, so healthy and so fecund, can only make girls with him. But here we are, entering England a new royal family, a new queen for crowning, and she is with child. A wedding-night baby, conceived in the only night they were together! What a sign of grace! Who can doubt that it is our destiny to take the crown and for my father to see his grandson born a prince and live to be a king?

My father orders us to Warwick Castle, up the dry roads with the brightly coloured leaves whirling around us and the trees a treasury of gold and bronze and copper. The roads are dry and hard after the long summer; we leave a cloud of dust behind us. Isabel leads the way, resting in a litter drawn by white mules. She is not to live in London with her victorious husband. It does not matter if they are parted now since she is already with his child. She is to rest and prepare for her coronation. My father will call a parliament at York that will proclaim George Duke of Clarence as king and she will be queen. There will be a huge coronation in London. She will take the sceptre in her hand and lay it across her big belly, and her coronation gown is to be gathered thickly at the front to emphasise her pregnancy.

Chests of goods come north from the royal wardrobe. Isabel and I open them like children on New Year's Day in the best chamber of the castle and spill the contents all around the room, seeing the gold lacing and the encrusted stones sparkle in the firelight. 'He's done it,' Isabel says breathlessly, looking at the boxes of furs that Father has sent her. 'Father has taken her goods. These are her furs.' She buries her face in the thick pelts, and gives a little awestruck gasp. 'Smell them! They still smell of her perfume. He has taken her furs, he will have taken her perfume. I shall wear her perfume too. He says I am to have all her furs from the royal wardrobes to trim my gowns. He will send me her jewels, her brocades, her cloth-of-gold dresses to be fitted to me. He has done it.'

'You can't ever have doubted that he would?' I ask, stroking the creamy ermine with the dark spots, which only kings and queens are allowed to wear. Isabel will have all her capes trimmed with it. 'He defeated King Henry, and holds him prisoner. Now he has defeated King Edward and holds him. Sometimes I think of him, high on the back of his horse, Midnight, riding across the whole country, unbeatable.'

'Two kings in prison, and a new one on the throne?' Isabel questions, putting the furs aside. 'How can it be? How shall the third king be safer than the other two? And what if Father turns against George as he turned against Edward? What if my father's plans don't just neglect me but come to oppose me? What if the kingmaker wants a new king after George?'

'He won't do that; there is no-one for him but you and George now, and you are carrying the prince, his grandson,' I say certainly. 'He's done all this for you, Isabel. He will put you on the throne and keep you there, and then the next king of England will be a Neville. If he had done it for me I would be so happy. If he had done it for me I would have been the happiest girl in England.'

But Isabel is not happy. My mother and I cannot understand why she is not exultant. We think she is tired in her pregnancy for she will not walk out in the bright cold mornings, and takes no pleasure in the sharp autumnal air. She is anxious, though we and all our loyal household are triumphant, revelling in our rise to power. Then one day at dinner, my father's Master of Horse, the most trusted and reliable man of his household, is announced. He walks the length of the hall, which falls silent and whispers as he hands a letter to my mother across the high table, and she takes it, surprised that he should come into the hall still dirty from the road, but knowing from his grave face that it is urgent news. She looks at the seal – my father's standard of the bear and ragged staff – and then, without saying a word, she goes through the door at the back of the dais into the solar, leaving us in silence.

Isabel and I and the dozen ladies of her chamber eat our dinner, trying to look untroubled under the hushed scrutiny of the great hall, but as soon as we can we withdraw to wait in the presence chamber outside the solar, pretending to talk cheerfully among ourselves, horribly aware of the locked door and the silence behind it. If my father were dead, would my mother be weeping? Does she weep? Actually, can she weep? I have never seen my mother weep. I find I am wondering if she has that capacity, or if she is forever hard-faced and dry-eyed.

If my father's Master of Horse had given her a letter telling us to come to London at once for Izzy's coronation would she not have burst out through the door with the good news? Does she cry out in joy, I wonder? Have I ever seen her dancing with exultation? The red afternoon sun walks slowly along the tapestried walls lighting up one scene, and then another, and still there is no sound from her room.

Finally, in the evening as it is starting to get dark and the servants are bringing in the candles, the door opens, and my mother comes out, the letter in her hand. 'Fetch the captain of the castle,' she says to one of her ladies, 'and the commander of the personal guard. Command my lord's steward, and the groom of the chambers, and his Master of Horse.'

She sits in her great chair under the canopy embroidered with her noble crests, and waits for the men to come through the double doors, bow, and stand waiting. Obviously something important has happened but there is no way of telling from her impassive face whether we have triumphed or are ruined.

'You ask her,' Isabel mutters to me.

'No, you.'

We stand with the ladies. Our mother is seated like a queen. She does not order a chair for Isabel, which is odd. It is as if Isabel's baby is suddenly not the greatest baby that will ever be, as if Isabel herself is not one step from being queen. We wait for the men to come and line up before her to hear her orders.

'I have a message from my husband, your lord,' she says, her voice hard and clear. 'He writes that he has restored the King of England, Edward, to his throne. My husband, your lord, has made an agreement with King Edward and in future the king will be guided by the natural lords of the kingdom; there will be no newcomers.'

Nobody says anything. These are men who have served my father for many years, through good battlefields and bad; they are not likely to stir and comment at ominous news. But the ladies shake their heads and whisper. Someone nods at Isabel as if in sympathy that she is not to be Queen of England after all and need not think herself special any more. My mother does not even look at us; her gaze is fixed on the wall hangings above our heads, and her voice never trembles.

'We are going to London to demonstrate our friendship and loyalty to the rightful King Edward and his family,' she says. 'My daughter the duchess will meet with her husband George Duke of Clarence. Lady Anne will attend me of course. And my lord sends me more good news: our nephew John is to be betrothed to the king's daughter, Princess Elizabeth of York.'

I snatch a quick glance at Isabel. This is not good news at all; it is utterly terrible. My father has taken up another pawn just as Isabel feared, and she is put aside. He is marrying his nephew into the royal household, to the royal heir, little Princess Elizabeth. My father will get a Neville on the throne one way or another; this is his new way. Isabel is the old way that he has surrendered.

Isabel is biting her lower lip. I reach out for her and, hidden by the widely spread skirt of her gown, we grip hands together.

'My nephew will be given a dukedom,' my mother says steadily. 'He is to be the Duke of Bedford. This is an honour from the king and a gesture of his goodwill to our nephew, my husband's heir. It is proof of the king's friendship with us and his gratitude for our care of him. That is all. God save the king, and bless the House of Warwick.'

'God save the king and bless the House of Warwick!' everyone repeats as if it were possible to wish for two such contradictory things at once.

My mother rises to her feet and nods to Isabel and me to come with her. I walk behind Isabel, showing the respect due to a royal duchess: a royal duchess – but not a queen. In one moment Isabel has lost her claim to the throne. Who cares about being a royal duchess if our cousin John is to marry the heiress of York, the king's own daughter? Cousin John is to be a duke, and the king has signalled to his brother that he can easily make other dukes and bring them into his family. Father has other pawns to put on the board.

'What will we do in London?' I whisper to Isabel as I lean forwards and straighten her veil.

'Show our friendship, I suppose,' she says. 'Give back the furs to the queen, return the coronation gown to the royal wardrobe. Hope that Father is satisfied with marrying our cousin into the king's family, and doesn't take arms against the king again.'

'You won't be queen,' I say sorrowfully. Ignobly, I feel a secret little glow that my sister will not wear ermine, will not be the greatest woman in the kingdom, Queen of England and my father's favourite, the daughter who fulfils his greatest ambition, the pawn that can make the winning move.

'Not now, no.'

Once again Isabel and I walk into the queen's rooms sick with apprehension. The queen is in her great chair, her mother Jacquetta standing like sculpted ice behind her. Our mother comes behind Isabel but before me, and I wish that I were young enough to get my toes under her train and pass unnoticed. Nobody will think I am charming today. Isabel, though a married woman and this queen's sister-in-law, has her head down, her eyes down, like a child in disgrace longing for this moment to be over.

My mother curtseys as low as she must do to a Queen of England and comes up, standing before her, hands quietly clasped, as composed as if she were in her own castle of Warwick. The queen looks her up and down and her eyes are as warm as grey slate in icy rain.

'Ah, Countess of Warwick,' she says in a voice as light and cold as drifting snow.

'Your Grace,' my mother replies through gritted teeth.

The queen's mother, her lovely face blank with grief, wearing white, the royal colour of mourning of her house, looks at the three of us as if she would cut us down where we stand. I do not dare to do more than snatch a glance at her before I drop my eyes to my feet. She smiled at me at the coronation dinner; now she looks as if she will never smile again. I have never seen heartbreak engraved on a woman's face before; but I know that I am seeing it in the ravaged beauty of Jacquetta Woodville. My mother inclines her head. 'Your Grace, I am sorry for your loss,' she says quietly.

The widow says nothing, nothing at all. We all three stand as if we are frozen in the ice of her gaze. I think – well, she must say something, she will say something such as 'fortunes of war' or 'thank you for your sympathy' or 'he is with God' or any of the things that widows say when their husbands have been lost in battle. England has been at war with itself, on and off, for the last fourteen years. Many women have to meet each other and know that their husbands were enemies. We are all accustomed to new alliances. But it seems that Jacquetta, the widow of Richard Woodville, Lord Rivers, does not know these conventions, for she says nothing to make us any easier. She looks at us as if we are her enemies for life, as if she is cursing us in silence, as if this is the start of a blood feud that will never end, and I can feel myself start to tremble under the basilisk hatred of her gaze and I swallow, and wonder if I am going to faint.

'He was a brave man,' my mother volunteers again. In the face of Jacquetta's stony grief the comment sounds frivolous.

At last the widow speaks. 'He suffered the ignoble death of a traitor, beheaded by the Coventry blacksmith, and my beloved son John died too,' the queen's mother replies. 'Both of them innocent of any crime, in all their lives. John was just twenty-four years old, obedient to his father and his king. My husband was defending his crowned and ordained king yet he was charged with treason, and then beheaded by your husband. It was not an honourable death on the battlefield. He had been on dozens of battlefields and always come home safe to me. It was a pledge he made to me: that he would always come home safe from war. He didn't break it. God bless him that he didn't break his promise to me. He died on the scaffold, not on the battlefield. I shall never forget this. I shall never forgive this.'

There is a truly terrible silence. Everyone in the room is looking at us, listening to the queen's mother swear her enmity against us. I look up and find the queen's icy gaze, filled with hatred, is resting on me. I look down again.

'These are the fortunes of war,' my mother says awkwardly, as if to excuse us.

Then Jacquetta does an odd, a terrible thing. She purses her lips together and she blows a long chilling whistle. Somewhere outside, a shutter bangs and a sudden chill flows through the room. The candles bob and flicker throughout the chamber as if a cold wind has nearly blown them out. Abruptly one candle in the stand beside Isabel winks and goes out. Isabel gives a little scream of fright. Jacquetta and her daughter the queen both look at us as if they would whistle us away, blow us away like dirty dust.

My formidable mother shrinks before this extraordinary inexplicable behaviour. I have never seen her turn from a challenge before but she flees from this, as she ducks her head and walks to the window bay. Nobody greets us, nobody breaks the silence that follows the unearthly whistle, nobody even smiles. There are people here who danced at the wedding at Calais Castle where this whole terrible plan was set in motion; but to look at them you would think they were utter strangers to us three. We stand in stony shame, quite alone, while the gust of air slowly dies down and the echo of Jacquetta's long whistle goes silent.

The doors open and the king comes in, my father at his side, George his brother on the other side, Richard the younger York duke a little behind him, his dark head high and proud. He has every reason to be pleased with himself; this is the brother who did not betray the king, the brother whose loyalty was tested and stayed true. This is the brother who will have wealth and favour poured over him while we are in disgrace. I look towards him to see if he will acknowledge us and smile at me; but it seems that I am invisible to him, as we are to the rest of the court. Richard is a man now, his boyhood in our keeping far behind him. He was loyal to the king, when we were not.

George slowly comes over to our lonely little corner, looking away from us, as if he is ashamed to be with us, and Father follows him with his long loping stride. Father's confidence is unshaken, his smile still bold, his brown eyes shining, his thick beard neatly trimmed, his authority untarnished by defeat. Isabel and I kneel for Father's blessing and feel his hand lightly touch our heads. When we rise he is taking Mother's hand as she smiles thinly at him, and then we all go into dinner, walking behind the king as if we were still his dearest friends and dedicated allies and not defeated traitors.

After dinner there is dancing and the king is cheerful, handsome and buoyant as always, like the lead actor in a masque, playing the role of the merry good king. He claps my father on the back, he puts his arm around his brother George's shoulders. He, at least, will play his part as if nothing has gone wrong. My father, no less cunning than his former ally, is also at his ease, glancing around the court, greeting friends who all know that we are traitors and are only here on the king's goodwill and because we own half of England. They smirk behind their hands at us, I can hear the laughter in their voices. I don't look to see the hidden smiles; I keep my eyes down. I am so ashamed, I am so deeply ashamed of what we have done.

We failed, that was the worst of it. We took the king but we could not hold him. We won a little battle, but nobody supported us. It was not enough for my father to hold the king at Warwick, at Middleham; the king simply ruled from there and behaved as if he were an honoured guest, and then rode out and away when it suited him.

'And Isabel must join the queen's court,' I hear the king say loudly, and my father replies without taking breath: 'Yes, yes, of course, she will be honoured.'

Both Isabel and the queen hear this and look up at the same

moment and their gazes meet. Isabel looks utterly shocked and afraid, her lips parting as if to ask Father to refuse. But the days when we could claim to be too good for royal service are long gone. Isabel will have to live in the queen's rooms, wait on her every day. The queen turns her head with a little gesture of disdain, as if she cannot bear to see the two of us, as if we are something unclean, as if we are lepers. Father is not looking at us at all.

'Come with me,' Isabel whispers urgently to me. 'You have to come with me if I have to serve her. Come and live in her household with me, Annie. I swear I can't go on my own.'

'Father won't let me . . .' I reply rapidly. 'Don't you remember Mother refusing us last time? You'll have to go, because of being her sister-in-law, but I can't come, Mother won't let me, and I couldn't bear it . . .'

'And Lady Anne too,' the king says easily.

'Of course,' Father says agreeably. 'Whatever Her Grace desires.'

The queen is never rude to us: it is far worse than that. It is as if we are invisible to her. Her mother never speaks to us at all, and if she passes us in the gallery or in the hall she steps back against the wall as if she would not let the skirt of her gown so much as touch us. If another woman stepped back like this I would take it as a gesture of deference, giving me the way. But when the duchess does it, with a quick step aside without even looking at me, I feel as if she is drawing her skirts away from foul mud, as if I have something on my shoes or my petticoat that stinks. We see our own mother only at dinner and at night when she sits with the queen's ladies, a little circle of unfriendly silence around her, while they talk pleasantly among themselves. The rest of the time we wait on the queen, attending her when she is dressing in the morning, following her when she goes to the nursery to see her three little girls, kneeling behind her in chapel, sitting below her place at breakfast, riding out with her when she goes hunting. We are constantly in her presence and she never, by word or glance, ever acknowledges that we are there.

The rules of precedence mean that we often have to walk immediately behind her, and then she is simply blind to us, speaking over our heads to her other ladies. If the two of us happen to be the only ones with her, she behaves as if she is quite alone. When we carry her train she walks at the same speed as if there were no-one behind her, and we have to scuttle along to keep up with her, looking foolish. When she hands her gloves to us she does not even look to see if one of us is ready to take them. When I drop one she does not demean herself to notice. It is as if she would let the priceless perfumed and embroidered leather lie in the mud rather than ask me to pick it up. When I have to hand something to her, a book of tales or a petition, she takes it as if it had come out of thin air. If I pass her a posy of flowers or a handkerchief she takes it so that she does not touch my fingers. She never asks me for her prayer book or her rosary, and I do not dare to offer them. I am afraid she would think them defiled by my bloody hands.

Isabel sinks into a white-faced sullenness, does as she must do, and sits in silence, never volunteering a remark while the ladies chatter around her. As Isabel's belly grows the queen asks her to do less and less, but not as a courtesy. With one disdainful turn of her head she suggests that Isabel is not able to serve her, is no good as a lady in waiting, is good for nothing but to breed like a pig. Isabel sits with her hands folded over her belly as if to hide the curve, as if she is afraid that the queen will cast her eye on the baby.

But still, I cannot see the queen as my enemy, because I cannot rid myself of the sense that she is in the right and we are in the wrong, and that her visible contempt for me and my sister has been earned by my father. I cannot be angry, I am too ashamed. When I see her smile at her daughters or laugh with her husband I am reminded of the first time I saw her when I thought her the most beautiful woman in the world. She is still the most beautiful woman in the world but I am no longer an awestruck little girl; I am the daughter of her enemy and the murderer of her father and brother. And I am sorry, deeply sorry for all that has happened – but I cannot tell her so, and she makes it clear she would hear nothing from me.

After a month of this I cannot eat my dinner at the ladies'

table. It sticks in my throat. I cannot sleep at night; I am always cold as if my bedroom in her household is whistling with a chill draught. My hands shake when I have to pass something to the queen, and my sewing is hopeless, the linen covered with spots of blood where I have pricked my fingers. I ask our Lady Mother if I may go to Warwick, or even back to Calais, I tell her that I feel ill, living at the court among our enemies is making me sick.

'Don't you complain to me,' she says shortly. 'I have to sit beside her mother at dinner and be chilled to my soul by that witch's ice. Your father risked everything and lost. He could not hold the king a prisoner on his own, the lords would not support him and without them, nothing could be done. We are lucky the king did not have him executed. Instead we are in a fine place: at court, your sister married to the king's brother and your cousin John betrothed to the king's daughter. We are close to the throne and may get closer still. Serve the queen and be grateful that your father is not dead on a scaffold like hers. Serve the queen and be glad that your father will seek a good marriage for you and she will approve it.'

'I can't,' I say weakly. 'Really, Lady Mother, I can't. It's not that I don't want to, nor that I could disobey you or Father. It is that I simply can't do it. My knees will give way rather than walk behind her. I can't eat when she watches me.'

The face she turns to me is as kindly as stone. 'You come from a great family,' she reminds me. 'Your father took a great risk for the good of his family and for the benefit of your sister. Isabel is lucky that he thought her worth the effort. We may now be in some discomfort but that will change. You show your father that in your turn it is worth us making an effort for you. You will have to rise to your calling, Anne, there is no point being weak and sickly now. You were born to be a great woman – be one now.'

She sees I am pale and shaking. 'Oh, cheer up,' she says roughly. 'We're to go to Warwick Castle for your sister's confinement. It will be easier for us there, and we can stay away from court for four months at least. There is no pleasure in this for any of us, Anne. It's as bad for me as it is for you. I will keep us at Warwick as long as I can.'

WARWICK CASTLE, MARCH 1470

I thought we would be happier every mile we were away from the court; but only weeks after we get to the castle, my father sends the groom of his chamber to tell us that he wants to see the two of us in his room. We enter his privy chamber, Isabel leaning heavily on my arm and holding her swelling belly as if to remind anyone who might forget for even a moment that she is still carrying the child of the heir of the King of England, and he will be born next month.

Father is seated in his carved chair with the Warwick crest of the bear and the ragged staff bright in gold leaf behind his head. He looks up when we come in and points with his quill pen at me. 'Ah, I don't need you.'

'Father?'

'Stand back.'

Isabel quickly releases me and stands perfectly well on her own, and so I take my place at the back of the room, put my hands behind my back and trace the linenfold panelling with my fingers, waiting until I am called on to speak.

'I am telling you a secret, Isabel,' Father says. 'Your husband the duke and I are riding out to support King Edward as he marches on a rebellion in Lincolnshire. We go with him to show our loyalty.'

Isabel murmurs a reply. I can't hear what, but of course it

doesn't matter what she says, or what I think, this is what the men have planned to do, and it will happen whatever our opinion may be.

'When the king lines up his men on the battlefield we will turn on him,' my father says bluntly. 'If he puts us behind him we will attack from the rear, if he has me on one wing and George on another we will come together from both sides and crush him between us. Our forces outnumber his and this time we will take no prisoners. I shall not be merciful and try to come to an agreement with him this time. The king will not survive this battle. We will finish it on the battlefield. He is a dead man. I will kill him with my own sword, I will kill him with my own hands if I have to.'

I close my eyes. This is the worst thing. I hear Isabel's muted gasp: 'Father!'

'He is not a king for England, he is a king for the Rivers family,' he continues. 'He is a cat's-paw of his wife. We did not risk our lives and our fortunes to put the Rivers in power and their child on the throne. I did not throw my fortune and my life into his service to see that woman queen it around England like a drab in borrowed velvets with your ermine stitched to her collar.'

His chair scrapes as he gets to his feet and pushes it back and walks round the table towards her. Ignoring her belly Isabel drops to her knees before him. 'I am doing this for you,' he says quietly. 'I will make you Queen of England, and if that child you are carrying is a son, he will be a royal prince and then king.'

'I will pray for you,' Isabel whispers almost inaudibly. 'And for my husband.'

'You will take my name and my blood to the throne of England,' Father says with satisfaction. 'Edward has become a fool, a lazy fool. He trusts us and we will betray him, and he will die on the battlefield like his father, who was a fool as well. Here, child, get up.' He put his hand under her elbow and hauls her ungently to her feet. He nods at me. 'Guard your sister,' he says with a smile. 'The future of our family is in her belly. She could be carrying the next King of England.' He kisses Isabel on both cheeks. 'Next time we meet you will be the Queen of England and I shall kneel to you.' He laughs. 'Think of that! I shall kneel to you, Isabel.'

The whole household goes to our chapel and prays for Father to be victorious. The whole household, thinking that he is fighting for the king against the rebels, prays without understanding the real danger he is in, the great risk he is running, challenging the King of England in his own kingdom. But Father has prepared the ground; Lincolnshire is alive with rebels, one of our kinsmen has roused the country complaining of the king's ill-judged rule and false councillors. George has an army of his own sworn to him whatever side he takes, and Father's men would follow him anywhere. But still, the fortunes of war are changeable and Edward is a formidable tactician. We pray for Father's success morning and night, and we wait for news.

Isabel and I are sitting in her chamber, Isabel resting on her bed and complaining of a pain in her belly. 'It's like a gripping pain,' she says. 'Almost as if I had eaten too much.'

'Maybe you have eaten too much,' I reply unsympathetically.

She pulls a face. 'I am nearly eight months into my time,' she says plaintively. 'If Father were not marching out I should be going into confinement this very week. I should have thought you would be kinder to me, your own sister.'

I grit my teeth. 'Yes,' I say. 'I am sorry. Shall I call the ladies, shall I tell Mother?'

'No,' she says. 'I probably ate too much. There's no room in my belly, and every time he moves or turns I can't breathe.' She turns her head. 'What's that noise?'

I go to the window. I can see a troop of men coming down the road towards the castle, out of their lines, stumbling like a weary crowd not marching together like a force, and ahead of them the mounted knights going slowly, wearily. I recognise my father's warhorse Midnight with his head bowed, and a bleeding wound deep in his shoulder. 'It's Father, coming home,' I say.

Isabel is up from her bed in a moment, and we run down the stone stairs to the great hall and fling open the door as the servants of the castle pour into the yard outside to greet the returning army.

My father rides in at the head of his troop on his weary horse, and as soon as they are safe inside the castle walls, the drawbridge creaks up and the portcullis rattles down and my father and his son-in-law, the handsome duke, dismount from their horses. Isabel at once leans on my arm and puts her hand to her belly, to make a tableau of maternity, but I am not thinking of how we appear, I am looking at the faces of the men. I can tell at one glance that they are not victorious. My mother comes up behind us and I hear her quiet exclamation and I know that she too has seen weariness and defeat in this army. Father looks grim, and George is white with unhappiness. Mother's back straightens as she braces herself for trouble and she greets Father briefly with a kiss on each cheek. Isabel greets her husband in the same way. All I can do is curtsey to them both and then we all go into the great hall and Father steps up on the dais.

The ladies in waiting are standing in a line, and they bow as my father comes in. The senior men of the household follow us into the room to hear the news. Behind them come the servants, the garrison of the castle and those of the troop who chose to come to listen rather than go to rest. Father speaks clearly enough so that everyone can hear. 'We rode in support of my kinsmen Lord Richard and Sir Robert Welles,' he says. 'They think, as I do, that the king is under the control of the queen and her family and that he has reneged on his agreements to me, and that he is no king for England.'

There is a murmur of approval; everyone here resents the power and success of the Rivers family. George clambers up on the dais to stand beside my father as if to remind us all that there is an alternative to this faithless king. 'Lord Richard Welles is dead,' Father says bleakly. 'This false king took him out of sanctuary –' he repeats the terrible crime done against the laws of God and man '– he took him out of sanctuary, and threatened him with death. When Lord Richard's son Sir Robert was arrayed for battle this false king killed Lord Welles before the battle even started, killed him without a trial, on the field of battle.'

George nods, looking grave. To break sanctuary is to undermine the safety and power of the church, to defy God Himself. A man who puts his hand on the altar of a church has to know that he is safe there. God Himself takes such a criminal under his protection. If the king does not recognise the power of sanctuary then he is setting himself up as greater than God. He is a heretic, a blasphemer. He can be very sure that God will strike him down.

'We were defeated,' my father says solemnly. 'The army mustered by the Welles' was broken in Edward's charge. We withdrew.'

I feel Isabel's cold hand come into mine. 'We've lost?' she asks disbelievingly. 'We've lost?'

'We will retreat to Calais and regroup,' Father says. 'This is a setback but not a defeat. We will rest tonight and tomorrow we will pack up and march out. But let no-one mistake, this is now war between me, and the so-called King Edward. The rightful king is George of the House of York, and I shall see him on the throne of England.'

'George!' the men shout, raising their fists in the air.

'God save King George!' my father prompts them.

'King George!' they reply. In truth they would swear to anything that my father commanded.

'À Warwick!' My father gives his battle cry and they bellow with one voice after him: 'À Warwick!'

DARTMOUTH, DEVON, APRIL 1470

We travel at the steady speed of the mules that carry Isabel's litter. Father has scouts following behind our retreating army and they report that Edward is not chasing us out of his kingdom. Father says that he is a lazy fool and he has gone back to the queen's warm bed in London. We go by easy stages to Dartmouth where Father's ship is waiting for us. Isabel and I stand on the quayside as the wagons and the horses are loaded. The sea is so calm it could be a lake, the day is hot for April, with the white seagulls wheeling in the air and calling; there is a pleasant smell of the quayside, the tang of salt, of drying seaweed from the nets, of tar. This could almost be a summer day and Father planning a pleasure voyage for us.

Midnight, Father's black warhorse, is one of the last to be led up the gangplank. They put a sack on his head so he cannot see the ridged plank and the water beneath. But he knows they are putting him on board a ship. He has gone criss-crossing the seas many times, he has invaded England twice. He is a veteran of Father's many battles but now he behaves like a nervous colt, pulling back from the gangplank, rearing up so that the men scatter from his flailing hooves, until they put him in a sling and load him on board and he cannot resist them.

'I'm afraid,' Isabel says. 'I don't want to sail.'

'Izzy, the sea is as calm as a pond. We could practically swim home.'

'Midnight knows there is something wrong.'

'No he doesn't. He's always naughty. And anyway, he is on board now, he's in his stall eating hay. Come on, Izzy, we can't delay the ship.'

Still she won't go forwards. She pulls me to one side as the ladies go on board and Mother too. They are raising the sails, shouting commands and replies. The royal cabin door stands open for us. George goes past us, indifferent to Izzy's fears, Father is giving his last orders to someone on the quayside and the sailors are starting to release the ropes from the great iron rings on the quay.

'I'm too near my time to sail.'

'You'll be fine,' I say. 'You can lie in the bunk on the ship just as you would lie in your bed at home.'

Still she hesitates. 'What if she has whistled up a wind?'

'What?'

'The queen, and her mother the witch. Witches can whistle up a wind, can't they? What if she has whistled up a wind and it's out there, waiting for us?'

'She can't do a thing like that, Iz. She's just an ordinary woman.'

'She would, you know she would. She will never forgive us for the death of her father and her brother. Her mother said as much.'

'Of course they were angry with us, but she can't do it, she's not a witch.'

Father is suddenly beside us. 'Get on board,' he says.

'Izzy is frightened,' I say to him.

He looks at her, his oldest, his chosen daughter; and though she has her hand on her swelling belly and her face is white, he looks at her with hard brown eyes, as if she were nothing to him but an obstacle between him and his new plan. Then he glances back inland, as if he might see the billowing standards of the king's army trotting down the road to the quayside. 'Get on board,' is all he says and he leads the way up the gangplank without looking back, and gives the order to cast off as we scurry after him.

They cast off the ropes, and the barges come and take their lines on board to tow us out to sea. The rowers in the barges lean forwards and pull as the little drummer boy starts a steady beat to keep them in time and they edge the ship away from the cobbled quayside and out into the river. The sails flap and start to fill with wind, and the boat rocks in the slapping waves. Father is beloved in Devon, as in all the ports of England, for his protection of the narrow seas and there are many people waving, kissing their hands to him, and calling their blessing. George immediately goes and stands beside him on the poop deck, raising his hand in a kingly salute, and my father calls Izzy to his side and puts his arm around her shoulders, turning her so that everyone can see her big pregnant belly. Mother and I stand in the bow of the ship. Father does not call me to his side, he does not need me there. It is Isabel who is to be the new Queen of England, going into exile now, but certain to return in triumph. It is Isabel who is carrying the child that they all hope will be the son who will be the King of England.

We reach the open sea and the sailors drop the ropes to the barges, and reef the sails. A little breeze comes up and the sails fill and then the timbers creak as the wind takes the boat and we start to plough through the blue water with the waters singing along the prow. Izzy and I have always loved sailing and she forgets her fear and comes and stands with me at the side of the boat, looking over the rail for dolphin in the clear water. There is a line of cloud on the horizon like a string of milky pearls.

In the evening, we heave to off the port of Southampton where the rest of Father's fleet is at anchor, waiting for the command to join us. Father sends a little rowing boat to tell them to come, and we wait, wallowing a little in the swirling currents of the Solent, looking towards land expecting to see, at any moment, a moving forest of sails, our wealth and pride and the source of Father's power – the command of the seas. But only two ships appear.

They come alongside us and Father leans over the side of our ship as they bawl to him that we were expected, that the Rivers' son, Anthony Woodville, with his family's cursed foresight rode like a madman with his troop to get here before us, and that he has commanded the crews, arrested some, killed others; but at any rate he has all of Father's ships, including our brand-new flagship the *Trinity*, in his grasping hands. Anthony Woodville has the command of Father's fleet. The Rivers have taken our ships from us, as they took our king from us, as they will take everything we own from us.

'Go below!' Father shouts furiously to me. 'Tell your mother we will be at Calais in the morning and that I will come back for the *Trinity* and all my ships, and Anthony Woodville will be sorry he stole them from me.'

We will sail all evening and all night, running before the wind in the narrow seas to our home port of Calais. Father knows these waters well, and his crew have sailed and fought over every inch of these deeps. The ship is newly commissioned, fitted out as a fighting vessel but with quarters worthy of a king. We are sailing east before the prevailing wind and the skies are clear. Isabel will rest in the royal cabin on the main deck, I will stay with her. Mother and Father will have the large cabin beneath the poop deck. George has the first officer's cabin. In a little while they will serve dinner and then we will play cards in candlelight which flickers and moves with the roll of the ship, then we will go to bed and I will sleep, rocked by the rise and fall of the waves, listening to the creaking of the timbers and smelling the salt of the sea. I realise that I am free: my time in service to the queen is over, completely over. I will never see Elizabeth Woodville again. I will never serve her again. She will never forgive me, she will never hear my name; but equally I will never again have to bear her silent contempt.

'The wind's getting up,' Izzy remarks as we are taking a stroll around the main deck before dinner.

I raise my head. The standard at the top of the sails is flapping wildly, and the seagulls that were following the wake of the ship have wheeled away and gone back towards England. The little pearly clouds strung out along the horizon have massed and now lie grey and thick, like feathers.

'It's nothing,' I say. 'Come on, Iz, we can go into the cabin. We've never had the best cabin before.'

We go to the door that opens onto the main deck but as she puts her hand on the brass lock the ship dips and she staggers and falls against the door, which yields suddenly, making her tumble into the cabin. She falls against the bed and I scramble in behind her and get hold of her. 'Are you all right?'

Another big heave of a wave sends us tottering to the other side of the little room and Izzy falls against me and knocks me against the wall.

'Get to the bed,' I say.

The floor rises up again as we struggle towards the bed and Isabel grabs the raised edge. I cling to the side. I try to laugh at the sudden swell that made us stagger like fools, but Iz is crying: 'It's a storm, a storm like I said!' Her eyes are huge in the sudden gloom of the cabin.

'It can't be, it's just a couple of big waves.' I look towards the window. The clouds that were so light and pale on the horizon have darkened, and lie in black and yellow stripes across the sun, which is itself growing red and dark though it is still the afternoon.

'Just clouding up,' I say, trying to sound cheerful though I have never seen a sky like this in my life before. 'Shall you get into bed for a rest? You might as well.'

I help her into the swaying bed but then the sudden drop of the boat into the trough of a wave, and the smack of the impact as it hits the bottom, throws me to my knees on the floor.

'You come in too,' Izzy insists. 'Come in with me. It's getting cold, I'm so cold.'

I heel off my shoes and then I hesitate. I wait and it feels as if everything is waiting. Suddenly, everything goes still as if the world has suddenly paused, as if the sky is silently waiting. The ship falls quiet, becalmed on an oily sea, and the wind that was blowing us homeward, steadily east, sighs as if exhausted and ceases. In the calm we hear the sails flap and then hang still. Everything is ominously horribly quiet.

I look out of the window. The seas are flat, as flat as if they were an inland marsh and the ship wallowing on silt. There is not a breath of wind. The clouds are pressing on the mast of the boat, pressing down on the sea. Nothing is moving, the seagulls are gone, someone seated on the crosstrees of the main mast says 'Dear Jesus, save us' and starts to scramble down the ropes to the deck. His voice echoes strangely as if we were all trapped under a glass bowl. 'Dear Jesus, save us,' I repeat.

'Take down sail!' the captain bellows, breaking the silence. 'Reef in!' and we hear the bare feet of the crew thundering on the decks to get the sails taken in. The sea is glassy, reflecting the sky, and as I watch it turns from dark blue to black and starts to stir, and starts to move.

'She is taking a breath,' Izzy says. Her face is haunted, her eyes dark in her pallor.

'What?'

'She is taking a breath.'

'Oh no,' I say, trying to sound confident but the stillness of the air and Isabel's premonition are frightening me. 'It's nothing, just a lull.'

'She is taking her breath and then she will whistle,' Izzy says. She turns away from me and lies on her back, her big belly rounded and full. Her hands come out and grip either side of the beautifully carved wooden bed, while she stretches her feet down to the bottom of the bedframe, as if she were bracing herself for danger. 'In a moment now, she will whistle.'

I try to say cheerfully: 'No, no, Izzy . . .' when there is a scream of wind that takes my breath away. Howling like a whistle, like a banshee, the wind pours out of the darkened sky, the boat heels over and the sea beneath us suddenly bows up and throws us up towards the clouds that split with sickly yellow lightning.

'Close the door! Shut her out!' Izzy screams as the boat rolls and the double doors to the cabin fly open. I reach for them and then stand amazed. Before the cabin is the prow of the ship and beyond that should be the waves of the sea. But I can see nothing before me but the prow, rising up and up and up as if the ship is standing on its stern and the prow is vertical in the sky above me. Then I see why. Beyond the prow is a mighty wave, towering as high as a castle wall, and our little ship is trying to climb its side. In a moment the crest of the wave, icy white against the black sky, is going to turn and crash down on us, as a storm of hail pours down with a rattle that makes the deck white as a snowfield in a second, and stings my face and bare arms, and crunches beneath my bare feet like broken glass.

'Close the door!' Izzy screams again and I fling myself against it as the wave breaks on us, a wall of water crashes down on the deck, and the ship shudders and staggers. Another wave rears above us and the door bursts open to admit a waist-high wall of water which pours in. The door is banging, Isabel is screaming, the ship is shuddering, struggling under the extra weight of water, the sailors are fighting for control of the sails, clinging to the spars, hanging like puppets with flailing legs, thinking of nothing but their own fragile lives, as the ship rears, the captain screaming commands and trying to hold the prow into the towering seas, while the wind veers against us, whipping up enemy waves that come towards us like a succession of glassy black mountains.

The ship reels and the door bangs open again, and Father comes in with a cascade of water, his sea cape streaming, his shoulders white with hail. He slams the door behind him, and steadies himself against the frame. 'All right?' he asks shortly, his eyes on Isabel.

Isabel is holding her belly. 'I have a pain, I have a pain!' she shouts. 'Father! Get us into port!'

He looks at me. I shrug. 'She always has pains,' I say shortly. 'The ship?'

'We'll run for the French shore,' he says. 'We'll get in the shelter of the coast. Help her. Keep her warm. The fires are all out, but when they are lit again I'll send you some mulled ale.'

The ship gives a huge heave and the two of us fall across the cabin. Isabel screams from the bunk. 'Father!'

We struggle to our feet, clinging to the side of the cabin, hauling ourselves up on the side of the bunk. As I pull myself forwards I blink, thinking I must be blinded by the flashes of lightning outside the cabin window, because it looks as if Izzy's sheets are black. I rub my eyes with my wet hands, tasting the salt of the waves on my knuckles and on my cheeks. Then I see her sheets are not black, I am not dazzled by the lightning. Her sheets are red. Her waters have broken.

'The baby!' she sobs.

'I'll send your mother,' Father says hastily and plunges through the door, fastening it behind him. He disappears at once into the hail. Now and then the lightning shows the hail as a wall of white, smashing against us, and then it is black again. The black nothingness is worst.

I grab Isabel's hands.

'I have a pain,' she says pitifully. 'Annie, I have a pain. I do have a pain.' Her face suddenly contorts and she clings to me, groaning. 'I am not making a fuss. Annie, I am not trying to be important. I do have a pain, a terrible pain. Annie, I do have a pain.'

'I think the baby is coming,' I say.

'Not yet! Not yet! It's too early. It's too early. It can't come here! Not on a ship!'

Desperately I look towards the door. Surely my mother will come? Surely Margaret will not fail us, surely the ladies will come? It cannot be that Isabel and I are clinging to each other in a thunderstorm as she gives birth without anyone to help us.

'I have a girdle,' she says desperately. 'A blessed girdle for help in childbirth.'

Our chests of things have all been loaded into the hold. There is nothing for Isabel in the cabin but a little box with a change of linen.

74

'An icon, and some pilgrim badges,' she continues. 'In my carved box. I need them, Annie. Get them for me. They will protect me ...'

Another pain takes her and she screams and grips my hands. The door behind me bursts open and a wash of water and a blast of hail comes in with my mother.

'Lady Mother! Lady Mother!'

'I can see,' my mother says coldly. She turns to me. 'Go to the galley and tell them they must get a fire lit, that we need hot water and then mulled ale. Tell them it is my command. And ask them for something for her to bite on, a wooden spoon if nothing else. And tell my women to bring all the linen we have.'

A great wave tosses the boat upwards and sends us staggering from one side of the cabin to the other. My mother grabs the edge of the bed. 'Go,' she says to me. 'And get a man to hold you on the ship. Don't get washed overboard.'

At the warning I find I dare not open the door to the storm and the heaving sea outside.

'Go,' my mother says sternly.

Helplessly, I nod and step out of the cabin. The deck is knee-deep in water, washing over the ship; as soon as it drains away another wave crashes on us, the prow climbs and then crashes, shuddering, as it falls into the sea. For sure, the ship cannot take this pounding for much longer, it must break up. A figure, shrouded in water, staggers past me. I grab his arm. 'Take me to the ladies' cabin and then the galley,' I shriek against the shrieking of the wind.

'God save us, God save us, we are lost!' He pulls away from me.

'You take me to the ladies' cabin and then to the galley!' I scream at him. 'I command you. My mother commands you.'

'This is a witch's wind,' he says horrifyingly. 'It sprung up as soon as the women came on board. Women on board, one of them dying, they bring a witch's wind.' He pulls away from me and a sudden heave of the ship throws me onto the rail. I cling to it as a mighty wall of water stands before the stern and then washes down on us. It takes me, lifting me clear off my feet, only my hands snatching at the ropes and my gown caught on a cleat save me, but it takes him. I see his white face in the green water as it plucks him over the rail and he goes past me, turning over and over in the wave, his arms and legs flailing, his white mouth opening and closing like a cursing fish. He is out of sight in a moment, and the ship shudders under the hammer blow from the sea.

'Man overboard!' I shout. My voice is a little pipe against the pounding drums of the storm. I look round. The crew are lashed to their stations; nobody is going to help him. The water drains off the deck past my knees. I cling to the railing and look over the side, but he is gone into the darkness of the black waters. The sea has swallowed him up and left no trace. The ship wallows in the trough of the waves but there is another towering wave coming. A sudden crack of lightning shows me the door to the galley, and I tear my gown from the cleat that saved me and make a dash for the doors.

The fires have been washed out, the room is filled with smoke and steam, the pans are clashing on their hooks as they lurch one way and then the other, the cook is wedged behind his table. 'You have to light the fire,' I gasp. 'And get us mulled ale, and hot water.'

He laughs in my face. 'We're going down!' he says with mad humour. 'We're going down and you come in here wanting mulled ale!'

'My sister is in labour! We have to have hot water!'

'To do what?' he demands of me, as if it is an entertainment of question and answer. 'To save her, so that she can give birth to fishes' meat? For without a doubt her baby will drown and her with it, and all of us with them.'

'I command you to help me!' I say through clenched teeth. 'I, Anne Neville, the kingmaker's daughter, command you!'

'Ach, she'll have to do without,' he says, as if he has lost interest. As he speaks the boat yaws violently and the door bursts open. A wave of water sweeps down the stairs and breaks into the fireplace.

'Give me some linen,' I persist. 'Rags. Anything. And a spoon for her to bite on.'

Bracing himself he reaches under the table and heaves out a basket of bleached cloths. 'Wait,' he says. From another box he brings a wooden spoon and from a cupboard he produces a dark glass bottle. 'Brandy,' he says. 'You can give her that. Take some yourself, bonny maid, might as well drown merry.'

I take the basket in my arms and start up the steps. A heave of the ship throws me forwards and I am out in the storm, my arms full, and dashing to the cabin door before another wave breaks over the deck.

Inside the cabin my mother is bending over Isabel, who is moaning steadily. I fall inwards and bang the door shut behind me as my mother straightens up. 'Is the galley fire out?' she asks.

Mutely I nod. The ship heaves and rocks, and we stagger as it shudders. 'Sit down,' she says. 'This is going to take a long time. It is going to be a long hard night.'

All through the night my only thought is that if we can plough through these seas, if we can survive this, then at the end of the voyage there is the outstretched arm of the Calais harbour wall and the shelter behind it. There is the familiar quayside where people will be looking for us, anxiously waiting with hot drinks and dry clothes, and when we come ashore they will gather us up, and rush us up to the castle, and Isabel will be put in our bedroom and the midwives will come, and she will be able to tie her holy girdle around her straining belly, and pin the pilgrim badges to her gown.

Then she will have a proper confinement, locked in her rooms and I locked in with her. Then she will give birth with half a dozen midwives at her beck and call, and physicians at the ready, and everything prepared for the baby: the swaddling board, the cot, the wet nurse, a priest to bless the baby the moment that he is born and cense the room.

I sleep in the chair as Isabel dozes and my mother lies beside her. Now and then Isabel cries out and my mother gets up and feels her belly which stands up square, like a box, and Isabel cries that she cannot bear the pain, and my mother holds her clenched fists and tells her that it will pass. Then it goes again and she lies down, whimpering. The storm subsides but rumbles around us, lightning on the horizon, thunder in the seas, the clouds so low that we cannot see land even though we can hear the waves crashing on the French rocks.

Dawn comes but the sky hardly lightens, the waves come rounded and regular, tossing the ship this way and that. The crew go hand over hand to the prow of the ship where a sail has been torn down and they cut it away, bundling it overboard as waste. The cook gets the galley fire working and everyone has a tot of hot grog and he sends mulled ale to Isabel and all of us. My mother's three ladies with my half-sister Margaret come to the cabin and bring a clean shift for Isabel to wear, and take away the stained bedding. Isabel sleeps until the pain rouses her; she is getting so tired that now only the worst racking contractions can wake her. She is becoming dreamy with fatigue and pain. When I put my hand on her forehead she is burning up, her face still white but a hot red spot on each cheek.

'What's the matter with her?' I ask Margaret.

She says nothing, just shakes her head.

'Is she ill?' I whisper to my mother.

'The baby is stuck inside her,' my mother says. 'As soon as we land she will have to have a midwife turn it.'

I gape at her. I don't even know what she is talking about. 'Is that bad?' I ask. 'Turning a baby? Is that bad? It sounds bad.'

'Yes,' she says baldly. 'It's bad. I have seen it done and it is a pain beyond pain. Go and ask your father how long before we get to Calais.'

I duck out of the cabin again. It is raining now, steady heavy rain that pours down out of a dark sky, and the sea is running strongly under the ship and pushing us on our way though the wind is buffeting against us. Father is on deck beside the steersman, the captain beside him.

'My Lady Mother asks when we will get to Calais?' I say.

He looks down at me and I can see he is shocked at my appearance. My headdress is off and my hair tumbled down, my gown torn and bloodstained, and I am soaked through and barefoot. Also, there is a wild sort of desperation about me: I have watched through the night, I have been warned that my sister might die. I have been able to do nothing for her but wade through water to the galley to get her a wooden spoon to bite on in her agony.

'In an hour or two,' he says. 'Not long now. How is Isabel?'

'She needs a midwife.'

'In an hour or two she will have one,' he says with a warm smile. 'You tell her, from me. She has my word. She will have her dinner at home in our castle. She will make her confinement with the best physicians in France.'

The very words cheer me, and I smile back at him.

'Set yourself to rights,' he says shortly. 'You're the sister of the Queen of England. Put your shoes on, change out of that gown.'

I bow, and duck back to the cabin.

We wait. It is a very long couple of hours. I shake out my gown; I have no change of clothes, but I plait my hair and put on my headdress. Isabel moans in the bed, sleeps, and wakes in pain; and then I hear the lookout shout, 'Land ho! Starboard bow! Calais!'

I jump up from my chair and look out of the window. I can see the familiar profile of the high walls of the town, the vaulted roof of the Staple Hall, and the tower of the cathedral, then the castle on top of the hill, the battlements, and our own windows with the lights shining. I shade my eyes against the driving rain, but I can see my bedroom window, and the candles lit for me, the shutters left open in welcome. I can see my home. I know we will be safe. We are home. The relief is extraordinary, I feel my shoulders lighten as if they have been hunched against the weight of fear. We are home and Isabel is safe.

There is a grinding noise and a terrible rattle. I look at the walls of the castle, where dozens of men are working at a great windlass, its gears clanking and screaming as they turn it, slowly. Before us, at the mouth of the harbour, I can see a chain coming out of the depths of the sea, trailing weed from the deepest depths, slowly rising up to bar our way.

'Quickly!' I scream, as if we could cram on sail and get over the chain before it is too high. But we don't need to race the barrier; as soon as they recognise us they will drop the chain, as soon as they see the standard with the ragged staff of Warwick they will let us in. Father is the most beloved captain that Calais has ever had. Calais is his town, not a town for York nor Lancaster, but loyal to him alone. This is my childhood home. I look up to the castle, and just below my bedroom window I can see the gun placements are being manned, and the cannon are rolling out, one after another, as if the castle is preparing for attack.

It is a mistake, I say to myself. They must have mistaken us for King Edward's ship. But then I look higher. Above the battlements is not Father's flag, the ragged staff, but the white rose of York, and the royal standard, flying together. Calais has remained true to Edward and the House of York, even though we have changed. Father declared that Calais was for York, and it has remained loyal to York. Calais does not shift with the tides. It is loyal as we were once loyal; but now we have become the enemy.

The steersman sees the danger of the rising chain just in time and shouts a warning. The captain leaps down to bellow at the sailors. Father flings himself on the wheel, heaving at it with the steersman to turn the ship away from the deadly snare of the taut chain. The sails flap dangerously as we turn sideways to the wind and the heaving sea pushes the ship sideways and looks likely to overturn us.

'Turn more, turn more, reef the sail!' Father shouts and, groaning, the ship comes round. There is a sickening explosion from the castle and a cannonball drops into the sea near the bow. They have our range. They have us in their sights. They will sink us if we don't get away.

I cannot believe that our own home has turned against us but Father gets the ship round and out of range at once, without hesitation. Then he reefs the sail and drops the anchor. I have never seen him more angry. He sends an officer in a little boat with a message into his own garrison demanding entrance of the men he commanded. We have to wait. The sea stirs and heaves, the wind blows us so that the anchor chain is taut, the ship pulls angrily, dips and rolls. I leave the cabin and go to the side of the ship to look back at my home. I cannot believe they have shut us out. I cannot believe that I will not be going up the stone stairs to my bedroom and calling for a hot bath and clean clothes. Now I can see a small boat coming out of the harbour. I hear it bump as it comes alongside and the shouts of the sailors who let down ropes. Up come some barrels of wine, some biscuits and some cheese for Isabel. That is all. They have no message; there is nothing to say. They sheer off and sail back to Calais. That is all. They have barred us from our home and sent wine to Isabel out of pity.

'Anne!' my mother calls, shouting into the wind. 'Come here.'

I stagger back to the cabin, as I hear the anchor chain creak protestingly, and then the rattle as it comes on board and sets us free. The ship is groaning, released again to the mercy of the sea, pounded by the waves, pushed along by the wind. I don't know what course Father will set. I don't know where we can go now that we have been banned from our own home. We cannot return to England, we are traitors to England's king. Calais will not admit us. Where can we go? Is there anywhere that we will be safe?

Inside the cabin, Isabel is up on the bed on her hands and knees, lowing like a dying animal. She looks at me through a tangle of hair and her face is white and her eyes rimmed red. I can hardly recognise her; she is as ugly as a tortured beast. My mother lifts her gown at the back and her linen is bloody. I have a glimpse and I look away.

'You have to put your hands in, and turn the baby,' my mother says. 'My hands are too big. I can't do it.'

I look at her with utter horror. 'What?'

'We have no midwife, we have to turn the baby ourselves,' my mother says impatiently. 'She's so small that my hands are too big. You'll have to do it.'

I look at my slender hands, my long fingers. 'I don't know what to do,' I say.

'I'll tell you.'

'I can't do it.'

'You have to.'

'Mother, I am a maid, a girl – I shouldn't even be here . . .'

A scream from Isabel as she drops her head to the bed interrupts me. 'Annie, for the love of God, help me. Get it out! Get it out of me!'

My mother takes my arm and drags me to the foot of the bed. Margaret lifts Isabel's linen; her hindquarters are horribly bloody. 'Put your hand in there,' my mother says. 'Push in. What can you feel?'

Isabel cries out in pain as I put my hand to her yielding flesh and slide it in. Disgust – disgust is all I feel through the hot flesh, and horror. Then something vile: like a leg.

Isabel's body contracts on my hand like a vice, crushing my fingers. I cry out: 'Don't do that! You're hurting me!'

She gasps like a dying cow. 'I can't help it. Annie, get it out.'

The slithery leg kicks at my touch. 'I have it. I think it's a leg, or an arm.'

'Can you find the other?'

I shake my head.

'Then pull it anyway,' my mother says.

I look at her aghast.

'We have to get it out. Pull gently.'

I start to pull. Isabel screams. I bite my lip, this is disgusting, horrifying work and Isabel disgusts and horrifies me that she should be here like this, like a fat mare, labouring like a whore, forcing me to do this. I find I am grimacing, my head turned aside as if I don't want to see, standing as far as I can from the bed, from her, from my sister, this monster, touching her without pity, holding tight onto this limb as I am ordered, despite my loathing.

'Can you get your other hand in?'

I look at my mother as if she is mad. This is not possible.

'See if you can get your other hand in, and get hold of the baby.'

I had forgotten there was a baby, I am so shocked by the horror of the stench and the sensation of the slippery little limb in my hand. Gently I try to press my other hand in. Something yields horribly, and I can feel, with the tips of my fingers, something that might be an arm, a shoulder.

'An arm?' I say. I grit my teeth so I don't retch.

'Push it away, feel down, get the other leg.' My mother is wringing her hands, desperate to get the work done, patting Isabel's back as if she were a sick dog.

'I've got the other leg,' I say.

'When I tell you – you have to pull both legs,' she commands. She steps sideways and takes Isabel's head in her hands. She speaks to her: 'When you feel your pain is coming you have to push,' she says. 'Push hard.'

'I can't,' Isabel sobs. 'I can't, Mother. I can't.'

'You have to. You must. Tell me as the pain comes.'

There is a pause and then Isabel's groans gather strength and she screams: 'Now, it is now.'

'Push!' my mother says. The ladies get hold of her clenched fists and heave on her arms, as if we are tearing her apart.

Margaret slips the wooden spoon in her mouth and Isabel howls and bites down on it. 'You pull the baby,' my mother shouts at me. 'Now. Steady. Pull.'

I pull as I am ordered, and horribly I feel something click and give under my hands. 'No! It's broken, broken!'

'Pull it. Pull it anyway!'

I pull, there is a rush and a gout of blood, a stink of liquid and two little legs are dangling from Isabel and she screams and pants.

'Once more,' Mother says. She sounds oddly triumphant, but I am filled with terror. 'Nearly there now, once again, Isabel. As the pain comes.'

Isabel groans and heaves herself up.

'Pull, Anne!' Mother commands and I hold the thin little slippery legs and pull again, and there is a moment when nothing moves at all and then one shoulder comes and then another and then Isabel shrieks as the head comes and I clearly see her flesh tear, as if she were a crimson and blue brocade, red blood and blue veins tear as the head comes out and then the slithery cord, and I drop the baby on the bedding and turn my head away and am sick on the floor.

The ship heaves, we all stagger with the movement, and then Mother comes hand over hand down the bed, and gently takes up the child and wraps him in the linen. I am shuddering, rubbing my bloody hands and arms on some rags, rubbing the vomit from my mouth but waiting for the words that will tell us a miracle has happened. I am waiting for the first miraculous little cry.

There is silence.

Isabel is moaning quietly. I can see that she is bleeding but nobody staunches her wounds. My mother has the baby wrapped warmly. One of the women looks up smiling, her face stained with tears. We all wait for the little cry, we wait for my mother's smile.

My mother's exhausted face is grey. 'It's a boy,' she says

harshly: the one thing we all want to hear. But oddly, there is no joy in her voice and her mouth is grim.

'A boy?' I repeat hopefully.

'Yes, it's a boy. But it's a dead boy. He is dead.'

The sailors take down the sails and cart them to the sailyards for repair, and scrub out the royal cabin where the boards are stained with Izzy's blood and my vomit. They say that it is a miracle we were not drowned in the storm, they speak of their own horror when the chain went up across the Calais harbour entrance. They say only my father's weight on the wheel made it possible for the steersman to get the ship round. They say they never want to take a voyage like that again, but if they had to, they would only do it with my father at the wheel. They say that he saved them. But never again will they sail with women on board. They shake their heads. Never again with women who are chased by a witch's wind. They are exultant in their survival. They all think that the ship was cursed with a woman in labour and a dead baby on board. They all believe that the ship was chased by a witch's wind whistled up by the queen to blow us to hell. Everywhere I go on board there is an immediate and total silence. They think the witch's wind was hunting us, will follow us still. They blame us for everything.

They get up the chests from the hold and at last we can wash and change our clothes. Isabel is still bleeding but she gets up and gets dressed, though her gowns hang oddly on her. Her proud belly has gone, she just looks fat and sick. Izzy's holy girdle and pilgrim badges for her confinement are unpacked with her jewels. She puts them in the box at the foot of our bed without comment. There is a wordless awkwardness between the two of us. Something terrible has happened, so terrible that we don't even know how to name it or speak of it. She disgusts me, she disgusts herself, and we say nothing about it. Mother takes the dead baby away in a box and someone blesses it and throws it into the sea, I think. Nobody tells us, and we don't ask. I know that it was my inexperienced tugging that pulled his leg from the socket; but I don't know if I killed him. I don't know if Izzy thinks this, or Mother knows it. Nobody says anything to me either way, and I am never going to speak of it again. The disgust and the horror lies in my belly like seasickness.

She should be in confinement until she has been churched, we should all be locked in her rooms with her for six weeks, and then emerge to be purified. But there are no traditions for giving birth to a dead baby in a witch's storm at sea; nothing seems to be as it should. George comes to see her when the cabin is clean and her bed has fresh linen. She is resting as he comes in and he leans over the bed to kiss her pale forehead, and smiles at me. 'I am sorry for your loss,' he says.

She hardly looks at him. 'Our loss,' she corrects him. 'It was a boy.'

His handsome face is impassive. I guess that Mother has already told him. 'There will be others,' he says. It sounds more like a threat than a reassurance. He goes to the door as if he cannot wait to get out of the cabin. I wonder if we smell, if he can smell death and fear on us.

'If we had not been nearly wrecked at sea I think the baby would have lived,' she says with sudden viciousness. 'If I had been at Warwick Castle I would have had midwives to attend me. I could have had my holy girdle and the priest would have prayed for me. If you had not ridden out with Father against the king and come home beaten, I would have had my baby at home and he would be alive now.' She pauses. His handsome face is quite impassive. 'It's your fault,' she says.

'I hear that Queen Elizabeth is with child again,' he remarks, as if this is an answer to her accusation. 'Please God she gets another girl, or a dead baby herself. We have to have a son before she does. This is just a setback, it is not the end.' He tries to smile cheerfully at her. 'It's not the end,' he repeats and goes out.

Isabel just looks at me, her face blank. 'It is the end of my baby,' she observes. 'Certainly, it is the end of him.'

Nobody knows what is happening but Father; and though we seem to be homeless and defeated, washed up at the mouth of the Seine, he is strangely cheerful. His fleet of warships escapes from Southampton and joins us, so he has fighting men and his great ship the *Trinity* under his command once more. He is writing constantly and sending messages to King Louis of France; but he does not tell us what he plans. He orders new clothes for himself, and has them cut in the French fashion, a velvet cap on his thick brown hair. We move to Valognes, so that the fleet can prepare in Barfleur for an invasion of England. Isabel makes the move in silence. She and George are given beautiful rooms on the upper floor of the manor house, but she avoids him. Most of the day she spends with me in Mother's presence chamber where we open the windows for air and close the shutters against the sun and sit all the day in warm gloom. It is very hot, and Isabel feels the heat. She complains of a constant headache, fatigue even in the morning when she first wakes. Once she remarks that she cannot see the point of anything, and when I ask her what she means she just shakes her head and her eyes fill with tears. We sit on the stone windowsill of the big chamber and look out at the river and the green fields beyond and neither of us can see the point of anything. We never say anything about the baby who was taken away by Mother in the little box and thrown in the sea. We never say anything about the storm, or the wind, or the sea. We never say much at all. We sit in silence for a lot of the time, and there is no need to talk.

'I wish we were back in Calais,' Isabel says suddenly one hot quiet morning, and I know she means that she wishes none of this had ever happened – not the rebellion against the sleeping king and the bad queen, not Father's victory, not his rebellion against King Edward, and most of all: no marriage to George. It is to wish away almost every event of our childhood. It is to wish away every attempt at greatness.

'What else could Father have done?' Of course, he had to struggle against the sleeping king and the bad queen. He knew they were in the wrong, they had to be pushed from the throne. Then, when they were defeated and thrown down, he could not bear to see the couple that replaced them. He could not live in an England ruled by the Rivers family; he had to raise his standard against King Edward. He is driven to see the kingdom under the rule of a good king, advised by us; George should be that king. I understand that Father cannot stop striving for this. As his daughter I know that my life will be shaped by this unending struggle to get us where we should be: the first power behind the throne. Isabel should realise this. We were born the kingmaker's daughters; ruling England is our inheritance.

'If Father had not turned against the king, I would have had my baby at home,' she goes on resentfully. 'If we had not set sail on that day, into that wind, I would have a baby in my arms now. Instead of nothing. I have nothing, and I hardly care at all.'

'You will get another baby,' I say – as Mother has told me to. Isabel is to be reminded that she will have another child. Isabel is not allowed to indulge herself in despair.

'I have nothing,' she repeats simply.

We hardly stir when there is a hammer at the door, the double doors are opened by one of the guards, and a woman comes quietly in. Isabel raises her head. 'I am sorry, my Lady Mother is away,' she says. 'We cannot grant requests.'

'Where is the countess?' the woman asks.

'With my father,' Isabel says. 'Who are you?'

'And where is your father?'

We don't know, but we are not going to admit it. 'He is away. Who are you?'

The woman puts back her hood. With a shock I recognise one of the York ladies in waiting: Lady Sutcliffe. I jump to my feet and stand before Isabel as if to protect her. 'What are you doing here? What d'you want? Have you come from the queen?' I have a pang of sudden terror that she has come to kill us both and I look at her hands, tucked in her cloak as if she is holding a knife.

She smiles. 'I have come to see you, Lady Isabel, and you too, Lady Anne, and to speak with your husband George, the duke.'

'What for?' Isabel asks rudely.

'Do you know what your father is planning for you now?'

'What?'

The woman looks towards me as if she thinks I am too young to be present. 'Perhaps Lady Anne should go to her room while I talk to you?'

Isabel clutches my hand. 'Anne stays with me. And you shouldn't even be here.'

'I have come all the way from London as a friend to warn you, to warn you both. The king himself does not know I am here. Your mother-in-law, the Duchess Cecily, sent me to speak with you, for your own good. She wants me to warn you. You know how she cares for you and for your husband, her favourite son George. She told me to tell you that your father is now dealing with England's enemy: Louis of France.' She ignores our shocked faces. 'Worse even than that: he is making an alliance with Margaret of Anjou. He is planning to make war on the true king, Edward; and restore King Henry to the throne.'

I shake my head in instant denial. 'He never would,' I say. Father's victories over the bad queen, Margaret of Anjou, and the sleeping king, Henry VI, were the stories of my childhood. Father's hatred and contempt for them were my lullabies. He fought battle after battle to throw them down from the throne and replace them with the House of York. He would never, never make an alliance with them. His own father died fighting them, and Margaret of Anjou spiked the heads of my grandfather and my uncle on the walls of York, as if they were traitors. We will never forgive her. We will never forgive her for this, if we forgave her for every other sort of corruption and evil. Father would never make an alliance with her after that. She was the nightmare of my childhood; she is our enemy till death. 'He would never ally with her,' I say.

'Oh yes, he would.' She turns to Isabel. 'I have come in friendship to warn your husband George Duke of Clarence. And to reassure him. He can return to England; his brother the king will receive him. His mother has arranged this and wants to welcome you too. You are both beloved of the House of York, now and always. George is next in line to the throne of England, he is still heir to the throne. If there is no son born to the king and queen then you could be queen one day. But – think of this – if your father puts the old king back on the throne you will be nothing, and all that you have suffered will be for nothing.'

'We can't join Lancaster,' I say almost to myself. 'Father cannot be thinking of it.'

'No,' she agrees shortly. 'You cannot. The idea is ridiculous. We all know that; everyone knows it but your father. This is why I have come to warn you. I have come to you, not to him, and you must consult your husband and see where your best interests lie. Duchess Cecily – your mother-in-law – wants you to know that you are to come home and she will be as a mother to you, even if your father is the enemy of the House of York and all of England. She says come home and she will see that you are properly cared for. She is appalled – we were all appalled – to hear of your ordeal at sea. We were shocked that your father would take you into such danger. The duchess is grieved for you and heartbroken for the loss of her grandson. It would have been her first grandson. She went into her room and prayed all night for his little soul. You must come home and let us all take care of you.'

The tears start into Isabel's eyes when she thinks of Duchess Cecily praying for the baby's soul. 'I want to come home,' she whispers.

'We can't,' I say at once. 'We have to be with Father.'

'Please tell Her Grace that I thank her,' Isabel stammers. 'I am glad of her prayers. But of course, I don't know what ... I shall have to do as my fa ... I shall have to do as my husband commands me.'

'We are afraid that you are grieving,' the woman says tenderly. 'Grieving and alone.'

Isabel blinks away the tears that come so quickly to her these days. 'Of course I feel my loss,' she says with dignity. 'But I have the comfort of my sister.'

Lady Sutcliffe bows. 'I shall go to your husband and warn him of what your father is planning. The duke must save himself, and he must save you from the Lancastrian Queen Margaret. Don't mention my visit to your father. He would be angry to know that you received me and that now you know that he is faithless.'

I am about to declare stoutly that Father is not faithless, that he could never be faithless, and that we would never keep a secret from him. But then I realise that I don't know where he is now in his new French clothes – nor what he is doing.

ANGERS, FRANCE, JULY 1470

Father orders us to join him at Angers and sends a handsome liveried guard for the long ride. He sends no explanation as to why
we are to travel nor where we will stay, so when we arrive, after five
long days on the dusty roads, we are surprised that he is waiting to
meet us outside the town, looking handsome and proud, high on
Midnight, with a mounted guard beside him, and he escorts us
through the walled gates, through the streets where people doff
their hats as we go by, into the courtyard of a great manor house
on the wide main square, which he has requisitioned. Isabel is
white with fatigue and yet he does not give her permission to go to
her bedroom but says that we are to go straight into dinner.

In the great hall my mother is waiting for us before a square
table laden with food; it is like a banquet. She greets me and
Isabel with a kiss and her blessing and then looks to my father.
He seats Isabel on one side of the table, while George comes in
and takes his place beside her with a murmured greeting. We
bow our heads for grace, and then Father smiles on us all and
bids us eat. He does not thank Isabel for making the long journey, nor commend her courage to her husband.

Me, he praises for my looks that he says are blooming in
France – how is it that experiences which exhaust my sister make
me so pretty? He pours the best wine into my glass, he places me
between my mother and himself. He cuts slices of meat for me

93

and the server puts them before me, serving me before Isabel, before my mother. I look at the food on my plate and I don't dare to taste it. What does it mean when the best cut of meat is served to me before anyone else? Suddenly, having spent my life following Isabel and my mother into every room we ever enter, I am going first.

'My Lord Father?'

He smiles and at the warmth in his face I find I am smiling back. 'Ah, you are my clever girl,' he says tenderly. 'You always were the brightest cleverest girl. You are wondering what plans I have for you.'

I don't dare to look at Isabel, who will have heard him call me the brightest cleverest girl. I don't dare to look at George. I never dare to look at my mother. I know that George has met Lady Sutcliffe in secret, and I guess that he is afraid that Father knows. This sudden favour to me might be Father's warning to George that he cannot play us false. I see Isabel's hands are trembling and she puts them under the table out of sight.

'I have arranged a marriage for you,' my father says quietly.

'What?'

This is the last thing I expected. I am so shocked that I turn to my mother. She looks back at me, perfectly serene; clearly she knows all about this.

'A great marriage,' he continues. I can hear the excitement under the level tones of his voice. 'The greatest marriage that could be got for you. The only marriage for you now. I daresay you can guess who I mean?'

At my stunned silence he laughs merrily, laughs in our dumbstruck faces. 'Guess!' he says.

I look at Isabel. For a moment only I think perhaps we are going home, we will reconcile with the House of York and I will marry Richard. Then I see George's sulky face and I am certain it cannot be that. 'Father, I cannot guess,' I say.

'My daughter, you are going to marry Prince Edward of Lancaster, and you will be the next Queen of England.'

There is a clatter as George drops his knife to the floor. He and Isabel are frozen as if enchanted, staring at my father. I realise that George has been hoping – desperately hoping – that Lady Sutcliffe was reporting false rumours. Now it looks as if she was telling only part of the truth, and the whole of it is worse than any of us could have imagined.

'The bad queen's son?' I ask childishly. In a rush, all the old stories and fears come back to me. I was brought up thinking of Margaret of Anjou as all but a beast, a she-wolf who rode out at the head of wild men, destroying everything in their path, in the grip of her terrible ambition, carrying with them a comatose king who slept through everything, as she tore England apart, murdered my grandfather, my uncle, tried to assassinate my own father in the kitchen with a roasting spit, in the court with swords; and was finally only defeated by him and Edward, our Edward, fighting uphill through snow in the most terrible battle that England has ever seen. Then like a blizzard herself, she blew away with the bloodstained snow into the cold North. They captured her husband and let him sleep in the Tower where he could do no harm; but she and the icy boy, who was inexplicably conceived by a wolf mother and sleeping father, were never seen again.

'Prince Edward of Lancaster, the son of Queen Margaret of Anjou. They live in France now and are supported by her father René of Anjou, who is King of Hungary, Majorca, Sardinia and Jerusalem. She is kinswoman to King Louis of France.' My father carefully ignores my exclamation. 'He will help us put together an invasion of England. We will defeat the House of York, free King Henry from the Tower, and you will be crowned Princess of Wales. King Henry and I will rule England together until he dies – saints preserve him! – and then I will guide and advise you and Prince Edward of Lancaster who will be King and Queen of England. Your son, my grandson, will be the next King of England – and perhaps of Jerusalem too. Think of that.'

George is choking as if drowning on his wine. We all turn to him. He whoops and flails and cannot catch his breath. My father waits until his fit subsides, watching him without sympathy. 'This is a setback for you, George,' my father concedes fairly. 'But you will be heir to the throne after Prince Edward, and you will be brother-in-law to the King of England. You will be as close to the throne as you have always been, and the Rivers will have been thrown down. Your influence will be clear, and your rewards great.' My father nods at him kindly. He does not even look at Isabel who was going to be Queen of England but will now give precedence to me. 'George, I shall see that you keep your title and all your lands. You are no worse off than you were before.'

'I am worse off,' Isabel remarks quietly. 'I have lost my baby for nothing.'

Nobody answers her. It is as if she has become so unimportant that nobody needs to reply.

'What if the king is still asleep?' I ask. 'When you get to London? What if you can't wake him?'

My father shrugs. 'It doesn't matter. Whether he is sleeping or awake I shall command in his name until Prince Edward and –' he smiles at me '– Princess Anne take their thrones and become King Edward and Queen Anne of England.'

'The House of Lancaster restored!' George leaps to his feet, malmsey wine staining his mouth, his face flushed with rage, his hands shaking. Isabel tentatively puts out her hand and rests it on his clenched fist. 'Have we gone through all this to restore the House of Lancaster? Have we faced such dangers on land and sea in order to put Lancaster back on the throne? Have I betrayed my brother and deserted my House of York to put Lancaster on the throne?'

'The House of Lancaster has a good claim,' my father concedes, throwing away the alliance with York that his family forged and defended for two generations. 'Your brother's claim for York is a poor one if he is indeed, as you suggest, a bastard.'

'I named him as a bastard to make me the next heir to the

throne,' George shouts. 'We were fighting to put *me* on the throne. We discredited Edward to prove *my* claim. We never discredited my house, we never slandered York! We never said that anyone should be king but me!'

'It couldn't be done,' my father says with mild regret as if speaking of a battle that was lost long, long ago, in a country far away, rather than England, and only this spring. 'We tried it twice, George, you know. Edward was too strong for us, there were too many people on his side. But with Queen Margaret in alliance with us she will bring out half of England, all the old Lancaster lords will flock to us, the Lancaster gentry who have never taken to your brother. She has always been strong in the North and Midlands. Jasper Tudor will bring out Wales for her. Edward will never be able to defeat an alliance of you and me and Margaret of Anjou.'

It is so strange to me to hear her name no longer cursed but cited as an ally – I used to have nightmares about this woman, yet now she is to be our trusted friend.

'Now,' my father says. 'You, Anne, have to go with your mother and meet the seamstresses. Isabel, you can go too, you are all to have new gowns for Anne's betrothal.'

'My betrothal?'

He smiles as if he thinks to give me the greatest joy. 'Betrothed now, and then the wedding as soon as we have the permission from the Pope.'

'I am to be betrothed straightaway?'

'The day after tomorrow.'

ANGERS CATHEDRAL, 25 JULY 1470

There are two silent figures at the high altar in the cathedral, handfast, plighting their troth. A light from the great window behind them illuminates their grave faces. They incline towards each other as if they are promising love as well as loyalty to death. They hold each other close, as if to be certain of each other. Someone watching might think this a love match from the intensity of their gaze and the closeness of their pose.

It is those great enemies, my father and Margaret of Anjou, side by side. This is the great union; her son and I will merely enact with our bodies this plighting of our parents. First she puts her hand on a fragment of the True Cross – the real cross brought here from the kingdom of Jerusalem – and even from the back of the cathedral I can hear her clear voice reciting an oath of loyalty to my father. Then it is his turn. He puts his hand on the cross and she adjusts it, making sure that every part of his palm and his fingers are on the sacred wood as if, even now, in the very act of swearing their alliance, she doesn't trust him. He recites his oath, then they turn to one another and give each other the kiss of reconciliation. They are allies, they will be allies till death, they have sworn a sacred oath, nothing can part them.

'I can't do it,' I whisper to Isabel. 'I can't marry her son, I can't be a daughter to the bad queen, to the sleeping king. What if their son is as mad as everyone says? What if he murders me, orders me beheaded as he did to the two York lords who guarded his father? They say he is a monster, with blood on his hands from childhood. They say he kills men for sport. What if they cut off my head as they did our grandfather's?'

'Hush,' she says, taking my cold hands in hers and rubbing them gently. 'You're talking like a child. You have to be brave. You're going to be a princess.'

'I can't be in the House of Lancaster!'

'You can,' she says. 'You have to be.'

'You once said that you were afraid that our father used you as a pawn.'

She shrugs. 'Did I?'

'Used you as a pawn and might let you fall.'

'If you are going to be Queen of England he won't let you fall,' she observes shrewdly. 'If you are going to be Queen of England he will love you and serve you every moment of the day. You've always been his pet – you should be glad that now you are the centre of his ambition.'

'Izzy,' I say quietly. 'You were the centre of his ambition when he nearly drowned you at sea.'

Her face is almost greenish in the dim light of the church. 'I know,' she says bleakly.

I hesitate at this, and our mother comes up and says briskly, 'I am to present you to Her Grace the queen.'

I follow her up the long aisle of the cathedral, the dazzling stained-glass window making a carpet of colour beneath my feet, as if I were walking over the sun in splendour. It strikes me it is the second time that my mother has presented me to a Queen of England. The first time I saw the most beautiful woman I have ever known. This time: the most ferocious. The queen sees me coming, turns towards us and waits, with a killer's patience, for me to reach the chancel steps. My mother sinks into a deep curtsey and I go down too. When I come up I see a short plump woman, magnificently gowned in cloth-of-gold brocade, a towering headdress on her head draped in gold lace, a gold belt slung low around her broad hips.

Her round face is stern, her rosebud mouth unsmiling. 'You are Lady Anne,' she says in French.

I bow my head. 'Yes, Your Grace.'

'You are to marry my son, and you will be my daughter.'

I bow again. Clearly, this is not an inquiry as to my happiness. When I look at her again her face is bright as gold with triumph. 'Lady Anne, you are only a young woman now, a nobody; but I am going to make you Queen of England and you will sit on my throne and wear my crown.'

'Lady Anne has been prepared for such a position,' my mother says.

The queen ignores her. She steps forwards and takes both my hands between hers, as if I am swearing fealty to her. 'I will teach you to be a queen,' she says quietly. 'I will teach you what I know of courage, of leadership. My son will be king but you will stand beside him, ready to defend the throne with your life, you will be a queen as I have been – a queen who can command, who can rule, who can make alliances and hold to them. I was just a girl, not much older than you, when I first came to England and I learned quickly enough that to hold the throne of England you have to cleave to your husband and fight for his throne, night and day, Anne. Night and day. I will hammer you into a sword for England, just as I was hammered into a blade. I will teach you to be a dagger at the throat of treason.'

I think of the horrors that this queen unleashed on the country with her court favourites and her ambition. I think of my father swearing that the king had flung himself into a sleep like death because he could not bear waking life with her. I think of the years when my father ruled England and this woman raged in Scotland, raising an army which came south like a band of brigands, half-naked, stealing, raping and murdering wherever they went until the country swore that they would have no more of this queen, and the citizens of London closed their gates to her and begged her best friend Jacquetta Woodville to tell her to take the army of the North back to their home.

Something of this shows in my face for she laughs shortly, and says to me: 'It is easy to be squeamish when you are a girl. It is easy to be principled when you have nothing. But when you are a woman and you have a son destined for the throne, after years of waiting, and when you are a queen and you want to keep your crown, you will be ready to do anything; anything. You will be ready to kill for it: kill innocents if need be. And you will be glad then that I have taught you all that I know.' She smiles at me. 'When you can do anything – anything – to keep your throne and keep your crown and keep your husband where he should be, then you will know that you have learned from me. Then you will be my daughter indeed.'

She repels me, she absolutely terrifies me. I dare say nothing.

She turns to the high altar. I see a slight figure standing beside my father: Prince Edward. There is a bishop before him with his missal open at the page of the marriage service.

'Come,' the bad queen says. 'This is your first step, I will guide all the others.' She takes me by the hand and leads me towards him.

I am fourteen years old, the daughter of an arraigned traitor in exile with a price on his head. I am about to be betrothed to a boy nearly three years older than me, the son of the most terrifying woman England has ever known, and through this marriage my father will bring her back into England like the wolf that they call her. And from this moment I will have to call this monster my mother.

I glance back at Isabel, who seems a long way away. She tries to smile encouragingly at me but her face is strained and pale in the darkness of the cathedral. I remember her saying to me on her wedding night: 'Don't go.' I mouth the words to her and then I turn and walk towards my father to do his bidding.

I cannot believe the life that is unfolding before me. In the cold light of the winter mornings I wake beside Isabel and have to lie still and look around the stone walls of the room and the tapestries, dull-coloured in the early light, to remind myself of where I am, how far we have come, and my dazzling incredible future. Then I tell myself once more: I am Anne of Warwick; still me. I am betrothed to Prince Edward of Lancaster, I am Princess of Wales while the old king lives, and on his death I will be Queen Anne of England.

'You're muttering again,' Isabel says crossly. 'Muttering like a mad old woman. Shut up, you sound ridiculous.'

I press my lips together to silence myself. This has become my ritual, as regularly observed as Prime. I cannot start the day without running through the changes in my life. It is as if I cannot believe that I am here, without reciting my expectations, my unbelievable hopes. First I open my eyes and see again that I am in one of the best rooms of the beautiful chateau of Amboise. In this fairytale castle we are the guests of the man who was once our greatest enemy: Louis King of France, now our greatest friend. I am betrothed to marry the son of the bad queen and the sleeping king, only now I must always remember to call her Lady Mother, and him, my royal father: King Henry. Isabel is not to be Queen of England, George is not to be king. She will be my chief lady in waiting and I am to be queen. Most extraordinary of all, Father has already taken England by storm, marched on London, released the sleeping king – King Henry – from the Tower, taken him out before the people and had him loudly proclaimed as King of England, returned to his people, restored to his throne. The people welcome this. Incredulously, in France, we learn to celebrate the triumph of Lancaster, say 'our house' when we mean the red rose, reverse all the loyalties of my life.

Queen Elizabeth, in terror of the open enmity of my father, has fled into sanctuary and is in hiding with her mother and her daughters, pregnant with another child, abandoned by her husband. It does not matter now if she has a boy, a girl, or the miscarriage that George wished on her – her son will never sit on the throne of England, for the House of York is utterly thrown down. She is cowering in sanctuary, and her husband, the handsome and once-powerful King Edward, our friend, our former hero, has fled from England like a coward, accompanied only by his loyal brother Richard and half a dozen others, and they are kicking their heels and fearing for their futures somewhere in Flanders. Father will make war on them there, next year. He will hunt them down and kill them like the outlaws they now are.

The queen who was so beautiful in her triumph, who was so steely in her dislike, is back to where she started, a penniless widow with no prospects. I should be glad, this is my revenge for the thousands of slights that she paid to Isabel and me, but I cannot help but think of her, and wonder how she will survive childbirth in the dark rooms of sanctuary beneath Westminster Abbey, and how she will ever get out?

Father has won England – he has returned to his irresistible winning form. George was faithfully at his side throughout the campaign, despite the temptations to treachery from the House of York, and Father has done all that he said he would do. I am to join him, as soon as Prince Edward and I are married; we wait only for a dispensation from the Pope to confirm our betrothal. As a young husband and wife, we will join Father in England,

and we will be proclaimed Prince and Princess of Wales. I will be at the side of Queen Margaret of Anjou; she is my mentor and my guide. They will send Queen Elizabeth's ermines from the wardrobe once again, only this time they will stitch them on my gowns.

'Shut up!' Isabel says. 'You are doing it again.'

'I can't believe it. I can't understand it,' I tell her. 'I have to say it over and over again to make myself believe it.'

'Well, in a little while you can mutter at your husband and see if he likes waking to a mad girl whispering away,' she says brutally. 'And I will be able to sleep in the mornings.'

That silences me, as she knew it would. I see my betrothed husband every day, when he comes to sit with his mother in the afternoon, and when we all go in to dinner in the evening. He takes her hand, I walk behind them. She takes the precedence of a queen, I am only a princess-to-be. He is three years older than me of course, so perhaps that is why he behaves as if he can hardly be troubled with me at all. He must have thought of my father with the same horror and hatred that we were taught to think of his mother; perhaps that is why he is so cold to me. Perhaps that is why I feel that we are still strangers, almost enemies.

He has his mother's fair hair, fair almost copper. He has her round face and her little spoiled mouth. He is lithe and strong, he has been raised to ride and fight, he has courage I know, for people say he is a good jouster. He has been on battlefields since he was a child, perhaps he has become hardened and cannot be expected to feel affection for a girl, the daughter of his former enemy. There is a story about him, aged only seven, calling for the York knights who protected his father to be beheaded, though they had kept his father safe during the battle. Nobody tells me that it is untrue. But maybe this is my fault – I have never asked anyone of his mother's court if such a young boy could do such a thing, if, in fact, it ever happened: if he blithely gave such a murderous order. I dare not ask his mother if it is true that she asked her seven-year-old son to name what death two honourable men should die. Actually, I never ask her anything.

His face is always guarded, his eyes veiled by his eyelashes, and he rarely looks at me, he always looks away. When someone speaks to him he looks downwards as if he does not trust himself to meet their gaze. Only with his mother does he ever exchange a glance, only she can make him smile. It is as if he trusts no-one but her.

'He has spent his life knowing that people denied him the throne, some even denied he was his father's son,' Isabel says to me reasonably. 'Everyone said he was the son of the Duke of Somerset, the favourite.'

'It was our grandfather who said that,' I remind her. 'To dishonour her. She told me so herself. She said that was why she put his head on a spike on the walls of York. She says that to be queen is to face a life of constant slander and that you have no-one to defend you but yourself. She says . . .'

' "She says! She says!" Does nobody else say anything but her? You speak of her all the time and yet you used to have nightmares about her when you were a little girl,' Isabel reminds me. 'You used to wake up screaming that the she-wolf was coming, you thought she hid in the chest at the end of our bed. You used to ask me to wrap you tight and hold you tight so that she couldn't get you. Funny that you should end up hanging on her every word and betrothed to her son, and forgetting all about me.'

'I don't believe he wants to be married to me at all,' I say desperately.

She shrugs. Nothing interests Isabel these days. 'He probably doesn't. He probably has to do as he is ordered: like all of us. Perhaps it will turn out better for you two than the rest of us.'

Sometimes he watches me when I dance with the ladies, but he does not admire me, there is nothing warm in his look. He watches me as if he would judge me, as if he would understand me. He looks at me as if I were a puzzle that he wants to translate. The queen's ladies in waiting tell me that I am beautiful: a little queen in miniature. They praise the natural curl of my auburn hair, the blue of my eyes, my lithe girl's figure and the rosy colour of my skin; but he never says anything to make me think that he admires me.

Sometimes he comes riding with us. Then he rides alongside me and never speaks. He rides well, as well as Richard. I glance at him and think that he is handsome. I try to smile at him, I try to make conversation. I should be glad that my father has chosen a husband who is so near my age and looks so fine and princely on a horse. And he will be King of England; but his coldness is quite impenetrable.

We speak together every day, but we never say very much. We are always under the eye of his mother and if I say anything to him that she cannot hear, she calls out: 'What are you whispering about, Lady Anne?' and I have to repeat something that sounds utterly foolish, such as 'I was asking His Grace if there were fish in the moat,' or 'I was telling His Grace that I like baked quinces.'

When I say something like this she smiles at him as if it is incredible that he is going to have to endure such a fool for the rest of his life. Her face is warm with humour and sometimes he laughs shortly. She always looks at her son like the wolf they call her, like a she-wolf looks at her cub, with fierce ownership. He is everything to her, she would do anything for him. Me, she has bought for him, through me she has bought the only commander who could defeat King Edward of York: his former guardian, the man who taught him how to fight. Prince Edward the wolf-cub has to be married to this tediously mortal girl so that they can get back to the throne. They endure me because I am the price exacted for the services of the great general, my father, and she dedicates herself to make me a fit wife for him, a fit queen for England.

She tells me about the battles that she fought for her husband's throne: her son's inheritance. She tells me that she learned to be hardened to suffering, to rejoice in the death of her enemies. She teaches me that to be a queen you have to see any obstacle in your way as your victim. Sometimes fate will command that only one person can survive, your enemy or you, or sometimes it might be your enemy's child or your child. When you have to choose, of course you will choose your life, your future, your child – whatever the price.

Sometimes she looks at me with a smile and says, 'Anne of Warwick, little Anne of Warwick! Who would ever have thought that you would be my daughter-in-law, and your father my ally?' This is so close to my own puzzled mutterings that once I reply: 'Isn't it extraordinary? After all that has been?'

But her blue eyes snap at my impertinence, and she says at once: 'You know nothing of what has been, you were a child shielded by a traitor when I was fighting for my life, trying to hold the throne against treason. I have seen fortune's wheel rise and fall, I have been ground to dust beneath the wheel of fortune; you have seen nothing, and understand nothing.'

I drop my head at her harsh tone, and Isabel who sits beside me leans slightly forwards so that I can feel the support of her shoulder, and be less ashamed at being scolded in front of all the ladies, including my mother.

At other times she summons me to her privy chamber and teaches me the things she thinks I should know. Once I go there and there is a map of the kingdom spread out on the table. 'This,' she says, smoothing it with her hand, 'this is a precious thing indeed.'

I look at it. Father has maps in his library at Warwick Castle, one of them of the kingdom of England; but it is smaller than this and only shows the midlands around our home. This is a map of the southern coast of England as it faces France. The southern ports are carefully drawn, though to the west and north it becomes vague and sketchy. Around the ports it is marked whether there is good farmland to feed troops or victual a fleet, at the entrance to the ports it shows the bed of the river or sandbanks. 'Sir Richard Woodville, Lord Rivers, my friend, made this map,' she says, putting her finger on his signature. 'He made a survey of the southern ports to keep me safe when we feared that your father would invade. Jacquetta Woodville was my dearest friend and lady in waiting, and her husband was my great defender.'

I bow my head in embarrassment; but it is always like this. My father was her greatest enemy, everything she ever tells me is a story of warfare against him.

'Lord Rivers was my dearest friend then, and Jacquetta his wife was like a sister to me.' She looks wistful for a moment and I dare not say anything at all. Jacquetta changed sides like everyone else after this queen's defeat and did well from it. Now she is the mother of the queen, her granddaughter a princess and she even has a prince as a grandson; her daughter Elizabeth has given birth to a son in sanctuary and named him Edward for his father, the exiled king. Jacquetta and this queen parted when my father won the final battle at Towton for Edward. The Rivers surrendered on the battlefield and turned their coats and joined York. Then Edward chose their widowed daughter for his bride. That was the moment he acted without my father's advice, the first mistake he made; that was his first step towards defeat.

'I will forgive Jacquetta,' the queen promises. 'When we enter London, I will see her again and forgive her. I shall have her at my side again, I will comfort her for the terrible loss of her husband.' She looks resentfully at me. 'Killed by your father,' she reminds me. 'And he accused her of witchcraft.'

'He released her.' I swallow.

'Well, let's hope she is grateful for that,' she says sarcastically. 'One of the greatest women in the kingdom and the dearest friend I ever had – and your father named her as a witch?' She shakes her head. 'It beggars belief.'

I say nothing. It beggars belief for me too.

'D'you know the sign for fortune's wheel?' she asks abruptly. I shake my head.

'Jacquetta herself showed it to me. She said that I would know a life when I rose very high and fell very low. Now I am going to rise again.' She extends her forefinger as if pointing and then she draws a circle in the air. 'You rise and you fall,' she says. 'My advice to you is to guard yourself as you rise and destroy your enemies as you fall.'

Finally, after several applications, we receive the dispensation from the Pope, so that Edward and I, though we are distant kin, can marry, and there is a quiet ceremony with little celebration, and we are put to bed by my mother and his. I am so afraid of my mother-in-law the queen that I go to the room without protest, without really thinking of the prince or what is to come in the night, and sit up in bed and wait for him. I hardly see him when he comes in, as I am watching his mother's avid face as she takes his cloak from his shoulders and whispers 'goodnight' to him, and goes from the room. It makes me shudder, the way she looks at him, as if she wishes she could stay and watch.

It is very quiet when everyone has gone. I remember Isabel telling me that it was horrible. I wait for him to tell me what to do. He says nothing. He gets into bed and the thick feather mattress sinks at his side and the ropes of the bed creak under his weight. Still, he says nothing.

'I don't know what to do,' I say awkwardly. 'I am sorry. Nobody has told me. I asked Isabel but she would say nothing. I couldn't ask my mother . . .'

He sighs, as if this is yet another burden that has been put on him by this essential alliance of our parents. 'You don't do anything,' he says. 'You just lie there.'

'But I . . .'

'You lie there and you don't say anything,' he repeats loudly. 'The best thing you can do for me, right now, is to say nothing.

Most of all don't remind me who you are, I can't stand the thought of that . . .' and then he heaves up in the bed and drops on me with his full weight, plunging into me as if he was stabbing me with a broadsword.

PARIS, CHRISTMAS 1470

The King of France, King Louis himself, is so delighted with our wedding that he bids us come to Paris before the Christmas season and celebrate with him. I open the dancing, I am seated on his right hand at dinner. I am the centre of attention for everyone: the kingmaker's daughter who will be Queen of England.

Isabel comes behind me. Every time we walk into a room she follows me, and sometimes she bends and frees my train if it is caught in a doorway or sweeping up the scented rushes. She serves me without a smile; her resentment and envy is obvious to everyone. Queen Margaret, my Lady Mother, laughs at Isabel's sulky face, pats my hand, and says: 'Now you see it. If a woman rises to greatness she becomes every woman's enemy. If she fights to keep greatness then everyone, men and women, simply hate her. In your sister's green face you see your triumph.'

I glance sideways at Isabel's sulky pallor. 'She's not green.'

'Green with jealousy,' the queen says, laughing. 'But no matter. You will be rid of her tomorrow.'

'Tomorrow?' I ask. I turn to Isabel as she sits beside me in the window seat. 'You are going tomorrow?'

She looks as stunned as I am. 'Not that I know.'

'Oh yes,' the queen says smoothly. 'You are going to London to join your husband. We will follow almost immediately, with the army.'

'My mother has not told me,' Isabel challenges the queen. 'I am not ready to go.'

'You can pack this evening,' the queen says simply. 'For you are going tomorrow.'

'Excuse me,' my sister says weakly, and rises to her feet and curtseys low to the queen, and briefly to me. I curtsey and scuttle out after her. She is tearing down the gallery to my rooms, I catch her in one of the beautiful oriel windows.

'Iz!'

'I can't stand another storm at sea.' Isabel rounds on me. 'I would rather kill myself on the quayside than go to sea again.'

Despite my reassurance, I put my hand to my belly as if I fear that I too might be with child and my baby too would be put in a box and thrown into the dark heaving waters, just as they did to Isabel's little son.

'Don't be ridiculous,' Isabel says shortly. 'You aren't pregnant, and you aren't just about to give birth. I should never have gone on board. I should have refused. You should have helped me. My life was ruined then ... and you let it happen.'

I shake my head. 'Iz, how could I refuse Father? How could either of us?'

'And now? Now I have to go to England to join him and George, and just leave you here? With her?'

'What can we do?' I ask her. 'What can we say?'

'Nothing,' she says furiously. She turns and walks away from me.

'Where are you going?' I call after her.

'To tell them to pack,' she throws over her shoulder. 'To tell them to pack for me. They can put in a shroud for all I care. I don't care if I drown this time.'

King Louis has provided an elegant little merchant ship, for Isabel to go with a couple of ladies to keep her company. My mother, Queen Margaret and I are on the quayside to see her leave.

'Really, I can't. I can't go on my own,' Isabel pleads.

'Your father says he needs you to be with your husband,' my mother rules. 'He says you must go at once.'

'I thought I was to sail with Annie. I should stay with Annie and tell her how to behave. I am her lady in waiting, she needs me.'

'I do,' I confirm.

'Queen Margaret has the command of Anne now, and Anne keeps the queen faithful to our agreement. She does that just by being there, being married to Prince Edward. She doesn't have to do anything more. She needs no advice, she just has to obey the queen. But you must go to do your work with George,' my mother tells her. 'Your task is to keep him faithful to our cause and keep him away from his family. Intercept any messages they send him, make sure he is true to your father. Remind him that he is sworn to your father and to you. We'll be only a few days behind you, and your father is victorious in England.'

Isabel reaches for my hand. 'Oh go on,' Mother says irritably. 'Stop clinging to your sister. It just means you will be in London, with your father, making merry at court while we are stuck with the army in Dorset, making our way slowly to London. You will be at Westminster Palace picking your clothes from the royal wardrobe, while we trudge up the Fosse Way.'

They take her chests of clothes and bags of things.

'Don't go,' I say in an urgent whisper. 'Don't leave me with the bad queen and her son.'

'How can I refuse?' she asks. 'Don't anger her, or him, just do as you are told. I'll see you in London. We'll be together then.' She finds a smile. 'Think, Annie, you'll be Princess of Wales.'

Her smile dies, and we look bleakly at one another. 'I have to go,' she says as Mother beckons her impatiently, and with our half-sister Margaret and two other ladies in waiting she walks along the dock to the little ship. She glances back as she goes up the gangplank, and raises her hand to me. I think that nobody but me cares that she will be seasick.

HARFLEUR, FRANCE, MARCH 1471

The winds are holding us in harbour though we said we would set sail more than two weeks ago. My mother-in-law, Queen Margaret, is desperately impatient, and every dawn finds her on the quayside arguing with the captains of her fleet. They assure her that since we are held in port by winds that blow so strongly onshore that we cannot get our ships out to sea, then the very same winds will be blowing the invasion fleet of King Edward further along the coast in Flanders, against his harbour walls, holding him powerlessly in port, like us.

For it turns out that he has not been wasting his time in exile. While my father has taken England under his command, released the king from the Tower and crowned him again, restored the lords of Lancaster to glory and announced that Prince Edward and I are married, the vanquished King Edward has scrounged for money, raised a fleet, recruited a ragtail army, and is waiting for good winds – just like us – to get back to England. Since his wife Elizabeth has given birth to a boy in sanctuary his friends and supporters claim this as a sign of their destiny, and urge him to attack my father's peace. So now we have to get to England before him, so that we can support my father against the invasion of Edward of York. We have to get to England ahead of King Edward, his loyal brother Richard, his friends and his fleet. This is a necessity, not a matter of choice; it must be done, and yet the wind blows steadily and powerfully against us. For sixteen days it has held us here, on the quayside, while the queen rages at her captains, and clings white-faced to the clenched fists of her son, and looks at me as if I am a heavy burden to ship across a stormy sea.

She is regretting now that she waited in France for our wedding. She is thinking that we should have marched at once and invaded alongside my victorious father. If we had gone then, we would be in London now, receiving oaths of fealty. But she did not trust my father, and she did not trust me. She delayed to see me married to her son; she had to see my father pin me, like a pledge into her hat, without chance of retreat. Only our marriage and my bedding reassured her that neither he nor she could play false. And secretly, she wanted the delay. She wanted to see that my father could capture England before she wasted her precious son on me. Now, because she delayed to see Father win, because she had to wait to secure me, she is trapped on the wrong side of the narrow seas and an inexplicable wind blows against her every day.

HARFLEUR, FRANCE, 12 APRIL 1471

'We sail tomorrow at dawn,' the queen says as she walks past Mother and I, standing on the quayside as usual, as we do every day, looking out to sea. This is all any of us has done for the past two weeks – we look to the horizon and we wait for the wind to die down and the seas to quiet. 'They think the wind will drop overnight. Even if it does not, we have to sail tomorrow. We cannot delay.'

I wait for my husband to tell his mother that we cannot risk sailing into a storm but he has her hard eyes and fixed mouth. He looks as if he would drown rather than stay any longer. 'And then we will be waiting for him when he lands,' he says. 'As the false king Edward steps off his ship we will put him to the sword, and he will go face down into the shingle. We will see his head on a pike on London Bridge.'

'We cannot sail against the wind,' I suggest.

His eyes are quite blank. 'We will.'

In the morning the wind has dropped but the waves are still capped with white, and outside the bar of the harbour we can see the sea is grey and heaving, as if ready for a storm. I have a sense of foreboding, but I can tell no-one, and anyway nobody cares how I feel.

'When will we see my father?' I ask Mother. It is only the thought that he is victorious on the other side of these seas that makes me feel I dare set sail. I so want to be with him, I want him to know that I have done my part in this great venture, I have wedded and bedded the prince he found for me, I did not shrink from the altar nor from the bed. My husband never speaks to me and does his duty on me as if I were a mare that must foal. But I have done all that my father asks, and when I call the bad queen 'My Lady Mother', and kneel for her blessing I do more than he asked of me. I am ready to take the throne that he has won for me. I am his daughter, I am his heir, I will cross the seas that are so fearsome and I will not fail him. I will become a queen like Margaret of Anjou with a will like a wolf. 'Will he meet us when we land?'

'We are to meet him in London,' my mother says. 'He has arranged a state entry for us into the city. They will throw down green boughs and flowers before you, there will be poets to sing your praises, your father will have the king greet you on the steps of Westminster Palace. There will be parades and pageants to celebrate your arrival, the fountains will run with wine. Don't worry, he has everything planned for you. This is the pinnacle of his ambition. He has won what he has wanted for years. He has won for himself what he fought for – and first gave to others. When you have a son, your father will have put a boy of Warwick – a Neville – on the throne of England. He is the king-maker indeed, and you will be the mother of a king.'

'My son, my father's grandson, will be King of England,' I repeat. I still cannot believe it.

'Guy of Warwick.' My mother names the great founder of our house. 'You will call him Guy Richard of Warwick and he will be Prince Guy of Warwick and Lancaster.'

A shrill whistle from the boatswain warns us that we must leave. My mother nods to the ladies of her household. 'Get aboard,' she says. 'We are taking that ship.' She turns to me: 'You sail with the queen.'

'Aren't you coming with me?' I am immediately frightened. 'Surely you will come with me, Lady Mother?'

My mother laughs. 'You can sail across the narrow seas on your own with her, I should think,' she says. 'She spends all her time telling you how to be queen. You spend all your time listening to her. The two of you will hardly miss me.'

'I . . .' I cannot tell my mother that without her and without Isabel I feel quite abandoned. Being Princess of Wales is no compensation, being coached by a woman of mad ambition is no substitute for being cared for by my mother. I am only fourteen, I am afraid of the heaving sea, and afraid of my husband, and afraid of his fierce mother. 'Surely you will travel with me, Lady Mother?'

'Go on with you,' my mother says briskly, 'go to the queen and sit at her feet like her lapdog, like you always do.' She goes up the gangplank of her ship, and does not look back at me, as if she has half-forgotten me already. She is in a hurry to join her husband, she is eager to get back to our London house; she wants to see him where he was born to be, at the right hand of the throne of England. I look around for my new husband, who is arm in arm with his mother, and they are laughing together. He waves for me to go on board our ship and I grip the rope and go up the gangplank, feeling my shoes slip on the damp timbers. The ship is small and poorly appointed; it is not one of my father's great flagships. It has been supplied by King Louis for his kinswoman Margaret, and he has equipped it to transport soldiers and horses, not for our comfort. The queen's ladies and I go into the master cabin and sit awkwardly on stools in the cramped space, leaving the best chair vacant for the queen. We sit in silence. I can smell the scent of my fear on my rich gown.

We hear the shouts of the sailors as they cast off the ropes then the door of the cabin bangs open and the queen comes in, her face alight with excitement. 'We are sailing,' she says. 'We will be there before Edward.' She laughs nervously. 'We must get there before Edward and raise our troops to face him. He will be racing to catch this wind, just like us, but we must outsail him. It is a race now; we must get there before him.'

CERNE ABBEY, WEYMOUTH,
15 APRIL 1471

The queen sits in state in the great hall of the Cerne Abbey, her son standing behind her chair as if he is her personal guard, his hand on her shoulder, his handsome face grave. I am seated beside her on a lower chair – really, a stool – as if I were a little mascot, to remind everyone that the Warwick name and fortune is attached to this venture. We are waiting for the Lancaster lords to welcome us to the kingdom. Seated like this we present them with a tableau of unity. Only my mother is missing, as her ship and a few others of our fleet made landfall further up the coast at Southampton. She will be riding to join us now.

The double doors at the end of the hall swing open and the brothers of the House of Beaufort come in together. The queen rises to her feet and first gives her hands and then her cheek to Edmund Duke of Somerset, the son of the man that people said was her only love, then she greets his brother: John the Marquis of Dorset. John Courtenay the Earl of Devon kneels to her. These are men who were her loyal favourites when she was queen, who stayed faithful to her when she was in exile, and who rallied to my father for her sake.

I had expected them to come in shouting greetings, filled with excitement, but they look grim, and their entourage and the other lords behind them are not beaming either. I look from one dark face to another and I know already that something has gone wrong. I glance at the queen and see that her face has lost its rosy colour. The excitement of greeting is draining away, leaving her pale and stony. So she knows it too, though she greets one man after another, often by name, often asking after friends and family. Too often they shake their head, as if they cannot bear to say that a man is dead. I start to wonder if these are new deaths, if there has been some sort of attack in London, an ambush on the road? They look like men with new fears, with fresh grief. What has happened while we waited at the quayside in France? What disaster happened while we were at sea?

She makes up her mind to know the worst and turns, sweeping the train of her gown, to her throne, and seats herself. She clasps her hands in her lap, she grits her teeth. I see her screw up her courage. 'Tell us,' she says shortly. She indicates her son and even me. 'Tell us.'

'The York claimant, the impostor Edward, landed in the North a month ago,' Edmund Beaufort says bluntly.

'A month ago? He can't have done. The seas must have held him in port . . .'

'He set sail into the very teeth of the storm and he was all but wrecked, he lost his fleet at sea, but they found each other again and marched on York and then London. As always, he has a witch's luck: his fleet scattered and then found each other again.'

Her son looks at her as though she has failed him. She says again, 'The seas must surely have held him in port as they did us.'

'Not him.'

She makes a small gesture with her hand as if to push away the bad news. 'And my lord Warwick?'

'Stayed true to you. Mustered his army and marched out against Edward. But he was betrayed.'

'Who?' The one word is like a cat's spit.

Somerset throws a quick sideways glance at me. 'George Duke of Clarence turned his coat and joined with his brother, Edward.

The younger son Richard brought them together. They were, all three, reconciled. It was the three sons of York together again and George's army and wealth was thrown onto the side of Edward. All George's affinity stood behind him, the Yorks were reunited.'

She turns a burning glance on me as if I am to blame. 'Your sister Isabel! We sent her ahead to keep him faithful! She was there to hold him to his word!'

'Your Grace . . .' I shrug. What could she do? What could she make George do, if he chose to change his mind?

'They met near the village of Barnet, on the Great North Road.'

We wait. There is something terrible about the slow unfolding of this story. I clench my hands in my lap to prevent myself shouting out: 'But who won?'

'There was a mist like a low cloud that rolled in through the night, which they said was a witch's mist. All night it grew thicker and darker, you couldn't see your hand in front of your face. One army couldn't see the other. At any rate – we couldn't see them.'

We wait, as they waited.

'They could see us though. At dawn when they came at us out of the mist, they were far closer than we thought – they were on top of us. They had been hiding in the mist, as close as a stone's throw, all night. They had known where we were when we were like blind men. We had been shooting cannon all night far over their heads. We parried the charge, we took them on, then through the day the battle lines shifted and though we locked forces with Edward and held him, the Earl of Oxford, our faithful ally, broke through them and then came back to the battle through the mist and our men thought the earl had turned traitor and was coming against them. Some thought it was re-inforcements for Edward, coming at them again from behind, Edward often keeps a battle in reserve . . . at any rate, they broke and fled.'

'They fled?' She repeats the word as if she does not understand it. 'Fled?'

'Many of our men were killed, thousands. But the rest fled back to London. Edward won.'

'Edward won?'

He goes down on one knee. 'Your Grace, I am sorry to say that in this first battle he was victorious. He defeated your commander the Earl of Warwick; but I am confident we can defeat him now. We have mustered the army again, they are on their way.'

I wait. I expect her to ask where my father is, when he will arrive with those of his army who managed to get away.

She turns to me. 'So Isabel did nothing for us, though we sent her ahead to be with her husband. She didn't keep George to our alliance,' she says spitefully. 'I will remember this. You had better remember this. She failed to keep him faithful to you, to me, to your father. She is a poor daughter and a poor wife, a wretched sister. I think she will regret this. I will make sure that she regrets the day her husband betrayed us.'

'My father?' I whisper. 'Is my father coming now?'

I see the Duke of Somerset wince and look at the queen for permission to speak.

'My father?' I ask more loudly. 'What of my father?'

'He died in the battle,' he says quietly. 'I am sorry, my lady.'

'Died?' she demands baldly. 'Warwick is dead?'

'Yes.'

She starts to smile, as if it is funny. 'Killed by Edward?'

He bows in assent.

She cannot help herself. She lets out a peal of laughter, clapping her hand over her mouth, trying to silence herself but not able to cease laughing. 'Who would have thought it?' she gasps. 'Who would ever have thought such a thing? My God! The wheel of fortune – Warwick killed by his own beloved protégé! Warwick against his own wards and they kill him. And Edward with his two brothers at his side again – after all we have done and sworn . . .' Slowly she subsides. 'And my husband, the king?' She moves onto the next question as if there is nothing more to be said about the death of my father.

'How did he die?' I ask, but nobody answers me.

'The king?' she repeats impatiently.

'Safe in London, back in the Tower. They picked him up after the battle and took him as their prisoner.'

'He was well?' she asks quickly.

Somerset shifts uncomfortably. 'Singing,' he says shortly. 'In his tent.' The mad king's son and his wife exchange one brief look.

'Did my father die in battle?' I ask.

'The York brothers went back to London victorious, but they will rest and arm and come on here,' Beaufort warns her. 'They will have heard that you have landed, just as we did. They will be marching after us as fast as they can come.'

She shakes her head. 'Ah, dear God! If we had only come sooner!'

'George Duke of Clarence might still have proved untrue. The Earl of Warwick might still have been killed,' the duke says steadily. 'As it is, your coming now brings us a fresh army, newly landed, and people gathering to support you as a new cause. Edward has marched, and fought, and is now marching again. He has drawn on all his credit, he has been joined by all his friends, there is no-one left to recruit and they have fought a heavy battle and suffered losses, and they are all tired. It was a hard battle and a long march. Everything is in our favour.'

'He'll be coming here?'

They all nod; there is no doubt that the House of York is coming to the table for a final throw of the dice.

'For us?'

'Yes, Your Grace – we have to move out.'

For a moment she draws a breath, then she makes a small gesture with her hand, drawing a circle in the air. 'The wheel of fortune,' she says almost dreamily. 'Just as Jacquetta said. Now her son-in-law is coming to attack me, having killed my ally; and her daughter and my son are rivals for the throne and she and I are far apart. I suppose we are enemies.'

'My father . . .' I say.

'They took his body to London, Your Grace,' the duke says quietly to me. 'Edward captured his body, and also that of your uncle Lord Montagu. I am sorry, Your Grace. He will show the bodies to the people of London, so that everyone knows he is dead and his cause lost.'

I close my eyes. I think of my grandfather's head on the spike on the walls of York, put there by this queen. Now my father's dead body will be put on show to the people of London by the boy who loved him like a brother. 'I want my mother,' I say. I clear my throat and say it again: 'I want my mother.'

The queen hardly hears me. 'What do you advise?' she asks Edmund Beaufort.

I turn to my husband, the young prince. 'I want to be with my mother,' I say. 'I have to tell her. I have to tell her of the death of her husband. I must go to her. I must find her.'

He is listening to the duke; he barely glances at me.

'We have to march north and west, join up with Jasper Tudor in Wales,' the duke replies to the queen. 'We have to go at once, get ahead of Edward. Once we join with Tudor's forces in Wales, we can come back into England in strength and attack Edward at a place of our own choosing. But we have to recruit men.'

'We should go now?'

'As soon as you are ready to travel. We need to start the march. Edward always travels fast, and so we need to be ahead and stay ahead of him. We have to get to Wales before he can cut us off.'

I see her change at once, from a woman receiving a warning into the commander who will drive the march. She has ridden at the head of an army before now, she has taken an army into battle. She responds to the call to action, she is quite without fear. 'We are ready! Order the men. They have disembarked and eaten and drunk, they are ready to march. Tell them to fall in.'

'I need to see my mother,' I say again. 'Your Grace, I need to see my mother, she may not even know of the death of her husband. And I need to be with her.' Like a child my voice quavers. 'I have to go to my Lady Mother! My father is dead, I have to go to my mother.'

At last she hears me. She glances at Edmund Beaufort. 'What of Her Grace the Countess of Warwick?'

One of his men comes in and whispers to him and he turns to me. 'Your mother has been told of the death of her husband. Her ship made landfall down the coast, and the men who were on board are just joining us now. They say they had the news in Southampton of the battle. She was told.'

I get to my feet. 'I must see her. Excuse me.'

'She did not come with the men.'

Queen Margaret clicks her tongue in irritation. 'Oh, for God's sake! Where is she?'

The messenger speaks to the duke again. 'She has retired to Beaulieu Abbey. She has sent word to say that she will not ride with you. She says she has taken sanctuary.'

'My mother?' I cannot understand what they are saying. 'Beaulieu Abbey?' I look from the duke to the queen and then to my young husband. 'What am I to do? Will you take me to Beaulieu Abbey?'

Prince Edward shakes his head. 'I can't take you. There's no time.'

'Your mother has abandoned you,' the queen says flatly. 'Don't you understand? She is in hiding in fear of her life. Clearly she thinks that Edward is going to win and we will be defeated and she doesn't want to be with us. You will have to come with us.'

'I don't . . .'

She rounds on me, her face white with fury. 'Understand this, girl! Your father has been defeated, his army all but destroyed. He is dead. Your sister cannot keep her husband on our side. Your mother has hidden herself away in an abbey. Your influence is worthless, your name means next to nothing. Your family do not stand by you. I have bound my son in marriage to you thinking that your father would defeat Edward but it is Edward who has defeated him. I thought your father was the man to destroy the House of York – the kingmaker as they call him! – but his protégé turns out to be the better man. Your father's promises are empty, your father is dead. Your sister is a turncoat and your mother has tucked herself up safely in sanctuary, while we fight for our lives. I don't need you, you can do nothing for me. I don't want you particularly. If you want to go to Beaulieu Abbey you can go. You mean nothing to me. Go to Beaulieu Abbey and wait to be arrested as a traitor. Wait for Edward's army to come in, and rape you with the rest of the nuns. Or ride with us with the chance of victory.'

I am trembling at her sudden rage.

'You can decide,' her son says indifferently, as if I am not his wife, bound to be with him. 'We can send a couple of men to ride with you. Later, we can get the marriage annulled. What do you want to do?'

I think of my father, dying to put me on the throne, fighting against an army that came out of the mist. I think of his burning constant ambition that a Neville girl should take the throne of England, that we should make a king. He did that for me. He died for me. I can do this for him. 'I'll come,' I say. 'I'll come with you.'

We set off on a punishing march, men flocking to our standards every time we halt. The queen is beloved in the western counties and her friends and allies have long promised that she would land on their shores and lead an army against the House of York. We go north and west. The city of Bristol supports us with money and cannon, and the citizens pile out into the narrow streets with their caps filled with gold coins for us. Behind us, Edward has to recruit soldiers on the run, in a country that has no love for the House of York. We hear that he finds it hard going and is lacking the support he needs; his army is tired, and every day the gap between our forces widens as we get away from him. Our spies tell us that he is falling behind, delayed by the need to get more men, incapable of catching us. Margaret laughs and jumps down from the saddle at the end of the day like a girl. I climb down wearily, aching all over, my knees and my buttocks red and sore.

We rest for a few hours only. I fall asleep lying on the ground wrapped in my riding cloak and I dream that my father comes, stepping carefully around the sleeping guard, and tells me that I can come home to Calais, that the bad queen and the sleeping king are defeated and I can be safe at home once more behind the high castle walls, guarded by the seas. I wake smiling and look around for him. It is raining slightly and I am chilled, and my gown is damp. I have to get up and mount on a wet saddle on a wet horse and go on with nothing to eat. We dare not wait and light fires for breakfast.

We are marching up the broad valley of the Severn, and as the sun comes up it is hot and weary; there are no trees and no shade. The wide green fields seem to stretch forever, and there are no roads, just tracks of dried mud, and so the riders stir up a cloud of dust which chokes everyone who comes behind them. The horses droop their heads and stumble through the dried ruts and stones. When we come to a stream the men fling themselves down on their bellies and try to drink before the horses go in and foul the river. When my guard brings me a cup of water it tastes dirty, and in the afternoon the flies come out and swarm around my face and eyes. My horse shakes his head all the time against the biting of the insects and I brush my face and rub my nose, and feel myself flushed and sweaty and so weary that I wish I could fall out, like some of the men do, and fling themselves on the side of the road and let the march go past them, beyond caring.

'We'll cross the river at Gloucester,' the queen says. 'Then Edward will drop back – he won't dare to attack us in Wales. Once we are over the river we are safe.' She gives a little excited laugh. 'Once we are over the river we are halfway to victory.

Jasper Tudor will raise men for me, we will come into England like a broadsword to the throat.' She is jubilant, beaming at me. 'This is what it is to be a queen militant,' she tells me. 'Remember this march. You have to fight for what you own by right, sometimes. You have to be ready to fight, to do anything.'

'I am so tired,' I say.

She laughs. 'Remember how it feels. If we win you will never have to march again. Let the tiredness, let the pain come into your soul. Swear to yourself you will never fight for your throne again. You will win once and forever.'

We come to the city of Gloucester from the south and as we approach we can see the great gates of the city swing to shut in our faces. I remember my father telling me that London once locked its gates to this queen and begged her to take her wild army of northern men away. This mayor comes out on the wall of Southgate himself and calls down his apologies, but he has an order from Edward – he calls him King Edward – and he will not disobey. Even while marching, even while recruiting, even while chasing after us, thirsty in the hot sun, Edward thought to send scouts ahead and round us to get to Gloucester and hold them to their loyalty to him. Perversely, I want to smile. It was my father who taught Edward to think ahead, to see an army in the field like a game of chess. My father will have told Edward not just to secure your own river crossing, but block your enemy.

The duke goes forwards to argue but the city's cannon look down on him with the mayor who just repeats that he is commanded by the king. The bridge across the great River Severn is the western gate out of the city; there is no other way to get to it but through the city. There is no way across the Severn but their bridge. We have to get inside the city walls to get to the bridge. The duke offers money, favour, the gratitude of the woman who was once queen and will be again. We can see the mayor shake his head. The city commands the crossing of the river, and if they won't let us in we cannot get across the River Severn here.

Clearly, they won't let us in. The queen bites her lip. 'We'll go on,' is all she says, and we ride on.

I start to count the paces of my horse. I lean forwards in the saddle trying to ease the pain in my thighs and buttocks. I wrap my hands in the horse's mane and grit my teeth. Before me, I see the queen riding straight-backed, indomitable. I fall into a daze of fatigue as it gets darker and then, as the stars are coming out, and the horse's pace is slower and slower, I hear her say: 'Tewkesbury. We'll cross the river here. There's a ford.'

The horse halts, and I stretch out of the saddle to lean along its neck. I am so weary I cannot care where we are. I hear a scout come and speak urgently to her and to the Duke of Somerset and to the prince. He says that Edward is behind, close behind, closer than a mortal man could have marched. He has the speed of the devil and he is on our heels.

I raise my head. 'How can he have gone so fast?' I ask. Nobody answers me.

We cannot rest, there can be no time for rest. But we cannot cross the river in the dark – you have to go from sandbank to sandbank, carefully staying in the shallows. We can't go into the cold deep water without lights. So we cannot escape him. He has caught us on the wrong side of the river and we will have to fight him here, as soon as it is light tomorrow. We must remember that he can turn his army in a moment, prepare them in darkness, conquer in mist, in snow. He has a wife who can whistle up a wind for him, who can breathe out a mist, whose icy hatred can make snow. We have to get into battle lines now, we must prepare for battle at dawn. No matter how tired and thirsty and hungry, the men must make ready to fight. The duke rides off and starts to order where the troops are to be deployed. Most of them are so weary that they drop down their packs and sleep where they are ordered to make their stand, in the shelter of the ruins of the old castle.

'This way,' the queen says and a scout takes her horse and leads us downhill, a little way out of the town, to a small nunnery where we can sleep for the night, and we ride into the stable yard and someone at last helps me from my horse and when my legs buckle beneath me, the almoner guides me into the guest house to the oblivion of a little truckle bed made up with coarse clean sheets.

TEWKESBURY, GLOUCESTERSHIRE,
4 MAY 1471

As soon as it grows light reports come to us almost hourly, but it is hard to tell what is happening, just a few miles away. The queen paces up and down the little hall of the priory where we have taken up our quarters. They say that Edward's army is fighting uphill, against our force that is well-positioned behind the half-ruined walls of the old Tewkesbury castle. Then they come and say that the York armies are advancing, Richard Duke of Gloucester on one wing, Edward in the centre fighting side by side with his brother George, and his great friend William Hastings bringing up the rear, protecting them from ambush.

I wonder if Isabel has come with her husband and is nearby, waiting for news as I am waiting for news. She will be wondering about me; I can almost sense her nearby, anxious as I am. I look out of the window of the priory, almost as if I expect to see her, riding up the road to me. It seems impossible that we should be close to each other and not together. The queen looks coldly at me when we hear that George is at the very centre of the army that is coming against us. 'Traitor,' she says quietly. I don't reply. It is meaningless to me that my sister is now a traitor's wife, she is my enemy, her husband is trying to kill my husband, she has abandoned the cause that my father gave his life for. None of this makes any sense to me. I cannot believe that my father is dead, I cannot believe that my mother has abandoned me, I cannot believe that my sister is married to a traitor to our cause, has become a traitor herself. Most of all I cannot believe that I am alone without Izzy, though she is just a few miles away.

Then the messengers fail to arrive, and nobody comes to tell us what is happening. We go out to the little physic garden of the priory and we can hear the terrible noise of the cannon, which sounds just like summer-day thunder; but there is no way of knowing whether it is our gunners, getting the white rose in their sights, mowing them down, or whether Edward has managed to bring his own artillery, even on a forced march, even at that speed, and they are shooting uphill at us.

'The duke is an experienced soldier,' the queen says. 'He will know what to do.'

Neither of us remark that my father was far more experienced, and won almost all his battles, but his pupil Edward defeated him. Suddenly we hear the rattle of a galloping horse and a rider with the Beaufort colours approaches the stable yard. We run to the open gate. He does not even dismount, he does not even enter the yard, but his horse wheels and rears on the road, sweat-stained and labouring for breath. 'My lord said I was to tell you, if ever I thought the battle lost. So I have come. You should get away.'

Margaret runs forwards and would grab his reins but he puts his whip-hand down to prevent her from touching him. 'I won't stay. I promised him I would warn you and this I have done. I'm off.'

'The duke?'

'Run away!'

The shock makes her shrill. 'The Duke of Somerset!'

'That's him. Run like a deer.'

'Where is Edward?'

'Coming!' is all he shouts, and he wheels his horse and gallops off down the road, the sparks flying from the horseshoes.

'We must go,' Margaret says flatly.

I am overwhelmed by the sudden defeat. 'Are you sure? Shouldn't we wait for Prince Edward? What if that man was mistaken?'

'Oh yes,' she says bitterly. 'I am sure. This is not the first time I have run from a battlefield and perhaps it will not be the last. Get them to bring our horses. I will get my things.'

She dashes into the house and I run to the stable and shake the old groom and tell him to bring my horse and the queen's horse at once.

'What's the matter?' His gummy old smile breaks his wrinkled face into a thousand cracks. 'Battle too hot for you, little lady? Want to get away now? I thought you were waiting to ride out in triumph?'

'Get the horses out,' is all I say.

I hammer on the door of the hayloft for the two men who are supposed to guard us and order them to get ready to leave at once. I run inside to fetch my cloak and my riding gloves. I hop on the wooden floor as I cram my feet into my riding boots. Then I scramble out into the yard, one glove on, one in my hand, but as I get to the yard and shout for them to bring my horse to the mounting block, there is a thunder of hooves outside and the gate to the yard is suddenly filled with fifty horses and I can see, amid them all, the black curly head of Richard Duke of Gloucester, my childhood friend, the ward of my father, and the brother of Edward of York. Beside him, I recognise at once, is Robert Brackenbury, his childhood friend, still faithful. Our two men have handed over their pikes, they are stripping off their jackets as if they are glad to be rid of the insignia of the red rose and my husband, Prince Edward's, badge of the swan.

Richard rides his great grey horse right up to me, as I stand, like a martyr, on the mounting block, as if he thinks I might mount behind him and ride pillion. His young face is grim. 'Lady Anne,' he says.

'Princess,' I say weakly. 'I am Princess Anne.'

He takes off his hat to me. 'Dowager princess,' he corrects me.

For a moment his meaning does not sink in. Then I sway and he puts out a hand to steady me so that I do not fall. 'My husband is dead?'

He nods.

I look around for his mother. She is inside the priory still. She does not know. The horror of this is quite beyond me. I think she will die when she hears this news. I don't know how I am going to tell her.

'At whose hands?'

'He died during the battle. He had a soldier's death: honourable. Now I am taking you into safe-keeping, according to the orders of my brother King Edward.'

I draw close to his horse, I put one pleading hand on his horse's mane and I look into his kind brown eyes. 'Richard, for the love of God, for my father's love for you, let me go to my mother. I think she is in an abbey somewhere called Beaulieu. And my father is dead. Let me go to my mother. There is my horse, let me mount it and go.'

His young face is stern; it is as if we are strangers, as if he had never seen me in his life before. 'I am sorry, Dowager Princess. My orders are clear. To take you and Her Grace Margaret of Anjou into my keeping.'

'And what of my husband?'

'He'll be buried here. With the hundreds, thousands of others.'

'I will have to tell his mother,' I say. 'Can I tell her how he died?'

His sideways glance, as if he is too afraid to meet my eyes, confirms my suspicions. That was how he used to look when he was caught out in some misdemeanour in the schoolroom. 'Richard!' I accuse him.

'He died during the battle,' he says.

'Did you kill him? Or Edward? Or George?'

The York boys stick together once more. 'He died in battle,'

Richard repeats. 'A soldier's death. His mother may be proud of his courage. You too. And now I must bid you get on your horse and come with me.'

The door of the priory opens and he looks up and sees her as she comes slowly down the steps in the sunshine. She has her travelling cape over her arm and a little satchel on her back; they caught us only by moments, we had nearly got away. She sees the fifty cavalrymen, and looks from Richard's grim face to my shocked one, and she knows at once the news that he brings. Her hand goes out to the stone doorway to steady herself, and she holds the arch at the height where she used to hold her son's little hand when she was Queen of England and he was her precious only boy.

'My son, His Grace the Prince of Wales?' she asks, clinging to the title now that she will never hold the young man again.

'I regret to tell you that Edward of Westminster died in the battle,' Richard says. 'My brother, the King of England, King Edward, has won. Your commanders are dead, or surrendering, or fled. I am here to take you to London.'

I jump down from the mounting block and go towards her with my hands out to hold her; but she does not even see me. Her pale blue eyes are stony. 'I refuse to come with you, this is hallowed ground, I am in sanctuary. I am a Princess of France, and Queen of England, you cannot lay hands on me. My person is sacred. The dowager princess is in my keeping. We will stay here until Edward comes to parley, and I will speak to none other but him.'

Richard is eighteen years old, born nothing more than the youngest son of a duke. She was born a princess and has fought half her life as a queen. She faces him down, and he drops his gaze. She turns from him and snaps her fingers at me to follow her inside the nunnery. I obey, falling in behind her, aware of his eyes on my back, wondering if we will get away with this magnificent gamble of prestige against power.

'Your Grace, you will get on your horse and ride with us to

London or I will have you bound and gagged and thrown in a litter,' he says quietly.

She rounds on him. 'I claim sanctuary! You heard me! I am safe here.'

His face is grim. 'We are dragging them out of the sanctuary of Tewkesbury Abbey and slitting their throats in the church-yard,' he says without raising his voice, without a trace of shame in his voice. 'We don't recognise sanctuary for traitors. We have changed the rules. You should thank God that Edward wants to show you as part of his triumph in London or you would be down in the dirt with them with your head staved in by an axe.'

In a second she has changed her tactics and she is off the steps and at his side, her hand on his rein. The face she turns up to him is warm and inviting. 'You are young,' she says gently. 'You are a good soldier, a good general. You will be nothing while Edward lives, you will always be a younger son, after Edward, after George. Come to me and I will name you as my heir, get us away from here and you shall marry Her Grace Anne, the princess dowager, I shall name you Prince of Wales, my heir, and you can have Anne. Put me back on the throne and I will give you the Neville fortune and then make you the next king after my husband.'

He laughs out loud, his laugh warm and genuine, the only healthy noise in the stable yard today. He shakes his young curly head in amusement at her persistence, at her refusal to give up. 'Your Grace, I am a boy of York. My motto is *loyauté me lie*. I am faithful to my brother as to my own self. I love nothing in the world more than honour. And I would as soon put a wolf on the throne of England as you.'

She is still for a moment. In his proud young voice she hears her defeat. Now, she knows she is beaten. She drops her hands from his rein, she turns away. I see her put her hand to her heart and know that she is thinking of the son she adored, whose inheritance she just threw on the ground for a final last desper-ate cast.

Richard looks over her head to me. 'And the princess dowager and I will make our own arrangements,' he says surprisingly.

She takes hours to pack her things. I know she has been kneeling before her crucifix in speechless weeping for her son; she begs the nuns to say mass for him, to get hold of his body if they can and bathe it and wrap it and bury him with the honours of a prince. She orders me to ask Richard for his body, but he says that the prince will be buried in Tewkesbury Abbey when the soldiers have scrubbed the blood from the chancel steps and the church has been re-consecrated. The Yorks have fouled a holy place with the blood of Lancastrian martyrs and my young husband will lie beneath bloodstained stones. Oddly, this is one of my family churches, endowed by the Nevilles for generations, our family resting place. So, as it happens, my young husband will lie near my ancestors, in a place of honour below our chancel steps, and his memorial stone will be bright with sun shining through the stained glass of our windows.

The queen has the priory turned upside down until we can find two gowns of white – the colour of royal mourning in France. She wears a bleached wimple and coif that drains her stricken face of any colour so that she looks indeed like the queen of ice that they once called her. Three times Richard sends to the door of her chamber to demand that she come now, and three times she sends him away saying she is preparing for the journey. Finally, she can delay no longer.

'Follow me,' she says. 'We will ride, but if they want to bind us to our horses we will refuse. Do as I do, obey me in everything. And don't speak unless I say you can.'

'I have asked him if I could go to my mother,' I say.

She turns on me a face like stone. 'Don't be a fool,' she says. 'My son is dead, his widow will have to pay the price too. He is dead and you are dishonoured.'

'You could ask for me to be released to my mother.'

'Why would I do anything for you? My son is dead, my army defeated, the struggle of my life is overthrown. Better for me to bring you into London at my side. Edward is more likely to pardon us as two women in mourning.'

I follow her out to the stable yard. I cannot deny her bleak logic, and there is nowhere else for me to go. The guard is drawn up, and Richard sits on his grey horse to one side. He is red-faced and trembling with anger at the delay, his hand clenched on the hilt of his sword.

She looks at him indifferently, as if he were a moody pageboy, whose temper is of no interest to her. 'I am ready now. You may lead the way; the princess dowager will ride beside me. Your guard will come behind us. I will not be crowded.'

He nods shortly. She gets onto her horse and they bring mine to the mounting block. I get on and one of the elderly nuns straightens my borrowed white gown so that it falls either side of the horse, covering my worn boots. She looks up at me: 'Good luck, Princess,' she says. 'God speed and a safe ending to your journey. God bless you, poor thing – little more than a child in a hard world.' Her kindness is so sudden, and so surprising, that the tears flood into my eyes and I have to blink them away to see.

'Ride out!' Richard of Gloucester says sharply. The guards fall in before, behind, and on either side of the queen, and when she is about to protest Robert Brackenbury leans over, pulls the reins out of her hands and leads her horse. They clatter out through the arch. I gather my reins and kick my horse forwards to join her but Richard wheels his big battle horse between the queen's cavalcade and me, and he leans over and puts his gauntleted hand on my reins.

'What?'

'You're not going with her.'

She turns to look back. The guard has closed up around her and I cannot hear her voice but I see that she is calling my name.

I pull my reins from Richard and say: 'Let go, Richard. Don't be stupid, I have to go with her. She ordered me.'

'No you don't,' he contradicts me. 'You're not arrested, though she is. You're not going to the Tower of London, though she is. Your husband is dead; you're not of the House of Lancaster any more. You are a Neville once more. You can choose.'

'Anne!' I hear her shout to me. 'Come now!'

I wave at her, gesturing to show her Richard, holding my reins. She tries to pull up her horse but the guard close around her and force her onward, a cloud of dust billowing up from the hooves of their horses as they drive her onward like a herded swan, down the road to London, away from me.

'I have to go, I am her daughter-in- law,' I say urgently. 'I swore fealty to her, she commands me.'

'She is going to the Tower,' he says simply. 'To join her sleeping husband. Her life is over, her cause is lost, her son and heir is dead.'

I shake my head. Too much has happened, too quickly. 'How did he die?'

'That doesn't matter. What matters is what happens to you next.'

I look at him; I am simply bereft of all will. 'Richard, I am lost.'

He doesn't even answer. He has seen such horrors today that my tears count for nothing. 'You say I cannot go with the queen?'

'No.'

'Can I go to my mother?'

'No. And anyway, she will be tried for treason.'

'Can I stay here?'

'No.'

'Then what can I do?'

He smiles as if at last I have realised that I have to consult with him, I am not free. I am the pawn in possession of another player. A new game has started and he is going to make a move. 'I am going to take you to your sister, Isabel.'

Of course, Isabel is now the victor. Isabel is of the House of York, a faithful wife to the most handsome York brother. Isabel is the wife of the victor of Barnet, of Tewkesbury. Isabel's husband is next in line to the throne after Edward's baby son, only two heartbeats away from greatness. If Edward were to die, mopping up the fighting, if Edward's son were to die – and even now the queen and the royal nursery are besieged in the Tower by Lancaster loyalists – then George will be King of England and Isabel would fulfil my father's ambition and her own destiny. Then, I suppose, my father would not have died in vain. He would have a daughter on the throne of England. It would not be me; it would be Isabel. But he would not have minded that. He never minded which one of us achieved the throne as long as it was a girl from the House of Warwick.

Isabel receives me in her privy chamber with three ladies in waiting. I know none of them. It is like meeting a stranger in awkward circumstances. I walk in and curtsey; she inclines her head.

'Iz.'

She has gone deaf with greatness. She just looks at me.

'Iz,' I say more urgently.

'How could you do it?' she demands. 'How could you come with her and invade us like that? How could you, Anne? You were bound to fail and face disgrace or death.'

For a moment I am aghast, and I stare at her as if she is speaking Flemish. Then I look at the avid ladies seated around her and realise we are speaking for the enjoyment of the House of York, we are a tableau of remorse and loyalty. She is playing Loyalty; I am to play Remorse.

'My Lady Sister, I had no choice,' I say quietly. 'My father ordered my marriage to the son of Margaret of Anjou, and she commanded that I go with them. You remember that I did not seek the marriage, it was at my father's command. As soon as we landed in England I asked at once to join my mother. There are witnesses to that.'

I thought that the mention of our mother, mourning in sanctuary, would soften Isabel but it turns out it is the wrong thing to say. Her face darkens at once. 'Our mother is to be arraigned for treason. She will lose her estates and fortune. She knew of the plot against King Edward and she did nothing to warn him. She is a traitor,' Isabel rules.

If my mother loses her estates then Isabel and I will lose our inheritance. Everything my father owned was lost on the battlefield. All we have left is the fortune that stayed in my mother's name. Isabel cannot want to throw this away, it is to make herself a pauper. I shoot an anxious glance at her. 'My mother was guilty of nothing but obedience to her husband,' I try.

Izzy scowls at me. 'Our father was a traitor to his king and his friend. Our mother is guilty with him. We will throw ourselves on the mercy and wisdom of Edward. God save the king!'

'God save the king!' I repeat.

Isabel waves the women to leave us and beckons me to come and sit beside her. I sink to a low stool and wait for her to tell me what I am to do, what she means by this. I am so weary and so overwhelmed by defeat that I wish I could put my head in her lap, like I used to do, and let her rock me to sleep.

'Iz,' I say miserably. 'I am so tired. What do we have to do now?'

'We can do nothing for Mother,' she says quietly. 'She made

her choice. She will be in the abbey for life now she has walled herself in there.'

'Walled?'

'Don't be stupid. I don't mean she's really walled in. I mean she has chosen to live there and claimed sanctuary. She cannot just come out now that the fighting is over and expect to carry on as normal.'

'What about us?'

'George is a favoured brother, a son of the House of York. He was on the right side in the last two battles. I'm going to be all right.'

'What about me?'

'You're going to live with us. Quietly, to start off with, until the fuss about the Prince of Lancaster and the battle is over. You will be my lady in waiting.'

I observe that I am brought so low that I am relieved to be in service to my sister, and she in the House of York. 'Oh, so now I am to serve you,' I say.

'Yes,' she says shortly. 'Of course.'

'Did they tell you about the battle at Barnet? When Father was killed?'

She shrugs. 'Not really. I didn't ask. He's dead, isn't he? Does it matter how?'

'How?'

She looks at me and her face softens as if beneath this battle-hardened young woman is the sister that loves me still. 'You know what he did?'

I shake my head.

'They say that he wanted the soldiers to know that he would not ride off and leave them. The soldiers, the common men, know that the lords have their horses held by their grooms behind the battle lines, and if they are losing, the lords can call for their horses and get away. Everyone knows that. They leave foot soldiers to be killed and they ride away.'

I nod.

'Father said he would face death with them. They could trust him to take the risk that they were taking. He called for his beautiful warhorse—'

'Not Midnight?'

'Yes, Midnight who was so handsome and brave, that he loved so much, that had carried him so often in so many battles. And before all the men, all the commoners who would never be able to get away if they were defeated, he drew his great battle sword and he plunged it into Midnight's loyal heart. The horse went down to its knees and Father held his head as he died. Midnight died with his big black head in Father's arms. Father stroked his nose as he closed his black eyes.'

I am horrified. 'He did that?'

'He loved Midnight. He did it to show them that this was a battle to the death – for all of them. He laid Midnight's head on the ground and stood up and said to the men: "Now I am like you, a foot soldier like you. I cannot gallop away like a false lord. I am here to fight to the death."'

'And then?'

'Then he fought to the death.' The tears are pouring down her face, and she does not wipe them away. 'They knew he would fight to the death. He didn't want anyone to ride away. He wanted this to be the last battle. He wanted it to be the last battle in the cousins' wars for England.'

I put my face in my hands. 'Iz – ever since that terrible day at sea everything has gone wrong for us.'

She does not touch me, she does not put her arm around my shoulders or reach for my tear-drenched fingers. 'It's over,' she says. She takes a handkerchief from her sleeve, and she dries her eyes, folds it, and puts it back. She is resigned to grief, to our defeat. 'It's over. We were fighting against the House of York and they were always certain to win. They have Edward before them and they have witchcraft behind them, they are unbeatable. I am of the House of York now, and I will see them rule England forever. You, in my household, will be faithful to York too.'

I keep my hands over my mouth and I direct my frightened whisper to her ears only. 'Do you know for sure that they won by witchcraft?'

'It was a witch's wind that nearly drowned me and killed my baby,' she says, her voice so low that I have to lean against her cheek to hear her words. 'The same witch's wind raged all spring and kept us in port but blew Edward to England. At the battle of Barnet, Edward's armies were hidden by a mist that swirled around them, only them, as they crept forwards. Father's army was on a ridge in plain view, it was Her magic that hid the York troops. It is not possible to defeat Edward as long as he has Her at his side.'

I hesitate. 'Our father died fighting them. He sacrificed Midnight to fight them.'

'I can't think about him now,' she says. 'I have to forget him.'

'I won't,' I say, almost to myself. 'I won't ever forget him. Not him or Midnight.'

She shrugs, as if it does not matter very much, gets to her feet and smooths her gown over her slim hips, arranging her golden belt. 'You have to come to the king,' she says.

'I do?' I am frightened at once.

'Yes. I am to take you. Make sure you don't say anything wrong. Don't do anything stupid.' She looks me over with a hard critical glare. 'Don't cry. Don't talk back. Try and act like a princess though you are not.'

Before I can say another word she beckons her ladies and leads the way out of her rooms. I follow her and the three ladies in waiting fall in behind me. I watch very carefully that I don't step on her gown as she leads the way through the castle to the king's apartments. Her train slips down the stairs, trails through the sweet-scented rushes across the great hall. I follow it like a kitten follows a skein of wool: blindly, like a fool.

We are expected. The doors swing open and Edward is there, tall, fair and handsome, seated behind a table that is spread with papers. He does not look like a man who has just fought a bloody battle, killed his guardian, and then led a desperate forced march to another battle to the death. He looks full of life, tireless. As the doors open he looks up and sees us, and he smiles his open-hearted beam as if we were still all friends, as if we were still the little daughters of his greatest friend and mentor. As if we adored him as the most glamorous older brother a girl could ever have.

'Ah, Lady Anne,' he says, and he rises from his seat and comes round the table and gives me his hand. I sink down into a deep curtsey and he raises me up and kisses me on both cheeks, first one then the other.

'My sister begs for your pardon,' Isabel says, her voice tremulous with sincerity. 'She is only young, she is not yet fifteen, Your Grace, and she has been obedient to my mother who judged ill, and she had to obey her father who betrayed you. But I will take her into my keeping and she will be faithful to you and yours.'

He looks at me. He is as handsome as a knight in a storybook. 'You know that Margaret of Anjou is defeated and will never ride out against me again?'

I nod.

'And that her cause was without merit?'

I can sense that Isabel is flinching with fear without looking at her.

'I know that now,' I say carefully.

He gives a short laugh. 'That's good enough for me,' he says easily. 'Do you swear to accept me as your king and liege lord and support the inheritance of my son and heir, Prince Edward?'

I close my eyes briefly at the name of my husband, in the place of my husband. 'I do,' I say. I don't know what else I can say.

'Swear fealty,' he says quietly.

Isabel pushes me on the shoulder and I go down to my knees to him, who has been like a brother to me, then a king, then an enemy. I watch him to see if he will gesture that I have to kiss his boot. I wonder how low I am going to have to go. I put up my hands together in a gesture of prayer and Edward puts his hands on either side of them. His hands are warm. 'I forgive you, and I pardon you,' Edward says cheerfully. 'You will live with your sister and she and I will arrange for your marriage when your year of widowhood is over.'

'My mother . . .' I start.

Isabel makes a little movement as if to stop me. But Edward holds up his hand for silence, his face stern. 'Your mother has betrayed her position and her obedience to her king,' he says. 'It is as if she were dead to me.'

'And to me,' says Isabel hastily, the turncoat.

THE TOWER OF LONDON,
21 MAY 1471

It is another tableau, played out by the House of York for the benefit of the citizens of London. The Queen of England, Elizabeth Woodville, stands on a great wooden stage that they have built before the door of the White Tower, her three daughters beside her, her baby son in a gown of cloth of gold, held lovingly in the arms of his grandmother: the named witch Jacquetta. Isabel stands beside the queen, I stand beside Isabel. The queen's brother Anthony Woodville, who now inherits his father's title and is Lord Rivers, who rescued his sister when she was besieged in the Tower and defeated the remnants of the Lancaster forces, is at the head of his personal guards, drawn up at the foot of the steps. The queen's own guards are on the other side. Behind railings of blue and murrey, York colours, the people of London wait for the show as if they had come to see a joust and are cheerfully impatient for it to begin.

The great gates in the Tower wall creak open, the drawbridge goes down over the moat with a heavy thud, and in rides Edward, gloriously dressed in enamelled armour with a gold circlet around his helmet, on a beautiful chestnut warhorse, at the head of his lords, his brothers on either side of him, his guards behind him. The trumpets sound, the York banners ripple in the wind that blows off the river, showing the embroidered white rose of York and their insignia of the sun in splendour: the three suns together, which signify the three reunited sons of York. Behind the victorious York boys comes a litter hung with cloth of silver, drawn by white mules, the curtains tied back so that everyone can see, seated inside, the former queen, my mother-in-law, Margaret of Anjou, in a white gown, her face utterly devoid of any emotion.

I look at my feet, at the rippling standards of the sun in splendour, anywhere but at her, for fear of meeting her blank furious eyes. Edward dismounts, hands his warhorse to his squire, and comes up the steps of the Tower. Elizabeth the queen comes towards him and he takes both her hands and kisses her on her smiling mouth. Jacquetta steps forwards and then there is a great bellow of applause as he takes his little son and heir and turns to the crowd and presents him. This will be Edward, Prince of Wales, the next King of England, Prince Edward of Wales, a baby to take the place of the dead Lancaster prince that neither his mother nor I saw buried. This baby will be king, his wife will be queen. Not me, not Isabel.

'Smile,' Isabel prompts me softly and at once I smile and clasp my hands together as if I too am applauding the triumph of York, so thrilled I can barely speak.

Edward hands his baby to his wife and goes down the steps to where the litter has halted. I see the oldest princess, little Elizabeth, aged only five years old, press close to her mother and clutch a handful of her gown for safety. The queen puts a gentle hand on her daughter's shoulder. The little girl will have been haunted from the cradle by tales of Margaret of Anjou, just as I was; and now the woman we so feared is imprisoned, and enslaved. Edward the victor takes her by the hand to help her from her litter, and leads her up the broad wooden steps to the stage where he turns her, as if she were a captured animal brought to join the collection of wild beasts at the Tower. She faces the crowd and they yell in triumph to see the she-wolf finally brought in.

Her face is quite impassive as she looks over their heads at the blue May sky, as if she cannot hear them, as if nothing that they can shout could ever make any difference to her. She is every inch a queen before them. I cannot help but admire her. She taught me that to fight for the throne may cost you everything, may cost your enemy everything. But it is worth it. Even now, I imagine she regrets only losing; she will never regret fighting and going on fighting. She smiles slightly at her defeat. Her hand, held firmly by Edward, does not shake, not even the veil from her high headdress trembles in the wind. She is a queen of graven ice.

He keeps her there, to make sure that everyone can see that he has her captive, while every boy in the crowd is raised in his father's arms to see that the House of Lancaster is reduced to this: one powerless woman on the steps of the Tower and hidden inside like an old bat, in his rooms, a sleeping king. Then Edward bows his head slightly, chivalrously, and turns Margaret of Anjou towards the entrance door to the White Tower and gestures that she shall go in to join her husband in prison.

She takes one step towards the door and then she pauses. She looks us over, and then, as if inspired, she walks slowly past us, looking at each one. She inspects the queen and her daughters and her ladies as if we were her guard of honour. It is a magnificent long-drawn-out insult from the utterly defeated to her victors. The little Princess Elizabeth shrinks back behind her mother's skirts to hide her face from the unswerving gaze of the white-faced prisoner. Margaret looks from me to Isabel and gives a slight nod as if she understands that I am now to be played in a new game, by a new player. She narrows her eyes at the thought of me being bought and sold all over again. She almost smiles as she realises that her defeat has knocked all the value off me; I am spoiled goods, destroyed goods. She cannot hide her amusement at that thought.

And then slowly, terribly, she turns her gaze to Jacquetta, the queen's mother, the witch whose wind destroyed our hopes by keeping us in port for all those long days, the sorceress whose mist hid the York army at Barnet, the wise woman who delivered her grandson when they were hiding in sanctuary and came out to victory.

I am holding my breath, straining to hear what Margaret will say to the dearest friend she ever had, who abandoned her at the battle of Towton and has never seen her again till this, the moment of her utter defeat; whose daughter married the enemy and changed sides, and who is now Margaret's enemy and is witnessing her shame.

The two women look at each other and in both faces there is a glimpse of the girls that they were. A little smile warms Margaret's face and Jacquetta's eyes are filled with love. It is as if the years are no more than the mists of Barnet or the snows at Towton: they are gone, it is hard to believe they were ever there. Margaret puts out her hand, not to touch her friend but to make a gesture, a secret shared gesture, and, as we watch, Jacquetta mirrors the movement. Eyes fixed on each other they both raise their index finger and trace a circle in the air – that's all they do. Then they smile to each other as if life itself is a joke, a jest that means nothing and a wise woman can laugh at it; then, without a word, Margaret passes silently into the darkness of the tower.

'What was that?' Isabel exclaims.

'It was the sign for the wheel of fortune,' I whisper. 'The wheel of fortune which put Margaret of Anjou on the throne of England, heiress to the kingdoms of Europe, and then threw her down to this. Jacquetta warned her of this long ago – they knew. The two of them knew long ago that fortune throws you up to greatness and down to disaster and all you can do is endure.'

That night the York brothers, working together as one dark assassin, go to the room of the sleeping king and hold a pillow over his face, ending the line of the House of Lancaster and bringing into their own home the treacherous death that they practise on the battlefield. With his wife and his innocent son sleeping under the same roof Edward commissioned the death of a King of England in a nearby room. We none of us knew that he had done it until the morning when we woke to the announcement that poor King Henry was dead – dead of sorrow, Edward said.

I don't need to be a soothsayer to predict that no-one will ever sleep safe in the king's keeping after that night. This is the new nature of making war for the crown of England. It is a battle to the death, as my father knew when Midnight fell to his knees and put his black head down on the field of Barnet. The House of York is ruthless and deadly, no respecter of place or person; and Isabel and I will do well to remember it.

L'ERBER, LONDON, AUTUMN 1471

I serve as my sister's lady in waiting in the house that belonged to my father and has now come, with all his fortune, to my brother-in-law George. I am given all the honours due to my kinship to her in her household. I am not yet expected to serve the Queen of England as I am still in mourning, but when we get past this dark autumn into Christmas and spring, then I will have to go to court, serve both the queen and my sister, and the king will arrange for my marriage. My late husband's title has been given to the son, born to the queen when she was hiding in sanctuary. He is Edward, Prince of Wales, just like my Edward, Prince of Wales. I have lost my husband and my name.

I remember being a little girl when my father told me that the queen had asked for Isabel and me as maids in waiting, and that he had refused her, for we were too good for her court; and I hug his pride to me, like a burning coal in a warming pan.

I have little cause for pride. I feel that I am falling very low and I have no protector. I have neither fortune, nor affinity, nor great name. My father died as a traitor, my mother is all but imprisoned. No man will want me as a wife to further his line. Nobody can be certain that I could give him sons, for my mother had only two girls, and I conceived nothing during my brief marriage to the prince. As soon as I am out of mourning I think that King Edward will grant some low knight a tiny share of my father's lands and my hand with it, as a reward for some shameful deed on the battlefield, and I shall be sent off to the country to raise hens, keep sheep and breed children if I can do it.

I know that my father would not have wanted this for me. He and my mother put a fortune together for the two of us, their treasured daughters. Isabel and I were the richest heiresses in England, and now I have nothing. My father's fortune is to be given to George, and my mother's fortune is to be taken from us without a word of protest. Isabel lets them call my mother a traitor and confiscate her fortune so that we are both paupers.

Finally I ask her why.

She laughs in my face. She is standing before a great tapestry tied tight on a loom, weaving the final gold threads herself, and her ladies are admiring the design. The weavers will come in later to finish the work and cut the threads, Isabel is playing at work with priceless gold thread on her shuttle. Now, a duchess of the famously cultured House of York, she has become a connoisseur.

'It's obvious,' she says. 'Obvious.'

'Not to me,' I reply steadily. 'It's not obvious to me.'

Carefully she threads the shuttle through the tapestry and one of the ladies cards it for her. They all step back and admire the result. I grit my teeth on my irritation.

'It's not obvious to me why you leave my mother in Beaulieu Abbey and let her fortune be seized by the king. Why do you not ask him to share it between the two of us if it has to be taken from her? Why don't you petition the king to return us at least some of Father's lands? How can it be that we don't at least keep Warwick Castle, our home? There have been Nevilles at Warwick Castle since the beginning of time. Why do you let everything go to George? If you will not petition the king, then I will. We cannot be left with nothing.'

She hands the shuttle and thread to one of her ladies and takes me by the arm and leads me away, so that nobody can hear her quiet words. 'You will not petition the king for everything; it has all been arranged. Mother keeps writing to him, and to all the royal ladies, but it makes no difference. It has all been arranged.'

'What has been arranged?'

She hesitates. 'Father's fortune goes to the king as he was attainted of treason.'

I open my mouth to protest: 'He wasn't attainted . . .'

But she pinches my arm. 'He would have been. He fell as a traitor, it doesn't make any difference. The king has granted it all to George. And Mother's fortune is taken from her.'

'Why? She's not been tried for treason. She's not even been accused.'

'Her fortune will be passed on to her heir. To me.'

I take a moment to understand. 'But what about me? I am joint heir with you. We have to share everything.'

'I will give you a dower on your marriage, from my fortune.'

I look at Isabel, who turns her gaze from the window and looks nervously back at me. 'You have to remember that you were the wife of a pretender to the throne. You are bound to be punished.'

'But it is you that are punishing me!'

She shakes her head. 'It is the House of York. I am just a duchess of the house.' Her sly little smile reminds me that she is on the winning side while I was married to the losers.

'You cannot take everything and leave me with nothing!'

She shrugs. Clearly, she can.

I pull away from her. 'Isabel, if you do this, you are no sister to me!'

She takes my arm again. 'I am, and I am going to make sure that you make a wonderful marriage.'

'I don't want a wonderful marriage, I want my own inheritance. I want the lands that my father would have given me. I want the fortune that my mother intended for me.'

'If you don't want to marry then there is another way . . .' She hesitates.

I wait.

'George says that he can get permission for you to join a

convent. You could join our mother if you like, at Beaulieu Abbey.'

I stare at her. 'You would have our mother imprisoned for life and then lock me up with her as well?'

'George says . . .'

'I don't want to know what George says. George says whatever the king tells him to say, and the king says whatever Elizabeth Woodville tells him to say! The House of York are our enemies and you have sided with them, as bad as any of them!'

In an instant she pulls me closer and puts her fingers firmly across my mouth. 'Shut up! Don't speak like that of them! Ever!'

Without thinking I nip her hand, and she gives a yowl of pain and rears back to slap me hard across the face. I scream at the blow and push her back. She rocks against the wall and we both glare at each other. Suddenly I am aware of the stunned silence in the room and the delighted gaze of the audience of ladies. Isabel stares at me, her cheeks red with rage. I feel my own temper drain away. Sheepishly, I pick up her ornate headdress from the floor and offer it to her. Isabel smooths her gown and takes her headdress. She does not look at me at all. 'Go to your room,' she hisses.

'Iz—'

'Go to your room and pray to Our Lady for guidance. I think you must have run mad, biting like a rabid dog. You are not fit to be in my company, you are not fit for the company of ladies. You are a stupid child, a wicked child, you may not come into my company.'

I go to my room but I don't pray. I pull out my clothes and I put them in a bundle. I go to my chest and I count out my money. I am going to run away from Isabel and her stupid husband and neither of them will ever tell me what I shall or shall not do, ever again. I pack in a feverish haste. I have been a princess, I have been the daughter-in-law of the she-wolf queen. Am I going to allow my sister to make me into a poor girl, depending on her and her husband for my dowry, depending on my new husband for a roof over my head? I am a Neville of the House of Warwick – shall I become a nothing?

I have my bundle in my hand and my travelling cloak around my shoulders, I creep to the door and listen. There is the usual bustle in the great hall as they prepare the room for dinner. I can hear the fire-boy bringing in the logs and carrying out the ashes, and the clatter as they slam down the trestles and bang the table-tops on them, then the squeak of wooden feet on floorboards, as they drag the benches from the sides of the room. I can slip through everyone and be out of the door before anyone notices that I am gone.

For a moment I stand, poised on the threshold, my heart hammering, ready to run. And then I pause. I don't go anywhere. The resolve and the excitement drain from me. I close the door and go back into my room. I sit on the edge of my bed. I don't have anywhere to go. If I go to my mother it is a long journey, across half of England, and I don't know the way, and I have no guard, and then at the end of it is a nunnery and the certainty of imprisonment. King Edward for all his handsome smile and easy pardons will just lock me up with her and consider it a little problem well solved. If I go to Warwick Castle I might be greeted with love and loyalty by my father's old servants but for all I know George has already put a new tenant in my father's place, and he will simply hold me under arrest and return me to Isabel and George, or worse, hold a pillow over my face as I sleep.

I realise that although I am not imprisoned like my mother-in-law Margaret of Anjou in the Tower, nor like my mother in Beaulieu Abbey, equally I am not free. Without money to hire guards and without a great name to command respect I cannot go out into the world. If I want to get away I have to find someone who will give me guards and fight for my money. I need an ally, someone with money and a retinue of fighting men.

I drop my bundle and sit cross-legged on the bed and sink my chin into my hands. I hate Isabel for allowing this – for colluding with this. She has brought me down very low – this is worse than the defeat at Tewkesbury. There it was a battle on an open field, and I was among the many defeated. Here I am alone. It is my own sister against me, and only I am suffering. She has let them reduce me to a nothing and I will never forgive her.

WESTMINSTER PALACE, LONDON, CHRISTMAS 1471

Isabel and George attend the king and his queen at their triumphant Christmas feast, restored to their beautiful palace, at ease among their friends and allies, a byword for beauty, for chivalry, for royal grace. The country has never seen anything like it, ever before. The citizens of London can speak of nothing but the elegance and extravagance of this restored court. The king spends his newly won fortune on beautiful clothes for the queen and her pretty princesses; every new fashion from Burgundy graces the royal family from the turned-up toes of their shoes, to the rich colours of their capes. Elizabeth the queen is a blaze of precious stones at every great dinner, and they are served from trenchers of gold. Every day sees a new celebration of their power. There is music, and dancing, jousts and boating on the cold river. There is masquing and entertainments.

The queen's brother Anthony Woodville, Lord Rivers, holds a crusade of scholars in which theologians of the Bible argue with the translators of Arabic texts. The king comes disguised into the ladies' chamber and amid much screaming and pretend terror holds them up like a pirate and steals their jewels from their arms and necks and replaces them with finer gifts. The queen, with her son in her arms, her mother at her side, and her daughters in her train, laughs with relief every day of the Christmas feast.

Not that I see any of this. I am in Isabel and George's household living in the rambling village that is Westminster Palace, but I am not bidden to dinner, not as the daughter of a formerly great man, nor as a dowager princess. I am kept out of sight as the widow of a failed pretender, the daughter of a traitor. I have rooms in the palace overlooking the river, near to the gardens, and at mealtimes my food is brought privately to me. I go to the royal chapel twice a day and sit behind Isabel, my head penitently bowed, but I do not speak with the queen nor with the king. When they go past me I sink into a curtsey and neither of them see me at all.

My mother is still imprisoned in Beaulieu Abbey. There is no pretence any longer that she is in sanctuary, that she has sought a life of retreat. Everyone is absolutely clear that she is held as a prisoner and that the king will never release her. My mother-in-law is held in the Tower, in the rooms that belonged to her dead husband. They say she prays for him daily, and constantly for the soul of her son. I know how bereft she feels, and I did not even love him. And I – the last woman standing after the attempt to throw Edward from the throne – I am held in this twilight world by my own sister: I am her prisoner and her ward. The agreeable fiction is that George and Isabel are caring for me, have rescued me from the battlefield, they serve as my guardians, and I am living with my family at peace and in comfort. They are helping me recover from the terror of battle, from the ordeal of my forced marriage and widowhood. The truth, as everyone secretly knows, is that they are my gaolers just as the guards in the Tower hold my mother-in-law, and the lay brothers at Beaulieu secure my mother. We are all three imprisoned women, we are all three without friends, money, or hope. My mother writes to me and demands that I speak with my sister, with George, with the king himself. I answer her briefly that nobody ever speaks to me but to give me orders and that she will have to free herself, that she should never have locked herself away.

But I am fifteen years old – I cannot help but hope. Some

afternoons I lie on my bed and dream that the prince my husband was not killed but escaped from the battle and will come for
me right now – climb through the window and laugh at my
astounded face, and tell me that there is a wonderful plan, an
army outside waiting to overthrow Edward, and I will be Queen
of England as my father wanted. Sometimes I imagine that his
death was wrongly reported, that Father still lives and that the
two of them are mustering an army in our lands in the North and
will come to rescue me, my father high on Midnight, his eyes
bright under his helmet.

Sometimes I pretend that none of it ever happened, and when
I wake in the morning I keep my eyes closed so that I cannot see
the small bedroom and the lady in waiting who sleeps in the bed
with me, and I can pretend that Iz and I are at Calais, and that
soon Father will come home and say that he has defeated the bad
queen and the sleeping king and that we are to come with him to
England and be the greatest ladies in the land and marry the York
dukes.

I am a girl, I cannot help but hope. My heart lifts at the crackle
of the fire in the grate. I open the shutters and see the milky
clouds of the early morning, and sniff the air and wonder if it will
snow. I cannot believe that my life is over, that I have made my
great gamble and lost. My mother may be on her knees at
Beaulieu, my mother-in-law may pray for the soul of her son, but
I am only fifteen and I cannot help but think every day – perhaps
today something will change. Perhaps today a chance will come
for me. Surely, I cannot be held here, without a name, without a
fortune, forever?

I am on my way back from chapel with Isabel's ladies when I
realise I have left my rosary on the floor where I was kneeling. I
say a brief word to my companions and go back. It is a mistake,
the king is coming out of the chapel as I am coming in, his arm
linked with his great friend William Hastings, his brother
Richard behind him, a long stream of friends and hangers-on
behind them.

I do as I have been commanded, I shrink back, I sink down, I look down. I do everything to indicate my penitence and my lack of worthiness to tread the same rushes as this king, who walks here in pomp only because he killed my father and my husband on the battlefield and my father-in-law by treachery. He goes past me with a pleasant smile: 'Good day, Lady Anne.'

'Dowager princess,' I say to the rushes under my knees, but I make sure that no-one can hear me.

I keep my head down as the many pairs of beautifully embossed boots dawdle past and then I get up. Richard, the king's nineteen-year-old brother, has not gone. He is leaning against the stone frame of a doorway and smiling at me, as if he has finally remembered that once we were friends, that he was my father's ward and every night he used to kneel for my mother's kiss as if he were her son.

'Anne,' he says simply.

'Richard,' I reply, giving him no title if he gives me none, though he is the Duke of Gloucester, and a royal duke, and I am a girl with no name.

'I'll be quick,' he says, glancing along the corridor where his brother and his friends are strolling away speaking of hunting and a new dog that someone has brought from Hainault. 'If you are happy living with your sister, with your inheritance robbed from you and your mother imprisoned, then I will not say another word.'

'I'm not happy,' I say rapidly.

'If you see them as your gaolers, I could rescue you from them.'

'I see them as my gaolers and my enemies and I hate them both.'

'You hate your sister?'

'I hate her even worse than I hate him.'

He nods, as if this is not shocking, but utterly reasonable. 'Can you get out of your rooms at all?'

'I walk in the privy garden in the afternoon most days.'

'Alone?'

'Since I have no friends.'

'Come to the yew arbour this afternoon after dinner. I'll be waiting.'

He turns without another word and runs after his brother's court. I walk swiftly to my sister's rooms.

In the afternoon my sister and all her ladies are preparing for a masque, and they are going to try their costumes in the wardrobe rooms. There is no part for me to learn, there is no ornate costume for me to try. They forget all about me in the excitement of the gowns and I take my chance and slip away, down a winding stone stair that leads directly to the garden, and from there to the yew arbour.

I see his slight form, seated on a stone bench, his hound beside him. The dog turns his head and pricks his ears at the sound of my shoes on the gravel. Richard rises to his feet as he sees me.

'Does anybody know you are here?'

I feel my heart thud at this, a conspirator's question. 'No.'

He smiles. 'How long do you have?'

'Perhaps an hour.'

He draws me into the shade of the arbour, where it is cold and dark but the thick green branches hide us from view. Anyone would have to come to the very entrance of the circular planting of trees and peer inside to see us. We are hidden as if enclosed in a little green room. I draw my cloak around me and sit on the stone bench and look up at him, expectantly.

He laughs at my excited face. 'I have to know what you want, before I can suggest anything.'

'Why would you suggest anything at all for me?'

He shrugs. 'Your father was a good man, he was a good guardian to me when I was his ward. I remember you with affection from childhood. I was happy in your house.'

'And for this you would rescue me?'

'I think you should be free to make your own choices.'

I look at him sceptically. He must think I am a fool. He was not thinking of my freedom when he led my horse to Worcester and handed me over to George and Isabel. 'Then why didn't you let me go to my mother, when you came for Margaret of Anjou?'

'I didn't know then that they would hold you as a prisoner. I thought I was taking you to your family, to safety.'

'It's because of the money,' I tell him. 'While they hold me, Isabel can claim all the inheritance from my mother.'

'And while your sister does not protest they can hold your mother forever. George gets all your father's lands, and if Isabel gets your mother's lands that great inheritance is made one again, but inherited by only one of the Warwick girls: by Isabel, and her wealth is in George's keeping.'

'I am not allowed to even speak to the king, so how can I put my case?'

'I could be your champion,' Richard suggests slowly. 'If you wanted me to serve you. I could speak to him for you.'

'Why would you do this?'

He smiles at me. There is a world of invitation in his dark eyes. 'Why d'you think?' he says quietly.

'Why d'you think?' The question haunts me like a love song, as I hurry from the chilly garden and go up to Isabel's rooms. My hands are freezing and my nose is red from the cold but nobody notices as I slip off my cloak and sit by the fire, pretending to listen to them talk about the gowns for the masque, though all I hear in my head is his question: 'Why d'you think?'

It is time to dress before dinner. I have to wait on Isabel as her maids lace her gown. I have to hand her little flask of perfume to her, open her jewel box. For once I serve her without resentment; I hardly even notice that she asks for a collar of pearls and then changes her mind, and then changes back again. I just take the things from the box and put them back and then get them out again. It does not matter to me if she wears pearls that her husband has stolen from someone else. She is not going to steal anything from me, ever again, for I have someone on my side.

I have someone on my side now and he is a king's brother just as George is a king's brother. He is of the House of York and my father loved him and taught him like a son. And, as it happens, he is heir to the throne after George, but more beloved than George, and more steadfast and loyal than George. If you were going to pick one of the York boys it would be George for looks, Edward for charm, but it would be Richard for loyalty.

'Why d'you think?' When he asked me he gave me a naughty smile, his dark eyes were so bright; he almost winked at me as if it were a private joke, as if it were a delightful secret. I thought I was being clever and guarded to ask him why he would help me – and then he looked at me as if I knew the answer. And there was something about the question, about the gleam of his smile, that made me want to giggle, that even now, as my sister moves to her hand-beaten silver mirror and nods for me to tie the pearls around her neck, makes me want to blush.

'What's the matter with you?' she says coldly, her eyes meeting mine in the silvered looking glass.

I steady myself at once. 'Nothing.'

Isabel rises from the table and goes to the door. Her ladies gather around her, the door opens and George and his household are waiting to join her. This is my signal to go to my room. It is generally agreed that I am in mourning so deep that I cannot be present in mixed company. Only George and Isabel and I know that it is they who have made this rule: they don't allow me to see anyone or speak to anyone, they keep me like a mewed hawk that should be flying free. Only George and Isabel and I know this – but Richard knows it too. Richard guessed it because he knows what I am like, what Isabel is like. He was like a son to my father, he understands the House of Warwick. And Richard cared enough to think about me, to wonder how I was faring in Isabel's household, to see through the façade of guardianship to the truth: that I am their prisoner.

I curtsey to George and keep my eyes down so he cannot see that I am smiling. In my head I hear again my question: 'Why would you do this?' and his answer: 'Why d'you think?'

When there is a knock at the door of the privy chamber I open it myself, expecting it to be one of the grooms of the servery with dishes for my dinner, but the presence chamber is empty except for Richard, standing there, magnificently dressed in red velvet doublet and breeches, his cape trimmed with sables slung around his shoulder as if it were nothing.

I gasp. 'You?'

'I thought I would come and see you while they are serving dinner,' he says, strolling into the privy chamber and seating himself in Isabel's chair under the cloth of estate by the fireside.

'The servers will come with my dinner at any moment,' I warn him.

He makes a careless gesture with his hand. 'Have you thought about our talk?'

Every moment of this afternoon. 'Yes.'

'Would you like me to be your champion in this matter?' Again he smiles at me as if he is proposing the most delicious game, as if asking me to conspire against my guardian and my sister is like inviting me to dance.

'What would we do?' I try to be serious but I am smiling in reply.

'Oh,' he whispers. 'We would have to meet often, I am sure.'

'Would we?'

'Once a day at least. For a proper conspiracy I should want to see you once a day, probably twice. I don't know that I wouldn't need to see you all the time.'

'And what would we do?'

He pulls a stool towards the chair with the toe of his boot and gestures that I should sit near him. I obey: he is mastering me as he would pet a hawk. He leans towards me as if to whisper, his breath warm on my bare neck. 'We would talk, Lady Anne, what else?'

If I were to turn my head just a little then his lips would touch my cheek. I sit very still, and will myself not to turn to him at all.

'Why? What would you like to do?' he asks me.

I think: I would like to do this, all day, this delicious play. I should like to have his eyes on me all day, I should like to know that he has moved at last from a nonchalant childhood acquaintance to lovemaking. 'But how would this get my fortune restored to me?'

'Oh yes, the fortune. For a moment I had quite forgotten the fortune. Well, first I must talk with you to make sure that I know exactly what you want.' Again he draws close. 'I would want to do exactly what you want. You must command me. I will be your cavalier, your chevalier-servant – isn't that what girls want? Like out of a story?'

His lips are against my hair, I can feel the warmth of him.

'Girls can be very silly,' I say, trying to be adult.

'It's not silly to want a man devoted to your service,' he points out. 'If I could find a lady that would accept my service, who would give me her favour, a lady of my choice, I would pledge myself to her safety and happiness.' He moves back a little so that he can study my face.

I cannot stop myself looking into his dark eyes. I can feel the colour rising in my cheeks but I cannot take my eyes from him.

'And then I will speak to my brother for you,' he says. 'You cannot be held like this against your will, your mother cannot be held against her will.'

'Would the king listen to you?'

'Of course. Without a doubt. I have been at his side ever since I was strong enough to hold a sword in battle. I am his faithful brother. He loves me. I love him. We are brothers in arms as well as in blood.'

There is a tap at the door and Richard goes in one fluid motion to stand behind it so that when the serving man bangs it open and comes in, with another behind him, carrying half a dozen dishes and a pitcher of small ale, they don't see him. They fuss at the table, putting out the plate and pouring the ale, and then they wait to serve me.

'You can go,' I say. 'Close the door behind you.'

They bow and leave the room, as Richard steps out of the shadow and pulls up a stool to the table. 'May I?'

We have the most delightful meal together, just the two of us. He shares the cup for the ale, he eats from my plate. The dinners I have endured in loneliness, eating for hunger with no pleasure, are forgotten. He picks little pieces of stewed beef from the dish and offers them to me, and mops up the gravy for himself with a piece of bread. He praises the venison and insists that I have some, and shares the pastries with me. There is no awkwardness between us, we could be children together again, with this constant bubble of laughter, and something beneath it – desire.

'I had better go,' he says. 'Dinner will be over in the hall and they will be looking for me.'

'They will think I have grown greedy,' I remark, looking at the empty dishes on the table.

He gets up and I stand too, suddenly awkward. I want to ask when we will see each other again, how we are to meet? But I feel that I cannot ask him that.

'I'll see you tomorrow,' he says easily. 'Will you go to mass early?'

'Yes.'

'Stay behind after Isabel leaves and I will come to you.'

I am breathless. 'All right.'

His hand is on the door, about to go. I put my hand on his sleeve, I cannot resist touching him. He turns with a little smile, and gently bends to kiss my hand where it rests on his arm. That's all, that's all. That one touch, not a kiss on my mouth, not a caress, but that one touch of his lips that makes my fingers burn. And then he slips from the room.

Wearing my widow's gown of dark blue, I follow Isabel into chapel and glance towards the side of the church where the king and his brothers sit to hear mass. The royal box is empty, nobody is there. I feel a sickly lurch of disappointment and think that he has failed me. He said he would be here this morning and he is not. I kneel behind Isabel and try to keep my mind on the service but the Latin words roll on and I hear them as if they were mean-ingless, a patter of sounds which say: 'I will see you tomorrow. Will you go to mass early?'

When the service is finished and Isabel rises I don't get up with her, but lower my head as if in prayer. She glances over at me impatiently, and then leaves me alone. Her ladies follow her from the chapel and I hear the door close behind them. The priest arranges his things on the altar behind the screen, his back to me, as I kneel devoutly, my hands together and my eyes closed, so I don't see Richard as he slips into the pew and kneels beside me. Tantalisingly, I let myself sense him before I open my eyes to see him – the light scent of soap from his skin and the clean smell of new leather of his boots, the little noise as he kneels, the smell of lavender as he crushes a flower head beneath his knee, and then the warmth of his hand over my clasped fingers.

I open my eyes slowly, as if I am waking, and he is smiling at me. 'What are you praying for?'

This moment, I think. You. Rescue. 'Nothing, really.'

'Then I will tell you that you should pray for your freedom and for the freedom of your mother. Shall I ask Edward for you?'

'Would you ask for my mother to be freed?'

'I could do. Would you want me to?'

'Of course. But do you think she could go to Warwick Castle? What is there for her here? Or could she go to one of our other houses? Do you think she would still stay at Beaulieu even if she were free to leave?'

'If she were to decide to stay in the abbey, in honourable retirement, then she might keep her fortune and you would still have nothing, and still have to live with your sister,' he says quietly. 'If Edward will forgive her and set her free then she will be a lady of great wealth, but never welcome at court: a wealthy recluse. You will have to live with her, and you will have nothing of your own until her death.'

The priest cleans the cup and puts it carefully in a case, turns the pages of the Bible and puts a silk marker on the page, then bows reverently to the cross and goes out of the door.

'Iz will be furious with me if she doesn't get my mother's fortune.'

'And how would you manage if you had nothing?' he asks.

'I could live with my mother.'

'Would you really want to live in seclusion? And you would have no dowry. Only what she chooses to give you. If you wanted to marry in the future.' He pauses, as if the idea has just occurred to him. 'Do you want to marry?'

Limpidly I look at him. 'I see no-one,' I say. 'They don't allow me to be in company. I am a widow, in my first year of mourning. Who would I marry, since I meet no-one?'

His eyes are on my mouth. 'You're meeting me.'

I see his smile. 'I am,' I whisper. 'But it is not as if we are courting or thinking of marriage.'

The door at the back of the chapel opens and someone comes in to pray.

'Perhaps you need both your share of the fortune and your freedom,' Richard says very quietly in my ear. 'Perhaps your mother may stay where she is and her fortune be given equally to you and your sister. Then you could be free to live your own life, and make your own choice.'

'I couldn't live alone,' I object. 'I wouldn't be allowed. I'm only fifteen.'

Again he smiles at me and moves a little so that his shoulder is against mine. I want to lean on him, I want his arm around me.

'If you had your fortune you could marry any man of your choice,' he says softly. 'You would bring your husband an enormous estate and great wealth. Any man in England would be glad to marry you. Most of them would be desperate to marry you.' He pauses to let me think about that.

He turns to me, his brown eyes honest. 'You should be sure of this, Lady Anne. If I can get your fortune restored into your hands then any man in England would be glad to marry you. He would become one of the greatest landowners of the kingdom through your wealth and related to a great English family. You could take your pick of the very best of them.'

I wait.

'But a good man wouldn't marry you for your fortune, and perhaps you shouldn't choose such a one as that.'

'Shouldn't I?'

'A good man would marry you for love,' he says simply.

The Christmas feast ends and the Duke of Clarence, my brother-in-law George, bids the fondest of goodbyes to his brother the king and especially to his young brother Richard. Iz kisses the queen, kisses the king, kisses Richard, kisses anyone who looks as if they might be important and might accept her kisses. She watches her husband as she does all this, his glance is a command to her. I see her behave like a good hunting dog that does not even need a whistle but watches for the master's nod and the abrupt move of his hand. George has her well-trained. She has learned to be as devoted to him as she was to my father: he is her lord. She has been so frightened by the power of the House of York – on the battlefield, at sea, and in the hidden world of mysteries – that she is clinging to him as her only safety. When she left us in France to join him she chose to go wherever George took her, rather than fight to keep him faithful to us.

Her ladies mount their horses, me among them. King Edward raises his hand to me. He does not forget who I was, though his court is engaged in a great effort of forgetting that there was ever a king and a queen before these, ever a Prince Edward before the baby that goes everywhere with the queen, that there was ever an invasion, a march and a battle. Elizabeth the queen looks at me levelly with her beautiful grey eyes like dark ice. She does not forget that my father killed her father, my father killed her brother. These are debts of blood that will have to be paid some day.

I get on my horse and I shake out my gown and gather the reins in my hands. I busy myself with my whip and I brush my horse's mane to one side. I make myself delay the moment when I will look for Richard.

He is beside his brother. He is always beside his brother – I have learned that there is a love and a fidelity here that nothing will ever change. As he catches my eye he beams at me, his dark face bright with affection. Anyone can see it who cares to look at him, he is hopelessly indiscreet. He puts his hand to his heart as if swearing fidelity to me. I look to left and right, thank God no-one is looking, they are all getting on their horses and George the duke is shouting for the guard. Recklessly, Richard stands there, his hand on his heart, looking at me as if he wants the world to know that he loves me.

He loves me.

I shake my head as if reproving him, and I look down at my hands on the reins. I look up again and he is still fixing his gaze on me, his hand still on his heart. I know I should look away, I know I should pretend to feel nothing but disdain – this is how the ladies in the troubadour poems behave. But I am a girl, and I am lonely and alone, and this is a handsome young man who has asked how he may serve me and now stands before me with his hand on his heart and his eyes laughing at me.

One of the guard stumbled while mounting his horse and his horse shied, knocking the nearby horseman. Everyone is looking that way, and the king puts his arm around his wife. I snatch off my glove and, in one swift gesture, I throw it towards Richard. He catches it out of the air and tucks it in the breast of his jacket. Nobody has seen it. Nobody knows. The guardsman steadies his horse, mounts it, nods his apology to his captain, and the royal family turn and wave to us.

Richard looks at me, buttoning the front of his jacket, and smiles at me warmly, assuredly. He has my glove, my favour. It is a pledge that I have given in the full knowledge of what I am doing. Because I don't want to be anybody's pawn again. The next move that is made will be mine. I will choose my freedom and I will choose my husband.

George the duke and Isabel his duchess keep great state in London, where their house is as grand as a palace, with hundreds of servants and George's own guard in his livery. He prides himself on his generosity and copies my father's rule that anyone who calls at the kitchen door at dinner time can spear his dagger with slices of meat. There is a constant stream of petitioners and tenants asking favours and needing help and the door to George's presence chamber stands open, since he will be denied to no man, not even to the poorest tenant on his lands. Everyone is to know that if they give George their fealty they can trust him to be a good lord to them. So dozens of people, hundreds, who would otherwise be indifferent, think of George as a good lord to have, a true ally on their side, a friend they would like – and George's power and influence widens like a flooding river.

Isabel shows herself as a grand lady, processing to her chapel, giving alms to the poor, interceding for George's mercy whenever she may be observed to do good. I trail behind her, one of the many objects of her ostentatious charity, and from time to time someone remarks how good my sister and my brother-in-law are to me, that they took me in when I was disgraced, and that they keep me in their home though I am penniless.

I wait until I can speak to George, since I think Isabel has become nothing more than his mouthpiece, and one afternoon I happen to be passing the stable yard when he comes in and dismounts from his horse and for once there is not a great crowd around him.

'Brother, may I speak with you?'

He starts, for I am standing in a shadowed doorway and he thought he was alone.

'Eh? Sister, of course, of course. It is always a pleasure to see you.' He smiles at me, his confident handsome smile, and he runs his hand through his thick blond hair in his practised gesture. 'How may I serve you?'

'It is about my inheritance,' I say boldly. 'I understand that my mother is going to stay in the abbey and I wonder what is going to happen to her lands and fortune?'

He glances up at the windows of the house as if he wishes Isabel would see us in the stable below her, and hurry down. 'Your mother chose to take sanctuary,' he says. 'And her husband was a warranted traitor. Their lands are forfeit to the crown.'

'*His* lands would be forfeit, if he was an arraigned traitor,' I correct him. 'But he was not arraigned. And his lands were not lawfully confiscated, I don't think. I believe the king simply gave them all to you, did he not? You are holding my father's lands as a gift from the king without the rule of law.'

He blinks. He did not know that I knew this. Again he glances around; but though the lads come to take his horse and his whip and his gloves there is no-one to interrupt me.

'And, anyway, my mother's lands are still in her keeping. She has not been declared a traitor.'

'No.'

'I understand that you propose to take her lands away from her and keep them for Isabel and for me?'

'This is business,' he starts to say. 'No need . . .'

'So when will I get my share of the lands?'

He smiles at me, he takes my hand, he draws it through his arm and he leads me from the stable yard, through the arched door into the house. 'Now, you should not be troubling yourself with this,' he says, patting my hand. 'I am your brother and your guardian, I will take care of these things for you.'

'I am a widow,' I say. 'I don't have a guardian. I have the right to own my own lands in my own right: as a widow.'

'The widow of a traitor,' he corrects me gently, as if he is sorry to say such things. 'Defeated.'

'The prince, being a prince, could not be a traitor in his own country,' I correct him. 'And I, though married to him, was not arraigned as a traitor. So I have a right to my lands.'

Together we walk into the great hall and, to his relief, Isabel is there with her ladies. She sees the two of us together and comes forwards. 'What's this?'

'Lady Anne met me in the stable yard. I am afraid she is grieving,' he says tenderly. 'And worrying about things that need not concern her.'

'Go to your room,' Isabel says abruptly to me.

'Not until I know when I will receive my inheritance,' I insist. I stand still. Clearly there is not going to be a graceful curtsey and withdrawal.

Isabel looks at her husband, unsure as to what she can do to make me go. She is afraid I may start brawling again and she can hardly ask the men of the household to take hold of me and drag me away.

'Ah, child,' George says gently. 'Leave this all to me, as I have told you.'

'When? When will I receive my inheritance?' Deliberately, I speak loudly. People are staring, the many hundreds of people that George and Isabel have as their court can hear.

'Tell her,' she says under her breath to him. 'She'll make a scene if you don't tell her. All her life she has been the centre of attention, she will throw a tantrum ...'

'I am your guardian,' he says quietly. 'Appointed by the king. You know this? You are a widow but you are also a child, you need to have someone to house you and care for you.'

I nod. 'I know that is what is said but—'

'Your fortune is in my keeping,' he interrupts. 'Your mother's estate will be transferred to you and Isabel. I will manage the estate for both of you until you are married, and then I will hand over your share to your husband.'

'And if I don't marry?'

'Then you will always have a home with us.'

'And you will always keep my lands?'

The swift guilty flicker across his handsome face tells me this is his plan.

'Then surely you will never permit my marriage?' I ask shrewdly; but he simply bows to me with great respect, kisses his hand to his wife and walks from the hall. People uncover their heads as he goes by, the women curtsey, he is a most handsome and beloved lord. He is quite deaf to me as I say again, loudly: 'I don't . . . I won't . . .'

Isabel is icy. 'Let this be the last we hear of this,' she says. 'Or I will have you locked in your room.'

'You have no rights over me, Isabel!'

'I am your guardian's wife,' she says. 'And he will lock you in your room if I tell him you are slandering us. You lost at Tewkesbury, Anne, you were on the wrong side and your husband is dead. You will have to get used to being defeated.'

There are always people coming and going through the great hall of L'Erber. The duke orders that the gates to the street are open during the day, that there are braziers burning before the doors at night. I go to the hall and look for a lad, any sort of lad – not a beggar and not a thief, but a lad that might run an errand for a groat. There are dozens of them, come to work for the day, mucking out the stables or carting away the ash, bringing little things from the market to sell to the maids of the wardrobe. I crook my finger at one of them, a tow-headed urchin with a leather jerkin, and wait for him to come to me and bow.

'D'you know the Palace of Westminster?'

''Course I do.'

'Take this, and give it to someone in the household of the Duke of Gloucester. Tell them to give it to the duke. Can you remember that?'

''Course I can.'

'And don't give it to anyone else, and don't say anything about it.'

I give him a twist of paper. Inside I have written:

I should like to see you, A

'If you get it to the duke himself he will give you a second groat,' I say and give him the coin. He takes it, nips it with his black tooth to check that it is good, and puts his knuckle to his forehead by way of a bow.

'Is it a love letter?' he asks impertinently.

'It's a secret,' I say. 'You shall have a groat from him if you will keep the secret.'

Then I have to wait.

Isabel makes an effort to be kind to me. She allows me to dine in the hall with her ladies and she sits me at her right-hand side. She calls me 'Sister' and one day she takes me to her wardrobe room and says that I must have my pick of her clothes. She is tired of seeing me in blue all the time.

She puts her arm around my shoulders. 'And you shall come to court with us,' she says. 'When your year of mourning is finished. And this summer we can go travelling with the court, and perhaps we can go to Warwick. It would be lovely to be home again, wouldn't it? You would like that? We might go to Middleham, and Barnard Castle. You will like to go to our old homes.'

I say nothing.

'We are sisters,' she says. 'I don't forget it. Anne, don't be so hard on me, don't be so hard on yourself. We have lost so much but we are still sisters. Let's be friends again. I want to live in sisterhood with you.'

I don't know how Richard will come to me, but I trust that he will come. As the days go on I start to think what I will do if he does not come. I think I am trapped.

In the cold dark days of February I hardly leave the house at all. George goes almost every day to the Palace of Westminster or out into the city. Sometimes men come to see him who enter by a side door and go straight to his room, as if they were meeting in secret. He maintains a great outward show as grand as a king. I wonder if he is planning to create a court to rival his brother's, if he hopes to amass such great lands and such a great affinity that he can set himself up as a prince in England. Isabel is always at his side, exquisitely dressed, as gracious as a queen. She goes with him when there are feasts or parties at Westminster, or when she is bidden to dine with the queen and her ladies. But I am neither invited nor allowed to go.

One day they are ordered to a special royal dinner. Isabel dresses in a blaze of emeralds, a green gown, a green veil and a belt of gold set with green emeralds. I help her dress, lacing the green ribbons with the gold points through the holes of her sleeves, and I know my face is sulky in her candlelit looking glass. All her ladies are buzzing with the visit to Westminster Palace; only I am to be left at L'Erber alone.

I watch from my bedroom window as they mount their horses in the yard before the great doors. Isabel has a white horse and a new saddle of green leather with green velvet trappings. George beside her is bareheaded, his blond hair shining in the sunlight as golden as a crown. He smiles and waves at the people who gather either side of the gate to shout their blessings. It is like a royal progress, and Isabel amid it all is like the queen that our father promised she would be. I step back from the narrow window to the deserted rooms. A manservant comes in behind me with a basket of wood. 'Shall I build up the fire, Lady Anne?'

'Leave it,' I say over my shoulder. They are through the gate and going at a jingling trot down Elbow Lane, the winter sun bright on George's pennants. He nods from left to right, raising his gloved hand in response to a cheer.

'But the fire's going down,' the man says. 'I'll put some wood on for you.'

'Just leave it,' I say impatiently. I turn around from the window and for the first time I see him. He has pulled off his hat and dropped the fustian cloak which was hiding his rich jacket and beautiful linen, his riding breeches and soft leather boots. It is Richard, smiling at my surprise.

I run to him, without thinking what I am doing. I run to the first friendly face that I have seen since Christmas, and in a moment I am in his arms and he is holding me tightly and kissing my face, my closed eyes, my smiling mouth, kissing me till I am breathless and have to pull away from him. 'Richard! Oh, Richard!'

'I have come to take you.'

'Take me?'

'Rescue you. They will keep you more and more close until they get your mother's fortune and then they will put you in a nunnery.'

'I knew it! He says he is my guardian, and will give me my share of the fortune when I am married; but I don't believe him.'

'They will never let you be married. Edward has put you in George's keeping, they will hold you forever. You will have to run away if you want to get out of this.'

'I'll go,' I say with sudden decision. 'I'm ready to go.'

He hesitates as if he doubts me. 'Just like that?'

'I'm not the little girl that you knew,' I say. 'I've grown up. Margaret of Anjou taught me not to hesitate, that there would be times when I have to see the best thing for myself and take that course without fear, without considering others. I have lost my father – there is no-one who can command me. I certainly won't be commanded by Isabel and George.'

'Good,' he says. 'I'll take you into sanctuary – it's the only thing we can do.'

'Will I be safe there?' I go into my little bedroom, just off the presence chamber, and he follows me without embarrassment and stands in the doorway, as I open my box and take out my jewellery case.

'They won't break sanctuary in London. I have a place for you at the college of St Martin's le Grand. They will keep you safe there.' He takes the box from my hands. 'Anything else?'

'My winter cloak,' I say. 'And I'll wear my riding boots.'

I sit on the bed and kick off my shoes, and he kneels before me and takes the riding boots, holding one open for my bare foot. I hesitate; it is such an intimate gesture between a young woman and a man. His smiling upward glance tells me that he understands my hesitation but is ignoring it. I point my toe and he holds the boot, I slide my foot in and he pulls the boot over my calf. He takes the soft leather ties and fastens the boot, at my ankle, then at my calf, and then just below my knee. He looks up at me, his hand gently on my toe. I can feel the warmth of his hand through the soft leather. I imagine my toes curling in pleasure at his touch.

'Anne, will you marry me?' he asks simply, as he kneels before me.

'Marry you?'

He nods. 'I will take you to sanctuary and then find a priest. We can marry in secret. Then I can care for you and protect you. You will be my wife and Edward will welcome you as his sister-in-law. Edward will grant your share of your mother's inheritance when you are in my keeping. He won't refuse my wife.'

He holds out the other boot, not even waiting for my reply. I point my toe and slide my foot in. Again he gently ties the laces at ankle, calf and knee. There is something very sensual about his careful tightening of the laces, working his way slowly up my leg.

I close my eyes, I am longing for the sensation of his fingers brushing gently on the inside of my thigh. Then he takes the hem of my skirt and pulls it down to my ankles, as if he will defend my modesty, as if I can trust him. He puts his hands on the bed either side of me, still kneeling before me, looking up at me, his face filled with desire.

'Say yes,' he whispers. 'Marry me.'

I hesitate. I open my eyes. 'You will get my fortune,' I remark. 'When I marry you, everything I have becomes yours. Just as George has everything that belongs to Isabel.'

'That's why you can trust me to win it for you,' he says simply. 'When your interests and mine are the same, you can be certain that I will care for you as for myself. You will be my own. You will find that I care for my own.'

'You will be true to me?'

'Loyalty is my motto. When I give my word, you can trust me.'

I hesitate for a moment. 'Oh Richard, ever since my father turned against your brother, nothing has gone right for me. Since his death I have not had one day without grief.'

He takes both of my hands in a warm grip. 'I know. I cannot bring your father back, but I can put you back in his world: at the court, in the palaces, in line for the throne, where he wanted you to be. I can win his lands back for you, you can be landlord to his tenants, you can fulfil his plans.'

I shake my head, smiling though there are tears in my eyes. 'We can never do that. He had very grand plans. He promised me that I would be Queen of England.'

'Who knows?' he says. 'If anything should happen to Edward and his son, and George – which God forbid – then I would be king.'

'It's not likely,' I say, my father's ambition prompting me like a whisper in my ear.

'No,' he says. 'It's not likely. But you and I of all people know that you cannot foresee the future; none of us knows what may happen. But think of what you might be right now. I can make you a royal duchess. You can make me a wealthy man. I can make you the equal of your sister and defend you from her husband. I will be a true husband to you. And – I think you know, don't you? – that I love you, Anne.'

I feel as if I have been living in a loveless world for too long. The last tender face I saw was my father's when he sailed for England. 'You do? Truly?'

'I do.' He rises to his feet and pulls me up to stand beside him. My chin comes to his shoulder, we are both dainty, long-limbed, coltish: well-matched. I turn my face into his jacket. 'Will you marry me?' he whispers.

'Yes,' I say.

My belongings go into one bundle, and he has a kitchen maid's cloak for me with a hood that I can pull forwards to hide my face.

I protest as he puts it round me. 'It stinks of fat!'

He laughs. 'All the better. We are walking out of here as a manservant and a kitchen maid and nobody will look twice at either of us.'

The great gates are open, the people are coming and going as they always do, and we slip out with some dairymaids driving their cows before them. Nobody sees us go, and nobody will notice that I have gone. The house servants will assume that I went to court with my sister and her ladies, and only when she comes home in a few days will they realise that I have escaped them. I laugh out loud at the thought and Richard, holding my hand as we go through the busy streets, turns and smiles at me and suddenly laughs too, as if we are embarking on an adventure, as if we are children running away and laughing as we go.

It is growing dark when we get to the college, which stands in the lee of St Paul's Cathedral, and the side door is open to the chancel and there are many people pushing their way in and out. There is a market inside, and stalls for people to sell all sorts of goods, money-changers and some secret business taking place in the corners. The people are hooded and shrouded against the cold mist that is rolling off the river, and they keep their heads down and look about them.

I hesitate; it feels unsafe. Richard glances down at me.

'I have a room prepared for you, you won't be with the common people,' he says reassuringly. 'They give sanctuary to all sorts of people here: criminals, coiners, and forgers, common thieves. But you will be safe. The college is proud of its power of sanctuary – they never give up anyone who claims the safety of the church. Even if George finds where you are and demands that they surrender you, they won't let him take you away. This college has a great reputation for being unhelpful.' He smiles. 'They would even defy my brother the king if they had to.'

He tucks my cold hand under his arm and leads me through the door. The curfew bell starts to sound in the tower above us, as one of the monks steps forwards, recognises Richard, and without a word leads the way to the abbey's guest house.

I tighten my grip on Richard's hand. 'You'll be safe here,' he repeats.

The monk stands to one side at the doorway and Richard takes me through into a small room, like a cell. Beyond that is another even smaller room like an alcove, and a narrow bed with a crucifix nailed to the wall at the head. A maid rises up from a stool at the fireside and bobs a curtsey to me.

'I'm Megan,' she says, her words almost incomprehensible because of her strong northern accent. 'My lord has asked me to make sure you are comfortable here.'

'Megan will stay with you, and if there is any trouble she will send for me, or come to me herself,' Richard says. His hands are on the ties of my cloak, under my chin. As he takes the cloak from my shoulders his fingers brush my chin in a gentle caress. 'You will be safe here and I will come tomorrow.'

'They will miss me when they get home to L'Erber,' I warn him.

He smiles in genuine amusement. 'They will go as mad as dogs,' he says. 'But there is nothing they can do; the bird has flown and soon she will find another nest.'

He bends his dark head and kisses me gently on the mouth. At his touch I feel a longing for more, I want him to kiss me as he did when I ran to him, when he came to me disguised, like a knight might come to a captured lady in a story. At the thought of this as a rescue, I take a breath and step closer to him. His arms come around me and he holds me for a moment.

'I shall come tomorrow at midday,' he says, and then he goes from the rooms and leaves me for my first night of freedom. I look from the little arched window into the busy streets outside, darkened by the shadow of St Paul's. I am free but I am barred from leaving the precinct of the church, and I may not speak to anyone. Megan is my servant but she is also here to guard me. I am free, but imprisoned in sanctuary, just like my mother. If Richard were not to come tomorrow I would be a prisoner, just like Queen Margaret in the Tower, just like my mother at Beaulieu.

He comes as he promised, his young face stern. He kisses my hands but he does not take me in his arms, though I stand beside him and long for his touch. This is an ache like hunger. I had no idea that this was what desire feels like.

'What's the matter?' I hear my voice is plaintive.

He gives me a swift, reassuring grin, and he sits at the little table beside the window, gesturing to me to take the opposite chair. 'Troubles,' he says shortly. 'George has discovered that you have run away, he has spoken to Edward about you, and is demanding your return. As a concession he says that I may marry you but we cannot have your inheritance.'

I gasp. 'He knows I am gone already? What does Isabel say? What about the king?'

'Edward will be fair to us. But he has to keep George his friend and keep him close. George has too much power and too great an affinity to risk his enmity. He is growing mighty. He may even now be plotting with your kinsmen the Nevilles, for another try at the throne. Certainly he has a lot of friends coming and going at L'Erber. Edward doesn't trust him, but he has got to show him favour to keep him at court.'

For only a moment do I fear that he will give me up. 'What will we do? What can we do?'

He takes my hand and kisses it. 'You will stay here, safe as you should be, and not worry. I will offer my office of Chamberlain of England to George.'

'Chamberlain?'

He grimaces. 'I know. It's a high price for me. I was proud to take up the office, it's the greatest post in England – and the most profitable – but this is worth more to me.' He corrects himself. '*You* are worth more to me.' He pauses. 'You are worth more than anything. And we have another difficulty: your mother is writing to everyone and saying that she is wrongly imprisoned and her lands are being stolen from her. She is demanding to be released. It looks bad. Edward has promised to be a just king. He can't be seen to rob a widow in sanctuary.'

I look at this young man who has promised to rescue me, and who now finds himself against the two most powerful men of the kingdom, his own brothers. It is going to cost him dear to stand by me. 'I won't go back,' I say. 'I'll do anything you want; but I won't go back to George and Isabel. I can't. I'll go away on my own if I have to, but I won't go back to that prison.'

Quickly he shakes his head. 'No, that won't happen,' he reassures me. 'We had better get married at once. At least then nobody can take you back. If we are married there is nothing they can do to you, and I can fight for your inheritance as your husband.'

'We'll need a dispensation from the Pope,' I remind him. 'Father had to apply twice for George and Isabel and they are related just as we are, but now, because of their marriage, we are even more closely connected. We are brother- and sister-in-law as well as cousins.'

He scowls, tapping at the table with his fingers. 'I know, I know. I have been thinking about it, and I will send an envoy to Rome. But it will take months.' He looks at me as if to measure my resolve. 'Will you wait for me? Will you wait here where you are safe but confined, till we hear from the Holy Father and have our dispensation?'

'I'll wait for you,' I promise him. I speak like a young woman in love for the first time, but in the back of my mind is the knowledge that I have nowhere else to go, and nobody else has the power or the wealth to protect me from George and Isabel.

As the mornings grow brighter and warmer I have to wait in sanctuary and grow more and more impatient to be free. I attend the services at St Martin's, and in the mornings I read in their library. Richard has loaned me his lute and in the afternoons I play, or sew. I feel like a prisoner, I am terribly bored and terribly anxious at the same time. I am utterly dependent on Richard for my safety, for visits, even for my keep. I am like a girl under a spell in an enchanted castle and he is the knight who comes to rescue me, and now I find that this is a most uncomfortable position to be in – utterly powerless and unable even to complain.

He visits me every day, sometimes bringing sprigs of trees with uncurling leaves, or a handful of Lenten lilies to show me the coming of the spring, the season of courtship, when I will be a bride again. He sends a seamstress to me to make me something new for my wedding day and I spend a morning being fitted with a gown of pale gold velvet with an underskirt of yellow silk. The tirewoman comes too and makes me a tall henin headdress with a veil of gold lace. I look in the dressmaker's mirror and see my reflection, a slim tall girl with a grave face and dark blue eyes. I smile at my reflection but I will never look merry like the queen, I will never have the warm easy loveliness of her mother Jacquetta, and all the women of that family. They were not raised in warfare as I was, they were always confident in their power – I have always been afraid of it, of them. The tirewoman gathers handfuls of my red-brown hair and piles it on top of my head. 'You'll be a beautiful bride,' she assures me.

One morning Richard comes, his face grave. 'I went to see Edward to tell him of our marriage plans as soon as the papal dispensation arrives, but the queen's baby is coming early,' he says. 'I couldn't see him, he's gone to Windsor to be near her.'

At once, my mind goes to Isabel's ordeal in childbirth: a nightmare because of the queen's witch's wind which threw the boat round like a peapod on a river and meant that we lost the baby, a boy, a grandson for my father. I have no sympathy for the queen at all, but I cannot show this to Richard who is loyal to his brother and tender to his wife and child. 'Oh, I am sorry,' I say insincerely. 'But does she not have her mother with her?'

'The dowager duchess is ill,' he says. 'They say it is her heart.' He glances at me with embarrassment. 'They say her heart is broken.'

He does not need to say any more. Jacquetta's heart was broken when my father executed her husband and her beloved young son. But she has taken her time in dying – more than two years. And she is not the only woman who has ever lost a loved one. My husband died in these wars and my father too – who has ever considered my grief?

'I am so sorry,' I say.

'Fortunes of war.' Richard repeats the usual comforting phrase. 'But it means that I couldn't see Edward before he left. Now he will be absorbed by the queen and her new baby.'

'What will we do?' Yet again, it seems that I can do nothing without the knowledge and permission of the queen, and she is hardly likely to bless my marriage to her brother-in-law when they all believe that her mother is dying of grief because of my father. 'Richard, I can't wait for the queen to advise the king in our favour. I don't think she will ever forgive my father.'

He slaps his hand on the table in sudden decision. 'I know! I know what we'll do. We'll marry now, and tell them, and get the Pope's dispensation later.'

I gasp. 'Can we do that?'

'Why not?'

'Because the marriage won't be legal?'

'It will be legal in the sight of God, and then the Pope's dispensation will come, and it will be legal in the sight of man too.'

'But my father—'

'If your father had married you to Prince Edward, without waiting for that dispensation, you could all have sailed together and he would have won at Barnet.'

Regret stabs me like a sword. 'Really?'

He nods. 'You know it. The dispensation came anyway, it didn't come any faster for you waiting in France for it. But if Margaret of Anjou and the prince and you had sailed together with your father then he would have had his full forces at Barnet. He would have defeated us with the Lancaster forces that she would have commanded. Waiting for the dispensation was a great mistake. Delay is always fatal. We'll marry and the dispensation will come and make the marriage safe in law. It is safe before God if we say our vows before a priest anyway.'

I hesitate.

'You do want to marry me?' He looks at me, his smile knowing. He is well aware that I want to marry him and that my heart goes faster when his hand touches mine, as it does now. When he leans forwards, as he is doing now, when his face comes towards me and he comes to kiss me.

'I do.' It is true, I am desperate to marry him, and desperate to be out of this half-life of sanctuary. Besides, there is nothing else that I can do.

For the second time in my life I am a bride, walking up the aisle towards the high altar, a young and handsome husband waiting for me at the chancel steps. I can't help but think of Prince Edward, waiting for me there, not knowing that our alliance would take him to his death, that we would be wedded and bedded for only twenty weeks before he had to ride out to defend his claim to the throne, and that he would never ride back again.

I tell myself that this is different – that this time I am marrying and it is my own choice, I am not dominated by a terrifying mother-in-law, I am not mindlessly obeying my father. This time I am making my own destiny – for the first time in my life I have been able to take matters into my own hands. I am fifteen, I have been married and widowed, the daughter-in-law of a Queen of England and then the ward of a royal duke. I have been a pawn for one player after another; but now I am making my own decision and playing my own cards.

Richard is waiting at the chancel steps; his kinsman and mine, Archbishop Bourchier, stands before him, with his missal open at the marriage service. I look around the chapel. It is as empty as for a pauper's funeral. Who would have thought this was the marriage of a dowager princess and a royal duke? No sister – she is now my enemy. No mother – she is still imprisoned. No father – I will never see him again. He died trying to put me on the throne of England and he and his hopes are finished. I feel very alone as I walk up the aisle, my leather shoes tapping on the memorial stones beneath my feet as if to remind me that here, lying in unending darkness, are all the other people who thought that they too would play their own cards.

We have nowhere to go. That is the great irony of our situation. I am the greatest heiress in England with an inheritance, if we can win it, of hundreds of houses and several castles and I have brought them all to my husband, himself a wealthy young man with revenues from some of the greatest counties in England – and we have nowhere to go. He cannot take me back to his London home – Baynard's Castle – for his mother lives there and the formidable Duchess Cecily frightened me enough as my sister's hard-faced mother-in-law; she will terrify me as my own. I dare not face her at all after making a secret wedding to one of her sons, against the wishes of the other two.

Obviously we cannot go to George and Isabel, who will be beside themselves with anger when they learn of this day's doings, and I absolutely refuse to return to the guest house of St Martin's in my kitchen maid's cloak. In the end, our kinsman the archbishop, Thomas Bourchier, invites us to his palace for as long as we want to stay. It identifies him even more closely with this secret marriage, but Richard whispers to me that the archbishop would never have opened the marriage service before us if he had not had Edward's private permission to perform it. Not much happens in England now without the knowledge of the York king and the assent of his queen. So though I had thought we were rebellious lovers, acting in secret, marrying for love and hiding for our honeymoon, it was not so. It was never so. I had thought I was planning my own life, without the knowledge of others; but it turns out that the king and my enemy, his grey-eyed queen, knew of it all, all the time.

This is our summer, this is our season. Every morning I wake to find golden sunshine streaming through the oriel window that looks out over the river, and the warm tumbled presence of Richard in my bed, sleeping like a child. The sheets are in a tangled knot from our lovemaking, the beautifully embroidered counterpane is in a heap half on the bed and half on the floor, the fire in the fireplace has fallen to ashes as he will allow no-one to come into the chamber until we call them: this is my summer.

Now I understand Isabel's slavish loyalty to George. Now I understand the passionate bond between the king and the queen. Now I even understand the queen's mother Jacquetta dying of heartbreak at the loss of the man she married for love. I learn that to love a man whose interests are mine, whose passion is given freely and openly to me, and whose battle-hardened young lithe body lies beside me every night as his only joy, is to utterly change my life. I was married before; but I was never shaken and touched and puzzled and adored before. I was a wife but I was no lover. With Richard I become wife and lover, counsellor and friend, partner in all things, comrade in arms, fellow-traveller. With Richard I become a woman, not a girl, I become a wife.

'What about the dispensation?' I ask him lazily, one morning, as he is kissing me carefully, counting as he goes, his ambition being to get to five hundred.

'You have interrupted me,' he complains. 'What dispensation?'

'For our wedding. From the Pope.'

'Oh, that – it's on the way. These things can take months, you know that. I have applied in writing and they will reply. I will tell you when they reply. Where was I?'

'Three hundred and two,' I volunteer.

Softly, his mouth comes down on my ribcage. 'Three hundred and three,' he says.

We spend every night together. When he has to visit the court, on its summer progress in Kent, he rides out at dawn with a group of his friends – Brackenbury, Lovell, Tyrrell, half a dozen others – and back at dusk so that he can see the king and come home to me. He swears we shall never be parted, not even for a night. I wait for him in the great guest chamber at Lambeth Palace with a supper laid ready for him and he comes in, dusty from the road, and eats and talks and drinks all at the same time. He tells me that the queen's new baby has died and the queen is quiet and sad. Jacquetta, her mother, is said to have died the very same afternoon as the baby; some people heard a lament sung around the towers of the castle. He crosses himself at that rumour and laughs at himself for being a superstitious fool. Under the table I clench my fist in the sign against witchcraft.

'Lady Rivers was a remarkable woman,' he concedes. 'When I first met her and I was just a boy I thought she was the most terrifying and the most beautiful woman I had ever seen. But when she acknowledged me as her kinsman, when Elizabeth married Edward, I came to love and admire her. She was always so warm with her children – and not just them, with all the children of the royal household – and loyal to Edward; she would have done anything for him.'

'She was my enemy in the end,' I say shortly. 'But I remember that when I first saw her I thought she was wonderful. And her daughter the queen too.'

'You would pity the queen now,' he says. 'She's very bereft without her mother, and she is lost without her baby.'

'Yes, but she has four other children,' I say hard-heartedly. 'And one of them a son.'

'We Yorks like to make a big family,' he says, with a smile at me.

'And so?'

'And so I thought we might go to bed and see if we can make a little marquess?'

I feel my colour rise, and I acknowledge my desire with a smile. 'Perhaps,' I say. He knows that I mean 'yes'.

Once again, I am waiting to go into the presence of the King and Queen of England, once again I am fearful and excited. This time there is no-one to precede me, no-one ready to scold me. I need not fear stepping on the train of my mother's gown for she is still held at Beaulieu and even if she were free she would not walk before me, for now I outrank her. I am a royal duchess. There are very few women whose train I will follow.

I need not fear Isabel's hard words for now I am her equal. I too am a royal duchess of the House of York. We have been forced to share our inheritance, our husbands now enjoy equal shares of our wealth. We have shared the boys of the House of York – she has George, the handsome older brother, but I have Richard, the loyal and beloved younger brother. He is at my side, and he gives me a warm smile. He knows I am nervous and he knows I am determined to walk into the great royal court and have them acknowledge me for what I now am: a royal duchess of York, and one of the greatest ladies of the kingdom.

I am wearing a gown of deep red. I bribed one of the ladies of the wardrobe to discover what Isabel is wearing tonight and she told me that my sister has ordered a gown of pale violet, that she will wear with her amethysts. My choice will make her colour fade into insignificance. I am wearing rubies around my throat and in my ears and my skin is creamy against the darkness of the gown and the fiery sparkle of the stones. I am wearing a head-dress so tall that it rises like a church spire above both me and my husband, and the veil is scarlet. The hem of my gown is embroidered with dark red silk and the sleeves are cut daringly high to show my wrists. I know that I look beautiful. I am sixteen and my skin is like the petal of a rose. The Queen of England herself, Edward's adored wife, is going to look old and tired beside me. I am at the very peak of my beauty and in the moment of my triumph.

The big doors before us swing open and Richard takes my hand, glances sideways at me and says 'forward march!' as if we were mustering on a battlefield, and we step into the blaze of light and warmth of the queen's presence chamber at Windsor Castle.

As always with Queen Elizabeth, her rooms are shining with the brilliant light of the very best candles, and her women beautifully dressed. She is playing bowls, and from the laughter and round of applause as we come in I guess that she is winning. At the far end of the room there are musicians, and the ladies are dancing a circle dance where they hold hands and form lines, and look around and smile at their favourite courtiers who lounge against the walls and inspect the ladies as if they were high-bred hunters, trotting out. The king is seated in the middle of the chamber talking to Louis de Gruthuyse, who was his only friend when my father drove him from the throne of England, and looked certain to be the victor. Louis was Edward's friend then, taking him into his court in Flanders, protecting him, and supporting him while he recruited men, raised ships and funds and came back to England like a storm. Now Louis has been made Earl of Winchester, and there are to be days of celebration to welcome him into his earldom. The king pays his debts, and always rewards his favourites. Luckily for me, he sometimes forgives his enemies.

King Edward looks up as we come in – his beloved brother and his pretty new wife – exclaims in pleasure and comes forwards to greet us himself. He is always informal and charming to those he loves and who amuse him, and now he takes my hand and kisses me on the mouth as if he had no recollection that the last time we met was when I was in such disgrace that I was not allowed to speak to him, but had to silently curtsey when he went by.

'Look who's here!' he calls delightedly to the queen. She comes to receive our bows and lets Richard kiss her cheeks and then turns to me. Clearly she and the king have decided that I am to be greeted as a kinswoman and a sister. Only the tiniest flicker of malice in her grey eyes shows me that she is amused to find me here – at the greatest feast of the year to welcome her husband's ally – rising up now having been down so very low. 'Ah, Lady Anne,' she says drily. 'I wish you joy. What a surprise. What a triumph for true love!'

She turns and gestures to the ladies behind her and my courage fails me as my sister Isabel stalks forwards. I cannot stop myself shrinking back against the comforting shoulder of Richard, my husband, who stands beside me as Isabel, pale and contemptuous, sweeps us both the most shallow curtsey.

'And here you are, Warwick's daughters, and yet both royal duchesses and both my sisters,' the queen says, her voice lilting with laughter. 'Who would ever have thought it? Your father gets his first choice of sons-in-law from the grave. How happy you must be!'

Her brother Anthony glances at her as if they are sharing a joke about us. 'Clearly, a joyous reunion of the Neville sisters,' he observes.

Isabel steps forwards as if she is embracing me and holds me close so that she can whisper fiercely in my ear. 'You have shamed yourself and embarrassed me. We didn't even know where you were. Running off like a kitchen slut! I can't imagine what Father would have said!'

I twist out of her grip and face her. 'You had me as your prisoner and you were stealing my inheritance,' I say hotly. 'What would he have thought of that? What did you think I would do? Bow down and worship George just because you do? Or did you wish me dead like you wish our own mother?'

In a quick gesture she raises her hand, and then instantly snatches it down again. But she has showed everyone that she longs to slap my face. The queen laughs out loud, Isabel turns her back on me, Richard shrugs, bows to the queen, and draws me away.

Across the room, someone tells George that there has been a quarrel and he comes quickly to stand beside Isabel and glare angrily at Richard and me. For a moment Isabel and I are open enemies, staring across the great hall at each other, neither of us ready to back down, Isabel standing beside her husband, me with mine. Then Richard touches my arm and we go to be introduced to the new earl. I greet him pleasantly and we talk for a few moments and then there is a lull. I turn, I cannot help but look back, as if I hope that she would call me over to her, as if I hope that we might make friends again. She is laughing and talking with one of the queen's ladies. 'Iz . . .' I say quietly. But she does not hear me, and only as Richard leads me away do I think I hear, like a tiny whisper, her call to me: 'Annie.'

This is not the last family greeting I undertake this autumn season, for I have to meet with Richard's formidable mother, the Duchess Cecily. We go to Fotheringhay, riding up the Great North Road in bright sunny weather to her home. She is in all but exile from the court, her hatred of her daughter-in-law the queen meant that she did not attend most of the major court festivities, and when she joined with George against his brother for the rebellion, she lost the remnants of love she had been able to exact from her son Edward. They all keep up appearances when they can; she still has a London house and visits court from time to time, but the queen's influence is clear. Duchess Cecily is not a welcomed guest; Fotheringhay is partly repaired and equipped, and given to her as her home. I am cheerful, riding beside Richard, until he says with a sideways glance at me: 'You know we go through Barnet? The battle was fought along the road.'

Of course I knew it; but I had not thought that we would ride along the actual road where my father died, where Richard, fighting with his brother, uphill against terrible odds, was able to come out of the mist, surprise my father's forces and kill him. It is the battlefield where Midnight did his last great task for his master: putting down his black head and taking a sword into his great heart to show the men that there would be no retreat, no running away and no surrender.

'We'll skirt round,' Richard says, seeing my face.

He orders his guard and they open a gate for us, so we leave the road to circle the battlefield by riding through the pastures and over the stubble of oat crops, and then rejoin the Great North Road on the northern side of the little town. Every step my horse takes I flinch, thinking that he is treading on bones, and I think of my betrayal, riding alongside my husband, the enemy who killed my father.

'There's a little chapel,' Richard volunteers. 'It's not a forgotten battle. He's not forgotten. Edward and I pay for masses to be said for his soul.'

'Do you?' I say. 'I didn't know.' I can hardly speak, I am so torn by guilt that I should be married into the house which my father named as his enemy.

'I loved him too, you know,' Richard says quietly. 'He raised me, like he raised all of his wards, as if we were more to him than boys for whom he would get a fee. He was a good guardian to all of us. Edward and I thought of him as our leader, as our older brother. We couldn't have done without him.'

I nod. I don't say that my father only turned against Edward because of the queen, because of her grasping family and her wicked advice. If Edward had not married her . . . if Edward had never met her ... if Edward had not been enchanted by her and her mother and their potent brew of sensuality and spells ... but this is just to open a lifetime of regret. 'He loved you,' is all I say. 'And Edward.'

Richard shakes his head, knowing as I do where the fault lay, where it still lies: with Edward's wife: 'It's a tragedy,' he says.

I nod, and we ride on to Fotheringhay in silence.

FOTHERINGHAY CASTLE, NORTHAMPTONSHIRE, AUTUMN 1472

The castle, Richard's birthplace and his family's house, is in disrepair, and has been ever since the wars started and the Yorks could only spend money fortifying the castles that they needed as bases for rebellion against the sleeping king and the bad queen. Richard frowns as he looks at the outer wall that is bowing dangerously over the moat, and scrutinises the roof of the castle where the rooks are making bundles of twiggy nests on the leads.

The duchess greets me warmly, though I am the third secret bride in her family. 'But I always wanted Richard to marry you,' she assured me. 'I must have discussed it with your mother a dozen times. That was why I was so pleased that Richard was made your father's ward, I wanted you to know each other. I always hoped you would be my daughter-in-law.'

She welcomes us into the smaller hall of the castle, a wood-panelled room with a great fire built at either end, and three huge tables laid for dinner: one for the menservants, one for the women servants and one table for the nobility. The duchess, Richard and I and a few of her kinswomen take the top table and oversee the hall. 'We live very simply,' she says, though she has hundreds of servants and a dozen guests. 'We don't try to compete with Her and Her court. Burgundian fashions,' she says darkly. 'And every sort of extravagance.'

'My brother the king sends you his good wishes,' Richard says formally. He kneels to his mother and she puts her hand on his head in blessing. 'And how is George?' she asks at once, naming her favourite. Richard winks at me. The overt favouritism of the duchess was an open joke in the family until the moment when it led her to favour George's claim to the throne. That was too far, even for the indulgent affection of the king.

'He is well, though we are still trying to settle the inheritance of our wives,' Richard says.

'A bad business.' She shakes her head. 'A good estate should never be broken up. You should make an agreement with him, Richard. You are the younger son after all. You should give way to your brother George.'

This favouritism is less amusing. 'I follow my own counsel,' Richard says stiffly. 'George and I will agree to share the Warwick fortune. I would be a poor husband to Anne if I let her inheritance be thrown away.'

'Better to be a poor husband than a poor brother,' she says smartly. 'Look at your brother Edward, under the cat's-paw and betraying his family every moment of the day.'

'Edward has been a good friend to me in this,' Richard reminds her. 'And he has always been a good brother to me.'

'It's not his judgement I fear,' she says darkly. 'It's Hers. You wait till your ambitions run counter to hers and then see whose advice Edward will take. She will be his ruin.'

'Indeed, I pray not,' Richard says. 'Shall we dine, Lady Mother?'

Her theme, the ruination of the family by the scheming of Elizabeth Woodville, is a constant one throughout our visit, and though Richard silences her as frequently and as politely as he can, it is impossible to deny the many cases she cites. It is apparent to everyone that the queen gets her way and Edward allows her to put her friends and family into places that belong to other men, she exploits her royal fees more than any queen has done before, and favours her brothers and sisters. Richard will not hear a word said against his brother the king; but at Fotheringhay nobody loves Elizabeth Woodville and the radiant young woman that I first saw on the great night of her triumph is quite forgotten in the picture of the grasping ill-wisher that the duchess describes.

'She should never have been crowned queen,' she whispers to me one day when we are sitting in her solar, carefully embroidering the cuffs of a shirt which the duchess will send to her favourite, George, for Christmas.

'Should she not?' I ask. 'I remember her coronation so well, I was only a little girl and I thought her the most beautiful woman I had ever seen in my life.'

A scornful shrug shows what this ageing beauty now thinks about good looks. 'She should never have been crowned queen because the wedding was never valid,' she whispers behind her hand. 'We all knew that Edward was secretly married before he even met her. He was not free to marry her. We all said nothing while your father planned the match with Princess Bona of Savoy because such a secret marriage could be denied – must be denied when such a great chance presents itself. But the oaths Edward swore with Elizabeth were just another secret marriage, actually a bigamous marriage – and it should have been denied too.'

'Her mother was witness ...'

'That witch would have sworn to anything for her children.'

'But Edward made her queen,' I point out. 'And their children are royal.'

She shakes her head and nips off the thread with her sharp little teeth. 'Edward has no right to be king,' she says, speaking very softly.

I drop my work. 'Your Grace ...' I am terrified of what she is going to say next. Is this the old scandal that my father circulated when he wanted to drive Edward from the throne? Is the duchess about to accuse herself of wanton adultery? And how much trouble will I be in if I know this enormous, this terrible state secret?

She laughs at my aghast face. 'Oh, you're such a child!' she says unkindly. 'Who would trust you with anything? Who would bother telling you anything? Remind me, how old are you?'

'I am sixteen,' I say with all the dignity I can muster.

'A child,' she mocks. 'I'll say no more. But you remember that George is not my favourite because I am a doting fool. George is my favourite for good reason, very good reason. He was born to be a king, that boy. That boy – and no other.'

WINDSOR CASTLE,
CHRISTMAS 1472

The season of the Christmas feast is always a great one for Edward and this is the year he celebrates his greatest triumph. Back at court Richard and I find we are caught up in the excitement of the twelve days. Every day there is a new theme and a new masque. Every dinner there are new songs, or actors or jugglers or players of one sort or another. There is a bear-baiting, and hunting in the cold riverside marshes every day. They go hawking, there is a three-day joust where every nobleman presents his standard. The queen's brother Anthony Woodville holds a battle of poets and everyone has to present a couplet, one after another, standing in a circle, and the first person to stumble over his rhyme bows and steps back, until there are only two men left, one of them Anthony Woodville – and then he wins. I see the gleam of his smile to his sister: he always wins. There is a mock sea battle in one of the courtyards, flooded for the occasion, and one night a dance of torches in the woods.

Richard, my husband, is always at his brother's side. He is one of the inner circle: comrades who fled with Edward from England and returned in triumph. He, William Hastings, and Anthony Woodville the queen's brother are the king's friends and blood brothers – together for life; they will never forget the wild ride when they thought that my father would catch them, they will never forget the voyage when they looked anxiously back over the stern of their little fishing boat for the lights of my father's ships following them. When they speak of riding through the dark lanes, desperate to find Lynn and not knowing whether there would be a boat there that they could hire or steal, when they roar with laughter remembering that their pockets were empty and the king had to give the boatman his furred gown by way of payment, and then they had to walk penniless in their riding boots to the nearest town, George shuffles his feet and looks around, and hopes that the conversation will take another turn. For George was the enemy that night, though they are all supposed to be friends now. I think that the men who thundered along the night roads in darkness, pulling up in a sweat of fear to listen for hoofbeats coming behind them, will never forget that George was their enemy that night, and that he sold his own brother and his own family, and betrayed his house in the hopes of putting himself on the throne. For all their smiling friendship now, for all the appearance of having forgotten old battles, they know that they were the hunted that night, and that if George had caught them he would have killed them. They know that this is the way of this world: you have to kill or be killed, even if it is your brother, or your king, or your friend.

For me, every time they speak of this time, I remember that it was my father who was their enemy, and their comradeship was forged in fear of him, their good guardian and mentor who suddenly, overnight, became their deadly enemy. They had to win back the throne from him – he had utterly defeated them and thrown them out of the kingdom. Sometimes, when I think of his triumph and then his defeat, I feel as alien in this court as my first mother-in-law, Margaret of Anjou, their prisoner in the Tower of London.

I know for sure that the queen never forgets her enemies. Indeed, I suspect that she thinks of us as her enemies now. Under instruction from her husband she greets me and Isabel with cool civility, and she offers us places in her household. But her little smile when she sees the two of us seated in stony silence, or when Edward calls George to bear witness to a battle and then breaks off realising that this was one where George was on the other side – those moments show me that this is a queen who does not forget her enemies, and will never forgive them.

I am allowed to decline a place in the queen's household as Richard tells me that we will live in the North for much of the time. At last, my share of the inheritance has been given to him. George takes the other half, and all Richard wants is to take up the great northern lands that he has won and rule them himself. He wants to take my father's place in the North and befriend the Neville affinity. They will be predisposed to him because of my name, and the love they had for my father. If he treats the northerners well, openly and honestly as they like to be treated, he will be as grand as a king in the North of England and we will make a palace at Sheriff Hutton, and at Middleham Castle, our houses in Yorkshire. I have brought him the beautiful Barnard Castle in Durham too, and he says that we will live behind the mighty walls that look down to the River Tees and up to the Pennine hills. The city of York – which has always loved the house that shares its name – will be our capital city. We will bring grandeur and wealth to the North of England, to a people who are ready to love Richard because he is of the House of York, and who love me already, for I am a Neville.

Edward encourages this. He needs someone to keep the North at peace, and to defend England's borders against the Scots, and there is no-one he trusts more than his youngest brother.

But I have another reason to refuse to stay at court, a reason even better than this. I curtsey to the queen and say: 'Your Grace must excuse me. I am . . .'

She nods coolly. 'Of course, I know.'

'You do?' At once I think that she has foreseen this conversation with her witch's gaze, and I cannot restrain my shiver.

'Lady Anne, I am no fool,' she says simply. 'I have had seven babies myself, I can see when a woman cannot eat her breakfast but still grows fatter. I was wondering when you were going to tell us all. Have you told your husband?'

I find I am still breathless with the fear that she knows everything. 'Yes.'

'And was he very pleased?'

'Yes, Your Grace.'

'He will be hoping for a boy, an earl for such a great inheritance,' she says with satisfaction. 'It is a blessing for you both.'

'If it is a girl I hope you will be godmother?' I have to ask her; she is the queen and my sister-in-law, and she has to assent. I don't feel any warmth or love for her and I don't think for one moment this means she will really bless me or my baby. But I am surprised by the kindness in her face as she nods. 'I shall be pleased.'

I turn so that her ladies can hear me. My sister, her head bent down to her sewing, is among them. Isabel is trying to look as if she has heard none of this conversation; but I have to believe that she is yearning to speak to me. I can't believe that Isabel would be indifferent to me, pregnant with my first child. 'If I have a girl I am going to call her Elizabeth Isabel,' I say clearly, pitching my voice for her ears.

My sister's head is turned away; she is looking out of the window at the swirling snow outside, pretending to be indifferent. But when she hears her own name, she looks around. 'Elizabeth Isabel?' she repeats. It is the first time she has spoken to me since she scolded me when I came to court as a runaway bride.

'Yes,' I say boldly.

She half-rises from her seat, and then sits down again. 'You will call a daughter: Isabel?'

'Yes.'

I see her flush and at last she gets up from her seat and comes towards me, away from the queen and her ladies. 'You would name her for me?'

'Yes,' I say simply. 'You will be her aunt, and I hope you will love her and care for her. And ...' I hesitate – of course Isabel of all the people in the world knows that I am bound to be afraid of childbirth. 'If anything should ever happen to me, then I hope you will raise her as your own child, and ... and tell her about our father, Iz ... and about everything that happened. About us ... and how things went wrong ...'

Isabel's face twists for a moment trying to hold back her tears, and then she opens her arms and we cling to each other, crying and laughing at the same time. 'Oh Iz,' I whisper. 'I have hated being at war with you.'

'I am sorry, I am so sorry, Annie. I should not have acted as I did – I didn't know what to do – and everything happened so fast. We had to get the fortune ... and George said ... and then you ran away ...'

'I'm sorry too,' I say. 'I know you couldn't go against your husband. I understand better now.'

She nods, she doesn't want to say anything about George. A wife owes obedience to her husband, she promises it on her wedding day before God; and husbands exact their full due, supported by the priest and by the world. Isabel is as much George's possession as if she was his servant or his horse. I too have promised fealty to Richard as if he were a lord and I was indeed a kitchen maid. A woman must obey her husband as a serf obeys his lord – it is the way of the world and the law of God. Even if she thinks he is wrong. Even if she knows he is wrong.

Isabel tentatively puts out her hand to where my belly is hard and swelling beneath the gathered folds of my gown. I take it and let her feel my broadening girth. 'Annie, you are so big already. Do you feel well?'

'I was sick at the start but I am well now.'

'I can't believe that you didn't tell me at once!'

'I wanted to,' I confess. 'I really wanted to. I didn't know how to begin.'

We turn away from the court together. 'Are you afraid?' she asks quietly.

'A little,' I say. I see the darkness of her glance. 'A lot,' I admit. We are both silent, both thinking of the rocking cabin on the storm-tossed ship with my mother screaming at me that I must pull the baby from her, the horror as the little body yielded inside her. The vision is so strong I am almost unsteady on my feet, as if the seas were throwing us around once more. She takes my hands in hers and it is as if we had just made landfall and I am telling her about the little coffin, and Mother letting it go into the sea.

'Annie, there's no reason that it should not be all right for you,' she says earnestly. 'There is no reason that it should go wrong for you as it did for me. My pains were so much worse for being at sea, and the storm, and the danger. You will be safe, and your husband . . .'

'He loves me,' I say certainly. 'He says he will take me to Middleham Castle and have the best midwives and physicians in the land.' I hesitate. 'Would you . . . I know that perhaps you . . .'

She waits. She must know that I want her to be with me for my confinement. 'I have no-one else,' I say simply. 'And neither do you. Whatever has passed between us, Iz, we have nobody but each other now.'

Neither of us mentions our mother, still imprisoned in Beaulieu Abbey, and her lands stolen from her by our husbands working together to rob her, and then competing to rob each other. She writes to us both, letters filled with threats, and complaints, swearing that she will write no more if we don't promise to obey her and get her set free. She knows, as we do, that both of us let this happen, powerless to do anything but our husbands' bidding. 'We are orphans,' I say bleakly. 'We have let ourselves be orphans. We have made orphans out of ourselves. And we have no-one else to turn to but each other.'

'I'll come,' she says.

MIDDLEHAM CASTLE, YORKSHIRE, SPRING 1473

Being in confinement with Isabel for six weeks in the Lady's Tower at Middleham Castle is like re-living the long days of our childhood again. Men are not allowed inside the confinement chamber, and so the wood for the banked-in fires, the platters for our dinner, everything that we want has to be handed over at the foot of the tower to one of the women attending me. The priest comes across the wooden bridge from the main keep of the castle and stands at the door behind a screen to read the mass, and gives me the Host through a metal grille, without looking at me. We hear almost no news. Isabel walks across to the great hall to dine with Richard once or twice and comes back to tell us that the little Prince of Wales is to take up his residence in Ludlow. For a moment I think of my first husband; the title of Prince of Wales was his, the beautiful castle of Ludlow would have been ours, Margaret of Anjou planned that we should live there for some months after our victory to impose our will on the people of Wales – but then I remember that all that is gone now, and I am of the House of York, and I should be glad that their prince has grown old enough to have his own household in Wales, even if it is under the management of his uncle, Anthony Woodville, the widower who now rises, through no skill of his own, to his dead wife's title of Baron Scales.

'It will mean that the Rivers run Wales in everything but name,' Isabel whispers to me. 'The king has handed his only heir into their keeping and Anthony Woodville is head of the prince's council and the queen rules everything. This is not the House of York, this is the House of Rivers. D'you think Wales will stand for it? They have always been for the House of Lancaster and the Tudors.'

I shrug. I am lapped in the serenity of the last weeks of pregnancy. I look out over the green fields nearby and beyond them the rough pasture with the lapwings wheeling and crying up to the moorland. London seems a long way away, Ludlow a lifetime. 'Who should rule her son but the queen?' I ask. 'And he couldn't have a better governor than his uncle Anthony. Whatever you think of the queen, Anthony Woodville is one of the finest men in Europe. They are a close family. Anthony Woodville will guard his nephew with his life.'

'You wait,' Isabel predicts. 'There will be many who fear to see the Rivers become over-mighty. There will be many who warn the king against trusting one family with everything. George is against them, even your husband Richard does not like to see all of Wales in their keeping.' She pauses. 'Father said they were bad advisors,' she reminds me.

I nod. 'He did,' I concede. 'The king was very wrong to prefer them to our father.'

'And She hates us still,' Isabel says flatly.

I nod. 'Yes, I suppose she always will; but she can't do anything. While George and Richard are in the favour of the king all she can do is be as cold as the fish-woman on her family's flag. She can't even change the order of precedence. She can't ignore us like she used to do. And anyway, when my baby is born I don't plan to go back to court.' I touch the thick wall beside the glazed window with satisfaction. 'Nobody can hurt me here.'

'I shall stay away from court too,' she says. She smiles at me. 'I shall have good reason to stay away. Do you notice anything about me?'

I raise my head and look at her more closely. 'You look—' I hunt for a phrase that is not impolite: 'Bonny.'

She laughs. 'You mean I am fat,' she says joyfully. 'I am getting good and fat. And I shall call on you to come to stay with me in August.' She beams at me. 'I shall want you to return the favour I am doing here.'

'Iz—' In a moment I understand what she means and then I take her hands. 'Iz – you are expecting a baby?'

She laughs. 'Yes, at last. I was starting to fear ...'

'Of course, of course. But you must rest now.' At once I drag her to the fireside and pull her into a seat, put a stool under her feet, and smilingly regard her. 'How wonderful! And you must not pick up things for me any more, and when you leave here, you must have a litter, and not go by horseback.'

'I am well,' she says. 'I feel far better than last time. I am not afraid. At any rate I am not very afraid ... and – oh, just think, Annie! – they will be cousins, my baby and yours, they will be cousins, born in the same year.'

There is a silence as we both think of the grandfather of our babies who will never see them, who would have regarded them as the fulfilment of his plans, who would at once have started new and ambitious plans for them, the minute that their little heads were in the cradle.

'Father would have had their marriages laid out, and their heraldry drawn up already,' Isabel says with a little laugh.

'He would have got a dispensation and married them to each other,' I say. 'To keep their fortunes in the family.' I pause. 'Will you write and tell Mother?' I ask tentatively.

She shrugs, her face closed and cold. 'What's the use?' she asks. 'She'll never see her grandchild. She'll never get out, and she has told me that if I cannot get her released then I am no daughter of hers. What's the use in even thinking of her?'

The pains start at midnight, just when I am going to sleep with Isabel in the big bed beside me. I give a little cry and within moments she is up, throwing a gown over her shoulders, lighting candles from the fire, sending the maid for the midwives.

I can see that she is afraid for me, and her white-faced ordering of ale and her sharp tone to the midwives make me afraid in my turn. They have a monstrance with the Host inside it set up on the little altar in the corner of my room. I have the girdle that was specially blessed for Isabel's first birth tied around my straining belly. The midwives have spiced ale for me and everyone else to drink, and they send orders to the kitchen for the cooks to be woken to make a great dinner, for it will be a long night and we will all want sustaining.

When they bring me a fricassee of game followed by some roast chicken and boiled carp the smell of the food turns my stomach and I order it from the room and prowl up and down, turning at the window and at the head of the bed while outside, in the presence chamber, I can hear them eating greedily and calling for more ale. Only Iz and a couple of maids stay with me. Iz has no appetite either.

'Are the pains bad?' she asks anxiously.

I shake my head. 'They come and go,' I say. 'But I think they're getting stronger.'

About two in the morning it gets a lot worse. The midwives, flushed and merry from the food and drink, come into the bedroom and walk me between the two of them. When I pause they force me to walk onward. When I want to lie down and rest, they cluck and push me on. The pains start to come more closely together and only then do they allow me to lean on one of them and groan.

At about three in the morning I hear footsteps coming across the bridge from the great chamber, and there is a knock at the door and I hear Richard calling: 'I am the duke! How is my wife?'

'Merrily,' says the midwife with rough good humour. 'She's doing merrily, my lord.'

'How much longer will she be?'

'Hours yet,' she says cheerfully, ignoring my moan of protest. 'Could be hours. You get yourself some sleep, Your Grace, we'll send to you the moment she takes to her bed.'

'Why, is she not in bed now? What is she doing?' he demands, puzzled, the door barred to him, knowing nothing of the midwives' arts.

'We're walking her,' the older one replies. 'Walking her up and down to ease the pain.'

Pointless to tell them that it does not ease the pain at all, for they will do this, as they have always done it, and I will obey them, for I can hardly think for myself now.

'You are walking her?' my young husband demands through the closed door. 'Is that helping much?'

'If the baby was slow in coming we would toss her in a blanket,' the younger one replies with a hard laugh. 'She is glad we are just walking her. This is women's work, Your Grace. We know what we are doing.'

I hear Richard's muffled expletive, but then his footsteps go away and Iz and I look bleakly at each other as the women take my arms and lead me from fireplace to doorway and back again.

They leave me as they go to take their breakfast in the great hall, and once again I find I cannot eat and Iz sits beside me as I rest on the bed, and strokes my forehead like she used to do when I was ill. The pains come so often and so powerfully that I think I cannot bear it any longer. Just then the door opens and the two midwives come back in, this time bringing with them the wet nurse, who sets the cradle to rights, and spreads the sheets on the birthing bed.

'Not long now,' says one of the midwives cheerfully. 'Here.' She offers me a wooden wedge, polished by use and indented with teeth marks. 'Bite on it,' she says. 'See those marks? Many a good woman has bitten on that and saved her own tongue. You bite on it when the pain comes, and then you take a good hold of this.'

They have tied a cord across the two bottom posts of my big bed and when I reach forwards from the day bed I can get hold of it and brace my feet against the foot of the big bed. 'You pull on that, and we pull with you. You bite on the wedge when you feel the pain rising, and we roar with you.'

'Do you have nothing you can give her to ease the pain?' Isabel demands.

The younger woman unstoppers a stone bottle. 'You take a drop of this,' she suggests, pouring it into my silver cup. 'Come to think of it, we'll all take a drop of this.'

It burns my throat and makes my eyes water but it makes me feel braver and stronger. I see Iz choke on her draught and she grins at me. She leans forwards to whisper in my ear: 'These are two greedy drunk old women. God only knows where Richard found them.'

'They are the best in the country,' I reply. 'God help the woman in travail with the worst.'

She laughs and I laugh too but the laugh catches in my belly like a sword thrust, and I give a great cry. At once the two women become businesslike, seating me on the birthing bed, putting the looped cord into my hand, telling the maid to pour hot water from the jug at the fireside. Then there is a long confused time when I am absorbed by the pain, and the firelight reflected on the side of the jug, the heat of the room, and Isabel's cool hand bathing my face. I feel as if I am fighting a pain in my very bowels and it is a struggle to breathe. I think of my mother, so far away from me, who should be here with me now, and I think of my father who spent his life fighting and who knew the final last terror of defeat and death. Oddly enough I think of Midnight, throwing up his big head as the sword went in his heart. At the thought of my father, going out on foot to put down his life in the fields outside Barnet so that I might be Queen of England I give a heave and I hear a crying, and someone saying urgently, 'Gently, gently now,' and I see Isabel's face blurred with tears and hear her say to me: 'Annie! Annie! You have a boy!' And I know that I have done the one thing that my father wanted, the one thing that Richard needs: I have given my father a grandson and my husband his heir, and God has blessed me with a baby boy.

But he is not strong. The midwives say cheerfully that many a frail boy makes a brave man, and the wet nurse says that her milk will make him grow fat and bonny in no time, but through the six weeks of my confinement after his birth, before my churching, my heart quails when I hear him cry, a little thin reedy sound, through the night, and in the day I look at the palms of his hands which are like little pale leaves.

Isabel is to go back to George in London after the baby's christening and my churching. We call him Edward for the king, and Richard says that he foretells a great future for him. The christening is small and quiet, as is my churching, the king and queen cannot come and although nobody says anything, the baby does not look likely to thrive, he is hardly worth the cost of a great christening gown, three days of celebration in the castle, and a dinner for all the servants.

'He will be strong,' Isabel whispers to me reassuringly as she climbs into her litter in the stable yard. She is not going to ride, for her belly is broadening. 'I thought he was looking much stronger this very morning.'

He is not, but neither of us admit this.

'And anyway, at least you know now that you can have a child, that you can have a live birth,' she says. The thought of the little boy who died at sea, who never even cried out, haunts us both, still.

'You can have a live child too,' I say staunchly. 'This one, for sure. And I shall come to your confinement. There is no reason that it should not go well for you this time. And you will have a little cousin for Edward, and please God they will both thrive.'

She looks at me, her eyes hollow in her face with fear. 'The

York boys are lusty stock but I never forget that our mother conceived only me and you. And I have had a child and lost him.'

'Now you be brave,' I order her, as if I am the older sister. 'You keep your spirits up, and all will be well with you as it was with me. And I will come to you in your time.'

She nods. 'God bless you, Sister, and keep you well.'

'God bless,' I say. 'God bless you, Iz.'

After Isabel has left I find that I am thinking of my mother, and that she may never see this, her first grandchild, the boy that we all wanted so much. I write her a brief note to tell her that the child is born, and that he is thriving so far, and I wait for a reply. She answers me with a tirade of rage. To her my child, my darling boy, is illegitimate; she calls him 'Richard's bastard', for she did not give permission for the wedding. The castle where he was born is not his home but hers, and so he is a usurper, like his father and mother. I must leave both child and husband at once and go to join her at Beaulieu. Or I must go to London and petition the king for her freedom. Or I must command my husband to set her free. George and Richard must return her fortune, they should be charged as thieves. And if I do none of these things then I will feel the coldness of a mother's curse, she will disown me, she will never write to me again.

Slowly, I fold the letter into smaller and smaller portions, and then I walk to the great hall where the fire is always burning and drop the wadded paper in the back of the fire and watch it smoulder and burn. Richard, coming by with his deerhound at his heels, pauses at my solemn face, and looks at the little flame in the grate.

'What was this?'

'Nothing,' I say sadly. 'It's nothing to me any more.'

It is the time of day that I love the best, the early evening before dinner, and Richard and I are walking around the walls which run around this great castle, a long square walk which takes us to all points of the compass and begins and ends at the prince's tower where my darling little Edward has his nursery. To our right is the deep moat. As I look down I can see them pulling a net from the moat gleaming with wriggling silver fish and I nudge Richard and say, 'Carp for dinner tonight.'

Beyond the moat is the jumble of stone and slate buildings of the little town of Middleham and all around the town the rich pasture that runs up to the moorland. I can see two milkmaids with their yoke and pails over their broad shoulders, carrying their three-legged stools, going out to milk the cows in the fields, and the cows raising their heads from the grass when they hear the call 'bonnie coo! bonnie coo!' and walking slowly towards them. Beyond the fields the lower slopes of the hills are dark green with bracken and beyond that, higher and higher, is the misty amethyst tinge of flowering heather. This has been my home, and my family's home, forever. Most of the boys in the cottages are named Richard after my father, and his father before him. Most of the girls are called Anne or Isabel after my sister and me. Almost everyone has sworn obedience to me or to the new Richard here – my husband. As we turn the corner on the walkway of the castle and go away from the town I see an early barn owl, white as a cloud, floating silent as a falling leaf along the bushy line of the hedge. The sun is sinking down into a layer of rose and gold clouds, my hand is tucked in Richard's arm, and I lean my head against his shoulder.

'Are you happy?' I ask.

He smiles at the question, which is not one he would ever pose. 'I am glad to be here.'

'You mean – not at court?'

I am hoping that he will say something about loving my company and loving being with me and the baby in this, our most beautiful home. We are still newly wed, we are still young, I still have a sense of playing the part of being the lord of the manor and his lady, as if I am not yet old enough or grand enough to take my mother's place. For Richard it is different. This life has been hard-won; he shoulders the responsibilities of being lord of the North of England. For me, being his wife, living here, in my family home, is a girl's dream. Often I cannot believe that such a dream has come true.

But Richard merely says: 'Court is like a general melee in a jousting tournament these days. The Rivers keep gaining, and George and the other lords keep fighting back. It is a constant unspoken struggle. Not a yard of land nor a coin in my pocket is safe. There is always some kinsman to the queen who thinks they should have it.'

'The king . . .'

'Edward agrees with the last person he spoke to. He laughs and promises anyone anything. He spends his days riding and dancing and gambling and his nights carousing on the streets of London with William Hastings, and even with his stepsons – and I swear that they are not his true companions but are there only to serve their mother. They go along with him, their stepfather, to be her eyes and ears, they lead him into all sorts of bawdy houses and stews, and then I swear they report back to her and tell her everything. He has no friends, only spies and toadies.'

'That's wrong,' I say with the stern morality of the young.

'It's very wrong,' Richard confirms. 'A king should set an example to his people. Edward is beloved and the people of London like to see him; but when he is drunk in the streets and chasing women—' He breaks off. 'Anyway, these are not matters for your ears.'

I match my steps to his, and I don't remind him that I spent much of my girlhood in a garrison town.

'And George seeks advantage at every moment,' Richard says. 'He cannot stop himself, he thinks of nothing but the crown he lost to Edward and the fortune he lost to me. His greed is phenomenal, Anne. He just goes on and on trying to get more land, trying to get more offices. He goes around court like a great carp with his mouth wide open gulping in fees. And he lives like a prince himself. God knows how much he spends on his London house buying friends and extending his influence.'

A skylark rises up from the meadow below the castle and sings as it beats upwards, and then pauses and then mounts again, going up and up as if it would never stop until it gets to heaven. I remember my father telling me to watch, watch carefully, for in a moment it will close its wings and drop silently, drop like a stone to the ground – and where it lands there will be its little down-lined nest and four speckled eggs, arranged point to the centre, for the skylark is a tidy bird, as any candidate for heaven should be.

We are coming down the winding stair of the gatehouse tower to the main courtyard of the castle as the doors are thrown open and a litter with curtains drawn and twenty outriders comes clattering through the gate.

'Who's this?' I ask. 'A lady? Visiting us?'

Richard steps forwards and throws a salute at the leader of the guard as if he has been expecting him. 'All well?'

The man takes off his bonnet and rubs his sweaty forehead. I recognise James Tyrrell, one of Richard's most trusted men of the household, Robert Brackenbury behind him. 'All well,' he confirms. 'Nobody followed us, as far as I know, and nobody challenged us on the road.'

I tug at Richard's arm. 'Who is this visitor?'

'You made good time,' Richard remarks, ignoring me.

A hand draws back the curtains of the litter, and Sir James turns to help the lady out. She puts aside the rugs that have kept her warm on the journey, and she takes his hand. He stands before her, hiding her face.

'Not your mother?' I whisper to Richard, horrified at the thought of a formal visit.

'No,' he says, watching as the lady steps out of the litter and straightens up with a little grunt of discomfort. Sir James steps aside. With a sensation like fainting, I recognise my mother, whom I have not seen for two long years, brought back from the grave, or at any rate from Beaulieu Abbey, stepping out of the litter like a living ghost, turning to smile a ghastly triumphant beam at me, the daughter who left her in prison, the daughter who left her for dead.

'Why is she here?' I demand.

We are in the privy chamber, completely alone, the door shut on the company in the great chamber outside who are waiting for us to lead them into dinner, the cooks in the kitchen down below cursing as meat is overdone and the pastries too crisp and brown.

'I rescued her,' he says calmly. 'I thought you would be pleased.'

I break off to look at him. He cannot have thought that I would be pleased. His bland expression tells me that he knows that bringing my mother to me is to stir up a war inside our family that has been raging in furious letters and painful apologies and excuses for two long years. After her last letter when she named my son, her own grandson, a bastard and my husband a thief she has not written to me again. She told me that I had shamed my father and betrayed her. She told me that I was no daughter of hers. She cursed me with a mother's curse and said that I would live without her blessing and she would go to her grave without saying my name. I did not reply – not so much as a single word. I decided when I married Richard that I had neither mother nor father. One had died on the battlefield, one had deserted me and sent me to a battle alone. Isabel and I call ourselves orphans.

Until now. 'Richard, for the love of God, why have you brought her here?'

Finally, he decides to be honest. 'George was going to take her,' he says. 'I am sure of it. George was going to kidnap her, appeal against the king's decision to share her fortune between the two of us, demand justice for her. Reclaim it all for her as if he was her knight errant, and then, when she had all the Warwick lands back in her keeping, he was going to take them from her. He was going to keep her in his household like he took you – and he would have got everything that we have, Anne. I had to get her before he did.'

'So to prevent George taking her – you have taken her,' I say drily. 'Doing the very crime that you suspect he would have done.'

He looks at me grimly. 'When I married you, I said I would protect you. I am protecting your interests now.'

The mention of our courtship silences me. 'I didn't think it would mean this.'

'Neither did I,' he says. 'But I promised to protect you and this is what it takes.'

'Where is she going to live?' My head is whirling. 'She can't go into sanctuary again, can she?'

'Here.'

'Here?' I almost scream at him.

'Yes.'

'Richard, I am frightened to even see her. She said I was no daughter of hers. She said I would never have a mother's blessing. She said I should not marry you. She called you things that you would never forgive! She said our son—' I break off. 'I won't repeat it. I won't think about it.'

'I don't need to hear it,' he says cheerfully. 'And I don't need to forgive her. And you don't need her blessing. She will live here as our guest. You need never see her if you don't want to. She can dine in her rooms, she can pray in her own chapel. We have enough space here, God knows. We can give her a household of her own. She need not trouble you.'

'How can she not trouble me? She is my mother! She is my mother who has set her face against me. She said that she would go to her grave without saying my name!'

'Think of her as your prisoner.'

I sink into a chair, staring at him. 'My mother is my prisoner?'

'She was a prisoner at Beaulieu Abbey. Now she is a prisoner here. She is never going to regain her fortune, she lost that when she claimed sanctuary at the moment that she heard of your father's death. She chose then to leave you to whatever danger the battle would bring. Now she has the life that she chose then. She can abide by her choice. She is a pauper, she is in prison. It just happens that she is a prisoner here rather than in Beaulieu. She might like that. She might prefer it here. This was her home, after all.'

'She came here as a bride, it was her family home,' I say quietly. 'Every stone in every wall will speak to her of her rights.'

'Well then . . .'

'It's still hers.' I look at his young handsome determined face, and realise that nothing I say will make any difference. 'We live here like thieves and now the true owner will be watching us collect her rents, claiming her dues, sheltered by her walls, living under her roof.'

He shrugs and I break off. I knew that he was a man of abrupt decision, a man who was capable – just like his brother – of powerful, rapid acts. The York boys spent their childhood in rebellion against the king, watching their father and then their brother risking everything at war. All the York brothers are capable of dauntless courage and stubborn endurance. I knew he was a man who would follow his own interests, without scruples. But I did not know that he was a man who could arrest his own mother-in-law and hold her, against her wishes, steal her lands from her as she sleeps under his roof. I knew that my husband was a hard man, but I did not know that he was granite.

'How long will she live here?'

'Till she dies,' he says blandly.

I think of King Henry in the Tower, who died the very night that the York brothers came home victorious from Tewkesbury, determined to end his line. I think of him when the three of them quietly walked into his darkened room as he slept. I think of him sleeping under their protection and never waking again; and I open my mouth to ask him a question, and close it again, saying nothing. I realise that I am afraid to ask my young husband how long he thinks that my mother may live.

Reluctantly, sick in my belly, I go to the rooms that have been allocated to my mother, that evening, after dinner. They have served her the best dishes from the evening meal, and presented them to her on one knee, with all the respect that a countess should receive. She has eaten well; they are taking out the empty plates as I come in. Richard has ruled that she shall be housed in the northwest tower, as far away from us as it is possible to be. There is no bridge from her corner tower to the main keep; if she were allowed out of her rooms, she would have to go all the way down the stairs and through the door to get into the courtyard, cross the courtyard, and then go up the stairs to the keep to get to the great hall. There are guards at every doorway. She will never visit us without invitation. She will never leave the tower without permission. For the rest of her life she will have a blinkered view. From her windows she can see only the roofs of the little town, the wide grey skies, the empty landscape and down to the dark moat.

I go in and curtsey to her – she is my mother and I have to show her respect – but then I stand before her, my chin up. I fear that I look like a defiant child. But I am only just seventeen and I am terrified of my mother's authority.

'Your husband intends to hold me as a prisoner,' she says coldly. 'Are you, my own daughter, serving him as his gaoler?'

'You know I cannot disobey him.'

'You should not disobey me.'

'You left me,' I say, driven to speak out. 'You left me with Margaret of Anjou and she led me to a terrible battle and to defeat, and to the death of my husband. I was little more than a child and you abandoned me on a battlefield.'

'You paid the price of overweening ambition,' she says. 'Your father's ambition, which destroyed us. Now you are following another ambitious man, like a dog, just as you followed your father. You wanted to be Queen of England. You would not know your place.'

'My ambition didn't take me very far,' I protest. 'Isabel imprisoned me, my own sister!' I can feel my anger and my tears welling up together. 'There was nobody to defend me. You let Isabel and George hold me against my will. You put yourself safely in sanctuary and you left me to be picked up from the battlefield! Anybody could have taken me, anything could have happened to me.'

'You let your husband and Isabel's husband steal my fortune from me.'

'How could I stop them?'

'Did you try?'

I am silent. I did not try.

'Return my lands to me, and release me,' my mother says. 'Tell your husband he must do this. Tell the king.'

'Lady Mother – I cannot,' I say weakly.

'Then tell Isabel.'

'She can't either. She is expecting a baby, she's not even at court. And anyway – the king does not hear petitions from Isabel and me. He would never listen to us in preference to his brothers.'

'I have to be free,' my mother says, and for a moment her voice trembles. 'I cannot die in prison. You have to set me free.'

I shake my head. 'I can't,' I say. 'There's no point even asking me, Lady Mother. I am powerless. I can't do anything for you.'

For a moment her eyes blaze at me; she can still frighten me. But this time, I hold her gaze and I shrug my shoulders. 'We lost the battle,' I say. 'I am married to my saviour. I have no power, nor does Isabel, nor do you. There is nothing I can do for you if it goes against my husband's will. You will have to reconcile yourself, as I do, as Isabel does, to being the defeated.'

It is a relief beyond measuring to leave my home with the silent brooding presence of my mother in the northwest tower, and go to Isabel for the birth of her baby in Norton St Philip, Somerset. Isabel is in confinement when I arrive and I join her in the shadowed rooms. The baby comes early and the two days of labour do not give her great pain, though by the end she is very tired. The midwife hands the baby to me. 'A girl,' she says.

'A girl!' I exclaim. 'Look, Iz, you've got such a pretty girl!'

She barely glances at the perfect face of the baby, though her face is as smooth and as pale as a pearl, and her eyelashes are dark. 'Oh, a girl,' she says dully.

'Better luck next time,' says the midwife drily, as she bundles up the bloodstained linen and rubs her hands on her soiled apron, and looks around for a glass of ale.

'But this is the best of luck already!' I protest. 'See how beautiful she is? Iz, do look at her – she's not even crying!'

The tiny baby opens her mouth and yawns, and she is as delightful as a kitten. Iz does not stretch out her arms for her. 'George was determined on a boy,' she says shortly. 'He will not thank me for this. He will see it as a failure, as my failure.'

'Perhaps a boy next time?'

'And She never stops giving birth,' Isabel says irritably.

'George says that her health must break down soon. They have a baby almost every year. Surely one of them will kill her in child-birth?'

I cross myself against her ill-will. 'Almost always girls,' I say to console her.

'One boy already, which is all she needs for a Prince of Wales, and another baby due this very month. What if she is carrying a second boy? Then she will have two sons to inherit the throne that their father usurped. And George will be pushed another step away from the crown. How will George ever get the throne if she has more sons?'

'Hush,' I say instantly. The midwife has her back to us, the wet nurse is coming into the birthing chamber, the maid is clearing away the linen and turning down the sheets of the big bed, but still I am afraid that we may be overheard. 'Hush, Isabel. Don't speak of such things. Especially not in front of people.'

'Why not? George was Edward's heir. That was their agreement. But She goes on having children, as if She would never stop, like a farrowing pig. Why would God give her a boy? Why would He make her fertile? Why does He not rain down pestilence on her and blow her and her baby to hell?'

I am so shocked at her sudden malice so soon after childbirth that I say nothing. I turn away from her to hand the baby to the wet nurse, who settles down in a rocking chair and takes the baby to her breast and coos over her dark downy head.

As I help Isabel into the big bed, my face is grim. 'These are not your thoughts, nor George's, I know,' I say firmly. 'For it is treason to speak against the king and his family. You are tired from the birth and drunk on the birthing ale. Iz, you must never say such things, not even to me.'

She beckons me close so that she can whisper in my ear. 'Do you not think that our father would want George to challenge his brother? Do you not know that our father would think that the very gates of heaven were opening if George were to take the crown and make me queen? And then your husband would be the next heir to the throne. This baby is a girl, she counts for nothing. If George took the throne, then Richard would come next. Have you forgotten that the one thing our father wanted above everything else in the world was to see one of us as Queen of England and his grandson as Prince of Wales? Can you imagine how proud and happy he would be if he saw me as queen and you as queen after me, and your son as king after us both?'

I pull away from her. 'It cost him his life,' I say harshly. 'He rode out to his death. And our mother is imprisoned, and you and I all but orphaned.'

'If George were to win then that would be the only thing that made it all worth while,' she says stubbornly. 'If George were to claim the throne then Father would be at peace.'

I flinch at the thought that my father is not at peace. 'Ah don't, Iz,' I say hastily. 'I pay enough for masses to be said for his soul in every one of our churches. Don't say such things. Look, I'll leave you to rest. The birthing ale has gone to your head. You shouldn't say such things and I won't hear them. I am married to a loyal brother of the king and so are you. Let that be the truth. Anything else will only lead us into danger and defeat. Anything else is a sword through the heart.'

We don't mention the conversation again and when I leave them, and George himself helps me onto my horse, thanking me for caring for Isabel in her time, I wish him every happiness and that the child grows strong and well.

'Perhaps she will have a boy next time,' he says. His handsome face is discontented, his charm quite overshadowed by such a setback, his smiling mouth is downturned. He is as sulky as a spoiled child.

For a moment I want to remind him that she had a boy, a beautiful baby boy, a boy who would have been the son and heir that he now wants so badly, a boy who would have been running around the hall now, a sturdy three-year-old with his nursemaid hurrying behind him; but that Iz was so shaken by the pounding waves on board my father's ship that she could not give birth to him, and she had no-one but me as a midwife, and the baby's little coffin was slipped into the grey heaving seas.

'Perhaps next time,' I say soothingly. 'But she is a very pretty girl, and feeding well and growing strong.'

'Stronger than your boy?' he asks nastily. 'What d'you call him: Edward? Was that in memory of your dead husband? Funny sort of tribute.'

'Edward for the king of course,' I say, biting my lip.

'And is our baby stronger than yours?'

'Yes, I think so.' It hurts me to say the truth but little Margaret is a wiry hungry baby and is doing well at once, and my baby is quiet, and is not thriving.

He shrugs. 'Well, it makes no odds. A girl's no good. A girl can't take the throne,' he says, turning away. I can hardly hear, but I am sure that is what he says. For a moment I think to challenge him, to dare him to repeat it, and warn him that this is to talk treason. But then I gather my reins in my cold hands and think better that he had never said it. Better that I never heard it. Better go home.

BAYNARD'S CASTLE, LONDON, SUMMER 1473

I meet Richard in Baynard's Castle, his family's London home, and to my relief the court is away from London and the city is peaceful. Elizabeth the queen has gone to Shrewsbury for the birth of her baby, another boy, the second son that Isabel feared, and the doting king is with her. Without doubt they will be joyfully celebrating the birth of another boy to give certainty to their line. It makes no difference to me if she has one boy more or twenty – Richard is three steps from the throne, a fourth step makes little odds, but I cannot help a twinge of irritation at her constant fertility which serves her so well.

They are calling him Richard, in honour of his grandfather and his uncle, my husband. Richard is pleased for them; his love for his brother means he delights in his success. I am only pleased that they are far away in Shrewsbury and I am not summoned with the rest of the ladies to hang over the crib and congratulate her on another strong son. I wish her and her newborn son well, just as I wish any woman in childbed well. I really don't want to see her in her triumph.

The rest of the lords and courtiers have gone to their lands for the summer, nobody wants to be in London during the hot plague months, so Richard and I will not stay long before we go on the long journey north to Middleham together, to see our baby again.

The day we are due to leave, I go to tell Richard that I will be ready within the hour, and find his presence chamber door is closed. This is the room where Richard hears petitions and applications for his judgement or generosity; the door always stands open as a symbol of his good lordship. It is his throne room, which is always visible so that people can see the youngest son of York about his business of ruling the kingdom. I open the door and go in. The inner door to his privy chamber is closed too. I go to turn the handle, and then I pause at the sound of a familiar voice.

His brother George Duke of Clarence is in there with my husband, talking very quietly and very persuasively. My hand drops from the ring of the handle and I stand still to listen.

'Since he is not a true son of our father, and since their marriage was undoubtedly brought about by witchcraft . . .'

'This? Again?' Richard interrupts his brother scornfully. 'Again? He has two handsome sons – one newly born this very month – and three healthy daughters against your dead boy and puling girl, and you say his marriage is not blessed by God? Surely, George, even you can see the evidence is against you?'

'I say they are all bastards. He and Elizabeth Woodville are not married in the sight of God, and their children are all bastards.'

'And you are the only fool in London who says it.'

'Many say it. Your wife's father said it.'

'For malice. And those who are not malicious are all fools.'

A chair scrapes on the wooden floor. 'Do you call me a fool?'

'Lord, yes,' Richard says scornfully. 'To your face. A treacherous fool, if you like. A malicious fool if you insist. Do you think that we don't know that you are meeting with Oxford? With every fool who still carries a grudge though Edward has done everything he can to settle with the embittered placemen who lost their positions? With the Lancastrians who rode against him? With every leftover out-of-place Lancaster follower that you can find? With every disgruntled squire? Sending secret messages to the French? D'you think we don't know all that you do, and more?'

'Edward knows?' George's voice has lost its bluster as if he has been winded. 'You said "we know"? What does Edward know? What have you told him?'

''Course he knows. Assume he knows everything. Will he do anything? He won't. Would I? In a moment. Because I have no patience with hidden enmity and I prefer to strike early and quick. But Edward loves you as only a kind brother could, and he has more patience than I can muster. But, brother mine, you bring me no news when you come here to tell me you have been a traitor before and you could be one again. That much I know already. That much we all know.'

'I didn't come here for that. Just to say . . .'

Again I hear the scrape of a chair as someone leaps to his feet and then Richard's raised voice: 'What does that say? Read it aloud! What does it say?'

Without opening the door to see him, I know that Richard will be pointing to his motto, carved in the massive wooden chimney breast.

'For God's sake!'

'*Loyauté me lie*,' Richard quotes. 'Loyalty binds me. You wouldn't understand such a thing, but I am sworn heart and soul to my brother Edward the king. I believe in the order of chivalry, I believe in God and the king and that they are one and the same thing and my honour is bound to both. Don't you even dare to question me. My beliefs are beyond your imagining.'

'All I am saying,' now George's voice is a persuasive whine, 'all I am saying is that there are questions about the king and questions about the queen and that if we are legitimate and he is not, then perhaps we should divide the kingdom, fairly – as you and I divided the Neville inheritance – and rule jointly. He has all but given you the North, he has allowed you to rule it almost as a principality. Why can't he give me the Midlands in the same way, and he can keep the south? Prince Edward has Wales. What is this if not fair?'

There is a moment's silence. I know that Richard will be tempted by the thought of a kingdom of the North, and him as its ruler. I take one tiny step closer to the door. I pray that he will resist temptation, say no to his brother, cleave to the king. Pray God that he does nothing to bring the enmity of the queen down on our heads.

'It's to carve up the kingdom that he won in a fair fight,' Richard says bluntly. 'He won his kingdom entire, by force of arms in honourable battle, with me and even you at his side. He will not divide it. It would be to destroy his son's inheritance.'

'I am surprised to see you defend Elizabeth Woodville's son,' George says silkily. 'You of all people, who are supplanted in your brother's love by their clan. You of all people, who was his best friend and most beloved; but now you come after her, and after her brother the saintly Anthony, and after her commoner sons, his constant companions in every whorehouse in London: Thomas and Richard. But I see that the Woodville boy has a champion in you. You are a loving uncle, as it turns out.'

'I defend my brother,' Richard replies. 'I say nothing about the Rivers family. My brother married the woman of his choice. She was not of my choosing; but I defend my brother. Always.'

'You can't be loyal to her,' George says flatly. 'You can't be.'

Again, I hear my young husband hesitate; it is true, he cannot be loyal to her.

'We'll talk,' George says finally. 'Not now; but later. When the Woodville boy wants to come to his throne. We'll talk then. When the boy from Grafton, the base-blooded bastard, wants to step up to the throne of England, and take our brother's crown which we won for him and for our house, not for them – we'll talk again then. I know you are loyal to Edward – I am too. But only to my brother, to my house and to the blood of kings. Not to that baseborn bastard.'

I hear him turn on his heel and walk across the room and I step back to a window bay. As they open the door, I look round with a little start as if I am surprised to find them there. George barely nods at me as he heads towards the door and Richard stands and watches him go.

MIDDLEHAM CASTLE, YORKSHIRE, JULY 1474

Richard keeps his word and although my mother and I live under the same roof I hardly ever see her. She has rooms in the north-west tower, near to the gatehouse for the convenience of the guards, overlooking the thatched roofs and stone gables of the little houses of Middleham, while our rooms are high in the central keep, with views all round like an eyrie. We come and go to London, to York, to Sheriff Hutton, Barnard Castle, accompanied by guards and our household of friends and companions, and she stays in the same rooms, watching the sun rise through the same windows every morning, and set on the opposite side, throwing shadows across her room in the same way every day.

I order that our son Edward shall never be taken along the walkway of the outer wall to see his grandmother. I don't want her to have anything to do with him. He bears a royal name, he is the grandson my father longed for. He is many steps now from the throne but I am raising him with the education and the courage of a king – as my father would have wanted, as my mother should have done. But she has cursed me and she has cursed my marriage – so I will not give her as much as one glimpse of my beautiful son. She can be dead to him, as she said I was dead to her.

In midsummer she asks to see Richard and me together. The

message comes from her chief lady in waiting and Richard glances at me as if asking me if I would like to refuse.

'We have to see her,' I say uncomfortably. 'What if she is ill?'

'Then she should send for a physician, not for you,' he says. 'She knows she can send for a physician, to London if she wishes. She knows I don't stint on her household.'

I look at Lady Worth. 'What does she want?'

She shakes her head. 'She told me only that she wants to see you,' she says. 'Both of you.'

'Bring her to us,' Richard decides.

We are seated in matching chairs, almost thrones, in the great chamber of Middleham Castle and I don't rise when my mother comes in the room though she pauses as if she expects me to kneel for her blessing. She looks about her as if to see what changes we have made to her home, and she raises an eyebrow as if she does not think much of our tapestries.

Richard snaps his finger at a manservant. 'Set a chair for the countess,' he says.

My mother sits before us and I see the stiffness of her movements. She is getting old; perhaps she is ill. Perhaps she wants to live with Isabel at Warwick Castle, and we can let her go. I wait for her to speak, and know that I am longing to hear her say that she has to go to London for her health and that she will live with Isabel.

'It's about the document,' she says to Richard.

He nods. 'I thought it would be.'

'You must have known I would hear about it sooner or later.'

'I assumed someone would tell you.'

'What is this?' I interrupt. I turn to Richard. 'What document?'

'I see you keep your wife in ignorance of your doings,' my mother observes nastily. 'Did you fear she would try to prevent you from wrongdoing? I am surprised at that. She is no champion of mine. Did you fear that this would be too much for even her to swallow?'

'No,' he says coldly. 'I don't fear her judgement.' To me he says briefly: 'This is the resolution to the problem of your mother's lands that George and I could finally agree. Edward has confirmed it. We passed it as an act of parliament. It has taken long enough for the lawyers to agree and to formulate it as a law. It is the only solution that satisfied us all: we have declared her legally dead.'

'Dead!' I stare at my mother who stares haughtily back at me. 'How can you call her dead?'

He taps his booted foot on the rushes. 'It's a legal term. It solves the problem of her lands. We could not get them any other way. Neither you nor Isabel could inherit them while she was still alive. So we have declared her dead and you and Isabel are her heirs and you inherit. Nobody steals anything from anyone. She is dead: you inherit. As your husbands, the lands are passed on to George and me.'

'But what about her?'

He gestures at her and he almost laughs aloud. 'As you see, here she is: living proof of the failure of ill-wishing. It would make a man disbelieve in magic. We called her dead and here she is, hale and hearty, and eating me out of house and home. Someone should preach a sermon on it.'

'I am sorry if you find me costly,' my mother says bitingly. 'But then I remember you have taken all of my fortune to pay for my keep.'

'Only half your fortune,' Richard corrects her. 'Your son-in-law and your other daughter have taken the other half. You need not blame Anne, Isabel has abandoned you too. But we have the cost of housing and guarding you. I don't ask for gratitude.'

'I don't offer any.'

'Would you prefer to be imprisoned in a nunnery?' he asks. 'For I could allow that. I can return you to confinement at Beaulieu if you wish.'

'I would prefer to live on my own lands in freedom. I would prefer that you had not abused the law to make away with me.

What is my life now? What can it be if I am declared dead? Am I in purgatory? Or is this hell?'

He shrugs. 'You posed an awkward problem. That's now resolved. I did not want to be seen to be stealing from my mother-in-law and the king's honour was at stake. You were a defenceless woman in sanctuary and he could not be seen to rob you. We have resolved this very neatly. The act of parliament declares that you are dead and so you have no lands, no house and I suppose no freedom. It is here, or a nunnery, or the grave. You can choose.'

'I'll stay here,' my mother says heavily. 'But I shall never forgive you for doing this to me, Richard. I cared for you as a boy in this very castle, my husband taught you all that you know about warfare and business. We were your guardians and we were good and kind guardians to you and to your friend Francis Lovell. And this is how you repay me.'

'Your husband taught me to march fast, kill without remorse, on and off the battlefield and sometimes outside the law, and take whatever I wanted. I am a good pupil to him. If he were in my shoes he would be doing just as I am doing now. In fact his ambition was greater. I have taken only half your lands but he would have taken all of England.'

She cannot disagree. 'I am weary,' she says. She gets to her feet. 'Anne, give me your arm back to my rooms.'

'Don't think you can suborn her,' Richard warns her. 'Anne knows where her loyalties lie. You threw her away into defeat, I rescued her from your neglect and made her a great heiress and a duchess.'

I take my mother's arm and she leans on me. Unwillingly, I lead her out of the presence chamber, down the stairs and across the great hall, where the servants are pulling out the tables for dinner, to the bridge which leads to the outer walls and her rooms.

She pauses under the archway to the tower. 'You know he will betray you and you will feel just like me, one day,' she says suddenly. 'You will be alone and lonely, you will be in purgatory, wondering if it is hell.'

I shudder and would pull away; but she has my arm in her grip and she is leaning heavily on me. 'He will not betray me,' I say. 'He is my husband and our interests lie together. I love him, we married for love and we love each other still.'

'Ah, you don't know then,' she says with quiet satisfaction. She sighs as if someone has given her a gift of great worth. 'I thought you did not know.'

Clearly, she will not take another step and for a moment, I stand with her. Suddenly I realise that it is for this moment, alone with me, that she asked for my arm. She did not want a moment alone with her daughter, she was not hoping for a reconciliation. No, she wanted to tell me some awful thing that I don't know, that I don't want to know. 'Come on,' I say. But she does not move at all.

'The wording of the law that makes me dead names you as his harlot.'

I am so shocked that I stop quite still and look at her. 'What are you saying? What madness are you speaking now?'

'It's the law of the land,' she laughs thinly, like a cackling witch. 'A new law. And you didn't know.'

'Know what?'

'The law that says that I am dead and you inherit goes on to say that if you and your husband divorce, then he keeps the lands.'

'Divorce?' I repeat the strange word.

'He keeps the lands, and the castles and the houses, the ships on the seas, and the contents of the treasure rooms, the mines and the quarries and the granaries and everything.'

'He has provided for our divorce?' I ask, stumbling on my speech.

'How could such a thing happen? How should you divorce?' she crows. 'The marriage has been consummated, you are proven to be fertile, you have given him a son. There can be no grounds for a divorce, surely? But in this act of parliament, Richard makes provision for a divorce. Why should he do that, if no divorce could ever take place? Why would he provide for a thing which is impossible?'

My head is whirling. 'Lady Mother, if you must speak to me at all, then speak plainly.'

She does. She beams at me as if she has good news. She is exultant that she understands this and I don't. 'He is providing for the denial of your marriage,' she says. 'He has prepared for his marriage to you to be set aside. If it was a true marriage it could not be set aside, there are no possible grounds. So my guess is this: you did not get a full dispensation from the Pope; but married without it. Am I right? Am I right, my turncoat daughter? You are cousins, you are brother- and sister-in-law, I am his godmother. Richard is even a kinsman to your first husband. Your marriage would need a full papal dispensation on many, many counts. But I don't think you had time to get a full dispensation from the Pope. My guess is that Richard urged you to marry and said that you could get a dispensation later. Am I right? I think I am right for here, in this very act where he shows why he married you – for your fortune – he also gets a ruling that he will keep your lands if he puts you aside. He shows it is possible to put you aside. It all becomes wonderfully clear!'

'It will be how the act is framed,' I say wildly. 'It will be the same for George and Isabel. There will be the same provision for George and Isabel.'

'No it is not,' she says. 'You are right. If George and Isabel had the same terms you could be reassured. But it is not the same for them. There is no provision for the annulment of their marriage. George knows that he cannot annul his marriage to Isabel so he does not provide for it. George knows that they got a dispensation for their kinship and their marriage is valid. It cannot be set aside. But Richard knows that he did not get a full dispensation and his marriage is not fully valid. It can be set aside. He has that in his power. I read the deed very carefully, as any woman might carefully read her own death certificate. My guess is that if I were to send to the Pope and ask him to show the legal dispensation for your marriage he would reply that there was none, full dispensation was never requested. So you are not married, and your son is a bastard and you a harlot.'

I am so stunned that I just stare at her. At first I think that she is raving but then one after another the pieces of what she is saying fall into place. Our driving urgent haste to marry and Richard telling me that we would do so without a dispensation, but get it later. And then I just assumed, like a fool, that the marriage was valid. I just forgot, like a fool, like a fool in the honeymoon month, that being married by an archbishop with the blessing of the king was not as good as a dispensation from the Pope. When I was greeted by his mother, when I was received by the court, when we conceived our son and inherited my lands, I assumed that everything was as it should be and I forgot to question it at all. And now I know that my husband did not forget, did not assume, but has provided that he can keep his fortune if he ever decides to set me aside. If he wants to rid himself of me he has only to say that the marriage was never valid. My marriage to him is based on our vows before God – at least those cannot be denied. But they are not enough. Our marriage depends on his whim. We will be husband and wife as long as he wishes it. At any moment he could denounce our marriage as a sham, and he would be free and I would be utterly shamed.

I shake my head in wonderment. All this time I thought that I was playing myself, both the player and the pawn, and yet I have never been more powerless, never more of a piece in someone else's game.

'Richard,' I say, and it is as if I am calling out to him to rescue me once more.

My mother regards me with silent satisfaction.

'What shall I do?' I whisper to myself. 'What can I do now?'

'Leave him.' My mother's voice is like a slap in the face. 'Leave him at once and come with me to London and we will overthrow the act, deny the false marriage, and get my lands back.'

I round on her. 'Don't you see yet that you will never get your lands back? D'you think you can fight against the King of England himself? Do you imagine you can challenge the three sons of York acting together? Have you forgotten that these were my father's enemies, Margaret of Anjou's enemies? And we were fatally allied to Father and to Margaret of Anjou? Have you forgotten that we were defeated? All you want to do is to throw yourself into prison in the Tower, and me alongside you.'

'You will never be safe as his wife,' she predicts. 'He can leave you whenever he wants. If your son dies, and you fail to get another, he can go to a more fertile woman and take your fortune with him.'

'He loves me.'

'He may do,' she concedes. 'But he wants the lands, this very castle, and an heir more than anything in the world. You have no safety.'

'I have no safety as your daughter,' I counter. 'I know that at least. You married me to a claimant to the throne of England and abandoned me when we had to go into battle. Now you call me to commit treason again.'

'Leave him!' she whispers. 'I will stand by you this time.'

'And what about my son?'

She shrugs. 'You will never see him again but as he is a bastard . . . does it matter?'

Fiercely, I take her by the arm and march her towards her rooms where the guard stands to one side to let us go in, and will then block the door so she cannot go out.

'Don't call him that,' I say. 'Don't you dare ever call him that. I stand by my son, and I stand by my husband. And you can rot in here.'

She wrenches her arm from me. 'I warn you, I will tell the world that you are not a wife but a harlot, and you will be ruined,' she spits.

I push her through the door. 'No you won't!' I say. 'For you will have no pen and no paper, and no way to send messages. No messengers and no visits. You have taught me only that you are my enemy and I will keep you straitly. Go in, Lady Mother. You will not come out again, and no word you say will ever be repeated outside these walls. Go and be dead – for you are dead to the world and dead to me. Go and be dead!'

I slam the door on her and I round on the guard. 'No-one to see her but her household,' I say. 'No messages passed, not even pedlars or tinkers to come to her door. Everyone coming or going to be searched. She sees no-one, she speaks to no-one. D'you understand?'

'Yes, Your Grace,' he says.

'She is an enemy,' I say. 'She is a traitor and a liar. She is our enemy. She is enemy to the duke, to me and to our precious son. The duke is a hard man on his enemies. Make sure you are hard on her.'

MIDDLEHAM CASTLE, YORKSHIRE, SPRING 1475

I think I am becoming a slate-hearted woman. The girl that I was – who dreaded her mother's disapproval, who clung to her big sister, who loved her father like her lord – is now an eighteen-year-old duchess who orders her household to guard her mother like an enemy, and writes with meticulous care to her sister. Richard warns me that his brother George is becoming a dangerously outspoken critic of the king, and that Isabel is known to agree with him; we cannot be seen to associate with them.

He does not have to convince me. I don't want to associate with them if they are walking into danger. When Isabel writes to me that she is going into confinement again, and would like me to come to her, I refuse. Besides, I cannot face Isabel with our mother in my keeping, gaoled for the rest of her life. I cannot face Isabel with my mother's terrible threats in my ears and in my dreams every night of my life. Isabel knows now, as I do, that we have declared our own mother a dead woman so that we could take her lands to give to our husbands. I feel that we are murderers, with blood on our hands. And what would I say if Isabel asked me if my mother is kept well? If she endures her imprisonment with patience? What could I say to her if she asked me to let our mother go?

I can never admit that my mother is kept in her tower so that she cannot speak about my marriage. I cannot tell Isabel that not only have our husbands declared our mother dead but that now even I wish her dead. Certainly I wish her silenced forever.

And now I am afraid of what Isabel thinks. I wonder if she has read the act that declares my mother dead with the care that my mother did. I wonder if Isabel has suspicions about my marriage, if one day George will tell everyone that I am the duke's whore just as much as Elizabeth Woodville is the king's whore: that there is only one son of York with an honest wife. I dare not see Isabel with these thoughts in my mind, so I write and say that I cannot come, the times are too difficult.

Isabel replies in March that she is sorry I could not come to her but that she has good news. At last she has a boy, a son and heir. He too is to be called Edward, but this boy will be named after the place of his birth and after his grandfather's earldom. He will be Edward of Warwick, and she asks me be happy for her. I try, but all I think is that if George makes an attempt on the throne he can offer any traitors who might join with him an alternative royal family: a claimant and now an heir. I write to Isabel that I am glad for her and for her son, and that I wish her well. But I don't send gifts, and I don't ask to be godmother. I am afraid of what George may be planning for this little boy, this new Warwick, the grandson of Warwick the kingmaker.

Besides, while I have been troubled by my mother's words, by my fears for my son, the country has been building up to war with France at a breakneck pace, and everything that was done in peace has been forgotten as taxes have to be raised, soldiers recruited, weapons forged, shoes cobbled, liveries sewn. Richard can think of nothing but mustering his army from our estates, drawing on tenants, retainers, household staff and everyone who has offered him their loyalty. Gentlemen have to bring their own tenants from their farms, towns have to raise funds and send apprentices. Richard hurries to recruit his men and join his brothers – both his brothers – as they go to invade France, with the whole of the kingdom for the re-taking, laid out like a rich feast before them.

The three sons of York are to march out in splendour again. Edward has declared himself determined to return to the glory of Henry V. He will be King of France again and the shame of England's failure under the bad queen and the sleeping king will be forgotten. Richard is cool with me as he prepares to leave. He remembers that the King of France, Louis, proposed and organised my first wedding, called me his pretty cousin and promised me his friendship when I would be Queen of England. Richard checks and double-checks the wagons which will carry everything to France, has his armourer pack two sets of armour, and mounts his horse in the stable yard at the head of about a thousand men. Even more will join him on the march south.

I go to say goodbye. 'Keep safe, my husband.' There are tears in my eyes and I try to blink them away.

'I am going to war.' His smile is distant; already his mind is on the work he must do. 'I doubt that I'll be able to keep safe.'

I shake my head. I so much want to tell him how afraid I am for him, that I cannot help but think of my father who barely said goodbye in his rush to get to his ships and go to war. I cannot help but think of my first husband whose life was cut so short on a battlefield so bloody that, even now, nobody talks about his death. 'I mean only that I hope you will come home to me and to your son Edward,' I say quietly. I go up to the side of his horse and put my hand on his knee. 'I am your wife, and I give you a wife's blessing. My heart will be with you every step of the way, I will pray for you every day.'

'I will come home safe,' he says reassuringly. 'I fight at the side of my brother Edward and he has never been defeated on the battlefield, only ever by treachery. And if we can reconquer the English lands in France it will be the most glorious victory in generations.'

'Yes,' I say.

He bends low in his saddle and kisses me on the lips. 'Be brave,' he says. 'You are the wife of a commander of England. Perhaps I will come home to you with castles and great lands in

France. Keep my lands and keep my son and I will come home to you.'

I step back and he wheels his horse and his standard bearer lifts his pennant that unfurls in the breeze. The sign of the boar, Richard's badge, raises a cheer from his men, and he gives the signal for them to follow him. He loosens the reins and his horse eagerly starts forwards, and they go, under the broad stone archway where the tramped feet echo over the drawbridge which spans the moat, as the ducks scutter away in fright, and then down the road past Middleham, and south, south to meet the king, south over the narrow seas, south to France to restore England to the days when the English kings ruled France and English farmers grew olives and grapes.

LONDON, SUMMER 1475

I move from Middleham Castle to our family house in London, Baynard's Castle, so that I can be close to the court and learn what is happening while my husband and his brothers are at war in France.

Queen Elizabeth keeps her court at Westminster. Her son, the little Prince Edward, is named as ruler of England in his father's absence, and she is glorying in her importance as the wife of a king on campaign, and as the mother of the prince. Her brother Anthony Woodville, the prince's guardian, has gone with the king to France, so her son is in her sole keeping. She is the leader of his council and his advisors and tutors are all chosen by her. The power of the kingdom is supposed to be vested in a council, but this is led by the newly appointed Cardinal Bourchier, and since he owes his red hat entirely to the king, he is at her beck and call. In the absence of anyone else, Elizabeth Woodville is leader of the House of York. She is all but regent, she is all but ruling. She is a self-made woman and has grown grand indeed: from squire's wife to all but queen regnant.

Like half of England, I cannot imagine the disaster that would overtake the country if our king were to die in France and the throne be inherited by this little boy. Like half of the country I suddenly realise what extraordinary power has been vested in this family from Northamptonshire. If the king were to die on this campaign, just as Henry V died on his campaign in France, it would put all of England into the hands of the Rivers family forever. They completely dominate the Prince of Wales and increase their power step by step across the country, as they appoint their friends or their kin into every place that becomes vacant. The prince's mentor and guardian is the queen's beloved brother Anthony Woodville Lord Rivers, the prince's council is headed by her and managed by him. The prince is richly endowed with Woodville brothers and sisters, as well as aunts and uncles for both Elizabeth Woodville and her mother, the witch Jacquetta, have been unnaturally – suspiciously – fertile. Those of us who are royal kin to the king hardly know the little princes – they are forever surrounded by the Rivers and their friends or their servants. The little boy is my husband's blood nephew and yet we never see him. He lives alone at Ludlow with Anthony Lord Rivers, and when he does come to court for Christmas or Easter he is dominated by his mother and his sisters who fall on him with joy and never let him out of their sight for the entire visit.

We have destroyed the House of Lancaster but in its place, as I now understand, we have allowed a new rival house, the House of Rivers, the Woodvilles who have their friends, their favourites or themselves in every position of power in the kingdom and the heir is a boy of their making.

If the king were to die in France it would be to make the Rivers the new royal family of England. Neither George nor Richard would be welcomed at court. And then, almost certainly, there would be war all over again. There is no doubt in my mind that George would oppose the usurpation of the Rivers, and he would be right to do so. They have no royal blood, they have not been chosen to rule. What Richard would do, I can hardly guess. His love and loyalty to his brother Edward runs very deep; but like everyone else who sees the queen's grasping ways, he cannot endure the power of his brother's wife and her family. I think it almost certain that the two brothers of York would turn on the

Rivers and England would be torn apart by a war of rival houses once again.

She invites me to a dinner to celebrate the good news that they have landed safely and started to march in France, and as I go in to the noise and bright lights of the queen's presence chamber I am surprised and delighted to see my sister Isabel at her side.

I curtsey to the queen and then when she offers me her cool cheek, I kiss her as my sister-in-law, I kiss all three York girls, and curtsey to the five-year-old prince, and the toddler his brother. Only then, when I have worked my way through this extensive family, can I turn to my sister. I had been afraid that she would be angry with me for failing to be with her in her confinement but she hugs me at once. 'Annie! I am so glad you are here. I have only just arrived or I would have come to your house.'

'I couldn't come, Richard wouldn't let me come to your confinement,' I say in a sudden rush of joy as I first hold her and then lean back to take in her smiling face. 'I wanted to; but Richard wouldn't allow it.'

'I know,' she says. 'George didn't want me to ask you. Have they quarrelled?'

I shake my head. 'Not here,' is all I say. The slightest tip of my head warns Isabel that Queen Elizabeth, who is apparently leaning down to speak to her son, is almost certainly listening to every word we say.

She slides her arm around my waist and we go as if to admire the new royal baby: another girl. The nursemaid shows her to us and then takes her to the nursery.

'I think my Edward is a stronger child,' Isabel remarks. 'But She always has such beautiful babies, doesn't she? How does she do it, do you think?'

I shake my head. I am not going to discuss the dangerous topics of the queen's remarkable fertility or the success of her child-rearing.

Isabel follows my lead. 'So – d'you know what is wrong between your husband and mine? Have they quarrelled?'

'I overheard them,' I confess. 'I listened at the door. It's not the money, Iz, not mother's inheritance. It's worse.' I lower my voice. 'I am very afraid that George may be preparing to challenge the king.'

She glances behind her at once, but in the noisy court we are alone and cannot be overheard. 'Did he say so to Richard? Are you sure?'

'Didn't you know?'

'He has men coming to him all the time, he is building up his affinity, he is taking advice from astrologers. But I thought it was for this invasion of France. He has brought more than a thousand men into the field. He and Richard have the greatest of the armies, they outnumber the king's men. But I thought that George was mustering his men for his brother Edward, for this invasion of France. He surely cannot be thinking of claiming the throne when he has just put an army together to support Edward?'

'Does he really think that Edward has no true claim to the throne?' I ask curiously. 'That's what he said to Richard.'

Isabel shrugs. 'We all know what is said,' she answers shortly. 'Edward looks nothing like his father, and he was born out of the country, during a time when his father was away fighting the French. There have always been rumours about him.' She glances over to the royal family, at the queen among her beautiful children, laughing at something her daughter Elizabeth is saying. 'And come to that, nobody witnessed their wedding. How do we know it was properly done, with a proper priest?'

I can't bear to speak of invalid weddings with Isabel. 'My husband won't hear a word of it,' I say. 'I can't speak of it.'

'Is your sister telling you all about her new baby?' the queen interrupts, calling across the room. 'We have a richness of Edwards, do we not? We all have an Edward now.'

'Many Edwards, but only one prince,' my sister replies gracefully. 'And you and His Grace the king are blessed with a fine nursery of many children.'

Queen Elizabeth looks complacently at the girls who are playing with their brother the Prince of Wales. 'Well, God bless them all,' she says pleasantly. 'I hope to have as many as my mother did, and she gave her husband fourteen children. Let us all hope to be as fertile as our mothers!'

Isabel freezes, the smile vanishing from her face. The queen turns away to speak to someone else, and I say urgently: 'What's the matter? What's the matter, Iz?'

'She cursed us,' she whispers to me, her voice a thread. 'Did you hear her? She cursed us to have children like our mother. Two girls.'

'She didn't,' I say. 'She was just talking about her mother's fourteen children.'

Isabel shakes her head. 'She knows that George would inherit the throne if her sons were to die,' she says. 'And she doesn't want my boy to succeed. I think she just cursed us. She cursed my son, in front of everyone. She wished that I would have the issue that my mother had: two girls. She cursed you too: two girls. She has just ill-wished our boys. She has just wished them dead.'

Isabel is so shaken that I take her out of sight of the queen, behind some people who are learning a new dance. They are making a lot of noise and practising the steps over and over. Nobody pays any attention to us at all.

We stand near an open window until the colour comes back into her cheeks. 'Iz – you cannot fear the queen like this,' I say anxiously. 'You cannot hear curses and witchcraft in everything she says. You cannot suspect her all the time and speak your fears. We are settled now, the king has forgiven George and rides with him at his side. You and I have our fortune. Richard and George may squabble about the future; but we should be at peace.'

She shakes her head, still frightened. 'You know that we are not at peace. And now I am wondering what is happening in France right now. I thought that my husband had mustered an army to support his brother the king in a foreign war. But he has a thousand men under his command and they will do whatever he wants. What if George plans to turn against the king? What if he has planned it all along? What if he is going to kill Edward in France and come back and take the throne from the Rivers?'

Isabel and I wait for anxious weeks, wondering if the English army, far from fighting the French, has fallen to fighting itself. Her terror and mine is that George is following my father's plan of marching in the vanguard and then closing in to attack. Then Richard sends me a letter to tell me that their plans have all gone wrong. Their ally, the Duke of Burgundy, has marched out to set a siege, far away, of no use to our campaign at all. His duchess, Margaret of York – Richard's own sister – has no power to recall him to support her brothers as they land in Calais and march to Reims for Edward's coronation as King of France. Margaret, born and bred a loyal York girl, is despairing that she cannot make her husband support her three brothers. But the duke seems to have lured them to fight with France so that he can make his own gains; all the allies seem to have their own ambitions. Only my husband would stick to the original plan if he could. He writes me a bitter account:

Burgundy pursues his own way. The queen's kinsman, our famed ally St Pol, the same. Now we are here ready for battle, we find that my brother has lost his desire to fight, and King Louis has offered him magnificent terms to leave the kingdom of France alone. Gold and the hand of his daughter the Princess Elizabeth so that she will be the next Queen of France turns out to be the price of our withdrawal. They have bought my brother.

Anne, only you will know how bitterly I am shamed by this. I wanted to win English lands in France for England again, I wanted to see our armies victorious in the plains of Picardy.

Instead we have become merchants, haggling over the price. There is nothing I can do to stop Edward and George snapping up this treaty, just as there was no way that I could drag my men out of the town of Amiens where King Louis served a feast of meats and an unending supply of wine, knowing that they would drink and eat until they were sick as dogs, and I am mortified that it is my badge on their collars. My men are poisoned with their own gluttony, and I am sick with shame.

I swear I will never trust Edward again. This is not kingly, this is not as Arthur of Camelot. This is behaviour as base as an archer's bastard and I cannot meet his eyes when I see him stuffing his mouth at King Louis' table and pocketing the gold forks.

BAYNARD'S CASTLE, LONDON, SEPTEMBER 1475

By September they are all home, richer than they dreamed, loaded with silver plate, jewels, crowns and promises of more to come. The king himself has seventy-five thousand crowns in his treasury as payment for his promise for a peace treaty to last for seven years, and the King of France will pay fifty thousand pounds a year, every year that Edward does not re-state his claim to English lands in France. George Duke of Clarence, who was always at his brother's side during the haggling, at the ready when there was easy money to be made, is named as the trustworthy councillor to arbitrate on this dishonourable pension, and he too is being paid a fortune. The only dissenting voice comes from my husband – of all the men who rode to France and came back richer, only my husband Richard warns Edward that this is no way to defeat the French king, cautions him that the commons of England will think that their taxes have been wasted, swears that the citizens of London and the gentry in parliament will turn against him for this dishonour, and begs him not to sell England's birthright for this pension. I think Richard is the only one in all of the great English army to speak against the treaty. Everyone else is too busy counting their own bribes.

'He knew I advised against it, he knew I wanted war, and yet the French king still gave me half a dozen hunters and a fortune in silver plate!' Richard exclaims in our private rooms, the door shut against eavesdroppers, his mother – thank God – at Fotheringhay and unable to add her voice to the complaints against the king.

'Did you accept it?'

'Of course. Everyone else has taken a fortune. William Hastings is taking two thousand crowns a year. And that's not all – Edward has agreed to release Margaret of Anjou!'

'Release the queen?'

'She's not to be called queen any more, she's to renounce her title and her claim on the crown of England. But she is to be released.'

A terrible fear strikes me. 'She wouldn't come to us? Richard, I really could not have her at one of our houses.'

He laughs out loud for the first time since his return home. 'God, no. She is going to France. Louis can take care of her if he wants her so much. They are well-suited. Both dishonourable, both greedy, both liars and both a disgrace to their thrones. If I had been Edward, I would have executed her and defeated him.' He pauses. 'But if I had been Edward I would never have stooped to this dishonourable truce.'

I put my hand on his shoulder. 'You did your duty. You mustered your men and you rode out to fight.'

'I feel as if my brother is Cain,' he says miserably. 'Both of them. Two Cains to sell their birthright for a mess of pottage. I am the only one that cares about honour. They laughed at me and called me a fool for chivalry, they said I dreamed of a better world that could never be; while they put their noses in the trough.' He turns his head and kisses my wrist. 'Anne,' he says quietly.

I bow my head and kiss his neck, his hairline, and then as he draws me into his lap, his closed eyes, his frowning eyebrows and his mouth. As he lies me down on the bed and takes me I reach for him and I pray that we are making another boy.

MIDDLEHAM CASTLE, YORKSHIRE, SUMMER 1476

Edward my son is three years old and released from the nursery, out of his gowns and into proper clothes. I have Richard's tailor make miniature copies of his father's dark handsome suits and I dress him myself every morning, threading the laces through the holes at the sleeves, pulling his riding boots on his little feet and telling him to stamp down. Soon his hair will have to be cut, but every morning of this summer I brush his golden-brown curls over his white lace collar and twist them around my fingers. I pray every month that another child comes, to be a brother to him, I even pray for a girl if that is the will of God. But month after month goes by and still my courses come and I never feel sick in the morning, and I never feel that wonderful faintness that tells a woman that she is with child.

I visit a herbalist, I summon a physician. The herbalist gives me the most vile potions to drink and a sachet of herbs to wear around my neck, the physician tells me to eat meat even on Fridays, and warns me that I am cold and dry in disposition and must become hot and moist. My ladies in waiting whisper to me that they know of a wise woman, a woman who has powers not of this world; she can make a baby, she can melt one away, she can call up a storm, whistle up a wind – I stop them there. 'I don't believe in such things,' I say stoutly. 'I don't think such things can be. And if they were, they would be against the will of God, and outside the knowledge of man, and I will have nothing to do with them.'

Richard never complains that our next child is a long time coming. But he knows that he is a fertile man; there are two children that I know of, from before we were married, and there may be more. His brother the king has bastards scattered round the three kingdoms and sired seven children with the queen. But Richard and I have only one: our precious Edward, and I have to wonder how the queen gets so many babies from one brother while I get only one; does she know things outside the will of God and the wisdom of man?

Every morning that I walk along the outer wall to the tower where Edward has his nursery I hear my heart beat a little faster for fear that he may be ill. He has gone through the childhood ailments, his little white teeth have come in, he grows, yet I always worry for him. He is never going to be a big-boned man, like his uncle the king. He is going to take after his father, lithe, short, slight of build. His father has made himself strong and powerful through constant practice and hard living, so perhaps Edward too can become strong. I love him completely, and I could not love him more than I do if we happened to be a poor family with nothing to leave to a son. But we are not. We are a great family, the greatest in the North, and I can never forget that he is our only heir. If we were to lose him, then we would lose not only our son but also our step into the future, and the massive fortune that Richard has put together by matching the grants from his brother the king with my vast inheritance would all be wasted, scattered among our kinsmen.

Isabel is far luckier than me. I cannot deny my jealousy of her easy conception of children, and the robust health of her babies. I cannot bear her to excel me in this. She writes to me that she had feared that our line was a weak one – our mother had only two girls, and that after a long wait. She reminds me that the queen cursed us, wishing our mother's weak seed on us. But the curse does not fix on Isabel, who already has two children, the pretty girl Margaret, and a son Edward, and she writes exultantly that she is pregnant again, and this time she is certain it will be another boy.

Her letter, scrawled in her wide hand, blotted with excessive ink in her joy, tells me that she is carrying the baby high, which is a certain sign of a boy, and that it kicks as strongly as a young lord. She asks me to tell our mother her good news and I write coldly in reply that while I am glad for her, and look forward to seeing her new baby, I do not visit our mother in her part of the castle, and that if Isabel wants her to have the good news she should tell her herself. She can write a letter to me and I will have it delivered for – as Isabel well knows – our Lady Mother is not allowed to receive any letters that we do not see first, and is not allowed to reply at all. As Isabel well knows, our Lady Mother is dead in the eyes of the law. Does Isabel want to challenge this now?

That silences her, as I knew it would. She is ashamed, as I am ashamed, that we have imprisoned our mother and stolen our inheritance from her. I never speak of Isabel to my mother, I never speak to her at all. I cannot bring myself to admit that she lives quite alone, our prisoner, in her rooms in the tower and that I never visit her, and she never sends for me.

I would always have had to keep her in strict confinement, there was no other choice. She could not be out in the world, leading a normal life as a widowed countess – it would have been to make a mockery of the act of parliament that declared her dead as Richard and George agreed. She could not be allowed to meet people and complain to them that she had been robbed. She could not be allowed to go on writing, as she did from Beaulieu Abbey, to every lady of the royal household calling on them as fellow ladies, in sisterhood, to defend her. We would never have been able to risk her living out in the world, challenging my inheritance and the very basis of our wealth, our ownership of this castle, the vast acres of our lands, my husband's great fortune.

Besides – what would she have lived on after George and Richard took everything? Where would have been her home since George and Richard took all her houses? But since she spoke to me, so terribly, so disturbingly, since she told me that she believes my marriage is invalid, since she named me, her own daughter, as a whore, since that day I cannot bear even to see her.

I never go to her room; I inquire after her health once a week from her lady in waiting. I ensure that she has the best dishes from the kitchen, the best wine from the cellar. She can walk in the courtyard before her tower, which is walled all round, and I keep a guard on the door. She can command musicians as long as I know who they are and they are searched when they arrive and leave. She goes to the chapel and takes mass, she goes to confession only with our priest, and he would tell me if she made any accusations. She has no cause to complain of her circumstances, and no-one can hear her complaint. But I make sure that I am never in the chapel when she comes in, I never walk in her garden. If I look down from the high window in the privy chamber and see her dully circling on the stony paths, I turn my head away. She is indeed as a dead woman, she is almost buried alive. She is – as I once feared she was – walled up.

I never tell Richard what she said about him, I never ask him is our marriage valid, is our son legitimate? And I never ask her if she is certain, or was she just speaking from spite to frighten me? I am never going to hear her say again that she thinks my marriage is invalid and that my husband tricked me into a false service and that I live with him now balanced on his goodwill, that he married me only for my fortune to him, and has made cold-hearted preparations to keep my fortune and lose me. To avoid her repeating this I am prepared to never hear her speak again. I will never let her say that to me – or to anyone else – as long as she lives.

I wish she had never said it, or that I had never heard it, or that having heard it I could simply forget it. I am sickened that she should say such a thing to me and I am unable to refute it. I am sickened that I should know, in my heart of hearts, that it is true. It eats away at my love for Richard. Not that he should marry me without a papal dispensation in the first place – I don't forget that we were so much in love and so steeped in desire that we could not wait. But that he should not apply for dispensation after our wedding, that he should keep that decision from me, and that – most chillingly and worst of all, far and away the worst thing – he should secure his rights to my inheritance even if he were to put me aside and deny his marriage to me.

I am bound to him, by my love, by my submission to his will, by my first passion, and since he is the father of my son and he is my lord. But what am I to him? That is what I want to know and what I can now – thanks to my mother – never confidently ask him.

In May Richard comes to me and says that he wants us to leave Edward at Middleham with his tutor and the lady of his household, and go to York to start the procession to Fotheringhay, for a solemn service: the reburial of his father.

'Margaret of Anjou's army beheaded him, and my brother Edmund, and put their heads on stakes above Micklegate Bar at York,' Richard says grimly. 'That's the sort of woman she was, your first mother-in-law.'

'You know I had no choice in my marriage,' I say, speaking steadily though I am irritated by the fact that he cannot forget or forgive that part of my life. 'And I was a child in Calais when that happened, and my father was fighting for York, fighting alongside your brother.'

He gestures with his hand. 'Yes, well, that doesn't matter now. What does matter is that I am going to have my father and brother honourably reburied. What d'you think?'

'I think it would be a very good thing to do,' I say. 'They lie at Pontefract now, don't they?'

'Yes. My mother would like them buried together in the family vault at Fotheringhay Castle. I should like him to be honoured properly. Edward has trusted me to arrange it all, he prefers me to George for this.'

'There could be no-one who would do it better,' I say warmly.

He smiles. 'Thank you. I know you are right. Edward is too careless and George has no love of chivalry and honour. But I shall take pride in doing it well. I shall be glad to see my father and brother properly buried.'

For a moment only I think of my own father's body dragged off the battlefield at Barnet, the blood pouring from his helmet, his head lolling, his great black horse lying down in the field, as if he were asleep. But Edward was a good enemy; he never abused the bodies of his foe. He showed them in public so that the people would know that they were dead, and then he allowed them to be buried. My father's corpse lies in Bisham Abbey, in the family vault, buried in honour but without ceremony. Isabel and I have never gone to pay our respects. My mother has never visited his grave, and now she never will. Bisham Abbey will not see her, till I bury her there, beside him: a better wife than she was a mother. 'What can I do to help?' is all I say.

He thinks. 'You can help me plan the route, and the ceremonies at each place. And you can advise me as to what people should wear and the ceremonies we should order. Nothing like this has ever been done before. I want it to go off perfectly.'

Richard, his Master of Horse and I plan the journey together, while our priest at Middleham advises as to the ceremonies of walking with the body and the prayers that should be said at each halt. Richard commissions a carved model of his father, to lie on top of his coffin, so that everyone can see the great man that he was, and adds a silver statue of an angel holding a golden crown over the effigy's head. This symbolises that the duke was a king by right, dying in his fight for his throne. It shows also how wise

Edward was, to trust only Richard with this ceremony and not his brother George. When George joined my father he denied that the duke was a king by right, and that his son Edward was legitimate. Only Richard and I know that George still says this, but now he speaks in secret.

Richard makes a beautiful procession to bring the body of his father and his brother from Pontefract to their home. The cortege travels south from York for seven days and at every stop it goes into great churches on the way to lie in state. Thousands of people file silently past it to pay their respects to the king who was never crowned, and are reminded of the glorious history of the House of York.

Six horses draped in black pull the carriages, and ahead of them rides a knight, quite alone, carrying the duke's banner as if he were going into battle. Behind him rides Richard, his head bowed, and behind him come the great men of the realm, all honouring our house, all honouring our fallen father.

For Richard this is more than a proper reburial of his father; this is a re-stating of his father's right to be King of England, King of France. His father was a great soldier who fought for his country, a greater commander, a greater strategist even than his son Edward. In this lengthy procession Richard honours his father, claims his kingship, reminds the country of the greatness and nobility of the House of York. We are everything the Rivers are not, and Richard shows this in the wealth and grace of this remembrance service.

Richard keeps watch by the coffins every night that they are on the road, rides before them every day on a black horse with dark blue trappings, his standard lowered before him. It is as if for the first time in his life he allows himself to grieve for the father he lost and for the world of nobility and honour that went with him.

I meet him at Fotheringhay and find him thoughtful and tender with me. He remembers that his dead father and mine were allies, kinsmen. His father died before my father's disastrous alliance with the bad queen, died even before he saw his son come to the throne, died before Richard had fought his first battle. That night, before Richard goes out for his last vigil by his father's coffin, we kneel in prayer together, side by side in the beautiful family church. 'He would have been glad of our marriage,' Richard says quietly as he rises to his feet. 'He would have been glad to know that we were married, despite everything else.'

For a moment, as he stands and I look up to him, the question *And is our marriage valid?* is on the tip of my tongue. But I see the grave sadness in his face, and then he turns and takes his place as one of the four knightly watchers who will stand all night around the coffin until dawn releases them from their vigil.

George and Isabel come to the funeral at Fotheringhay and she and I stand next to each other, both wearing beautiful gowns of the royal mourning colour of dark blue as the king and the queen and their family receive the two coffins at the cemetery at Fotheringhay church. Edward kisses the effigy's hand and I see George and then Richard follow suit. George is especially tender and pious in this scene, but nobody takes the eye more than the little princesses. The ten-year-old Princess Elizabeth, exquisitely beautiful, is in the forefront; she leads her sister Princess Mary by the hand, and behind them come ambassadors from all the countries in Christendom to honour the head of the royal family of York.

It is a masque – a performance rich in symbols as well as an act of mourning. Nobody can see the royal family burying their forebear as if he were a king without reflecting how kingly is Edward, and his brothers, how reverent is the little prince, and how enchanting and queenly are Elizabeth and her daughters. I cannot help but think that they are more like actors than real kings and queens. Elizabeth the queen is so poised and beautiful, and her girls – especially the Princess Elizabeth – so conscious of themselves and their place in the procession. At her age I was frightened that I might step on my mother's train, but little Princess Elizabeth walks with her head up, looking neither to left nor right, a little queen in the making.

I should admire her – everyone else seems to adore her, and perhaps if I had a daughter I would point to the princess and tell my little girl that she must learn the poise of her cousin. But since I don't have a little girl, though I pray for one, I cannot look at the Princess Elizabeth without irritation, and think her spoiled and artificial – a precocious pet who would be better confined to the schoolroom rather than walking through a serious ceremonial as if she were taking the steps of a dance, revelling in all the eyes on her.

'Minx,' my sister says briefly in my ear, and I have to lower my eyes and suppress my smile.

As ever, with anything that Edward does, there has to be a banquet and a great show. Richard sits beside his brother and drinks little and eats less, as more than a thousand guests dine in the castle, and thousands more in beautifully dressed tented pavilions outside. Throughout the dinner there is music playing and good wines poured, between each course there is a choir singing solemn beautiful anthems and fruit served. Elizabeth the queen sits on the right hand of her husband as if she were a fellow ruler of the kingdom and not merely a wife, a crown on her head, dark blue lace covering her hair, and she looks around her with the serene beauty of a woman who knows that her place is safe, and her life beyond challenge.

She catches me staring at her, and she gives me the glacial smile that she always shows me and Isabel, and I wonder if she is thinking, at this ceremonial reburial of her father-in-law, of her own father who died a hasty criminal death at the hands of my father. My father hauled hers into the town square at Chepstow, accused him of treason, and beheaded him – without trial, without rule of law – in public. His beloved son John died beside him, his last sight would have been his son's severed head.

Isabel, seated next to me, shivers as if someone had stepped on her grave. 'D'you see how she looks at us?' she whispers.

'Oh, Iz,' I reproach her. 'What can she do to hurt us now?

When the king loves George so much? When Richard is so honoured by them? When we two are royal duchesses? They went to France as allies, and they came home as good friends. I don't think she wastes much love on us but there is nothing she can do to us.'

'She can put us under an enchantment,' she says very softly. 'She can blow up a storm that nearly drowns us, you know that yourself. And every time my little Edward runs a fever, or is sleepless while he is cutting a tooth, I wonder if she has turned her evil gaze on us, and she is heating up his image, or putting a pin into his portrait.' Her hand covers the swell of her belly beneath her gown. 'I wear a specially blessed girdle,' she says. 'George got it from his advisor. It is specially blessed to ward off the evil eye, to protect me from Her.'

Of course my mind goes at once to Middleham and my own son, who could fall from his pony, or cut himself while practising jousting, catch a chill or take a fever, eat something bad, breathe a miasma, drink foul water. I shake my head to dismiss my fears. 'I doubt she even thinks about us,' I say stoutly. 'I bet she thinks of nothing but her own family, her two precious sons, and her brothers and sisters. We are nothing to her.'

Isabel shakes her head. 'She has a spy in every household in the land,' she says. 'She thinks about us, believe it. My lady in waiting told me that she prays every day that she never has to run into sanctuary again, that her husband holds his throne unchallenged. She prays for the destruction of her enemies. And she does more than pray. There are men who follow George everywhere he goes. She watches me in my household, I know she has a spy on me. She will have someone placed to watch you in yours.'

'Oh really, Iz, you sound like George!'

'Because he's right,' she says earnestly. 'He is right to watch the king and fear the queen. You'll see. One day you'll hear that I have died suddenly, without good reason, and it will be because she has ill-wished me.'

I cross myself. 'Don't say it!' I glance at the high table. The queen is dipping her fingers in a golden bowl of rosewater and wiping them on a linen towel held out to her by a kneeling manservant. She does not look like a woman who keeps herself safe by putting spies in the households of her sisters-in-law, and sticking pins in images. She looks like a woman who has nothing at all to fear.

'Iz,' I say gently. 'We fear her because we know what our father did to hers, and we know how wrong it was. His sin is on our conscience and we fear his victims. We fear her because she knows that we both hoped to steal her throne – one after the other – and we both were married to men who raised their standards against hers. She knows that both George and the prince, my first husband, would have killed Edward and put her in the Tower. But when we were defeated she received us. She didn't have us locked up. She didn't have us accused of treason and imprisoned. She has never shown anything but courtesy to us.'

'That's right,' she says. 'She has never shown anything but courtesy. No anger, no desire for revenge, no kindness, no warmth, no human feeling of any sort at all. Has she ever said to you that she can't forget what our father did to hers? After that first time? That terrible time when the witch her mother whistled up a cold wind that blew out all the candles?'

'One candle,' I correct her.

'Has she ever said she still feels rage? Has she ever said she forgives you? Has she ever said anything as a sister-in-law, as one woman to another, anything at all?'

Unwillingly, I shake my head.

'Nor to me. Not one word of anger, not one word of her revenge. Don't you think that proves that her malice is stored coldly inside her like ice in an ice house? She looks at us as if she is Melusina, the emblem of her house, half woman, half fish. She is as cold as a fish to me, and I swear to you that she is planning my death.'

I shake my head at the server who is offering us a dish.

'Take it,' Isabel prompts anxiously. 'She sent it from the high table to us. Don't refuse her.'

I take a spoonful of the potted hare. 'You don't fear it is poisoned?' I say, trying to laugh her out of her fears.

'You can laugh if you like; but one of her ladies told me that she had a secret enamel box, and in the box a scrap of paper with two names written on it. Two names written in blood, and that she swore the two named would not live.'

'What names?' I whisper, dropping the spoon in the dish, all appetite gone. I cannot go on pretending that I don't believe Isabel, that I am not afraid of the queen. 'What names does she have in secret?'

'I don't know,' she says. 'The lady in waiting didn't know. She only saw the paper, not the words. But what if they are our names? Yours and mine? What if she has a scrap of paper and the words written in blood are Anne and Isabel?'

Isabel and I have a week together at Fotheringhay before we go with the court to London. Isabel is going to give birth to this baby at their London home of L'Erber, and this time I will be allowed to share her confinement. Richard has no objection to me staying with Isabel in the London palace, as long as I visit court from time to time with him to keep on the best terms with the queen, and make sure to never hear one word against the royal family.

'It will be so nice to be together for a long time again,' Isabel says. 'And I like it best when you are there with me.'

'Richard says I can only stay for the last weeks,' I warn her. 'He does not want me under George's protection for too long. He says that George is talking against the king again and he doesn't want me to come under suspicion.'

'What does the king suspect? What does She suspect?'

I shrug. 'I don't know. But George is openly rude to her, Iz. And he has been far worse since the funerals.'

'It should have been him to organise the reburial of his father but the king did not trust him with it,' she says resentfully. 'It should be him at the side of the king but he is never invited. Do you think he does not notice that he is slighted? Slighted every day?'

'They do wrong to slight him,' I grant her. 'But it is more and more awkward. He looks sideways at the queen and whispers about her behind his hand, and he is so disrespectful of the king and careless with the king's friends.'

'Because She is always beside the king before anyone else can get there, or if not her then the king is with her Grey sons, or with William Hastings!' Isabel flares up. 'The king should cleave to his brothers, both his brothers. The truth is that though he says he has forgiven and forgotten George for following Father, he will never forgive and forget. And if he did ever forget, for even one minute, then She would remind him.'

I say nothing. The queen, though pointedly cool with Isabel and me, is icy with George. And her great confidant, her brother Anthony Woodville, smiles when George goes by as if he finds my brother-in-law's tinderbox temper amusing, and worthy of very little respect.

'Well, at any rate, I can come for the last three weeks,' I say. 'But send for me if you are ill. I will come at once if you are ill, whatever anyone says, and at least I shall be there for his birth.'

'You are calling the baby "him"!' she says gleefully. 'You think it will be a boy too.'

'How can I not, when you call it a boy all the time? What name will you give him?'

She smiles. 'We are calling him Richard for his grandfather, of course,' she says. 'And we hope your husband will stand as his godfather.'

I smile. 'Then you will have an Edward and a Richard, just like the royal princes,' I observe.

'That's what George says!' she crows. 'He says that if the king and the queen and her family were to disappear off the face of the earth then there would still be a Prince Edward Plantagenet to take the throne and a Prince Richard Plantagenet to come after him.'

'Yes, but it's hard to imagine what disaster could wipe the king and the queen off the face of the earth,' I say, lowering my voice cautiously.

Isabel giggles. 'I think my husband imagines it every day.'

'Then who is doing the ill-wishing?' I ask, thinking to score a point. 'Not Her!'

At once she looks grave and turns away. 'George is not ill-wishing the king,' she says quietly. 'That would be treason. I was speaking in jest.'

I should have taken a warning from that, but when we get back to London I am amazed at how George behaves around the court while Isabel rarely comes out of their private rooms to join everyone, as if to snub the queen and her household. George walks surrounded by his own particular friends; he is never seen without men of his choosing, and they stand guard around him, almost as if he feared attack within the high walls of Westminster Palace.

He comes to dinner in the great hall, as we all do, but once he is seated, in full view of everyone, he makes no pretence at eating. They set dishes before him and he glowers, as if he has been insulted, and does not even pick up his knife or spoon. He looks at the servers as if he fears the dish has been poisoned, and he lets everyone know that he eats only what his own cooks prepare, in his private rooms.

Any time of the day you can be certain to find the doors to the Clarence apartments bolted shut with a double guard on the door as if he thinks someone might storm the rooms and kidnap Isabel. When I visit her, I have to wait outside the double doors for someone to call my name, then a shouted order comes from behind the closed door, and the guards lower their pikes and let me in.

'He is behaving like a fool,' my husband rules. 'It is a performance of suspicion like a masque, and if Edward stands for it because he is lazy and indulgent with George, he can be very sure that the queen will not.'

'He cannot really think that he is endangered?'

Richard scowls. 'Anne, I really don't know what he thinks. He has not spoken to me about Edward since I told him that I took his warnings to be treason. But he speaks to many others. He speaks ill of the queen—'

'What does he say of her?'

'He constantly speaks ill of the king.'

'Yes, but what does he say?'

Richard turns and stares out of the mullioned window. 'I can hardly repeat it,' he says. 'I wouldn't stoop to repeat it. Let me leave it that he says the worst thing one can say of a man, and the worst thing one can say of a woman.'

I don't press him, as I have learned that his sense of honour is always alert. Besides, I don't need to ask, I can guess. George will have been saying that his brother Edward is a bastard – slandering and dishonouring his own mother in the attempt to show that he should be king. And he will be saying that Elizabeth got into the king's bed by witchcraft and that their marriage is not holy or valid, and that their children are bastards too.

'And I am afraid that George is taking money from Louis of France.'

'Everyone is taking money from Louis of France.'

Richard laughs shortly. 'None more than the king. No – I don't mean the pensions, I mean that Louis is paying George secretly to behave like this, mustering men and reciting his claims to the throne. I am afraid Louis will pay George to make an attempt on the throne. It would suit him to have the country at war again. God knows what George is thinking.'

I don't say that George will be thinking what George is always thinking – how he can get the most advantage from any situation. 'What is the king thinking?'

'He laughs,' Richard says. 'He laughs and says that George is a faithless dog, and that our mother will speak to him, and that after all, there is little that George can do except curse and glower.'

'And what does the queen say?' I ask, knowing that she will oppose any slur on her children, she would fight to the death for her son, and that it will be her advice that will control the king.

'She says nothing,' Richard replies drily. 'Or at any rate, she says nothing to me. But I think if George continues the way he is going she will see him as her enemy, and the enemy of her sons. I would not want to be her enemy.'

I think of the scrap of paper in the enamelled box and the two names written in blood. 'Neither would I.'

When I next go to the Clarence apartments the door is standing open and they are carrying boxes out, down the tower stairs to the stable yard. Isabel is sitting by the fire, with her travelling cloak around her shoulders, her hand on her big belly.

'What's happening?' I ask, coming into the room. 'What are you doing?'

She gets to her feet. 'We're leaving,' she says. 'Walk me down to the stable yard.'

I take her hand to keep her inside the chamber. 'You can't travel like this. Where are you going? I thought you were going to L'Erber for your confinement?'

'George says we can't stay at court,' she says. 'It's not safe. We won't be safe even at L'Erber. I'm going into confinement at Tewkesbury Abbey.'

'Halfway to Wales?' I exclaim in horror. 'Iz, you can't!'

'I have to go,' she says. 'Help me, Anne.'

I take her hand in my arm and she leans on me as we go down the winding stone stairs and out into the cold bright stable yard. She gives a little gasp at a stab of pain in her belly. I am certain that she is not fit to make the journey. 'Isabel, don't go. Don't travel like this. Come to my house if you won't go to your own.'

'We're not safe in London,' she whispers. 'She tried to poison George and me. She sent poisoned food to our rooms.'

'No!'

'She did. George says that we are not safe at court nor even in London. He says that the queen's enmity is too great a danger. Annie, you should leave too. Get Richard to take you home to Middleham. George says that she will turn Edward against both his brothers. He says she will strike against us this Christmas. She will bring the court together for the Christmas feast and then accuse both brothers and have them arrested.'

I am so frightened that I can hardly speak. I take both her hands in mine. 'Isabel, surely this is madness. George is making a war in his dreams, he constantly speaks against the king and his right to the throne, he whispers against the queen. The dangers are all of his own making.'

She laughs without humour. 'D'you think so?'

George's master of horse brings up her litter, drawn by matched mules. Her ladies in waiting draw back the curtains and I help her seat herself on the soft cushions. The maids put hot bricks beneath her feet and the kitchen boy comes with a brass tray of hot coals.

'I do,' I say. 'I do.' I am trying to suppress my fear for her, so near her time, travelling cross-country on muddy roads. I cannot forget that she had to travel near her time once before and that ended in a death and heartbreak and the loss of a son. I lean into the litter and whisper: 'The king and the queen are bent on pleasure this Christmas, and showing off their new clothes and their endless children. They're drunk on vanity and luxury. We're not in danger, neither of us are in danger, nor our husbands. They're the king's own brothers, they're royal dukes. The king loves them. We are safe.'

Her face is white with the strain. 'I have a dead lapdog who stole a piece of chicken from a dish meant for me,' she says. 'I tell you, the queen is set on my death, on yours too.'

I am so horrified I cannot speak. I just hold her hand and warm it between my own. 'Iz, don't go like this.'

'George knows, I tell you. He knows for certain. He's had a warning from someone in her household. She is going to have both brothers arrested and executed.'

I kiss her hands and her cheeks. 'Dearest Iz . . .'

She puts her arms around my neck and hugs me. 'Go to Middleham,' she whispers. 'For me: because I ask it of you. For your own safety: because I am warning you. For your boy: to keep him safe. For God's sake go. Get away from here, Annie. I swear they will have us all killed. She will not stop until your husband and my husband and both of us are dead.'

All through the cold days which grow increasingly dark and wintry I look for news of Isabel's confinement, and think of her in the guest rooms of Tewkesbury Abbey, waiting for her baby to come. I know that George will have provided her with the best of midwives, there will be a physician nearby, and companions to cheer her, and a wet nurse waiting, and the rooms will be warm and comfortable for her. But still I wish I could have been with her. The birth of another child to a royal duke is an important event, and George will have left nothing to chance. If it is a boy then it establishes him as a man with two heirs – as good as his brother the king. Still, I wish I had been allowed to go to her. Still, I wish that he had allowed her to stay in London.

I go to Richard as he sits at his table in his privy chamber to ask him if I may join Isabel in Tewkesbury, and he refuses me out of hand. 'George's household has become a centre of treason,' he says flatly. 'I have seen some of the sermons and chapbooks which are being written under his patronage. They question my brother's legitimacy, they name my mother as a whore, and my father as a cuckold. They suggest his marriage to the queen is invalid and that his sons are bastards. It is shameful what George is saying. I cannot forgive it, Edward cannot overlook it. Edward is going to have to act against him.'

'Would he do anything to Isabel?'

'Of course not,' Richard says impatiently. 'What has she to do with it?'

'Then can't I go to her?'

'We can't associate with them,' Richard rules. 'George is impossible. We cannot be seen near him.'

'She is my sister! She has done nothing.'

'Perhaps after Christmas. If Edward does not arrest him before then.'

I go to the door and put my hand on the brass ring. 'Can we go home to Middleham?'

'Not before the Christmas feast, it would be to insult the king and queen. George leaving the city so suddenly is insult enough. I won't make matters worse.' He hesitates, his pen raised over a document for signing. 'What is it? Are you missing Edward?'

'I am afraid,' I whisper to him. 'I am afraid. Isabel told me something, warned me . . .'

He does not try to reassure me. He does not ask me what was Isabel's warning. Later, when I think about it, that is the worst of it. He merely nods. 'You have nothing to fear,' he says. 'I am guarding us. And besides, if we left it would show that we were fearful too.'

In November I receive a letter from Isabel, travel-stained and delayed on the flooded roads. It is one of Isabel's exultant three-page scrawls.

I was right. I have a boy. He is a good size, long-limbed and fat, and fair like his father. He is feeding well and I am up and walking around already. The labour was quick and easy. I have told George that I will have another just like that! As many as he likes! I have written to the king and to the queen and she sent some very good linen with her congratulations.

George will attend court at Christmas after all, as he does not want to look as if he is afraid. Then he will meet me at Warwick Castle after the king's feast. You must come and see the baby after the twelfth night. George says there can be no objection to you visiting us on your way to Middleham, and that you are to tell your husband so, from him.

It has rained so much that I have not cared about being in confinement though I am getting tired of it now. I shall be churched in December and then we will go home. I can't wait to bring a new Richard into Warwick Castle. Father would have been so pleased, I would have been his favourite daughter forever – getting him a second grandson, and he would have plans for his greatness ...

And so on, and so on, over three crumpled pages, with afterthoughts in the margins. I put the letter to one side and place my hand on the softness of my belly as if the warmth of my hand could hatch a new baby as if it were a chick in a shell. Isabel is right to be happy and proud in the safe delivery of another baby, and I am glad for her. But she might have thought how her words would strike me: her younger sister, still only twenty years old, with only one little boy in the nursery, after four, nearly five years of marriage.

Her letter is not all boasting, for she writes one word at the end of the letter to show that she has not forgotten her fear of the queen.

Take care what you eat at the Christmas feast, my sister. You know what I mean – Iz

The door of my presence chamber opens and Richard comes in with his half-dozen friends, to escort me and my ladies to dinner. I stand and smile at him.

'Good news?' Richard asks, looking at the letter on the table beside me.

'Oh yes!' I say, holding my smile. 'Very.'

WESTMINSTER PALACE, LONDON, CHRISTMAS DAY 1476

It is the season of Christmas and the royal family will blaze in jewels and the bright colours of the new fabrics that they have bought in, at the price of a small fortune, from Burgundy. Edward plays the part of a king in a swirl of cloth of gold and colour and the queen is always at his side as if she were born to the place – and not the lucky upstart she truly is.

We wake early for mass in the king's chapel on this most holy day of the year. I have a great wooden bath, lined with the finest linen, rolled into my bedroom before the fire and the maids bring jugs of hot water and pour it around my shoulders as I wash my hair and my body with the rose-petal soap that Richard bought from the Moorish traders for me.

They wrap me in hot sheets while they lay out my gown for the day. I will wear deep red velvet trimmed with marten fur, a dark shiny pelt as good as anything the queen has. I have a new headdress that sits snugly on my head with coils of gold wire over my ears. They comb my hair dry as I sit before the warmth of the fire and then plait it and twist it up under the headdress. I have a new linen shift embroidered this summer by my ladies under my direction, and from the treasure room they bring my box and I pick out dark red rubies to match the gown.

When Richard comes to my presence chamber to accompany

me to mass he is dressed in black, his preferred colour. He looks handsome and happy and as I greet him I feel the familiar pulse of desire. Perhaps tonight he will come to my room and tonight we will make another child. What could be a better day than the day when the Christ-child was born, to make another heir for the dukedom of Gloucester?

He offers me his arm and the knights of his household, all richly dressed, escort my ladies to the king's chapel. We line up and wait, the king often keeps us waiting; but then there is a rustle and a little gasp from some of the ladies as he comes in, dressed in white and silver, and leading Her. She is in silver and white like him and she gleams in the shadows of the royal chapel as if she were lit by the moon. Her pale golden hair just shows beneath her crown, her neck is bare to the top of her gown, which is cut low and square and veiled with the finest lace. Behind them come their children, first the young Prince of Wales, six years old now, taller every time he comes to court, dressed to match his father, and then the nursemaid holding the hand of the little prince, still in his baby clothes of white and silver lace, then comes Princess Elizabeth dressed in white and silver like her parents, solemn with an ivory missal in her hand, smiling to one side and the other, poised and precocious as always, and behind her the rest of them, beautiful, royal, richly dressed little girls, all three of them and the new baby. I cannot watch them without envy.

I make sure that I am smiling, as the court smiles, to see this exquisite royal family walk by. The queen's grey gaze flickers over me and I feel the chill of her regard, and the astute measurement, as if she knows that I am envious, as if she knows that I am fearful; and then the priest comes in and I can kneel and close my eyes and spare myself the sight of them.

When we get back to our own presence chamber there is a man waiting outside the closed double doors, travel-stained with his wet and muddy cape thrown on the stone windowsill. Our household guard bars the door to him, waiting for our return.

'What's this?' Richard asks.

He drops to one knee, and holds out a letter. I see a red wax seal. Richard breaks it, and reads the few lines on the one page. I see his face darken and then he glances at me and back down at the page.

'What is it?' I cannot say what I fear – I think at once with horror that it might be a letter from Middleham about our son. 'What is it, Richard? My lord? I pray you . . .' I snatch a breath. 'Tell me. Tell me quickly.'

He does not answer me at once. He nods over his shoulder to one of his household knights. 'Wait there. Hold the messenger, I'll want to see him. See he speaks to no-one.'

Me, he takes by the arm and walks through our presence chamber, through my privy chamber and into my bedroom where no-one will disturb us.

'What?' I whisper. 'Richard, for God's sake – what is it? Is it our boy, Edward?'

'It's your sister,' he says. His quiet voice makes it sound almost like a question, as if he cannot believe what he has read himself. 'It's about your sister.'

'Isabel?'

'Yes. My love – I don't know how to tell you – George wrote to me, this is his letter, he told me to tell you; but I don't know how to tell you . . .'

'What? What about her?'

'My love, my poor love – she's dead. George writes that she is dead.'

For a moment, I cannot hear the words. Then I hear them, as if they are clanging like a bell right here, in my bedroom, where only two hours ago I was dressing in my gown and choosing my rubies. 'Isabel?'

'Yes. She's dead, George says.'

'But how? She was well, she wrote to me, she said it was an

easy labour. I had her letter, full of self-praise. She was well, she was very well, she told me to come and see ...'

He pauses, as if he has an answer, but does not want to put words to it. 'I don't know how. That's why I'm going to speak with the messenger.'

'Was she ill?'

'I don't know.'

'Did she have childbed fever? Did she bleed?'

'George doesn't say that.'

'What does he say?'

For a moment, I think he is going to refuse to answer me, but then he spreads the letter open, smoothing it flat on the table, and gives it to me, watching my face as I read the words.

22 December 1476
Brother and Sister Anne,

My beloved wife Isabel died this morning, may God keep her soul. There is no doubt in my mind that she was poisoned by an agent of the queen. Keep your wife safe, Richard, and keep yourself safe. There is no doubt in my mind that we are all in danger from the false family that our brother the king has brought about. My baby son yet lives. I pray for you and yours. Burn this.

Richard takes the letter from my hand and, leaning towards the fire, pushes it into the red embers and stands over it as the paper curls black and then suddenly flares into flame.

'She knew it would happen.' I find I am shaking, from my fingertips to my feet, as if the letter has frozen me with a whistle of an icy gale. 'She said it would happen.'

Richard takes hold of me and pushes me to sit on the bed as my knees give way beneath me. 'George said so too, but I wouldn't listen to him,' he says tersely.

'She said the queen had a spy in her house, and that she has a spy in our house too.'

'I don't doubt that. That's almost certainly true. The queen trusts no-one, and she pays servants for intelligence. So do we all. But why would she poison Isabel?'

'For revenge,' I say miserably. 'Because she has our names on a scrap of paper in an enamelled box hidden among her jewels.'

'What?'

'Isabel knew, but I wouldn't listen. She said the queen has sworn to be avenged on the murderers of her father – that would be our father. Isabel said she had written our names in blood on a scrap of paper and kept them hidden. Isabel said that one day I would hear she was dead and she would have been poisoned.'

Richard's hand is on his belt, where his sword would be, as if he thinks we might have to fight for our lives here, in the Palace of Westminster.

'I didn't listen!' The loss of her suddenly hits me and I am shaken by sobs. 'I didn't listen to her! And her baby! And Margaret! And Edward! They will have to grow up without a mother! And I didn't go to her! I told her she was safe.'

Richard goes to the door. 'I'm going to talk to the messenger,' he says.

'You wouldn't let me go to her!' I fire out.

'Just as well,' he says drily, and turns the handle of the door.

I scramble to my feet. 'I'll come too.'

'Not if you're going to cry.'

Roughly, I rub my wet face. 'I won't cry. I swear I won't cry.'

'I don't want this news getting about just yet, and not by accident. George will have written to the king also, announcing the death. I don't want us making accusations and you crying. You will have to be silent. You will have to be calm. And you will have to meet the queen and say nothing. We will have to act as if we think nothing against her.'

I grit my teeth and turn to him. 'If George is right, then the queen killed my sister.' I am not shaking any more and I am not sobbing either. 'If George's accusations are true, then she plans to kill me. If this is true then she is my mortal enemy and we are living in her palace and dining on the food that comes from her kitchen. See – I am not making accusations, and I am not crying. But I am going to protect me and mine, and I will see her pay for the death of my sister.'

'If it is true,' Richard says levelly.

It is like a pledge. 'If it is true,' I agree.

The court wears dark blue in mourning for my sister and I keep to my rooms as much as I can. I cannot bear to look at the queen. I truly believe that in her beautiful face I see the murderer of my sister. I am afraid for myself. Richard refuses absolutely to discuss anything until we meet with George and know more. But he sends his right-hand man Sir James Tyrrell to Middleham with instructions to guard our son, to examine every member of our household, especially any that are not Yorkshire born and bred, and to see that Edward's food is tasted before he eats anything.

I order my food to be cooked in our private rooms in the palace, and I stay in my privy chamber. I almost never sit with the queen. When I hear a sudden knock on the door I start from my chair and have to steady myself, holding the table by the fireplace. The guard on the door swings it open and announces George.

He comes in wearing deepest blue, his face drawn and tragic. He takes my hands and kisses me. When he draws back to look at me he has tears in his eyes.

'Oh, George,' I whisper.

All his smug confidence has gone; he is lean and handsome in grief. He leans his head against the carved chimney. 'I still can't believe it,' he says quietly. 'When I see you here – I can't believe that she is not here with you.'

'She wrote to me that she was well.'

'She was,' he says eagerly. 'She was. And so happy! And the baby: a beauty, as always. But then she suddenly weakened, fell away almost overnight, and in the morning she was gone.'

'Was it a fever?' I ask, hoping desperately that he will say yes.

'Her tongue was black,' he tells me.

I look at him aghast: it is a sure sign of poison. 'Who could have done it?'

'I have my physician inquiring into her household, into our kitchen. I know that the queen had a woman in Isabel's own confinement room, to report to her at once whether we had a boy or a girl.'

I give a little hiss of horror.

'Oh, that's nothing. I have known of it for months. She will have a servant set to watch you as well,' he says. 'And a man placed among the household, perhaps in your stables to warn her when you mean to travel, perhaps in your hall to listen to the talk. She has watched us all ever since we first came to her court. She will have watched you as well as Isabel. She trusts no-one.'

'Edward trusts my husband,' I protest. 'They love each other, they are faithful to each other.'

'And the queen?'

He laughs shortly at my silence.

'Will you speak to the king about this?' I ask. 'Will you name the queen's guilt?'

'I think he will offer me a bribe to buy me off,' George says. 'And I think I know what it will be. He will want to silence me, he will want me out of the way. He won't want me accusing his wife of being a poisoner, naming their children as bastards.'

'Hush,' I say, glancing at the door. I go to him at the fireplace so we are head to head, like conspirators, our words blowing up the chimney like smoke.

'Edward will want me out of the way, somewhere I can't speak against him.'

I am horrified. 'What will he do? He will not imprison you?'

George's smile is a grimace. 'He will command me to marry again,' he predicts. 'I know that is what he plans. He will send me to Burgundy to marry Mary of Burgundy. Her father is dead, our sister Margaret his widow has suggested my name. Mary is her step-daughter, she can give her in marriage to me. Edward sees this as a way of getting me out of the country.'

I can feel the tears spill down my cheeks. 'But Isabel has been dead less than a month,' I cry. 'Are you supposed to forget her at once? Is she to be buried and a new wife in her place within weeks? And what of your children? Are you supposed to take them with you to Flanders?'

'I'll refuse him,' George says. 'I will never leave my children, I will never leave my country, and I certainly will not leave the murderer of my wife to walk free.'

I am sobbing, the loss of her is so painful, the thought of George taking another wife so shocking. I feel so alone in this dangerous court without her. George puts his arm around my shaking shoulders. 'Sister,' he says tenderly. 'My sister. She loved you so much, she was so anxious to protect you. She made me promise that I would warn you. I will protect you too.'

As always, I have to wait in the queen's rooms in the hour before dinner for the king and his household to join us, so that we all go into the great hall together. The queen's ladies assume that I am quiet from grief, and leave me alone. Only Lady Margaret Stanley, recently come to court with her new husband Thomas, takes me to one side and tells me that she prays for the soul of my sister and for her blessed children. I am oddly touched by her goodwill and I try to smile and thank her for her prayers. She sent her own son, Henry Tudor, overseas, for his own safety, as she does not trust this king with his keeping. Young Tudor is of the House of Lancaster, a promising youth. She would not allow him to be raised by a York guardian in this country, and though she is now married to one of the lords of York and high in favour with both king and queen she still does not trust this royal family enough to bring her boy home. Of all the court she will understand what it is to fear the king that you serve, she knows what it is to curtsey to the queen, uncertain if she is your enemy.

When Richard comes in with his brother the king, all smiles, and takes me by the hand to lead me into dinner, I walk close to him and whisper that George has come to court and promised me that he will find the murderer of my sister.

'How will he do that from Flanders?' Richard asks caustically.

'He won't go,' I say. 'He refuses to go.'

Richard's crack of laughter is so loud that the king looks back and grins at him. 'What's the jest?' he asks.

'Nothing,' Richard calls to his brother. 'Nothing. My wife told me a jest about George.'

'Our duke?' the king asks, smiling at me. 'Our Duke of Burgundy? Our Prince of Scotland?' The queen laughs aloud and taps the king on the arm as if to reprove him for publicly mocking his brother though her grey eyes gleam. I seem to be the only person who does not understand the richness of the humour. Richard draws me to one side and lets the dinner procession go past us. 'It's not true,' he says. 'It's the reverse of the truth. It is George who is demanding a chance at the dukedom of Burgundy. He hopes to become the duke of one of the richest countries in Europe and marry Mary of Burgundy. Or if not her, then the Princess of Scotland. He's not particular as long as his next wife is wealthy and commands a kingdom.'

I shake my head. 'He told me himself he would not go. He is mourning Isabel. He doesn't want to go to Flanders. It is the king who is trying to get him out of the kingdom to silence him.'

'Nonsense. Edward would never allow it. He could never trust George as ruler of Flanders. The lands owned by the Dukes of

Burgundy are enormous. None of us would trust George with that power and wealth.'

I am cautious. 'Who told you that?'

Over his shoulder I can see the queen seating herself at the high table that looks over the great hall. She turns and sees me, head to head with my husband. I see her lean to the king and say one word, two, and then he turns and sees us both too. It is as if she is pointing me out, as if she is warning him about me. As her gaze flicks indifferently over me I shiver.

'What's the matter?' Richard asks.

'Who told you that George was trying to go to Flanders or to Scotland and that the king would not allow it?'

'The queen's brother, Anthony Woodville, Lord Rivers.'

'Oh,' is all I say. 'It must be true, then.'

She looks down the great hall at me and she gives me her beautiful inscrutable smile.

Rumours swirl around court and everyone seems to be talking about me, and about Isabel and George. It is generally known that my sister died suddenly, having come through the ordeal of childbirth, and people are starting to wonder if she could have been poisoned, and if so, who would have done such a thing. The rumours grow in intensity, more detailed and more fearful as George refuses to eat in the great hall, refuses to speak to the queen, takes off his hat but does not bow his head as she goes past, crosses his fingers behind his back so that anyone standing beside him can see that he is using the sign of protection against witchcraft against the queen as she goes by.

He is frightening her, in his turn. She goes pale when she sees him and she glances at her husband as if to ask what she should do in the face of this insane rudeness. She looks to her brother, Anthony Woodville, who used to laugh when he saw George stalking down the gallery, acknowledging no-one; but now he too scrutinises him, as if taking the measure of an adversary. The court is utterly divided between those who have benefited from the Rivers family's long ascendance, and those who hate them and are willing to suspect them of anything. More and more people watch the queen as if they wonder what powers she has, what she will be allowed to do.

I see George every day, for we are staying in London though I long to go home to Middleham. But the roads are too bogged down for travel and Middleham itself is snowed in. I have to stay at court though every time I walk into her rooms Elizabeth the queen receives my curtsey with a look of blank enmity, and her daughter, Princess Elizabeth, draws back her gown in a mirror copy of her grandmother the witch.

I am afraid of the queen now, and she knows it. I don't know the extent of her powers or what she would do to me. I don't know if she played any part in the death of my sister, or if that was nothing but Isabel's fearful imaginings – and now my own. And I am alone in these fears. I feel horribly alone in this merry beautiful flirtatious court, alert with gossip and rich with whispers. I cannot speak to my husband, who will hear nothing against his brother Edward, and I dare not be seen speaking to George, who swears to me in our one secret meeting that he will discover the murderer of my sister and destroy her – when he speaks of the murderer he always says 'her' – and then everyone will know what a woman of malice and evil powers can do.

George comes to our London home at Baynard's Castle to say farewell to his mother the duchess, who is leaving for Fotheringhay the next day. He is locked up with the duchess in her rooms for some time; he is her dearest son, and her enmity for the queen is well known. She does not discourage him of speaking ill of his brother or of the queen. She is a woman who has seen much of the world and she swears that the queen married Edward through enchantment, and that she has gone on using dark arts while the crown of England is on her head.

As George comes through the great hall he sees me at the doorway of my own rooms and hurries forwards. 'I hoped I would see you.'

'I am glad to see you, Brother.' I step back into my rooms and he follows me. My ladies move to one side and curtsey to George – he is a handsome man and I realise with a pang that he is now an eligible husband. I have to steady myself with a hand on the windowsill when I think that I may have to see another woman in Izzy's place. Her children will run to another woman and call her 'Mother'. They are so young, they will forget how Isabel loved them, what she wanted for them.

'Richard tells me that you are not going to marry Mary of Burgundy,' I say quietly to him.

'No,' he says. 'But who do you think is going to marry the sister to the Scottish king? They suggested the Scots princess for me, but who do you think is the king's preferred candidate?'

'Not you?' I ask.

He laughs shortly. 'My brother has decided I am safer kept close at hand. He will not send me to Flanders or to Scotland. The Scottish princess is to marry none other but Anthony Woodville.'

Now I am astounded. The queen's brother, born the son of a squire, surely cannot dream of marrying royalty? Is there no height that she will not attempt? Are we to accept anything that the Rivers propose for themselves?

George smiles at my astounded face. 'A daughter of a little manor in Grafton on the throne of England, her brother on the throne of Scotland,' he says drily. 'It is a climbing expedition. Elizabeth Woodville should carry her standard and plant a flag on the peaks. What next? Shall her brother become a bishop? Why should he not be Pope? Where will she stop? Can she become the Holy Roman Emperor?'

'How does she do it?'

His dark glance reminds me that we both know how she achieves her goals. I shake my head. 'She has the ear of the king because he loves her so dearly,' I say. 'He will do anything for her now.'

'And we all know how this woman, out of all the women that he could have had, took hold of his heart.'

BAYNARD'S CASTLE, LONDON, JANUARY 1477

The Christmas feast is over but many people are staying in London, trapped by the bad weather. The roads to the North are impassable, and Middleham is still closed in by snow. I think of its safety, guarded by storms, moated with the great rivers of the North, shielded by blizzards; and my son, safe and warm behind the thick walls before a roaring fire with the gifts I have sent him spread out on the rug before him.

In the middle of January there is a quiet tap on the door of my privy chamber, a little rat-a-tat-tat that is George's knock. I turn to my ladies. 'I'm going to the chapel,' I say. 'I'll go on my own.' They curtsey and stand as I leave the room and I take my missal and rosary and walk towards the chapel door. I sense George fall into step behind me and we slip into the shadowy empty chapel together. A priest is hearing confession in one corner of the church, a couple of squires muttering their sins. George and I step into one of the dark alcoves and I look at him for the first time.

He is as white as a drowned man in the gloom, his eyes hollow in his face. All his debonair good looks are wiped away. He looks like a man at the very end of his tether. 'What is it?' I whisper.

'My son,' he says brokenly. 'My son.'

My first thought is of my own son, my Edward. Pray to God

that he is safe at Middleham Castle, sledging in the snow, listening to the mummers, tasting a mug of Christmas ale. Pray God he is well and strong, untouched by plague or poison.

'Your son? Edward?'

'My baby, Richard. My baby, my beloved: Richard.'

I put my hand to my mouth, and beneath my fingers I can feel my lips tremble. 'Richard?'

Isabel's motherless baby is cared for by his wet nurse, a woman who had raised both Margaret and Edward, whose milk had fed them as if she were their mother. There is no reason why Isabel's third child should not thrive in her keeping. 'Richard?' I repeat. 'Not Richard?'

'He's dead,' George says. I can hardly hear his whisper. 'He's dead.' He chokes on the word. 'I just had a message from Warwick Castle. He's dead. My boy, Isabel's boy. He has gone to heaven to be with his mother, God bless his little soul.'

'Amen,' I whisper. I can feel a thickening in my throat, a burning in my eyes. I want to pitch down onto my bed and cry for a week for my sister and my little nephew and the hardness of this world, that one after another takes all the people that I love.

George fumbles for my hand, grips it tight. 'They tell me that he died suddenly, unexpectedly,' he says.

Despite my own grief, I step back, pulling my hand from his grasp. I don't want to hear what he is going to say. 'Unexpectedly?'

He nods. 'He was thriving. Feeding well, gaining weight, starting to sleep through the night. I had Bessy Hodges as his wet nurse, I would never have left him if I had not thought he was doing well, for his own sake as well as his mother's. But he was well, Anne. I would never have left them if I had any doubt.'

'Babies can fail very suddenly,' I say weakly. 'You know that.'

'They say he was well at bedtime and died before dawn,' he says.

I shiver. 'Babies can die in their sleep,' I repeat. 'God spare them.'

'It's true,' he says. 'But I have to know if he just fell asleep, if it is innocent. I am leaving for Warwick right now. I shall have the truth of this, and if I find that someone killed him, dripped poison into his little sleeping mouth, then I will take their life for it – whoever they are, however grand their position, however great their name, whoever they are married to. I swear it, Anne. I shall have vengeance on whoever killed my wife, especially if she killed my son too.'

He turns for the door and I grip his arm. 'Write to me at once,' I whisper. 'Send me something, fruit or something with a note to tell me. Write it in such a way that I will understand but nobody else can know. Make sure that you tell me that Margaret is safe, and Edward.'

'I will,' he promises. 'And if I see the need I will send you a warning.'

'A warning?' I don't want to understand his meaning.

'You are in danger too, and your son is in danger. There is no doubt in my mind that this is more than an attack on me and mine. This is not an attack solely on me, though it strikes me to the heart; this is an attack on the kingmaker's daughters and his grandsons.'

At his naming this fear I find I am cold. I go as white as him, we are like two ghosts whispering together in the shadows of the chapel. 'An attack on the kingmaker's daughters?' I repeat. 'Why would anyone attack the kingmaker's daughters?' I ask, though I know the answer. 'He has been gone six years this spring. His enemies have all forgotten.'

'One enemy has not forgotten. She has two names written in blood on a piece of paper in her jewel box,' he says. He does not need to name the 'she'. 'Did you know this?'

Miserably, I nod.

'Do you know whose names they are?'

He waits for me to shake my head.

'Written in blood it says: "Isabel and Anne". Isabel is dead, I don't doubt that she plans you will be next.'

I am shaking in my fear. 'For vengeance?' I whisper.

'She wants revenge for the death of her father and her brother,' he replies. 'She has sworn herself to it. It is her only desire. Your father took her father and his son, she has taken Isabel and her son. I don't doubt she will kill you and your son Edward.'

'Come back soon,' I say. 'Come back to court, George. Don't leave me here alone at her court.'

'I swear it,' he says. He kisses my hand and is gone.

'I can't go to court,' I say flatly to Richard, as he stands before me, in rich dark velvet, ready to ride to Westminster where we are bidden for dinner. 'I can't go. I swear I cannot go.'

'We agreed,' he says quietly. 'We agreed that until we knew the truth of the rumours that you would attend court, sit with the queen when invited, behave as if nothing has happened.'

'Something has happened,' I say. 'You will have heard that the little baby Richard is dead?'

He nods.

'He was thriving, he was born strong, and now he dies, only three months after his birth? Dies in his sleep with no cause?'

My husband turns to the fire and pushes a log into place with his booted foot. 'Babies die,' he says.

'Richard, I think She killed him. I can't go to court and sit in Her rooms and feel Her watching me, wondering what I know. I can't go to dinner and eat the food from Her kitchen. I cannot bring myself to meet Her.'

'Because you hate her?' he asks. 'My dearest brother's wife and the mother of his children?'

'Because I am afraid of Her,' I say. 'And perhaps you should be too, perhaps even he should be.'

George returns to London and comes at once to his mother's house to see Richard. My ladies tell me that the brothers are together, behind closed doors in Richard's council chamber. In a little while one of Richard's trusted grooms of the household comes and asks me will I attend my lord. I leave my ladies to their excited speculation and walk across the great hall to Richard's rooms.

When I enter I am shocked at George's appearance. He has grown even thinner during his absence, his face is lean and weary, he looks like a man who is undertaking work he can hardly bear to do. Richard glances up when I come in and holds out his hand to me. I stand beside his chair, handclasped.

'George has bad news from Warwick,' Richard says to me shortly.

I wait.

George's face is grim, far older than his twenty-seven years. 'I have found Isabel's murderer. I have arrested her and brought her to trial. She was found guilty and put to death.'

I feel my knees weaken, and Richard gets up from his chair and presses me into his seat. 'You have to be brave,' he says. 'There is more and it is worse.'

'What can be worse?' I whisper.

'I found the murderer of my son also.' George's voice is a hard monotone. 'He too was found guilty by the jury that I sent him to, and was hanged. These two, at least, will be no danger to you or yours.'

I tighten my grip on Richard's hand.

'I have been inquiring ever since Isabel's death as to her murderer,' George says quietly. 'Her name was Ankarette, Ankarette Twynho, she was a maidservant in my wife's rooms. She served Isabel's meals, she brought her wine when she was in labour.'

Briefly I close my eyes, thinking of Isabel accepting the service and not knowing that she was being cared for by an enemy. I knew that I should have been there. I would have seen the servant for what she was.

'She was in the pay of the queen,' he says. 'God knows how long she has been spying on us. But when Isabel went into childbirth and was so happy and confident that it would be another boy – the queen ordered her servant to use the powders.'

'Powders?'

'Italian powders: poison.'

'You are sure?'

'I have the evidence, and the jury found her guilty and sentenced her to death.'

'He has only proof that Ankarette named the queen as her employer,' Richard intercedes. 'We can't be sure the queen ordered the murder.'

'Who else would hurt Isabel?' George says simply. 'Was she not beloved, by everyone who knew her?'

I nod blindly, my eyes filling with tears. 'And her little boy?'

'Ankarette went to Somerset as soon as Isabel was dead and her household dismissed,' George says. 'But she left the powders with her friend John Thursby, a groom of the household at Warwick. He gave them to the baby. The jury found them both guilty, they were both executed.'

I give a shuddering sigh, and I look up at Richard.

'You must guard yourself,' George cautions me. 'Eat nothing that comes from her kitchens, no wine but from your own cellars, have them open the bottles before you. Trust none of your servants. That's all you can do. We cannot protect ourselves from her witchcraft except by hiring our own witch. If she uses dark forces against us, I don't know what we can do.'

'The queen's guilt is not proven,' Richard says doggedly.

George laughs shortly. 'I have lost a wife, a blameless woman that the queen hated. I don't need more proof than that.'

Richard shakes his head. 'We cannot be divided,' he insists. 'We are the three sons of York. Edward had a sign, the three suns in the sky. We have come so far, we cannot be divided now.'

'I am true to Edward and I am true to you,' George swears. 'But Edward's wife is my enemy, and she is the enemy of your wife too. She has taken the best wife a man could have had from me, and a boy of my making. I shall make sure she does not hurt me again. I will employ food tasters, I will employ guards, and I will employ a sorcerer to protect me from her evil crafts.'

Richard turns away from the fireside and looks out of the window as if he could find an answer in the sleety rain.

'I shall go to Edward and tell him of this,' George says slowly. 'I don't see what else I can do.'

Richard bows his head to his duty as a son of York. 'I'll come with you.'

Richard never tells me in detail what passes between the three brothers in the meeting when Edward accuses George of taking the law into his own hands, packing a jury, inventing charges and executing two innocent people and George replies to his brother that Elizabeth Woodville set murderers on Isabel and her baby boy. Richard only tells me that the gulf between George and Edward is perhaps fatally wide, and that his loyalty to one brother is on the brink of destruction because of his love for the other, and that he fears where this will take us all.

'Can we go home to Middleham?' I ask.

'We go to dine at court,' he says grimly. 'We have to. Edward has to see I stand by him, the queen cannot see that you are afraid of her.'

My hands start to shake, so I clasp them behind my back. 'Please . . .'

'We have to go.'

The queen comes to dinner white-faced and biting her lips; the look she shoots at George would fell a weaker man. He bows low to her, with ironic respect, a flowery court bow like a player might make as a joke. She turns her shoulder towards George's table, speaks constantly to the king as if to prevent him even glancing at his brother, leans close to the king at dinner, sits at his side as they watch an entertainment, allowing no-one else near him; certainly not George, who stands leaning back against the wall and stares at her as if he would put her on trial too. The court is agog with the scandal and horrified at the accusations. Anthony Woodville goes everywhere with his thumbs in his sword belt, walking on the balls of his feet as if ready to spring up to defend his sister's honour. Nobody is laughing at George any more, not even the careless Rivers family who have always taken everything so lightly. Matters have become serious: we all wait to see what the king will do, whether he will allow the murderous witch to guide him, yet again.

'I am not afraid,' George tells me. We are seated by the fireside in my privy chamber at Baynard's Castle. Unseasonal rain is running down the windows, the skies are heavily grey. We are head to head not for warmth but for fear. Richard is at court, consulting with his brother Edward, trying to reconcile his brothers, trying to balance the unending drip of poisonous advice that is the counsel of the queen, trying to counteract the unending gossip that comes from L'Erber, where George's household speaks of a bastard clinging to the throne, a king enchanted by a witch, and a poisoner at work in the royal family. Richard believes that the brothers can be reconciled. Richard believes that the House of York can stand with honour – despite the Rivers family, despite their death-dealing queen.

'I am not afraid,' says George. 'I have my own powers.'

'Powers?'

'I have a sorcerer to protect me from her spells. I have hired a cunning man named Thomas Burdett, and two others, two astronomers from Oxford University. They are very skilled, very serious scholars, and they have foreseen the death of the king and the throwing down of the queen. Burdett has traced the influence of the queen, he can see her path through our lives like a silver slime. He tells me what is to be, and he assures me that the Rivers will fall by their own hand. The queen will hand over her sons to their murderer. She will end her own line.'

'It's against the law to forecast the death of the king,' I whisper.

'It's against the law to poison a duchess, and the queen did that without reprisal. I should like to see her challenge me. I am armed against her now, I don't fear her.' He rises to go. 'You always wear your crucifix?' he asks. 'You wear the amulet I gave you? You always carry your rosary in your pocket?'

'Always.'

'I will get Burdett to write a spell for you to carry, deep magic to hold her at bay.'

I shake my head. 'I don't believe in such things. I won't believe in such things. We should not fight her with magic, it means we are no better than her. What are we to do? How far should we go? Invoke the devil? Call up Satan?'

'I would have called up Satan himself to defend Isabel against her,' he says bitterly. 'For I have lost a wife I loved, to the queen's poisoner, I have lost my baby to her accomplice, and before that a son, my first son, in a storm of a witch's wind. She uses magic. She uses dark arts. We have to use them against her. We have to turn her own weapons against her.'

There is a knock at the door. 'Message for the Duke of Clarence!' someone shouts from outside.

'Here!' George shouts, and the messenger comes into the room and my husband Richard strolls in behind him.

'I didn't know you were here,' he remarks to George, casting a frowning glance at me; he is determined that we must be neutral in the struggle between the two brothers. George does not reply, as he is reading the message over and over again. Then he looks up. 'Did you know of this?' he demands of Richard. 'Or are you a part of it? Are you here to arrest me?'

'Arrest you?' Richard repeats. 'Why would I arrest you? Unless endless gossiping and rudeness and glumness is a crime, in which case I should.'

George does not respond to this joke at all. 'Richard, do you know of this: yes or no?'

'Of what? What does it say?'

'The king has arrested my friend, Thomas Burdett, my protector, my advisor. Arrested him and charged him with treason and sorcery.'

Richard's face is grim. 'Damnation. Has he done so?'

'Arrested my closest advisor? Yes. This is to threaten me.'

'Don't say so, George. Don't make it worse than it is. I knew only that he was thinking of it. I know that you have pushed him so far that he doesn't know what he should do.'

'You didn't warn me?'

'I warned you that your accusations and your spreading of slander and your insulting behaviour would cause trouble.'

'He is in mourning for his wife!' I protest. 'He knows that she was murdered. How should he behave?'

'Richard, you must support me.' George turns to him. 'Of course I have advisors to protect me against the ill-wishing of the queen, to guard me from poison and enchantments. Why should I not? When the whole court knows what she did to my wife? I have done nothing more than you.'

'Not so fast! I have not accused the queen of murder.'

'No; but have you set someone to guard your house? Your kitchens? Your wife? Your son?'

Richard bites his lip. 'George—'

'Brother, you must stand by me against her. She has taken my wife, she has her sights on me. She will murder your wife and then you. She is a woman of most terrible enmity. Richard, I call on you as my brother to stand by me. I beg you not to abandon me to her enmity. She will not stop until we three are dead, and our children too.'

'She is the queen,' Richard says. 'And you're not making any sense at all. She is greedy, God knows, and she has overmuch influence with Edward, but . . .'

George flings himself to the door. 'The king shall not hurt one hair of the head of this innocent man,' he says. 'This is Her doing. She thinks to pay me back for the death of Ankarette. They think to take my honest servant in payment for the death of their spy and poisoner. But she will see that she dare not touch me. I am a royal duke – does she think my servants can be thrown into a common gaol?'

George dashes out to save Burdett; but he cannot save him. The royal inquiry into Burdett and his colleagues – for George has hired two other advisors, and possibly more – reveals a plot of spells and forecasting, threats and fears. Many wise people do not believe one word of this; but Thomas Burdett, Dr John Stacey and Thomas Blake, his chaplain, are found guilty of treason and sentenced to be beheaded. Thomas Blake is saved from the scaffold by an appeal to Edward, but the other two are sent to die, protesting their innocence to the last moment. They refuse the traditional confession of their guilt that buys a man a quicker death and protects the inheritance of his heirs. Instead, they go to the scaffold like innocent men who will not be silenced, shouting that they have done nothing but study, that they are innocent of any wrongdoing, that the queen has turned their learning against them and has had them killed to ensure their silence.

George tears into the king's council meeting at Westminster, protesting his innocence, protesting the innocence of the dead men, and has his spokesman read the words of their speeches from the gallows – powerful words from men about to meet their maker, saying they are innocent of any charge.

'This is a declaration of war,' Richard says shortly. We are riding side by side through the streets of London, on our way to dine at court. The queen is about to go into confinement yet again, to prepare for the birth of yet another baby; this is a dinner to honour her before she withdraws. She is leaving a court buzzing with gossip about witchcraft, sorcerers and poisonings. She must feel as if all the peace and elegance that she has worked for is falling apart. She must feel as if she is discovered, as if her true nature, the fish beneath the woman, is pushing its scaly head through her very skin.

It is a hot May afternoon and I am dressed very richly in red silks, and my horse has a saddle of red leather and a red leather bridle. Richard has a new jerkin of black velvet with embroidered white linen beneath. We may be going to dinner; but I have eaten already. I never take anything that comes from the queen's kitchens now, and when she glances over to me she can see me with my fork poised to eat, crumbling bread, spreading the sauce with a spoon, and then putting my plate to one side. I pretend that I am eating food that comes from her kitchen, she pretends that she does not see that I am eating nothing. We both know that I think she will poison me if she can. We both know that I am not like George or my sister; I don't have the courage to challenge her in public. My husband is determined to be her friend. I am easy prey to her ill-will.

'A declaration of war?' I repeat. 'Why?'

'George is saying openly that Edward was not our father's true-born son and heir. He is telling everyone that Edward's marriage was brought about by witchcraft and his sons are bastards. He is saying Edward prevented him from marrying Mary of Burgundy because he knows that he would claim the throne of England with her army. He says that many people would rise in his support, that he is better loved than the king. He is openly repeating everything he has whispered before. This is as bad as a declaration of war. Edward will have to silence him.'

We ride into the courtyard of Westminster Palace, the herald announces our titles and the trumpeters blow a blast of welcome. The standard bearers dip the flags to acknowledge the arrival of a royal duke and duchess. My horse stands still as two liveried servants help me down from the saddle and I rejoin Richard as he waits in a doorway.

'How can the king silence his brother?' I pursue. 'Half of London is now saying the same thing. How can Edward silence them all?'

Richard puts my hand on his arm and smiles around at the people who throng the gallery that leads to the stable yard. He leads me onward. 'Edward can silence George. At last, I think he is driven to do it. He is going to give him one last warning and then he will charge him with treason.'

The crime of treason carries a death sentence. Edward the king is going to kill his own brother. I stop still with the shock and feel my head swim. Richard takes my hand. We stand for a moment, handclasped as if we are clinging to each other in this new and terrifying world. We don't notice the passing servants, or the courtiers hurrying by. Richard looks into my eyes and once again I know us for the children that we were, who had to make our own destiny in a world we could not understand.

'The queen has told Edward that she will not feel safe, going into her confinement, if George is still at large. She has demanded his arrest for her own safety. Edward has to satisfy her. She is putting the life of his child against his brother.'

'Tyranny!' I breathe the word and for once Richard does not defend his brother. His young face is dark with anxiety.

'God knows where we are going. God knows where the queen has taken us. We are the sons of York, Edward saw our three suns in the sky. How can we be divided by one woman?'

We turn into the great hall of Westminster Palace and Richard raises his hands to acknowledge the cheers and bows from the people gathered there and in the gallery to watch the nobility arrive. 'Do you eat the food?' he asks quietly.

I shake my head. 'I never eat the food from the queen's kitchen,' I tell him in a whisper. 'Not since George warned me.'

'Neither do I,' he says with a sigh. 'Not any more.'

We leave London, with George's fate still unsettled. I might almost say we flee from London. Richard and I ride north away from the city, which is racked with rumour and suspicion, to get home, where the air is clear and where people speak their minds and not for their own advantage, and where the great northern skies bear down on the mossy green hills and we can be at peace, far from court, far from the Woodville family and the Rivers adherents, far from the lethal mystery that is the Queen of England.

Our son Edward greets us with joy, and has much to show us with the bursting pride of a four-year-old. He has learned to ride his little pony and tilt at the quintain; his pony is a skilled steady little animal that knows its business and rides at a bright trot at exactly the right angle for Edward's little lance to hit the target. His tutor laughs and praises him and glances at me to see me alight with pride. He is progressing in his studies and is starting to read Latin and Greek. 'So hard!' I protest to his tutor.

'The earlier he starts, the easier it is for him to learn,' he assures me. 'And already he says his prayers and follows the mass in Latin. It is just to build on that knowledge.'

His tutor allows him days at liberty so that he and I can ride out together and I buy him a little merlin falcon so that he can

come hunting with us with his own bird. He is like a little nobleman in miniature, astride his stocky pony with the pretty falcon
on his wrist, and he rides all day and denies that he is tired,
though twice he falls asleep on the ride home and Richard,
astride his big hunter, carries his little son in his arms, while I
lead the pony.

At night he dines with us in the great hall, sitting between us at
the top table, looking down over the beautiful hall crowded with
our soldiers, guards and manservants. The people come in from
Middleham to see us dine, and to carry away the scraps from the
dinners and I hear them comment on the bearing and charm of
the little lord: my Edward. After dinner, when Richard withdraws
to his privy chamber and sits by the fire to read, I go with
Edward to the nursery tower and see him undressed and put to
bed. It is then, when he is newly washed and smelling sweet,
when his face is as smooth and as pale as the linen of his pillow,
that I kiss him and know what it is to love someone more than life
itself.

He prays before he sleeps, little Latin prayers that his nurse
has taught him to recite, hardly understanding their meaning.
But he is earnest over the prayer that names me and his father,
and once he is in bed and his dark lashes are softly lying on his
little cheek, I get to my knees beside his bed and pray that he
grows well and strong, that we can keep him safe. For surely
there never was a more precious boy in all of Yorkshire – no, not
in all of the world.

I spend every summer day with my little son, listening to him
read in the sun-drenched nursery, riding out with him over the
moor, fishing with him in the river, and playing catch, and bat
and ball in the inner courtyard, until he is so tired that he goes to
sleep on my lap as I read him his night-time story. These are easy
days for me, I eat well, and sleep deeply in my richly canopied
bed with Richard wrapped around me, as if we were lovers still in
our first year of marriage; and I wake in the morning to hear the
lapwing calling over the moorland, and the ceaseless chatter and

twitter of the nesting swallows and martlets that have made their nests in cups of mud under every corbel.

But no baby comes to us. I revel in my son but I long for another baby, I am yearning for another child. The wooden cradle stands below the stairs in the nursery tower. Edward should have a brother or a sister to play with – but no child comes. I am allowed to eat meat on fast days, a special letter from the Pope himself gives me permission to eat meat during Lent or any day of fasting. At dinner Richard carves for me the best cuts of the spring lamb, the fat of the meat, the skin of the roast chicken, but still no little body is made from the flesh. In our long passionate nights we cling together with a sort of desperate desire but we do not make a child; no baby grows inside me.

I had thought we would spend all the summer and autumn in our northern lands, perhaps going over to Barnard Castle, or looking at the rebuilding work at Sheriff Hutton, but Richard gets an urgent message from his brother Edward, summoning him back to London.

'I have to go, Edward needs me.'

'Is he ill?' I have a pang of fear for the king, and for a moment I think the unthinkable: can She have poisoned her own husband?

Richard is white with shock. 'Edward is well enough; but he's gone too far. He says he is putting a stop to George and his unending accusations. He has decided to charge George with treason.'

I put my hand to my throat where I can feel my heart hammer. 'He will never ... he could not ... he would not have him executed?'

'No, no, just charge him, and then hold him. Certainly, I shall insist that he holds him with honour, in his usual rooms in the Tower, where George can be well-served by his own servants and kept quiet until we find an agreement. I know that Edward has to silence him. George is completely out of control. Apparently he was trying to marry Mary of Burgundy only so that he could mount an invasion against Edward from Flanders. Edward has evidence now. George was taking money from the French, as we suspected. He was plotting against his own country, with France.'

'This is not true, I would swear that he did not plan to marry her,' I say earnestly. 'Isabel was hardly buried, George was beside himself. Remember how he was when he first came to court and told us! He told me himself that it was a plan of Edward's to get him out of the country, and only forbidden by the queen, who wanted Mary for her own brother Anthony.'

Richard's young face is a mask of worry. 'I don't know! I can't tell the truth of it any more. It's the word of one brother against another. I wish to God that the queen and her family would stay out of the business of ruling the country. If she would only stick to having children and leave Edward to rule as he sees fit, then none of this would ever happen.'

'But you will have to go . . .' I say plaintively.

He nods. 'I have to go to make sure that George is not harmed,' he says. 'If the queen is speaking against my brother, who will defend him but me?'

He turns and goes into our bedroom where his servants are packing his riding clothes into a bag. 'When will you come back?' I ask.

'As soon as I can.' His face is dark with worry. 'I have to make sure that this goes no further. I have to save George from the queen's rage.'

MIDDLEHAM CASTLE,
YORKSHIRE, AUTUMN 1477

The summer days with my son turn to autumn, and I send for the tailor from York to come and fit him for his winter clothes. He has grown during the summer, and there is much exclaiming at the new length of his riding trousers. The cobbler comes with new boots, and I agree, despite my own fears, that he shall go on to a bigger pony, and the little fell pony that has served him so well will be turned out to grass.

It is like a sentence of imprisonment when Richard rides home and tells me that we have to return to London to be at court for Christmas. Elizabeth the queen has come out of her confinement, mother to a new boy, her third; and as if to add lustre to her triumph, she has arranged for the betrothal of her younger royal son Richard to a magnificent heiress, the richest little girl in the kingdom, Anne Mowbray, a cousin of mine, and the heiress to the mighty Norfolk estate. Little Anne would have been a great match for my Edward. Their lands would have tallied, they would have made a powerful alliance, we are kinswomen, I have an interest in her. But I did not even bother to ask the family if they might consider Edward. I knew Elizabeth the queen would not let a little heiress like Anne into the world. I knew that she would secure her fortune for the Rivers family, for her precious son, Richard. They will be married as infants to satisfy the queen's greed.

'Richard, can we not stay here?' I ask. 'Can we not spend Christmas here for once?'

He shakes his head. 'Edward needs me,' he says. 'Now that George is imprisoned Edward needs his true friends even more, and I am the only brother he has left. He has William Hastings as his right-hand man, but apart from William – who can he talk to but her kinsmen? She has him surrounded. And they are a choir of harmony – they all advise him to send George into exile and forbid him ever to come again to England. He is confiscating George's goods, he is dividing up his lands. He has made up his mind.'

'But their children!' I exclaim, thinking of little Margaret and Edward his son. 'Who will care for them if their father is exiled?'

'They would be as orphans,' Richard says grimly. 'We have to go to court this Christmas to defend them as well as George.' He hesitates. 'Besides, I have to see George, I have to stand by him. I don't want to leave him on his own. He is much alone in the Tower, nobody dares to visit him, and he has become fearful of what might happen. I am certain that She can never persuade Edward to harm his brother, but I am afraid . . .' He breaks off.

'Afraid?' I repeat in a whisper, even though we are safe behind the thick walls of Middleham Castle.

He shrugs. 'I don't know. Sometimes I think I am as fearful as a woman, or as superstitious as George has become with his talk of necromancy and sorcery and God knows what darkness. But . . . I find I am afraid for George.'

'Afraid of what?' I ask again.

Richard shakes his head; he can hardly bear to name his fears. 'An accident?' he asks me. 'An illness? That he eats something that turns out to be bad? That he drinks to excess? I don't even want to think about it. That she works on his sorrow and on his fears so that he longs to end his own life and someone brings him a knife?'

I am horrified. 'He would never hurt himself,' I say. 'That's a sin so deep . . .'

'He's not like George any more,' Richard tells me miserably. 'His confidence, his charm, you know what he is like – it's all gone from him. I am afraid she is giving him dreams, I am afraid she is draining his courage. He says that he wakes in a terror and sees her leaving his bedroom, he says he knows she comes to him in the night and pours ice water into his heart. He says he has a pain which no doctor can cure, in his heart, under his ribs, in his very belly.'

I shake my head. 'It can't be done,' I maintain stoutly. 'She cannot work on someone else's mind. George is grieving, well so am I, and he is under arrest which would be enough to make any man fearful.'

'At any rate, I have to see him.'

'I don't like to leave Edward,' I say.

'I know. But he has the best childhood a boy could have here – I know it. This was my own childhood. He won't be lonely; he has his tutor and his lady of the household. I know he misses you and loves you but it is better for him to stay here than be dragged down to London.' He hesitates again. 'Anne, you have to agree to this: I don't want him at court . . .'

He needs to say nothing more than that. I shudder at the thought of the queen's cold gaze on my boy. 'No, no, we won't take him to London,' I say hastily. 'We'll leave him here.'

The Christmas feast is as grand as ever, the queen exultant, out of the birthing chamber, her new baby with the wet nurse, her new boy paraded around the court and mentioned in every conversation. I can almost taste the bitterness in my mouth when I see her boy, carried everywhere behind her, and her six other children.

'She's naming him George,' Richard tells me.

I gasp. 'George? Are you sure?'

His face is grim. 'I am sure. She told me herself. She told me and smiled as if I might be pleased.'

The poisonous humour of this appals me. She has had this innocent child's uncle arrested for speaking ill of her, threatened him with a charge that carries a death sentence, and she names her son for him? It is a sort of malicious madness, if it is nothing worse.

'What could be worse?' Richard asks.

'If she thought she were replacing one George with another,' I say very low, and I turn from his aghast face.

All her children are gathered here at court for Christmas. She flaunts them everywhere she goes, and they follow behind her, dancing in her footsteps. The oldest daughter, Princess Elizabeth, is eleven years old now, up to her tall mother's shoulder, long and lean as a Lenten lily, the darling of the court, and her father's particular favourite. Edward the Prince of Wales is here for the Christmas feast, taller and stronger every time he comes back to London, kind to his brother Richard, who is just a little boy but a stronger and sturdier little boy than my own son. I watch them go by with the wet nurse bringing up the rear with the new baby George, and I have to remind myself to smile in admiration.

The queen at least knows the smile is as real and as warm as her cool nod to me, and the offer of her smooth cheek to kiss. When I greet her I wonder if she can smell fear on my breath, in the cold sweat under my arms, if she knows that my thoughts are always with my brother-in-law, trapped by her in the Tower; if she knows that I can't see her happiness and her fertility and not fear for my own solitary son, and remember my own lost sister.

At the end of the Christmas feast there is the shameful charade of the betrothal of little Prince Richard, aged only four, to the six-year-old heiress Anne Mowbray. The little girl will inherit all the fortunes of the Dukes of Norfolk: she is their only heir. Or rather she *was* their only heir. But now Prince Richard will get this fortune, for the queen writes a marriage contract for them that ensures that he will have the little girl's wealth even if she dies as a child before they are old enough to be married, before she reaches adulthood. When my ladies tell me of this I have to make sure I don't shudder. I cannot help but think that the Norfolks have signed her death warrant. If the queen gets a great fortune on Anne's death, how long will the little girl live, after the contract has been signed?

There is a great celebration of the betrothal, which we all must attend. The little girl and the little prince are carried by their nursemaids in procession and are stood side by side on the high table in the great hall like a pair of little dolls. Nobody seeing this tableau of greed could doubt for a moment that the queen is in the heyday of her power, doing exactly what is her will.

The Rivers of course are delighted with the match and

celebrate with feasting and dancing and masquing and a wonderful joust. Anthony Woodville, the queen's beloved brother, fights in the joust in the disguise of a hermit in a white gown with his horse caparisoned in black velvet. Richard and I attend the betrothal in our finest clothes and try to appear happy; but the table where George and Isabel used to sit with their household is empty. My sister is dead and her husband imprisoned without trial. When the queen looks down the hall at me I smile back at her, and under the table I cross my fingers in the sign against witchcraft.

'We don't need to attend the joust if you don't wish to,' Richard says to me that night. He has joined me in my bedchamber in the palace, sitting before the fireplace in his gown. I climb into bed and pull the covers around my shoulders.

'Why don't we have to?'

'Edward said we could be excused.'

I ask the question that matters more and more at the court in these days. 'What about Her? Will She mind?'

'I don't think so. Her son Thomas Grey is to be one challenger, her brother is the first knight. The Rivers are in full flood. She won't much care whether we are there or not.'

'Why did Edward say you could be excused?' I hear the caution in my own voice. We are all afraid of everything at court now.

Richard rises and takes off his robe, pulls back the covers and gets into bed beside me. 'Because he sees that I am sick to my heart at George's imprisonment, and sick with fear at what might come next,' he says. 'He has no stomach for merrymaking either when our brother is in the Tower of London and the Queen of England is pressing for his death. Hold me, Anne. I am cold to my bones.'

They keep George in the Tower without trial, without visitors, in comfortable rooms – but he is imprisoned as a traitor for the rest of the year. Not until January does the queen finally get her way and persuade the king to bring him before the court and charge him with treason. The Rivers adherents have got hold of the jurors at the trial of Ankarette the poisoner, and persuaded them to say that they thought her innocent all along, even while they sent her to the gallows. My sister, they now declare, died quite naturally of the consequences of childbirth. Suddenly, Isabel had childbed fever, though when they were last consulted, they swore she was poisoned. They now say that George exceeded his authority in charging Ankarette and acted like a king himself, in having her executed, they say that he presumed on the royal state, they make him a traitor for punishing the murderer of his own wife. In one brilliant move they have hidden the murder, hidden the murderer the queen, exonerated her instrument, and shifted the blame for everything onto George.

The queen is everywhere in this matter, advising the king, warning of danger, complaining very sweetly that George cannot serve as a judge and an executioner in his town of Warwick, suggesting that this is practically a usurpation. If he will order a jury, if he will command an execution, where will he stop? Should he not be stopped? And finally?

Finally the king is driven into agreement with her and he himself undertakes the work of prosecuting his brother, and nobody – not one single man – speaks in George's defence. Richard comes home after the last day of the hearing with his shoulders bowed and his face dark. His mother and I meet him in the great hall and he takes us into his privy chamber and closes the door on the interested faces of our household.

'Edward has accused him of trying to destroy the royal family and their claim to the throne.' Richard glances at his mother. 'It's proven that George told everyone that the king was base-born – a bastard. I am sorry, Lady Mother.'

She waves it away. 'This is an old slander.' She looks at me. 'This is Warwick's old lie. Blame him, if anybody.'

'And they have proof that George's men were paid to go round the country saying that Thomas Burdett was innocent, and was murdered by the king for foretelling his death. Edward heard the evidence for that and it was good. George certainly hired people to speak against the king. George says that the king is using black arts – everyone supposes this is to accuse the queen of witchcraft. Finally, and almost worst of all: George has been taking money from Louis of France to create a rebellion against Edward. He was going to mount a rebellion and take the throne.'

'He would not,' his mother says simply.

'They had letters from Louis of France addressed to him.'

'Forgeries,' she says,

Richard sighs. 'Who knows? Not I. I am afraid, Lady Mother, that some of it – actually, most of it – is true. George hired a tenant's son and put him in the place of his own son, Edward of Warwick. He was sending young Edward to Flanders for safe-keeping.'

I draw a breath. This is Isabel's son, my nephew, sent to Flanders to keep him safe. 'Why didn't he send him to us?'

'He says he did not dare to let the boy stay in England, and the queen's malice would be his death. They cited this as evidence of his plotting.'

'Where is Edward now?' I ask.

'The child is in danger from the queen,' his grandmother says. 'That's not proof of George's guilt, it is proof of the queen's guilt.'

Richard answers me: 'Edward's spies arrested the boy at the port as he was about to take ship, and took him back to Warwick Castle.'

'Where is he now?' I repeat.

'At Warwick, with Margaret, his sister.'

'You must speak with your brother the king,' Duchess Cecily tells Richard. 'You must tell him that Elizabeth Woodville is the destruction of this family. There is no doubt in my mind that she poisoned Isabel, and that she will destroy George too. You have to make Edward see that. You have to save George, you have to safeguard his children. Edward is your nephew. If he is not safe in England you have to protect him.'

Richard turns to his mother. 'Forgive me,' he says. 'I have tried. But the queen has Edward in thrall, he won't listen to me any more. I cannot advise him. I cannot advise him against Her.'

The duchess walks the length of the room, her head bowed. For the first time she looks like an old woman, exhausted by sorrow. 'Will Edward pass the death sentence on his own brother?' she asks. 'Am I to lose George as I lost your brother Edmund? To a dishonourable death? Will She have his head set on a spike? Is England ruled by another she-wolf as bad as Margaret of Anjou? Does Edward forget who his friends are, his brothers?'

Richard shakes his head. 'I don't know. He has removed me from my place as Steward of England, so that I don't have to rule on the death sentence.'

She is alert at once. 'Who is the new steward?'

'The Duke of Buckingham. He will do as his Rivers wife tells him. Will you go to Edward? Will you appeal to him?'

'Of course,' she says. 'I will go to one beloved son to beg for the life of another. I shouldn't have to do this. This is the consequence of a wicked woman, an evil wife, a witch on the throne.'

'Hush,' Richard says wearily.

'I will not hush. I will stand between her, and my son George. I will save him.'

BAYNARD'S CASTLE,
LONDON, FEBRUARY 1478

We have to wait. We wait and wait from January to February. The members of both houses of parliament send delegations to beg the king to pass a sentence and finish the case against his brother one way or the other. Finally, the sentence is passed and George is found guilty of treason. The punishment for treason is death but still the king hesitates to order his brother's execution. Nobody is allowed to see George, who appeals from his prison for the right to be tried by single combat – a chivalric resolution to a dishonourable charge. It is the final defence of an innocent man. The king, who claims to be the very flower of English chivalry, refuses. This seems to be a matter outside of honour, as well as outside of justice.

Duchess Cecily goes as she promised to see Edward, certain that she can make him commute the death sentence into exile. When she returns to Baynard's Castle from court, they have to help her out of her litter. She is as white as her lace collar and she can barely stand.

'What happened?' I ask her.

She clings to my hands on the steps of her great London home. She has never reached out to me before. 'Anne,' is all she can say. 'Anne.'

I call for my ladies and between us we help her into my rooms, seat her in my chair before the fire, and give her a glass of malmsey wine. With a sudden gesture she strikes the glass away and it shatters on the stone hearth. 'No! No!' she screams with sudden energy. 'Don't bring it near me!'

The bouquet of the sweet wine fills the room as I kneel at her feet and take her hands. I think she is raving as she shudders and cries: 'Not the wine! Not the wine!'

'Lady Mother, what is it? Duchess Cecily? Compose yourself!'

This is a woman who stayed at court while her husband plotted the greatest rebellion against a king that England has ever seen. This is the woman who stood at the market cross in Ludlow when her husband ran away and the Lancaster soldiers sacked the town. This is not a woman who cries easily, this is not a woman who has ever acknowledged defeat. But now she looks at me as if she can see nothing, she is blinded by tears. Then she lets out a great shaking sob. 'Edward said that all I could do was offer George his choice of death. He said that he must die. That woman was there all the time, she never let me say a thing in George's favour. All I could win for him was a private death in his room in the Tower, and he can choose the means.'

She buries her face in her hands and weeps as if she could never stop. I glance at my ladies. We are so shocked to see the duchess like this that we all stand in a helpless circle around the grieving mother.

'My favourite son, my own darling,' she whispers to herself. 'And he has to die.'

I don't know what to do. I put my hand gently on her shoulder. 'Will you not take a glass of something, Your Grace?'

She looks up at me, her beautiful old face ravaged with grief. 'He has chosen to be drowned in malmsey wine,' she says.

'What?'

She nods. 'That's why I didn't want to drink it. I will never touch it again as long as I live. I won't have it in my house. They will clear the cellar of it today.'

I am horrified. 'Why would he do such a thing?'

She laughs, a bitter dry sound that peals like a carillon of misery in the stone-walled room. 'It is his last gesture: to make Edward treat him, to make Edward pay for his drink. To make a mockery of the king's justice, to drink deep of the queen's favourite wine. He shows it is her doing, this is her poison for him, as it was her poison that killed Isabel. He makes a mockery of the trial, he makes a mockery of his death sentence. He makes a mockery of his death.'

I turn to the window and look out. 'My sister's children will be orphans,' I say. 'Edward, and Margaret.'

'Orphans and paupers,' Duchess Cecily says acutely, drying her cunning old face.

I look back at her. 'What?'

'Their father will die for treason. A traitor's lands are taken from him. Who do you think gets their lands?'

'The king,' I say dully. 'The king. Which is to say the queen – and her endless family – of course.'

We are a house in deep mourning but we cannot wear blue. George, the handsome irrepressible duke, is dead. He died as he requested, drowned in a barrel of the queen's favourite wine. It was his last bitter brilliant gesture of defiance to the woman who ruined his house. She herself never drank the wine again, as if she feared that she would taste sputum from his gasping lungs in the sweetness. I wish that I could see George in purgatory and tell him that he achieved that at least. He spoiled the queen's appetite for wine. Would to God that he could have drowned her too.

I go to court and wait for my chance to speak to the king. I sit in the queen's rooms with her ladies and I talk to them of the weather, and the likelihood of snow. I admire their fine lacework for which the queen herself drew the pattern, and I remark on her artistry. When she speaks to me briefly, I reply with pleasant courtesy. I don't let her see from my face or from any gesture, not even the turn of my hand or the set of my feet in my leather slippers, that I regard her as a murderer of my sister by poison, and my brother-in-law by politics. She is a killer and perhaps even a witch, and she has taken from me all the people that I love, except my husband and my son. I don't doubt that she would rob me of them but for my husband's position with the king. I will never forgive her.

When the king comes in, smiling and cheerful, he greets the ladies by name as usual and when he comes to me and kisses me as a brother on both cheeks I say quietly: 'Your Grace, I would ask you a favour.'

At once, he glances over to her and I see their swift exchange of looks. She half-rises to her feet as if she would intercept me; but I was prepared for this. I don't expect to get anything without the witch's permission. 'I should like the wardship of my sister's children,' I say quickly. 'They are at Warwick in the nursery there. Margaret is four, Edward nearly three. I loved Isabel dearly, I should like to care for her children.'

'Of course,' Edward says easily. 'But you know they have no fortunes?'

Oh yes, I know that, I think. For you robbed George of everything he had gained by accusing him of treason. If their wardship was worth anything your wife would already have claimed it. If they had been wealthy she would have the marriage contract already drawn up for their betrothal to one of her own children. 'I will provide for them,' I say.

Richard, coming towards me, nods his assent. 'We will provide for them.'

'I will raise them at Middleham with their cousin my son,' I say. 'If Your Grace will allow it. It is the greatest favour you could do me. I loved my sister and I promised her that if anything happened to her I would care for her children.'

'Oh, did she think she might die?' the queen asks, with pretend concern, coming up to the king and slipping her hand in his arm, her beautiful face solemn and concerned. 'Did she fear child-birth?'

I think of Isabel warning me that one day I would hear that she had died suddenly and that on that day I might know that she had been poisoned by this beautiful woman who stands before me in her arrogance and her power, and dares to tease me with the death of my sister. 'Childbirth is always dangerous,' I say quietly, denying the truth of Isabel's murder. 'As everyone knows. We all enter our confinement with a prayer.'

The queen holds my gaze for a moment as if she might challenge me, see if she can drive me into saying something treasonous or rebellious. I can see my husband tense as if readying himself for an attack, and he draws a little closer to his brother as if to take his attention from the she-devil who holds his arm. Then she smiles her lovely smile and looks up at her husband in her familiar seductive way. 'I think we should let the Clarence children live with their aunt, do you not, Your Grace?' she asks sweetly. 'Perhaps it would comfort them all in their loss. And I am sure that my sister Anne here will be a good guardian to her little niece and nephew.'

'I agree,' the king says. He nods at Richard. 'I am glad to grant your wife a favour.'

'Let me know how they go on,' the queen says to me as she turns away. 'What a sadness that her baby died. What was his name?'

'Richard,' I say softly.

'Did she call him after your father?' she asks, naming the murderer of her father, of her brother, the accuser of her mother, her lifelong enemy.

'Yes,' I say, not knowing what else I can say.

'What a pity,' she repeats.

BAYNARD'S CASTLE,
LONDON, MARCH 1478

I think I have won. That evening and in the days after I silently celebrate my victory. I celebrate without words, without even a smile. I have lost my sister; but her children will be in my keeping and I will love them as my own. I will tell them that their mother was a beauty and their father was a hero, and that Isabel put them into my keeping.

I write to Warwick Castle and tell them that as soon as the roads are clear enough for the journey the two children shall go to Middleham. Weeks later, delayed by snow and storms, I get a reply from the castle to tell me that Margaret and Edward have set off, well-wrapped in two litters with their nursemaids. A week later I hear from Middleham that they have safely arrived. I have Isabel's children behind the thick walls of our best castle, and I swear that I will keep them safe.

I go to my husband while he is hearing petitions in his presence chamber in Baynard's Castle. I wait patiently while the dozens of people present their applications and their grievances and he listens carefully and deals justly with each one. Richard is a great lord. He understands, as my father did, that each man has to be allowed to have his say, that each one will give his fealty if he can be sure that a lord will repay him with protection. He knows that wealth is not in land but in the men and women who work the land. Our wealth and our power depend upon the love of the people who serve us. If they will do anything for Richard – as they would do anything for my father – then he has an army on call, for whatever need. This is true power, this is real wealth.

When the very last of them has finished and has bent the knee, thanked Richard for his care, and gone, my husband looks up from signing his papers and sees me. 'Anne?'

'I too wanted to see you and ask a favour.'

He smiles and steps down from his throne on the dais. 'You can ask me anything, at any time. You don't have to come here.' He puts his arm around my waist and we walk to the window that overlooks the courtyard before the house. Beyond the great wall the trade and bustle of London goes on, beyond that is the Palace of Westminster and the queen sits behind those walls in her power and her mystery. Behind us, Richard's clerks clear away the papers that the petitioners have brought, carry away the writing tables with the quills and ink and sealing wax. Nobody is eavesdropping on our conversation.

'I have come to ask you if we can go home to Middleham.'

'You want to be with your sister's children?'

'And with little Edward. But it is more than that.'

'What is it?'

'You know what.'

He glances around to make sure that no-one can hear us. I observe the king's own loyal brother fearful of speaking in his own house. 'The truth is that I think that George was right to accuse Ankarette of being in the queen's pay, of poisoning Isabel,' I say bluntly. 'I think the queen set her spy to poison Isabel and perhaps even to kill the baby, because she hates Isabel and me and wanted her revenge for the murder of her father. It is a blood feud, and she is waging it against my father's children, Isabel, and her son Richard. I am certain that I, and the children, will be next.'

Richard's gaze does not leave my eyes. 'This is a grave allegation against a queen.'

'I make it only to you, in private,' I say. 'I would never publicly accuse the queen. We all saw what happened to George who publicly accused her.'

'George was guilty of treason against the king,' Richard reminds me. 'There was no doubt of his guilt. He spoke treason to me, I heard him, myself. He took money from France, he plotted a new rebellion.'

'There is no doubt of his guilt but he had always been forgiven before,' I say. 'Edward on his own would never have taken George to trial. You know it was on the advice of the queen. When your own mother went to beg for clemency she said it was the queen who insisted that George be put to death. The queen saw George as a danger to her rule, she would not let him accuse her. He named her as a murderer and to silence him she had him killed. It was not about a rebellion against the king, it was about his enmity to Her.'

Richard cannot deny this. 'And your fear?' he asks quietly.

'Isabel told me of the queen's jewellery case, and two names written in blood, that she keeps inside an enamel box.'

He nods.

'Isabel believed that it was our names: hers and mine. She believed that the queen would kill us both to avenge her father and her brother that were killed by our father.' I take his hands. 'Richard, I am sure that the queen will have me killed. I don't know how she will do it, whether by poison or something that looks like an accident, or some passing violence on the street. But I am sure she will contrive my death, and I am very afraid.'

'Isabel was poisoned at Warwick,' he says. 'She was far from London, and it didn't save her.'

'I know. But I think I would be safer at Middleham than right here, where she sees me at court, where you rival her in Edward's affections, where I remind her of my father every time I walk into her rooms.'

He hesitates.

'You yourself warned me not to eat the food that came from

the queen's kitchen,' I remind him. 'Before George was arrested. Before she pressed for his death. You warned me yourself.'

Richard's face is very grave. 'I did,' he says. 'I thought you were in danger then, and I think you are in danger now. I agree with you that we should go to Middleham and I think we should stay away from court. I have much to do in the North, Edward has given me all of George's Yorkshire lands for my own. We will leave London and we will only come to court when we have to.'

'And your mother?' I ask, knowing that she too will never forgive the queen for the death of George.

He shakes his head. 'She speaks treason, she says that Edward should never have taken the throne if he was going to make such a woman his queen. She calls Elizabeth a witch like her mother. She is going to leave London and live at Fotheringhay. She too dares not stay here.'

'We will be northerners,' I say, imagining the life we shall lead, far from the court, far from the constant fear, far from the edgy brittle amusement and entertainment that always now seems like a veneer over the manoeuvrings and plottings of the queen and her brothers and sisters. This court has lost its innocence; it is no longer joyful. This is a court of killers and I shall be glad to put miles and miles between them and me.

MIDDLEHAM CASTLE, YORKSHIRE, SUMMER 1482

We do not live at peace, as I hoped; for the king commands Richard to lead the armies of England against the Scots, and when the treaty between Scotland and England breaks down, and Anthony Woodville finds himself without his promised Scottish royal bride, it falls to Richard to lead the Rivers' revenge: taking a small English force, mostly our northerners, to victory, winning the town of Berwick and entering Edinburgh itself. It is a great victory; but even this does not persuade the court that Richard is a great soldier and worthy heir to his father. Within the month we hear that the Rivers are complaining at court that he should have gone further, and won more.

I hear Elizabeth's whispered counsel in this, and I grit my teeth. If she can persuade her husband to call this victory against the Scots a treasonous failure, then they will summon Richard to London to answer for it. The last royal brother accused of treason had a trial without a defence and choked away his life in a vat of the queen's favourite wine.

To comfort myself, I go to the schoolroom and sit at the back while the children wade through their Latin grammars, reciting the verbs that were taught to Isabel and me so long ago in the schoolroom at Calais. I can almost hear Isabel's voice, even now, and her triumphant crow when she gets through them without making a mistake. My boy Edward is nine years old, seated beside him is Isabel's daughter, Margaret, nine this year, and beside her is her brother Edward, who we all call Teddy, just seven.

Their tutor breaks off and says they can stop work for a little while to greet me and the three of them gather round my chair. Margaret leans against me and I put my arm around her and look at the two handsome boys. I know that these may be all the children I ever have. I am only twenty-six years old, I should be ready to bear half a dozen more children, but they never seem to come, and nobody, not the physicians, the midwives nor the priest, can tell me why not. In the absence of any others, these three are my children, and Margaret, who is as pretty and as passionate as her mother, is my darling and the only daughter I expect to raise.

'Are you all right, Lady Mother?' she asks sweetly.

'I am,' I say, brushing her unruly brown hair out of her eyes.

'Can we play at being at court?' she asks. 'Will you pretend to be queen and we can be presented to you?'

The return of the game that I used to play with my sister is too poignant for me today. 'Not this morning,' I say. 'And anyway, perhaps you don't need to practise. Perhaps you children won't go to court. Perhaps you will live like your father does: as a great lord on his lands, free of court and far from the queen.'

'Won't we have to go to court for Christmas?' Edward asks me with a worried frown on his little face. 'I thought that Father said that we would all three have to go to court for Christmas this year?'

'No,' I promise myself. 'Your father and I will go if the king commands it; but you three will stay safe here, at Middleham.'

'We had no choice,' Richard says to me as we pause before the royal presence chamber. 'We had to come for the Christmas feast. It is bad enough that you left the children behind. It looks like you don't trust them in London.'

'I don't,' I say bluntly. 'I will never bring them while she is on the throne. I won't put Isabel's children into her keeping. Look at the Mowbray child – married to Prince Richard, her fortune signed over to the Rivers family, and dead before her ninth birthday.'

Richard scowls at me. 'Not another word,' is all he says.

The great doors before us are thrown open and a blast of trumpets heralds our arrival. Richard recoils slightly – the court becomes grander and more glamorous every time we visit. Now every honoured guest has to be announced with trumpets and a bawled introduction, as if we did not know already that half the wealthy people in England are her brothers and sisters.

I see that Edward is walking about among the courtiers, a head taller than everyone, broader now, he will run to fat, and the queen is seated on a throne of gold. The royal children, from the new baby Bridget who is toddling at her mother's feet, to the oldest princess, Elizabeth, now a young woman of sixteen, are exquisitely dressed and seated around their mother. Prince

Edward, fair-headed and handsome as his father, a boy of twelve, back from Wales for the Christmas feast, is playing at chess with his guardian Anthony Woodville, whose handsome profile is turned to the puzzle of the board.

No-one could deny that they are the most handsome family in England. Elizabeth's famous face is sharper and more elegant as age wears her prettiness away to real beauty. She lost her fifteen-year-old daughter Princess Mary this year and her third son George a year after she won the execution of his namesake and uncle. I wonder if these losses have given her pause in her unending ambition and search for revenge. Sorrow has given her a single white streak in her golden hair, and grief has made her quieter and more thoughtful. She is still dressing like an empress, wearing a gown of cloth of gold, and gold chains are roped around her slim waist. As I enter, she whispers something to Anthony Woodville and he looks up and they both show me the same charming insincere smile. Inside the thick sleeves of my gown I can feel my hands tingle with cold as if her gaze is a chill wind.

'Onward,' Richard says, as he said once before, and we go in and bow to the king and queen and receive Edward's joyous greeting to his beloved brother, and her tepid welcome to the man she has named in secret as a traitor.

For everyone else at court, the Christmas feast is an opportunity to get close to the royal family and try to establish friendships and flirtations that may pay well in the future. There is a constant swirl of interest around the king, who still has fortunes to give away and great patronage in his gift. But it is even more obvious that the queen and her family, her brothers and sisters, even her sons from her first marriage, control the court and control access to the king. She allows him to take his mistresses, he even brags about them; she allows him to favour strangers. But the great gifts in the royal household go only to her family and her affinity. Not that she ever asserts herself. She never speaks in any discussion, she never gets to her feet or raises her voice, but all the power of the court is at her fingertips and her brothers Anthony, Lionel and Edward survey the comings and goings of the court at play as if they were card cheats watching a table and waiting for a fool to come to play. Her sons from her first marriage, Thomas and Richard, ennobled by the king, enriched by the king, control the access to the royal chamber. Nothing happens without their observation, and nothing is allowed without her smiling permission.

The royal family is always beautifully dressed, the royal rooms glow with wealth. Edward, neglecting ships and castles, ports and sea walls, has lavished money on his family palaces, especially on the grand rooms for the queen that he has enlarged and beautified in every place that she declares is her new favourite. Leaving Richard to guard the nation against Scotland with a scratch force of his own mustering, Edward has spent a fortune on a new suit of jousting armour, which will never see a real sword. A perfect king in looks and charm, I think this is all he can do now: outward façade. He looks like a king and he speaks like a king, but he does not rule like a king. Power is in the hands of the queen and she looks and speaks as she has always done – a beautiful woman, married for love, devoted to her children, and charming to her friends. She is, as she has always been, quite irresistible. No-one could tell by looking at her that this is a most unscrupulous schemer, the daughter of a known witch, a woman with blood on her beautiful white hands, her slim white fingers stained at the nails.

The twelve days of the Christmas feast would have been the most celebrated that the court has ever known but just after Christmas Day the news comes from Burgundy that the queen's kinsman Duke Maximilian has played her false. Seeking his own good, just as she always seeks hers, he has made peace with Louis of France, given his daughter to the king's son in marriage, and given him Burgundy and Artois as her dowry.

Richard is beside himself with anger and worry – Burgundy has always been the great power that we use to balance against the might of France. The countries that have been given to France – Burgundy and Artois – are English by right, and this will be the end of the French pensions which have made Edward and his court so wealthy.

In this desperate moment I have to laugh in my sleeve at the queen whose daughter Elizabeth was betrothed to the French prince and now finds herself jilted – and a cousin on her mother's side is preferred. Princess Elizabeth herself seems to be indifferent as she plays with her brothers and sisters in the frozen gardens, or goes hunting with the court in the cold marshes by the river; but I am sure that she must realise that she has been humiliated by France, since she has lost the chance to be Queen of France, and has failed to fulfil her father's ambition. Surely, this is the worst thing of all: she has failed to play her part in her father's plan.

In this crisis it is Richard who advises on policy – the queen has no idea what should be done – and he tells his brother that in the spring he will march again against the Scots. If they can be defeated and sworn to our cause then they can serve as our allies against France, and we can invade. It is Richard who takes this proposal to the houses of parliament. In return they give Richard a massive grant: the whole of the huge county of Cumberland. In addition, he is to keep any land he conquers in southwest Scotland. It is all to be his. It is a massive gift, it is the princedom that he deserves. For the first time Edward truly recognises what his brother has done for him and gives him great lands – in the North, where Richard is beloved and where we have made our home.

Edward announces this in council, but we hear of it in court when the brothers come back, arm in arm, to the queen's rooms. The queen hears Edward declare that Richard must set up a council of the North to help him rule his great lands, and I see the shock on her face and her quick glance of consternation to her brother Anthony. It is clear to me that the king has not consulted her, and that her first thought is how can he be overruled, and her first ally is her brother Anthony. Anthony is more diplomatic than his sister; he comes forwards to congratulate Richard on his new wealth, smiles and embraces him, and then turns and kisses my hand and says I will be as a princess among the snows. I smile and murmur nothing, but I think that I have seen much, and understood more. I have seen that the king does not trust her with everything, I have seen that she would overrule him if she could, and that she counts on her brother as her ally, even when she wants to act against the king. But there is still more; from the quick exchange of glances between brother and sister I know that neither of them loves or trusts Richard any more than we trust her. Worse, they suspect and fear him.

The king knows well enough she does not like this. He takes her hand and says to her: 'Richard will keep the North for me, and – please God – Richard's young strength on my side will make this a greater kingdom even than it is now.'

Her smile is as sweet as ever. 'Under your command,' she reminds him. I see Anthony Woodville stir as if he would say something, but then he shakes his head slightly at his sister and falls silent.

'He will be warden of the West Marches. And when my son comes to his throne, Richard will have guarded his borders for him, he will be his advisor and protector, and in heaven I shall be glad of that.'

'Ah! My lord, don't say it!' she exclaims. 'Your son will not sit on his throne for many years yet.'

I wonder if I am alone in feeling a prickle of unease, a shiver at her words.

That was his death sentence. I am sure of it, I would swear to it. She judged that his favour to Richard was growing, his dependence on Richard was greater than the dependence she had tried to create on her family. She might have made her brother

Anthony the guardian to the prince and so ruler of Wales, but the gift of land to Richard was far greater than this. Richard was given the command of the armies, Richard was given almost all of the North of England. She knew that if the king were to write his will, Richard would be made regent. She thought that in giving Richard the North of the country the king was on the way to dividing the country: the Rivers family would rule Wales and the south, and Richard would rule the North. I believe that she saw her power slipping away, that she thought the king favoured his brother, that he knew Richard would keep the border with Scotland, would hold the North. I believe she thought that Richard was his true heir and would only grow in power and prestige in the northern lands. And as soon as she came to that conclusion, she poisoned the king, her own husband, so that he could not favour Richard any more, so that Richard could not develop his power and threaten her own.

I don't think this all at once. At first, I ride out of London with the sense of relief that I always have when we put the Bishop's Gate behind us, and I go north to my boy and my little nephew and niece with my usual feeling of joy. I have an odd lingering sense that the queen's swift glance to her brother meant no good for us, and no good for anyone outside that tight pair – but I think nothing more than this.

I am in the hay meadow outside the castle walls, watching the children practising their riding. They have three strong horses, bred from the rugged wild ponies that live here on the moors, and they are trotting them over a set of little jumps. The grooms set the jumps higher and higher as each rider gets successfully clear. My task is to rule when it is too high for Teddy, but Margaret and Edward can continue, and then to declare a winner. I have picked half a dozen stems of foxgloves and I am winding them into a crown for the winner. Margaret jumps clear and throws a triumphant beam at me; she is a brave little girl and will set her pony at anything. My son follows her over the jumps, riding with less style but even more determination. I think that soon we must give him a bigger horse and he will have to learn to joust in the adult tiltyard.

The bells from the chapel start to toll with a sudden jangle. The rooks pour out of the rafters of the castle with a harsh black cawing, and I turn in alarm. The children pull up their ponies and look at me.

'I don't know,' I answer their puzzled faces. 'Back to the castle at the trot, quickly now.'

It is not the tocsin that sounds the alarm but the steady knell, which means a death, a death in the family. But who could have died? For a moment I wonder if they have found my mother dead in her rooms and ordered the tolling of the bell as if to announce a death that was actually declared years ago. But surely they would have come to tell me first? I hold my gown bunched in my hands, free of my feet, so that I can run sure-footed down the stony path to the castle gate and follow the children into the inner garth.

Richard is on the steps leading up to the great hall, and people are gathering round him. He has a paper in his hand; I see the royal seal and my first leaping hope is that my prayers have been answered and the queen is dead. I run up the steps to stand beside him and he says, his voice choked with grief: 'It is Edward. Edward, my brother.'

I gasp but wait as the bell slowly falls silent and the household looks to my husband. The three children come at a run from the stables and stand, as they should, on the steps before us. Edward has uncovered his head and Margaret takes Teddy's cap from his curly hair.

'Grave news from London,' Richard says clearly, so that everyone, even the labourers who have come running in from their fields, can hear him. 'His Grace the king, my beloved and noble brother, is dead.' There is a tremendous stir among the crowd. Richard nods as if he understands their disbelief. He clears his throat. 'He was taken ill some days ago and died. He received the last rites and we will pray for his immortal soul.'

Many people cross themselves, and one woman gives a little sob and puts her apron to her eyes. 'His son Edward, Prince of Wales, will inherit his father's crown,' Richard says. He raises his voice: 'The king is dead. God save the king!'

'God save the king!' we all repeat, and then Richard takes my arm and turns me in to the great hall, the children trailing behind us.

Richard sends the children to the chapel to pray for the soul of their uncle the king. He is fast and decisive, burning up with the vision of what must be done. This is a moment of destiny, and he is a Plantagenet – they are always at their best in a crisis or on the brink of an opportunity. A child of war, a soldier, commander, warden of the West Marches, he has worked his way up through the ranks of his brother's men to be ready for the moment now – the moment that his brother is no more, and Richard must protect his brother's legacy.

'Beloved, I must leave you. I have to go to London. He will have named me as regent and I have to make sure that his kingdom is secure.'

'Who should threaten it?'

He does not answer: 'the woman who has threatened the peace of England every day since the cursed May-day that she seduced and enchanted him'. Instead he looks seriously at me and says: 'As well as everything else, I fear a landing by Henry Tudor.'

'Margaret Stanley's son?' I say incredulously. 'A boy half-bred between the Houses of Beaufort and Tudor? You cannot fear him.'

'Edward feared him, and he was treating with his mother to bring him home as a friend. He is an heir to the House of Lancaster, however obscure, and he has been in exile since Edward took the throne. He is an enemy and I don't know what alliances he has. I don't fear him; but I will get to London and secure the throne for York so that there can be no doubt.'

'You will have to work with the queen,' I caution him.

He smiles at me. 'I don't fear her either. She will neither enchant nor poison me. She doesn't matter any more. At her worst she can speak against me; but no-one of importance will listen. The loss of my brother is her loss too, though she will only understand that when she sees she is thrown down. She is a dowager queen, no longer principal advisor to the king. I will have to work with her son, but he is Edward's boy as well as hers, and I will see that he knows my authority as his uncle. My task must be to take him in hand, guard his birthright, see him to the throne as my brother wanted. I am his regent. I am his guardian. I am his uncle. I am protector of the country and of him too. I shall take him into my keeping.'

'Shall I come too?'

He shakes his head. 'No, I will ride fast with my closest friends. Robert Brackenbury has already left to provide horses for us on the road. You wait here until I have Elizabeth Woodville and all the cursed Rivers family in quiet mourning at Windsor and out of the way. I will send for you when I have the seal of office and England is mine to command.' He smiles. 'This is my moment of greatness, as well as my moment of grief. For a little while – until the boy is old enough – I will rule England as a king. I will resolve the wars with Scotland and negotiate with France. I will see that justice runs through the land and that good men can get places – men who are not Rivers kinsmen. I shall take the Rivers out of their offices and out of their great estates. I shall set my stamp on England in these years and they will know that I was a good protector and a good brother. And I shall take the boy Edward and teach him what a great man his father was – and what a greater man he could have been if it had not been for that woman.'

'I'll come to London as soon as you send for me,' I promise. 'And here we will pray for the soul of Edward. He was a great sinner, but a loveable one.'

Richard shakes his head. 'He was betrayed by the woman that he put in the very highest place in the land,' he says. 'He was a fool for love. But I shall see that the finest parts of his legacy are passed on to his boy. I shall make the boy a true grandson to my father.' He pauses for a moment. 'And as for Her, I shall send her back to the village she came from,' he swears, in an unusual moment of bitterness. 'She shall go to an abbey and live in retirement. We have all seen enough of her and her endless brothers and sisters. The Rivers are finished in England, I shall throw them down.'

Richard rides out that very day. He pauses at York and he and all the city make an oath of loyalty to his nephew. He tells the city that they will honour the late king by their loyalty to his son, and he rides on to London.

Then I hear nothing from him. I am not surprised at the silence, he is on the road to London – what should he write to me about but the slowness of the going and the mud in these spring days? I know that he is meeting the Duke of Buckingham, young Henry Stafford, who was married against his will to the Woodville sister Catherine when they were both children, who passed down the death sentence on George, against his conscience, to oblige his wife and her sister. I know that William Hastings, the king's true friend, has written to Richard to come at once, and warned him of the enmity of the queen. The great lords will be gathering to protect the boy Edward, the heir to his father's throne. I know that the Rivers will be wanting to surround and protect their heir from anyone else – but who can refuse Richard, the king's brother, the named Protector of England?

MIDDLEHAM CASTLE,
YORKSHIRE, MAY 1483

Then in the middle of May I get a letter from my husband, written in his own hand and sealed with his private seal. I take it to my chamber away from the noise of the household and I read it by the bright light of the clear glass window.

> *You will hear that the coronation of my nephew will take place on 22 June, but do not come to London until I write in my own hand to tell you to do so. London is not safe for anyone who is not sworn or kin to the Rivers or their friends. Now she shows her true colours, and I am ready for the worst. She is refusing to be dowager queen, she hopes to make herself a king. I have to face her as an enemy, and I do not forget my brother George, your sister, or their baby.*

I go to the kitchen where the great fire stays lit night and day and I crush the letter into a ball and push it under the glowing logs and wait till it has burned away. There is nothing to do but wait for news.

In the stable yard outside the children are watching the farrier shoe their ponies. Everything is safe and ordinary: the flare of the forge, the smoke billowing from the hoof in an acrid cloud. My son Edward is holding the halter rope of his new horse, a handsome cob, as the farrier grips the horse's leg between his knees and taps in the nails. I cross my fingers in the old sign against witchcraft and I shudder as a cool draught blows in from the door to the dairy. If the queen is showing her true colours and my husband is ready for the worst, then her enmity to me and mine will be apparent for all to see. Perhaps even now she is whistling up a plague wind to blow against me. Perhaps even now she is laying a curse on my husband's sword arm, weakening his strength, suborning his allies, poisoning the minds of men against him.

I turn and go to the chapel, drop to my knees and pray that Richard is strong against Elizabeth Woodville and against all her kinsmen and women and the mighty affinity she has put together. I pray that he acts decisively and powerfully, I pray that he uses whatever weapons come to his hand, for certainly she will stop at nothing to get her son on the throne and see us thrown down. I think of Margaret of Anjou teaching me that there are times when you have to be ready to do anything to defend yourself or the position you deserve, and I hope that my husband is ready for anything. I cannot know what is happening in London, but I fear the start of a new war, and this time it will be the king's true brother against the false-hearted queen. And we must, we have to triumph.

I wait. I send one of our guard with a letter to Richard begging for news. I warn him against the ill-will of the queen.

You know she has powers, so guard yourself against them. Do whatever you have to do to protect your brother's legacy and our safety.

On my own at Middleham Castle, I spend every afternoon with the children as if only by constantly watching can I prevent a hot plague wind blowing towards them from London, stop the flight of a mistimed arrow, ensure that the new horse is well-trained and that Edward can manage it. If I could hold my son in my arms like the baby he once was, I would never let him go. There is no doubt in my mind that the queen's grey eyes are turned towards us, that her mind is set against my husband, that she will be plotting and conjuring our deaths, that it is finally, clearly, us against her.

MIDDLEHAM CASTLE,
YORKSHIRE, JUNE 1483

Every morning after chapel I go and stand on the top of the south tower, looking south down the road to London. And then I see the plume of dust that blows from the rough road after the passage of half a dozen horsemen. I call to my maid: 'Fetch the children to my room, and turn out the guard. Someone is coming.'

Her look of alarm and her sudden scurry down the steps tells me that I am not the only person to know that my husband, far from securing a safe succession for his nephew, is in danger, and that danger could come even to us, in this, our safest home.

I hear the portcullis rattle down and the drawbridge creak up, and the running footsteps of men dashing to man the walls of the castle. When I go to the great hall the children are waiting for me. Margaret has tight hold of her brother's hand; Edward is wearing his short sword and his pale face is determined. They all three kneel for my blessing and when I put my hand on their warm heads I could weep for fear for the three of them.

'There are horsemen coming to the castle,' I say as calmly as I can. 'Perhaps they are messengers from your father, but with the country so unsettled I dare take no risks. That is why I sent for you.'

Edward rises to his feet. 'I did not know the country was unsettled?'

I shake my head. 'I spoke wrongly. The country is at peace, waiting for your father's righteous rule as regent,' I say. 'It is the court which is unsettled for I think the queen will try to rule in the place of her son. She may try to make herself regent. I am anxious for your father, who is bound by his promise to the king to take Prince Edward into his keeping and teach him how to rule, and bring him to his throne. If the prince's mother is an enemy then your father will have to judge and to act swiftly and powerfully.'

'But what would the queen do?' little Margaret asks me. 'What could she do against us, against my lord uncle?'

'I don't know,' I say. 'That is why we are prepared for an attack in case one were to come. But we are safe here, the soldiers are strong and well-trained and the castle is loyal to us. The whole of the North of England would support your father as if he were king himself.' I try to smile at them. 'I am probably being anxious. But my own father was always ready in his own defence. My father always raised the drawbridge if he did not know the visitor.'

We wait, listening. Then I hear the shouted challenge from the captain of the guard and the indistinct reply. I hear the drawbridge rattle on its chains as they let it down and the thud as it hits the far side of the moat. The portcullis screeches as they haul it up.

'We are safe,' I say to the children. 'They will be friends bringing a message.'

I hear feet on the stone stairs that lead up to the hall, and then my guard opens the door and Sir Robert Brackenbury, Richard's childhood friend, comes in with a smile. 'I am sorry if I alarmed you, my lady,' he says, kneeling and proffering a letter. 'We came quickly. I should perhaps have sent someone ahead to tell you that it was my troop.'

'I thought it right to be careful,' I say. I take the letter, and gesture to my lady in waiting that she shall pour a glass of small ale for Sir Robert. 'You can go,' I say to the children and to my ladies. 'I will talk with Sir Robert.'

Edward hesitates. 'May I ask Sir Robert if my father is safe and well?'

Sir Robert turns to him and bends down so that the ten-year-old boy and he are at the same height. He speaks gently to all three children. 'When I left London your father was well and doing the very best he could,' he says. 'He has Prince Edward in his safe-keeping and he will make sure that he comes to his throne when the time is right.'

The children bow to me and leave the room. I wait until the door is closed behind them and I open the letter. Richard is brief as usual.

The Rivers are conspiring against us and against all of the old lords of England. They plan to replace the Plantagenet line with themselves. I have found hidden weapons and believe they are planning an uprising and all our deaths. I will defend us and my country against them. Come to London now, I need you to be seen here at my side, and I want your company. Leave a strong guard with the children.

I fold the letter carefully and tuck it inside my gown. Sir Robert is standing, waiting for me to speak to him.

'Tell me what is happening,' I command.

'The queen was mustering a troop and planning to put her son on the throne. She would have excluded our lord from the protectorate and there would have been no regency. She was going to put her son on the throne and she and her brother Anthony Woodville would have ruled England through the boy.'

I nod, hardly daring to breathe.

'Our lord captured Prince Edward, while he was being taken to London from Ludlow by the queen's kinsmen. Our lord arrested the queen's brother Anthony Woodville, and her son by her first marriage Richard Grey, and took the boy into his own keeping. When we got to London we found the queen had fled into sanctuary.'

I gasp. 'She has gone into sanctuary?'

'A clear admission of her guilt. She took her children with her. Our lord has the prince in the royal apartment in the Tower, preparing him for his coronation, and the council has declared our lord as Lord Protector – according to the wishes of his brother the king. The queen refuses to attend the coronation or release the royal prince and princesses out of sanctuary so that they can attend their brother.'

'What is she doing in there?'

Sir Robert grimaces. 'Without a doubt she is plotting to overthrow the protectorate under the shield of sanctuary. Her brother has commanded the fleet to sail and they are on the high seas; we are preparing for an attack from the river.' He glances at me. 'It is my lord's belief that she is practising witchcraft – hidden in sanctuary.'

I cross myself and feel in my pocket for the amulet that George gave me against her enchantments.

'He says his sword arm is giving him pain, tingling and aching. He thinks she is trying to weaken him.'

I find I am clenching my hands together. 'What can he do to defend himself?'

'I don't know,' Sir Robert says unhappily. 'I don't know what he can do. And the young prince constantly asks for his mother and for his governor, Anthony Woodville. Clearly, as soon as he is crowned he will command their presence, and they will rule England through him. My own view is that my lord will have to hold the prince as his ward, without a coronation, until he can make an agreement with the family. His own safety demands it. If the queen's son is on the throne then she takes power again. She is certain to act against our lord – and against you and your son. Once she seizes power through her son, my lord is as good as executed.'

At the thought of her secret silent malice against Richard and against me and the children my knees weaken and I lean against the stone of the chimney breast.

'Be of good cheer,' Sir Robert says encouragingly. 'We know the danger, we are armed against her. Our lord is going to muster his faithful men from the North. He will summon them to London. He has the prince in his hands, and he is ready for anything she might do. He need not crown him until he has an agreement. He can hold him until she will make an agreement.'

'He says I am to go to him.'

'I am ordered to escort you,' Sir Robert says. 'Shall we leave tomorrow morning?'

'Yes,' I say. 'At first light.'

The children come down to the stable yard to see me leave. I kiss each of them and they kneel for my blessing. Leaving them is the hardest thing to do, but to take them to London would be to lead them into unknown dangers. My son Edward stands straight and says to me: 'I will take care of my cousins, Lady Mother. You needn't fear for us. I will hold Middleham Castle for Father, come what may.'

I smile so that they can see I am proud of them but it is hard to turn away from them and get onto my horse. I brush the tears away with the back of my glove. 'I shall send for you as soon as I can,' I say. 'I shall think of you all every day, and pray for you every night.' Then Sir Robert gives the signal and our little company goes under the portcullis arch, over the drawbridge, and south down the road to London.

At every stop on the way we hear fresh confused rumours. At Pontefract the people are saying that the coronation has been delayed because the councillors were in a treasonous conspiracy with the queen. In Nottingham, when we spend the night at the castle, people say she was going to put her brother Anthony Woodville on the throne, and many more say that she was going to make him Lord Protector. Outside Northampton I hear someone swear that the queen has sent all her children overseas to our sister-in-law Margaret in Flanders, because she is afraid that Henry Tudor will come and seize the throne.

Outside St Albans a pedlar rides beside me for a few miles and tells me that he heard from one of his most respectable customers that the queen is no queen at all but a witch who enchanted the king, and their children are not true heirs but were got by magic. He has a new ballad in his pack: the story of Melusina, the water-witch who pretended to be mortal to get children from her lord and then was revealed as a nixie, a water-sprite. It is pointless to listen to him lustily singing the ballad, and foolish to listen to rumours which merely fuel my fear of the queen's malice, but I cannot stop myself. What is worse is that everyone in the country is doing the same – we are all listening to rumours and wondering what the queen will do. We are all praying that Richard will be able to prevent her putting her son on the throne, allowing her brother to command him, taking the country into war again.

As we ride through Barnet, where my father is still remembered fighting against this queen and her family, I turn aside to the little chapel that they have built at the battlefield and light a candle for him. Somewhere out there, under the ripening corn, are the bodies of his men who were buried where they lay, and somewhere out there is Midnight, the horse that gave his life in our service. Now I know that we are facing another battle, and this time my father's son-in-law is – must be – the kingmaker.

I am off my horse and up the stairs and into our apartments at a run and in a moment Richard's arms are tight around me and we are clinging to each other as if we have survived a shipwreck. We hold each other as we did when we were little more than children and had run away together to be married. Once again I remember him as the only man who could keep me safe, as he holds me as if I am the only woman he has ever wanted.

'I am so glad you are here,' he says in my ear.

'I am so glad you are safe,' I reply.

We step back to look at each other as if we cannot believe that we have got through these dangerous days. 'What's happening?' I ask.

He glances to see that the door is closed. 'I've uncovered part of a plot,' he says. 'I swear that it reaches throughout London, but I have it by the tail at least. Edward's mistress Elizabeth Shore has been playing the part of go-between between Elizabeth Woodville and the king's friend William Hastings.'

'But I thought it was Hastings who sent for you?' I interrupt. 'I thought he wanted the prince to be taken from the Rivers' keeping? I thought he warned you to come quickly?'

'He did. When I first came to London, he told me that he feared the power of the Rivers. Now he has turned his coat. I don't know how she has managed to get hold of him but she has enchanted him as she does everyone. At any rate, I know of it in time. She has created a ring of plotters against my brother's last words and against me. They are Hastings, perhaps Archbishop Rotherham, certainly Bishop Morton and perhaps Thomas, Lord Stanley.'

'Margaret Beaufort's husband?'

He nods. This is bad news for us, since Lord Stanley is famous for always being on the winning side; if he is against us, then our chances are not good.

'They don't want me to crown the boy and serve as his chief councillor. They want him in their keeping – not mine. They want to get him away from me, restore the power of the Rivers, and arrest me for treason. Then they'll crown him, or declare a regency with Anthony Woodville as Lord Protector. The boy has become a prize. The little prince has become a pawn.'

I shake my head. 'What will you do?'

He smiles grimly. 'Why, I shall arrest them for treason. Plotting against the Lord Protector is treason, just as if I were king. I am already holding Anthony Woodville and Richard Grey. I shall arrest Hastings and the bishops also, I shall arrest Thomas, Lord Stanley.'

There is a tap at the door and my ladies come in with my chests of clothes. 'Not in here,' my husband orders them. 'Her Grace and I will sleep in the rooms at the back of the house.'

They curtsey and go out again. 'Why are we not in our usual rooms?' I ask. We normally have the beautiful rooms that overlook the river.

'It's safer at the back of the house,' he says. 'The queen's brother has taken the fleet to sea. If he sails up the Thames and bombards us, we could take a direct hit. This house has never been fortified – but who would have thought that we would face an attack from the river by our own fleet?'

I look out of the wide windows at the view I love, of the river and the ships, the ferries, the little rowing boats, the barges and the scows all going by at peace. 'The queen's brother might bombard us? From our river, the Thames? In our own house?'

He nods. 'This is a time of wonders,' he says. 'I wake every morning and try to puzzle out what new hell she is devising.'

'Who is with us?' It is the question that my father would always ask.

'Buckingham has emerged as a true friend; he hates the wife that they forced on him and all the Rivers family. He commands a fortune and many men. I can also count on all of my men from the North of course; John Howard; my personal friends; my Lady Mother's affinity; your side of the family, of course, so all the Nevilles ...'

I am listening intently. 'It's not enough,' I say. 'And mostly based in the North. She can call out the royal household, and all her own family that she has put in such great positions. She can call on help from Burgundy, from her kinsmen in Europe. Perhaps she has made an alliance with the King of France already? France would back her rather than you, thinking they have a greater advantage to make trouble with a woman in power. And as soon as they know you are in London, the Scots will take the chance to rise.'

He nods. 'I know. But I have the prince in my keeping,' he says. 'That is my master card. Remember how it was with the old king Henry? If you hold the king then there is really no argument. You have the power.'

'Unless you simply crown another king,' I remind him. 'That's what my father did with your brother. He held Henry; but he crowned Edward. What if she puts her other boy on the throne? Even though you hold the true heir?'

'I know. I have to get her second son into my keeping too. I have to hold anyone who might claim to be king.'

Richard's mother and I sit together for company in the back rooms of Baynard's Castle. The nagging noise of the busy streets drifts through the open windows, the stink of London comes in on the hot air, but Richard has asked us to stay away from the cool gardens that lead down to the river, and never to go near the riverside windows. We may not go out into the streets without an armed guard. He does not know if the Rivers have hired assassins against us. The duchess is pale with anxiety; she has some sewing in her hands but she works at random, picking it up and putting it down again at the least noise from the streets outside the window.

'I wish to God he would put her to death,' she says suddenly. 'Make an end of her. Her and all her ill-gotten children.'

I am silent. It is so near to my own thoughts that I hardly dare to agree.

'We have not had one peaceful or happy day since she enchanted my son Edward,' she says. 'He lost the love of your father for her, he lost the chance of an honourable marriage that would have brought peace between us and France. He threw away the honour of his family by bringing her sturdy brood into our house, and now she will put one of her changeling sons on our throne. She told him to kill George – I know it, I was there as she advised him. Edward would never have decided on the death sentence on his own. It was her spy who killed your sister. And now she plots the death of my last living son, Richard. The day that he falls because of her enchantment she will have taken every single one of my sons.'

I nod. I dare not say anything out loud.

'Richard is ill,' she mutters. 'I swear it is her doing. He says that his shoulder aches and he cannot sleep. What if she is tightening a rope around his heart? We should warn her that if she harms so much as one hair of his head we will kill her boy.'

'She has two boys,' I say. 'She has two chances at the throne. All we would do by killing Prince Edward would be to give the throne to Prince Richard.'

She glances at me in surprise. She did not know I was so hardened. But she did not realise that I watched my sister scream in pain, trying to deliver a baby in a witch's wind, and die from a witch's poison. If I ever had a tender heart it has been broken and frightened too often. I too have a son to defend, I have his little cousins. I have a husband who walks up and down the bedroom at night, clutching his sword arm as the pain wakes him from sleep.

'Richard will have to get the other boy into his keeping,' she says. 'We have to hold both the Rivers heirs.'

That evening Richard comes in and greets me and his mother abstractedly. We go through the great hall to dine at the high table and Richard nods grimly as his men cheer him to his place. Everyone knows we are in danger; we feel like a house under siege. When he leans on his right arm as he goes to sit at his place it gives way beneath him and he stumbles and clutches at his shoulder.

'What is it?' I whisper urgently.

'My arm,' he says. 'I am losing the strength in it. She is working on me. I know it.'

I hide my fear and smile out over the hall. There will be people here who will report to the queen, hiding in the shadowy walls of sanctuary. They will tell her that her enemy is vulnerable. She is not far away, just down the river in the gloomy chambers below the Abbey of Westminster. I can almost feel her presence in the hall: like a cold diseased breath.

Richard dips his hands in the silver bowl that is presented to him and wipes his hands on the linen cloth. The servers bring out the food from the kitchen, and take the dishes round to all the tables.

'A bad business today,' Richard says quietly to me. From the other side his mother leans forwards to listen. 'I had proof of the plot that I suspected, between Hastings and the queen. His whore was go-between. Morton was in it too. I accused them in council and arrested them.'

'Well done,' his mother says at once.

'Will you have them tried?' I ask.

He shakes his head. 'No,' he says shortly. 'There was no time. These are the fortunes of war. I had Hastings beheaded at the Tower. Morton I have put in the care of Henry Stafford the Duke of Buckingham. Rotherham and Thomas, Lord Stanley I will hold under suspicion. I have had their homes searched for evidence, I will execute them if I find that they are plotting against me.'

I say not one word as a server offers us a fricassee of chicken. When he has moved on I whisper: 'Beheaded? William Hastings? Without trial? Just like that?'

His mother flares at me. 'Just like that!' she repeats. 'Why not just like that? You think that the queen demanded a fair trial for my son? You think that George had a fair trial when she called for his death?'

'No,' I say, acknowledging the truth of what she says.

'Well, anyway, it's done,' Richard says, breaking into a loaf of white bread. 'I could not put the prince on the throne with Hastings in league with the queen against me. As soon as he was crowned king and free to choose his advisors they would have taken him from me and put my death warrant before him. He would have signed it too. It is clear to me when I speak to him that he is utterly their boy, he is completely at their beck and call. I shall have to have Anthony Woodville, Richard Grey and Thomas Vaughan, their kinsman, executed too. They would all command the prince against me. When they are dead I will be safe.' He looks at my aghast face. 'This is the only way I can crown him,' he says. 'I have to destroy his mother's affinity. I have to make him a king with only one councillor – myself. When they are dead I have to face only her – the plot is broken.'

'You have to wade through the blood of innocent men,' I say flatly.

He meets my eyes without wavering. 'To get him on the

throne,' he says. 'To make him a good king and not their cat's-paw: yes, yes I do.'

In her dark sanctuary the queen makes her spells and whispers incantations against us. I know that she does. I can almost feel her ill-will pressing like river mist against the bolted windows of the back rooms of Baynard's Castle. I hear from my ladies in waiting that the queen has surrendered her second son into the care of her friend and kinsman Cardinal Bourchier. The cardinal swore to her that the boy would be safe, and took the boy Richard from her to join his brother Edward in the royal rooms in the Tower to prepare for the coronation.

I cannot believe that it is going ahead. Even if we hold the boys in our keeping, even if we take them to Middleham Castle and treat them as our own children, the prince is not an ordinary child. He can never be treated as an ordinary ward. He is a boy of twelve years old raised to be a king. He adores his mother and will never betray her. He has been educated and schooled and advised by his uncle Anthony Woodville; he will never transfer his love and loyalty to us, we are strangers to him, they may have told him we are his enemies. They have held him in their thrall from his babyhood, he is absolutely the child of their making, nothing can change that now. She has won him from us, his true family, just as she won her husband from his brothers. Richard is going to crown a boy who will grow up to be his deadliest enemy – however kindly we treat him. Richard is going to make Elizabeth Woodville the mother to the King of England. She is going to take my father's title of 'the king-maker'. There is no doubt in my mind that she will do just as my father would have done: bide her time and then slowly eliminate all rivals.

'What else can I do?' Richard demands of me. 'What else can I do but crown the boy who has been raised to be my enemy? He is my brother's son, he is my nephew. Even if I think he has been raised to be my enemy, what else, in honour, can I do?'

His mother at the fireside raises her head to listen. I feel her dark blue gaze on me. This is a woman who stood in the centre of Ludlow and waited for the riotous bad queen's army to burst through the gates. This is not a woman who has much fear. She nods at me as if to give me permission to say the one thing, the obvious thing.

'You had better take the throne,' I say simply.

Richard looks at me. His mother smiles, and lays aside her sewing work. There has not been a good stitch put in it for days.

'Do as your brother did,' I say. 'Not once but twice. He took the throne from Henry in battle not once but twice, and Henry had a far better right to it than the Rivers boy. The boy is not even crowned, not even ordained. He is nothing but one claimant to the throne and you are another. He may be the king's son but he is a boy. He may not even be his legitimate son, but a bastard, one of many. You are the king's brother, and a man, and ready to rule. Take the throne from him. It's the safest thing for England, it's the best thing for your family, it's the best thing for you.' I feel my heart suddenly pulse with ambition, my father's ambition – that I should be Queen of England after all.

'Edward appointed me as Lord Protector, not as his heir,' Richard says drily.

'He never knew the nature of the queen,' I say passionately. 'He went to his grave under her spell. He was her dupe.'

'The boy is not even Edward's heir,' his mother suddenly interjects.

Richard holds up his hand to stop her. 'Anne doesn't know of this.'

'Time she did,' she says briskly. She turns to me. 'Edward was married to a lady, a kinswoman of yours: Eleanor Butler. Did you know?'

'I knew she was . . .' I look for words. 'A favourite.'

'Not just his whore, they were married in secret,' the duchess says bluntly. 'Just the same trick as he played on Elizabeth Woodville. He promised marriage, went through a form of words with some hedge priest ...'

'Hardly a hedge priest,' Richard interrupts from his place, glowering into the fire, one hand resting on the chimney breast. 'He had Bishop Stillington perform the service with Eleanor Butler.'

His mother shrugs away the objection. 'So that marriage was valid. It was a priest with no name and perhaps no calling with the Woodville woman. His marriage to Elizabeth Woodville was false. It was bigamy.'

'What?' I interrupt, grasping none of this. 'Lady Mother, what are you saying?'

'Ask your husband,' she says. 'Bishop Stillington told the story himself – didn't he?' she demands of Richard. 'The bishop stood by and said nothing while Edward ignored Lady Eleanor and she went into a nunnery. Edward rewarded his silence. But when the bishop saw that the Rivers were putting their boy on the throne, and he a bastard, he went to your husband and told him all he knew: Edward was married when he made his secret agreement with Elizabeth Woodville. Even if it was a valid priest, even if it was a valid service, it still was nothing. Edward was already married. Those children, all those children, are bastards. There is no House of Rivers. There is no queen. She is a mistress and her bastard sons are pretenders. That is all.'

I turn in amazement to Richard. 'Is this true?'

He shoots a swift beleaguered look at me. 'I don't know,' he says shortly. 'The bishop says he married Edward to Lady Eleanor in a valid ceremony. They are both dead. Edward claimed Elizabeth Woodville as his wife and her son as his heir. Don't I have to honour my brother's wishes?'

'No,' his mother says bluntly. 'Not when he was wishing wrong. You don't have to put a bastard on the throne in preference to yourself.'

Richard turns his back to the fire. His hand cups his shoulder. 'Why did you never speak of this before? Why did I hear it first from Bishop Stillington?'

She takes up her sewing. 'What was there to tell? Everyone knows that I hate her and that she hates me. While Edward was alive and prepared to call her his wife and own the children, what difference would it make what I said? What anyone said? He had Bishop Stillington silenced, why should I speak out?'

Richard shakes his head. 'There have been scandals about Edward ever since he took the throne,' he says.

'And not one word against you,' his mother reminds him. 'Take the throne yourself. There is not one man in England who would defend Elizabeth Woodville unless he was one of her family or she had already bribed him into her service. Everyone else knows her for what she is: a seductress and a witch.'

'She will be my enemy for life,' Richard remarks.

'Then keep her in sanctuary for life,' she says, smiling, hag-like herself. 'Keep her on holy ground, in the half-darkness, and her little coven of daughters with her. Arrest her. Keep her there, the troglodyte with her bastard breed.'

Richard turns to me. 'What do you think?'

The room is silent, waiting for my decision. I think of my father who killed his great horse and then lost his own life fighting the battle to put me on the throne of England. I think of Elizabeth Woodville, who has been the bane of my days and the murderer of my sister. 'I think that you have a greater claim to the throne than her son,' I say out loud. And I think: 'And I have a greater claim to the throne than her. I shall be, as I was supposed to be, Queen Anne of England.'

Still he hesitates. 'It is a big step, to take the throne.'

I go to him and take his hand. It is as if we were handfasted, plighting our troth once more. I find I am smiling and I can feel my cheeks are warm. In this moment of decision I am indeed my father's daughter. 'This is your destiny,' I tell him, and I can hear my own voice ringing with certainty. 'By birth, by inclination, and by education, you are the best king that England could have in these times. Do it, Richard. Take your chance. It is my birthright as it is yours. Let us take it. Let us take it together.'

THE TOWER OF LONDON,
JULY 1483

Once more I am in the royal apartments of the Tower, looking through the slit windows at the moon laying a silver path on the dark waters of the river. Once more I am conscious of the silence of the night and from far away the distant sound of music playing. It is the night before our coronation, and I have come away from the celebration feast to pray and look out at the swiftly flowing water as the river rushes down to the sea. I am to be Queen of England. Once more I whisper to myself the promise that was first made to me by my father. I am to be Queen Anne of England, and I will be crowned tomorrow.

I know that She will be at her little window, peering out at the darkness outside the sanctuary, her beautiful face twisted with grief as she prays for her sons, knowing that we have them both in our keeping, and that neither of them will ever be king. I know she will be cursing us, twisting some bloody rag in her hands, moulding some wax figure, pounding herbs and burning them on the fire. Her whole attention will be on the Tower just like the moon that tonight makes a silvery path on the water that points to their bedroom.

Their bedroom, the bedroom of her boys. For they are here, both boys, in the Tower with me, on the floor above. If I went up only one turn of the circular stone stairs and told their guard to step aside I could go into their rooms and see them sleeping, in one bed, the moon pale on their pale faces, their eyelashes dark on their cheeks, their warm little chests in white lace-trimmed linen, rising and falling, in the deep peace of infant sleep. The prince is only twelve years old, with the faintest of fair down on his upper lip, his legs sprawled on the bed as gangly as a colt. His brother Richard is ten years old next month; he was born in the same year as my son Edward. How can I ever look at her son without thinking of my own? He is a merry little boy, even lost in sleep he smiles at some amusing dream. These boys are in our keeping now, they will be our wards until they grow into men. We will have to hold them at Middleham Castle or Sheriff Hutton, one of our northern homes where we can trust the servants to keep them close. I foresee that we will have to hold them forever. They will grow from enchanting boys to prisoners. We can never let them go.

They will always be a danger to us. They will always be a focus of any discontent, for anyone who wants to question our rule. Elizabeth Woodville will spend her life trying to get them away from us, trying to restore them to the throne. We will be taking our gravest threat into our own home. Their father, King Edward, would never have tolerated such a danger. My father would have felt the same. My father held King Edward once and said that after Edward escaped and put himself back on the throne he knew that there was no choice next time but to capture and kill him. Edward learned this lesson from my father. When he held the old king, Henry, he kept him safe only as long as there was a Lancaster heir. My husband Prince Edward's death was the death warrant for his father. When King Edward saw that he could end the House of Lancaster he did it that night: he killed King Henry and his brothers George and Richard aided the murder, the regicide. They realised that alive he would always be a focus of rebellion, a danger to them. Dead he could be mourned; but he was no threat. There is no doubt in my mind that the Woodville boy alive is a danger to us. Really, neither of these boys should be suffered to live. It is only my weak tender-ness and Richard's love of his brother that makes us decide that they should be spared. Neither my father nor Richard's brother would ever have been such soft-hearted fools.

I wrap my fur cloak a little closer around me though the night is warm; the breeze through my open window has the chill of the deep river. I think how Isabel would laugh to see me now, in Elizabeth Woodville's furs – the same priceless miniver that Isabel once put in her chest of gowns, and then had to give back. Isabel would laugh at our triumph. We have won tonight, in the end we have won, and the little girl that I was then, who played at being queen on the night of Elizabeth Woodville's coronation, in this very tower, will wear the crown tomorrow.

And the doubts that my mother whispered to me matter not at all. Whether my marriage was valid or not, my coronation will be done by an archbishop with sacred oil. I shall be Queen of England and I shall be at peace. Richard made me his wife in the eyes of God; he makes me his queen before all the world. I need wonder no more if he loves me. He has given me his ring in pri-vate and the crown in public. I shall be Queen Anne as my father wanted me to be.

I put aside the fur, dropping it on a chair as if it were of little value. I have a wardrobe full of furs now, I have the finest jewels, and I will have a fortune paid to me every year to maintain the queen's household as it should be. I shall live as grandly as the queen before me, I have all Elizabeth's gowns and I will have them cut down to my size. I slide between the warmed silky sheets of the great bed, with the cloth-of-gold canopy and the red velvet-lined curtains. From now on, I shall only have the finest things around me. From now on I shall only have the best. I was born the daughter of the kingmaker, and tomorrow his plan for me comes to fruition and I shall be queen. And when my hus-band dies, our son Edward, the kingmaker's grandson, will be king in his turn, and the House of Warwick will be the royal house of England.

A ROYAL PROGRESS,
SUMMER 1483

The welcome that we get along the road, at every halt, tells us that we have done the right thing. The country is almost mad with relief that the danger of war has been averted, and that my husband has led us to peace. Richard has gathered around him men that he can trust. Henry Stafford the Duke of Buckingham left his Woodville wife at home to lead Richard into the cathedral as Lord Chamberlain of England. John Howard, who recaptured the fleet from the Rivers for us, becomes the new first Howard Duke of Norfolk and keeps the ships he won; he is Lord Admiral. My kinsman the Earl of Northumberland is given the wardenship of the North to hold for a year. We travel without a guard, secure in the knowledge that there is no-one in England who does not welcome us. Our enemies are dead or cooped up in sanctuary, the Rivers boys are safely held in the Tower. And at every town where we stay, Reading, Oxford, Gloucester, they put on pageants and festivals to welcome us and to assure us of their loyalty.

The Rivers had made themselves so hated that the people would have taken almost any powerful ruler rather than a boy whose family would devour England. But better than this, the people have a Plantagenet on the throne again: my husband, who looks so like his namesake and well-loved father, whose brother rescued the country from the sleeping king and the bad queen, and who now rescues it once more from another ambitious woman.

Nobody even asks after the boys that we have left in the Tower in London. Nobody wants to remember them or their mother, who still skulks in the darkness of sanctuary. It is as if the whole country wants to forget that there were months of fear about what might happen, and weeks when nobody knew who would be king. Now we have a king crowned in the sight of the people and ordained by God, and he and I ride together through England at the very height of summertime, picnic under clumps of trees when the sun is hot, and enter the beautiful towns of England where they welcome us as their saviours.

Only one person asks me about the Rivers boys, left behind in the quiet Tower of London, asking for their mother in sanctuary, just three miles upriver. Sir Robert Brackenbury, now made Keeper of the Exchange and Constable of the Tower, has responsibility for guarding them. He is the only person to say to me in his blunt Yorkshire way: 'So what's to happen to the Rivers bastards, Your Grace? Now that we have them and they are in my keeping?'

He is an honest man, and I would trust him with almost anything. I take his arm as we walk in the courtyard of the beautiful college at Oxford. 'They have no future,' I tell him. 'They can be neither princes nor men. We will have to hold them forever. But my husband knows, as I do, that they will be a danger forever for us. They will be a danger just in their being. They will be a threat to us for as long as they live.'

He pauses and turns to me. His honest gaze meets mine. 'God save you, would you wish them dead, Your Grace?' he asks simply.

I shake my head in instant revulsion. 'I can't wish it,' I say. 'Not a couple of boys, not a pair of innocent boys.'

'Ah, you're too tender-hearted . . .'

'I can't wish it – but what life can they have? They will be prisoners forever. Even if they were to give up all claims to the throne there will always be someone who would claim it for them. And what safety can we have while they live?'

We are going to York where our son – Prince Edward as he now is – will be invested as Prince of Wales. It is a compliment to the city that has supported Richard from first to last and where he is loved better than in any other part of the country. We get a welcome into the walled city greater than anything we have yet seen. In the high-vaulted York Minster my boy Edward walks forwards, watched by his cousins Edward and Margaret, and takes the golden wand and little gold crown of the Prince of Wales. The cheers when he comes out on the steps of the Minster to greet the crowds send the birds whirling into the sky. I cross myself, and whisper, 'Thank God.' I know that my father is watching his grandson invested as Prince of Wales, and that in heaven he knows that his struggle has ended, at last, in victory. The kingmaker has made a prince of his grandson. There will be a Warwick boy on the throne of England.

We will stay in the North for some time, and this will always be our home, as we are happier here than anywhere else. We will rebuild the palace of Sheriff Hutton where the children will live, safely away from the diseases and plagues of London, safely distant, I think, from the brooding presence of the defeated queen in her damp holt under Westminster Abbey. We will make this a new palace in the North of England, a place to rival Windsor, or Greenwich, and the wealth from the court will spill out to our friends and neighbours, the northern affinity that we trust. We will make a golden kingdom of the North, great enough to rival the City of London itself. The heart of the country will be here, where the king and queen – northern by birth and inclination – live among the high green hills.

My son Edward and his cousins Margaret and Teddy and I go

to Middleham, riding merrily together, as if we are out for pleasure. I will stay with them for the rest of the summer, Queen of England and mistress of my own time. In winter we will all go back to London and I shall have the children with me at Greenwich. Edward will have to have more tutors and more training in horse-riding; we have to build up his strength for he is still a slight boy. He has to be prepared to be king in his own turn. In a few years he will go to live at Ludlow and his council will rule Wales.

As we take the road north for Middleham, Richard leaves us and starts the journey southwards once more with a tiny escort around him, among them our longstanding friends Sir James Tyrrell, now made Master of Henchmen, Francis Lovell, Robert Brackenbury and the others. Richard kisses the children and blesses them. He holds me in his arms and whispers to me to come to him as soon as the weather turns. I feel my heart warm with love for him. We are at last victorious, we are at last blessed. He has made me Queen of England, as I was born to be, and I have given him a prince and an heir. Together we have fulfilled my father's vision. This is victory indeed.

On the road going south, Richard writes me a hasty letter.

Anne,

The Rivers like a scotched snake are up and more dangerous than ever. They mounted an attack on the Tower to rescue their boys and were narrowly beaten off in a desperate battle. We can arrest no-one – they have melted away. Anne, I tell you, I had her so closely guarded that I thought that no-one could get in or out from her dark sanctuary but she somehow raised a small army up against us. Her army without livery or insignia came and went like ghosts, and now nobody can tell me where they are. Someone mustered troops and paid them – but who?

We still hold the boys, thank God. I have moved them into inner rooms in the Tower. But I am shocked at the extent of her hidden power. She will be biding her time and then she will flare up again. How many can she recruit? How many who cheered at our coronation sent men and weapons to her? I am betrayed and I don't know who to trust. Burn this.

'What is it, Your Grace?' Little Margaret is at my side, her dark blue eyes puzzled at my aghast face. I put my arm around her and feel her warmth and softness and she leans into my side. 'Not bad news?' she asks. 'Not the king, my uncle?'

'He has worries,' I say, thinking of the wickedness of the woman who hides in the darkness and made this little girl an orphan. 'He has enemies. But he is strong and brave and he has good friends who will help him against the bad queen and her bastard so-called sons.'

MIDDLEHAM CASTLE, YORKSHIRE, OCTOBER 1483

I speak to Margaret with confidence but I am mistaken. My husband has fewer friends than I thought, than he thought.

A few days later comes a hurried scrawl:

The falsest of friends, the most wicked of turncoats – the Duke of Buckingham is the most untrue creature living.

I drop the page for a moment, and can hardly bear to read on.

He has joined with two evil women, each as bad as the other. Elizabeth Woodville has seduced him to her side, and she has made a hags' alliance with Margaret Beaufort, who carried your train at our coronation, who was always so good and loving to you, the wife of my friend, the trusted Lord Thomas Stanley, whom I made Lord Chamberlain.

Falseness upon deceit.

Margaret has betrothed her son, Henry Tudor, to Elizabeth, the Rivers girl – and they are all up against us, mustering their affinity, sending for Henry Tudor to sail from Brittany. Henry Stafford Duke of Buckingham, the one man I would have trusted with my life, has turned his coat and is on their side. He is now

*raising his forces in Wales, and will march into England soon. I
leave at once for Leicester.*

*Worst of all – even worse than all of this – Buckingham is
telling everyone that the princes are dead and by my hand. This
means the Rivers will fight to put Tudor and Princess Elizabeth
on the throne. This means that the country – and history –
names me a murderer, a killer of children, a tyrant who turns on
his brother's son and takes his own blood. I cannot bear this slur
on my name and honour. This is a slander which will stick like
pitch. Pray for me and for our cause – Richard.*

I do as he bids me. I go straight to the chapel without a word to
anyone and I go down on my knees, my eyes fixed on the crucifix above the rood screen. I gaze at it unblinking, as if I would
burn away from my sight the letter which told me that the people
we had counted as friends – the handsome and charming Duke
of Buckingham, the winner Lord Thomas Stanley, his wife
Margaret who was so kind and welcoming to me when I first
came to London, who took me to the great wardrobe and helped
me to pick out my coronation gown – all these are false. Bishop
Morton, whom I have loved and admired for years – false too.
But the one sentence that stays with me, that rings in my ears
through my muttered Ave Maria, which I repeat over and over
again as if to drown out the sound of the few words, is –
*Buckingham is telling everyone that the princes are dead and by my
hand.*

It is dark when I rise to my feet, the early dark of autumn, and
I am cold and chilled as the priest brings in the candles and the
household follows him in for Compline. I bow my head as he
goes past but I stumble out of the chapel into the cold evening
air. A white owl hoots and goes low overhead and I duck as if it
is a spirit passing me by, a warning from the witch who is mass-
ing her forces against us.

*Buckingham is telling everyone that the princes are dead and by
my hand.*

I had thought that if the princes were dead then there would be no other claimant to the throne, that my husband's time on the throne would be untroubled, and my son would take his place when God saw fit to call us away. Now I see that every man is a kingmaker. A throne is not empty for a moment before someone is being measured for the crown. And fresh princes spring up like weeds in a crop as soon as the rumour goes out that those who wear the crown are dead:

Buckingham is telling everyone that the princes are dead and by my hand.

And now, another young man, calling himself heir, appears from nowhere. Henry Tudor, the son of Margaret Beaufort of the House of Lancaster and Edmund Tudor of the House of Tudor, should be out of mind as he has been out of sight. He has not set foot in this country for years, not since his mother hustled him abroad to keep him safe from the basilisk gaze of the House of York. When Edward was on the throne the boy was many steps from being an heir, yet even so Edward would have taken him to the Tower, would quietly have seen to his death. That is why Margaret Beaufort kept him far away, and negotiated very cautiously for his return. I even pitied her as she missed her son. She even sympathised with me when George was going to send his son away. I thought we had an understanding. I thought we were friends. But all the time she was waiting. Waiting and thinking when her son could return, an enemy to the King of England whether the king was Edward or my husband Richard.

Buckingham is telling everyone that the princes are dead and by my hand.

So Henry Tudor has a claim to the throne, through the House of Lancaster, and his mother is no longer my friend but throws off her cloak of obedient affection and becomes a war-maker. She will make war against us. She will tell everyone that the princes are dead, and my husband their murderer. She will tell everyone that the next heir is her son and that they should overthrow such a tyrant, a regicide.

I go up the dark stairs to the north tower, where I have walked so many times with Richard, in the evening sunlight at the end of the day, talking over the joys of the children, the land, the ruling of the North. Now it is dark and cold and the moon is coming up with a silvery glow on the far horizon.

Buckingham is telling everyone that the princes are dead and by my hand.

I do not believe that my husband gave the order for the murder of his nephews. I will never believe it. He was secure on his throne, he had declared them as bastards. Nobody on our progress even mentioned them. They were forgotten and we were accepted. It was only me, talking to the keeper of the Tower, who said that though I could not wish for their death, I knew that I must think of it. And it was the Constable of the Tower, their gaoler, who remarked that I was tender-hearted. Richard would not have given the order to kill the boys; of that I am sure. But I know I am not the only person who loves Richard and wants to keep him safe. I know I am not the only person to think that the boys will have to die.

Has one of our loyal friends stooped to such a dark sin as to kill a ten-year-old boy and his twelve-year-old brother while they were in our keeping? While they slept? And worse – has someone done it thinking to please us? Has someone done it thinking it was my wish? Thinking that I walked with him in the quadrangle of the Oxford college, and then and there actually asked him to do it?

MIDDLEHAM CASTLE,
YORKSHIRE, WINTER 1483

We wait for news, and Richard writes to me almost daily, knowing how anxious I am. He tells me of the mustering of his forces; men are flocking to serve him, and the great nobles of the realm are turning out to support their king against the duke who was once at his side. His childhood friend Francis Lovell never leaves him, Thomas, Lord Stanley, though his own wife Margaret Beaufort plotted with Elizabeth Woodville, joins Richard and promises his loyalty. This shows, I think, how little the former queen can appeal to good men. She may have won over Margaret Beaufort – ambitious for her son and hoping for the throne – but she cannot win Thomas, Lord Stanley, who stays true to us. I don't forget that Thomas Stanley is a bellwether, leading the flock where everyone follows. That he is on our side shows that he calculates we are likely to win. John Howard, our good friend, stays faithful too, and Richard writes to me that Howard is holding down rebels in Sussex and Kent to stop war breaking out against us.

And then God blesses us. It is as simple as that. God is on our side. He sends down the rain that washes the treason out of people's minds, and the anger out of their hearts as day after day it pours with cold wintry water as hard as sleet, and the men who were mustering in Kent go home to dry fires, the men who thought they would march out of Sussex learn that the roads are impassable, and the citizens of London are flooded from their riverside homes and can spare no thought for anything but the rising waters that threaten the low-lying sanctuary where Elizabeth Woodville has to wait, without news of her rebellion, her messengers stuck where they are, on roads that have churned into mires, gradually losing hope.

God sends rain on Wales and all the little mountain streams that play so prettily through the meadows in midsummer get faster and rougher as the dark waters pour off the mountains into the bigger streams and then into the rivers. The torrents flood and break their banks and pour into the Severn river, which rises and rises until it breaches all the river walls, spreads for miles in the valley, maroons one town after another, drowns the riverside villages and – best of all – holds the false Duke of Buckingham in Wales, while his men melt away as if they were sugar men in the wet, and his hopes become sodden, and he himself runs away from the men that he said he would lead, and his own servant turns him in to us as a traitor for a small reward.

God sends the rain on the narrow seas so they are dark and menacing and Henry Tudor cannot set sail. I know what it is to look out from port and see dark moving water and white caps on the waves and I laugh, in the warmth and dryness of landlocked Middleham Castle, to think of Henry Tudor, standing on the quayside and praying for fine weather while it rains down unstoppably on his young auburn head, and not even the woman he hopes will be his mother-in-law, the witch Elizabeth, can hold back the storm.

There is a break in the weather and he sets sail bravely enough, crossing the rough seas, but his hopes have been chilled by the long wait and he does not even land. He takes a look at the coast that he plans to call his own and he cannot even find within himself the courage to set foot on the wet sand. He reefs his sodden sails and turns his boat for home and runs before a cold wind back to Brittany, where he should stay forever, if he would take my advice, and die like all pretenders, in exile.

Richard writes to me from London.

It is over. It is over but for naming of the traitors and ordering their punishment. It is a joy to me that Wales was true to me, that the south coast offered no safe haven to Henry Tudor, not a single town opened its gates to a rebel force, not one baron or earl defied me. My kingdom is loyal to me and I shall punish lightly or not at all those who were drawn to this reckless last gasp of the Rivers and their new-found, ill-chosen ally, Henry Tudor. The boy's mother, Margaret Beaufort, cannot be expected to deny the cause of her son but she will live the rest of her days under house arrest – in the charge of her husband, Thomas, Lord Stanley. I have put her fortune in his keeping, which for a grasping ambitious woman will – I think – be punishment enough. He will keep her close, she has been stripped of her servants and her friends, not even her confessor can attend her. I have broken her affinity as I have broken the alliances around the Rivers.

I am victorious without raising my sword. This is my vindication as well as an easy victory. The country does not seek to restore the Rivers, they certainly don't want the stranger, Henry Tudor. Margaret Beaufort and Elizabeth Woodville are seen as foolish mothers conspiring together for their children, nothing more than that. The Duke of Buckingham is despised as a traitor and a false friend. I shall take care whom I befriend in future, but you can see this as an easy victory and – though a hard few weeks – part of our ascension to our throne. Please God we shall look back on this and be glad that we came to our royal estate so easily.

Come to London, we shall keep Christmas as royally as Edward and Elizabeth ever did, with true friends and loyal servants.

Just as we are readying ourselves for the Christmas feast – a feast which Richard swears will be the grandest that London has ever seen – just as people start to arrive at court and are allocated their rooms, told their parts in the entertainments, and learn the new dances, Richard comes looking for me and finds me in the great rooms of the wardrobe, looking over the gowns that belonged to the other queens, and now belong to me. I am planning to take apart two beautiful old-fashioned gowns of cloth of gold and deep purple to make a new one, layered in a new pattern with purple sleeves slashed to show the gold beneath, gathered with a gold braid at the wrist. On either side of me are great bales of cloth for more new gowns, and furs and velvets for new capes and jackets for Richard himself. He looks ill at ease, but he always looks ill at ease, these days. The crown sits heavily on him, and he can trust no-one.

'Can you leave this?' Richard asks, looking doubtfully at the mountains of priceless cloth.

'Oh yes,' I say, lifting my gown and picking my way over the cuttings on the floor. 'My lady wardrobe mistress knows far better than I what is to be done.'

He takes me by the arm and draws me to the little area off the main wardrobe room, where the wardrobe mistress usually sits to make her audit of the furs, gowns, robes and shoes in her keeping. There is a warm fire burning in the grate and Richard takes the seat by the table and I perch on the window seat and wait.

'I have taken a decision,' he says heavily. 'I did not take it lightly, and still I want to talk it over with you.'

I wait. It will be about the Woodville woman, I know it. I can tell by the way he is holding his right arm, between the elbow and the shoulder. This is a constant pain for him now, and no physician can tell him what is wrong. I know, though I have no proof, that the pain is of her doing. I imagine her knotting a rag around her own arm, feeling it prickle and go numb, and then wishing the pain on him.

'It's about Henry Tudor,' he says.

I stiffen in my seat. I did not expect this.

'He is going to hold a betrothal ceremony in Rennes cathedral. He is going to declare himself King of England and betrothed to Elizabeth.'

For a moment I forget the daughter in thinking of the ill-will of the mother. 'Elizabeth Woodville?'

'Her daughter, Elizabeth Princess of York.'

The familiar name of Edward's favourite daughter falls into the cosy little room, and I think of the girl with skin like a warm pearl, and the smiling charm of her father. 'He said she was his most precious child,' Richard says quietly. 'When we had to fight our way home from Flanders he said that he would do it for her, even if everyone else was dead. And that it would be worth any risk to see her smile again.'

'She was always terribly spoiled,' I say. 'They took her everywhere, and she always put herself forwards.'

'And now she is up to my shoulder and a beauty. I wish Edward could see her, I think she is even more beautiful than her mother was at that age. She is a woman grown – you would not know her.'

With a slow uncoiling of anger I realise that he is speaking of her as she is now. He has been to see her, he has been to see the

Woodville woman and he has seen Elizabeth. While I have been here, preparing for the Christmas court that is to celebrate our coming to power, he has slipped away to the dark hovel that is her choice. 'You have seen her?'

He shrugs as if it does not much matter. 'I had to go and see the queen,' he says.

I am the queen. It seems that he has made one visit to the Woodville woman and forgotten everything that we hold dear. Everything that we have fought to win.

'I wanted to ask her about the boys.'

'No!' I cry out, and then I put my hand over my mouth so that no-one can hear my arguing with my husband, the king. 'My lord, I beg you. How could you do such a thing? Why would you do such a thing?'

'I had to know.' He looks haunted. 'They told me of Buckingham's rebellion and his words at the same time. One was as bad as the other. I wrote to you at once.'

Buckingham is telling everyone that the princes are dead and by my hand.

I nod. 'I remember. But . . .'

'I sent at once to the Tower, as soon as I heard that everyone was saying they were dead. All they could tell me was that the boys were gone. As soon as I got to London, the first thing I did was go to the Tower. Robert was there—'

'Robert?' I ask, as if I have forgotten the name of the Constable of the Tower. Robert Brackenbury, who looked at me with his honest understanding and said, 'Oh, you're tender-hearted' when I said that the boys should be killed, but that I could not bring myself to give the order in so many words.

'Brackenbury,' he says. 'A true friend. He would be true to me. He would do anything for me.'

'Oh yes,' I say, and I can feel dread in my belly as if I have been drinking ice. 'I know he would do anything for you.'

'He doesn't know what has happened to the boys. He is the Constable of the Tower and he did not know. All he could say was that when he got to the Tower the boys were gone. All the guards would say was that they put them to bed one night and guarded the door all night and in the morning they were gone.'

'How could they just go?'

His old energy returns. 'Well, someone must be lying. Someone must have bribed a guard.'

'But who?'

'I thought perhaps the queen had taken them. I was praying that she had taken them. That's why I went to see her. I said to her, I won't even pursue them, I won't even try to find them. If you have smuggled them away somewhere, they can stay there in safety. But I have to know.'

'What did she say? The Woodville woman?'

'She went down on her knees and she wept like a woman who knows heartbreak. There is no doubt in my mind that she has lost her sons and she doesn't know who has them. She asked me if I had taken them. She said she would put a curse on whoever has killed them, if they are dead, that her curse would take the murderer's son and his line would die without issue. Her daughter joined with her in the curse – they were terrifying.'

'She cursed us?' I whisper through cold lips.

'Not us! I didn't order their deaths!' he shouts at me in a sudden explosion of rage that echoes off the wooden panelling of the little room. 'I didn't order their deaths! Everybody thinks I did. Do you think so too? My own wife? You think I would do that? You think that I would murder my own nephews when they were in my keeping? You think I would do something as sinful, as criminal, as dishonourable as that? You call me a tyrant with blood on my hands? You? Of all the people in the world who know what I am? You who know that I have spent my life pledging my sword and my heart to honour? You too think me a killer?'

'No, no, no, Richard.' I catch his hands and shake my head and swear that I know he would not do such a thing. I stumble over my words before his furious face and the tears come, and I cannot tell him – dear God, I cannot tell him – no, it is not you but it might have been me who ordered their deaths. It might have been my careless speech, my thinking aloud which prompted this. And so it is my sin that will draw the curse of the Woodville woman onto the heads of my Edward so that our line is without a son like hers. In that one moment, when I thought I was protecting us, when I dropped a word into Robert Brackenbury's ear, I destroyed my future and everything my father worked for. I have drawn on my beloved son's head the righteous enmity of the most dangerous witch in England. If Robert Brackenbury thought he heard an order in my words, if he did what he thought was my bidding, if he did what he thought was best for Richard, then I have killed her sons and her revenge will be thorough. I have destroyed my own future.

'There was no need for me to kill them,' he says. To my ears, his voice is an exculpatory whine. 'I had them safe. I had them declared bastards. The country supported my coronation, my progress was a success, we were accepted everywhere, acclaimed. I was going to send them to Sheriff Hutton and keep them there, safe. That's why I wanted it rebuilt. In a few years' time, when they were young men, I was going to release them and honour them as my nephews, command them to come to court to serve us. Keep them under my eye, treat them as royal kinsmen . . .' He breaks off. 'I was going to be a good uncle to them, as I am to George's boy and his girl. I was going to care for them.'

'It would never have worked!' I cry out. 'Not with her as their mother. George's boy is one thing, Isabel was my beloved sister; but none of the Woodville woman's children will ever be anything but our most deadly enemy!'

'We'll never know,' he says simply. He gets to his feet, rubbing his upper arm as if it has gone numb. 'Now, we'll never know what men those two boys might have been.'

'She is our enemy,' I tell him again, amazed that he is such a fool he cannot remember this. 'She has betrothed her daughter to Henry Tudor. He was all set to invade England and put the

Woodville bastard girl on the throne as queen. She is our enemy and you should be dragging her out of sanctuary and imprisoning her in the Tower, not going in secret to visit her. Not going to her as if you were not the victor, the king. Not going and meeting her daughter – that spoiled ninny.' I break off at the dark rage in his face. 'Spoiled ninny,' I repeat defiantly. 'What will you tell me: that she is a princess beyond price?'

'She is our enemy no more,' he says briefly, as if all his rage has burned out. 'She has turned her rage on Margaret Beaufort. She suspects her, not me, of kidnapping or killing the princes. Their deaths make Henry Tudor the next heir, after all. Who gains from the deaths of the boys? Only Henry Tudor, who is the next heir of the House of Lancaster. Once she acquitted me she had to blame Tudor and his mother. So she turned against the rebellion, and she will deny the betrothal to him. She will oppose his claim.'

I am open-mouthed. 'She is changing sides?'

He smiles wryly. 'We can make peace, she and I,' he says. 'I have offered to release her to house arrest, somewhere of my choosing, and she has agreed to go. She can't stay in sanctuary for the rest of her life. She wants to get out. And those girls are growing up as pale as little lilies in shade. They need to be out in the fields. The older girl is simply exquisite, like a statue in pearl. If we set her free she will bloom like a rose.'

I can taste jealousy in my mouth like the bile that rushes under my tongue when I am about to be sick. 'And where is this rose to bloom?' I ask acidly. 'Not in one of my houses. I will not have her under my roof.'

He is looking at the fire but now he turns his beloved dark face to me. 'I thought we might take the three oldest girls to court,' he says. 'I thought they might serve in your household, if you will agree. These are Edward's daughters, York girls, they are your nieces. You should love them as you do little Margaret. I thought you might keep them under your eye and when the time comes we will find good husbands for them and see them settled.'

I lean back against the stone windowframe and feel the welcome coldness against my shoulders. 'You want them to come and live with me?' I ask him. 'The Woodville daughters?'

He nods, as if I might find this an agreeable plan. 'You couldn't ask for a more beautiful maid in waiting than the Princess Elizabeth,' he says.

'Mistress Elizabeth,' I correct him through my teeth. 'You declared her mother a whore and her a bastard. She is Mistress Elizabeth Grey.'

He laughs shortly as if he had forgotten. 'Oh yes.'

'And the mother?'

'I will settle her in the country. John Nesfield is as trustworthy as any of my men. I will put her and the younger girls in his house and he can watch them for me.'

'They will be under arrest?'

'They will be kept close enough.'

'Kept in the house?' I press. 'Locked in?'

He shrugs. 'As Nesfield sees fit, I suppose.'

I understand at once that Elizabeth Woodville is to be a lady of a fine country house once more and her daughters will live as maids in waiting at my court. They are to be as free as joyous birds in the air and Elizabeth Woodville is to triumph again.

'When is all this going to happen?' I ask, thinking he will say in the spring. 'In April? May?'

'I thought the girls might come to court at once,' he says.

I round on him at that, I leap from my window seat and stand. 'This is our first Christmas as king and queen,' I say, my voice trembling with passion. 'This is the court where we stamp ourselves on the kingdom, where people will see us in our crowns and tell of our clothes and entertainments and joy. This is when people start to make a legend about our court and say it is as beautiful and as joyous and as noble as Camelot. You want Elizabeth Woodville's daughters to sit at the table and eat their Christmas dinner at this – our first Christmas? Why not tell everyone that nothing has really changed? It is you on the throne instead of Edward but the Rivers still hold court and the witch still holds sway, and the blood of my sister and your brother, and their little baby, is still on her hands, and nobody accuses her.'

He comes to me and takes me by the elbow, feeling me tremble with rage. 'No,' he says gently. 'No. I hadn't thought. I see it would not do. This is your court, not hers. I know that. You are queen, I know that, Anne. Be calm. Nobody will spoil your time. They can come after Christmas, later when all the agreements have been properly drawn up. We need not have them earlier, spoiling the feast.'

He soothes me, as he has always been able to do. 'Spoiling it?'

'They would spoil it.' He lulls me with the sweetness of his voice. 'I don't want them there. I only want to be with you. They can stay in their cellar until after Christmas and only when you think the time is right will we release them.'

I am quietened by his touch like a gentled mare. 'Very well,' I breathe. 'But not before.'

'No,' he says. 'Not until you think the time is right. It shall be you who judges the right time, Anne. You are Queen of England and you shall have no-one in your household but those of your choice. You shall only have the women that you like around you. I would not force you to have women that you fear or dislike.'

'I don't fear them,' I correct him. 'I am not jealous of them.'

'No indeed,' he says. 'And you have no cause at all. You shall invite them when you are ready and not before.'

We spend Christmas in London without the children. I had hoped up to the very last days of November that they would come. Edward is well enough but our physician advised that he is not strong enough for a long journey on bad roads. They said that he should stay at Middleham, where our physicians, who know his health, will take care of him. They say that such a long journey in such bad weather would be bound to strain his health.

I think of little Prince Richard when I last saw him, just the age of my Edward, but a good head taller and rosy-cheeked and full of high spirits. Edward does not bubble with life, he does not always have to be up and doing. He will sit quietly with a book, and he goes to bed without arguing. In the morning he finds it hard to rise.

He eats well enough, but the cooks take great trouble to send up dainty dishes with tempting sauces. I have never once seen him go with Margaret and Teddy down to the kitchens to steal offcuts of pastry from the table, or beg the bakers for a bread roll, hot from the oven. He never filches cream from the dairy, he never loiters for trimmings from the roasting spit.

I try not to fear for him; he does his schoolwork with pleasure, he rides out on his horse with his cousins, he will play at tennis with them, or archery, or bowls, but he is always the first to stop the game, or turn away and sit for a few moments, or laugh and say that he has to catch his breath. He is not sturdy, he is not strong, he is in fact just as you would expect a boy to be if he had spent his life under a curse from a distant witch.

Of course I don't know if she has ever cursed my son. But sometimes when he sits at my feet and leans his head against my knees and I touch his head, I think that since her ill-will has blighted my life, I would not be surprised to know that it has burdened my son. And now that Richard speaks of a new curse laid down by the witch Elizabeth and her apprentice-witch daughter, on the murderer of their princes, I fear even more that the Rivers' malice is directed at me and my boy.

I command the physicians at Middleham to send me a letter every three days telling me how the children are. The letters get through the snowy weather in the North and the thickly bogged roads in the south and assure me that Edward is in good spirits, playing with his cousins, enjoying the wintry weather, sledging and skating on the ice. He is well. I can be of good heart. He is well.

Even without the children Richard is determined that we shall have a merry Christmas at court. We are a victorious court; everyone who comes to feast, to dance, or merely to watch knows that this first Christmas of our reign is made more joyful by knowing that when we were challenged – challenged in the first weeks of our reign by the former queen herself, and an untried boy who calls himself king – we were supported. England does not want Henry Tudor, England has forgotten the Rivers boys, is content to leave the Woodville queen in sanctuary. She is finished. That reign is over and this Christmas proclaims that ours is begun.

Every day we have entertainments, hunts, boating, contests, jousts, and dances. Richard commands the best musicians and playwrights to court, poets come and write songs for us and the chapel is filled with sacred music from the choir. Every day there is a new amusement for the court, and every day Richard gives me a little gift – a priceless pearl brooch or a pair of scented leather gloves, three new riding horses to take North for the children, or a great luxury – a barrel of preserved oranges from Spain. He showers me with gifts and at night comes to my grand apartments and spends the night with me, wrapping me in his arms as if only by holding me tightly can he believe that he has indeed made me queen.

Sometimes in the night I wake, and look at the tapestry which is hung over the bed, woven with scenes of gods and goddesses victorious and lolling on clouds. I think that I too should feel victorious. I am where my father wanted me to be. I am the greatest lady in the land – never again need I fear treading on someone's train – for now everyone follows me. But just as I am smiling at that thought, my mind goes to my son in the cold dales of Yorkshire, to his slight frame and the pallor of his skin. I think of the witch who still lives in sanctuary and will be celebrating her release this Christmas, and I take Richard in my embrace and feel for his sword arm, gently spanning it with my hand, as he is sleeping, to see if it is indeed wasting and withering as he thinks. I can't tell. Is Elizabeth Woodville a defeated widow whom I can pity? Or is she the greatest enemy to my family and to my peace?

GREENWICH PALACE,
LONDON, MARCH 1484

Spring comes early to London, weeks earlier than in our northern home, and when I wake in the morning I can hear the cocks crowing and the dairy cows lowing as they are driven through the streets to the meadows beside the river. With spring comes the parliament and they pass a law which recognises that Edward was married to another woman before his false wedding with the Woodville woman, and so all their children are bastards. It is law, the parliament has passed it, and it must be so. Elizabeth Woodville is Elizabeth Woodville once again, or she can call herself by the name of her first husband – her only true husband – and be Lady Elizabeth Grey, and her girls can cower under that name too. Richard presents his agreement with the Woodville woman, who is released into the care of Sir John Nesfield with her two youngest girls and they go off to live in his beautiful country house at Heytesbury, Wiltshire.

He sends Richard regular reports and I have sight of one which tells of the queen – in a slip of the pen he calls her the queen, as if I did not exist, as if the law had not been passed – riding and dancing, commanding a troop of local musicians, attending the local church, educating her girls, and interfering in the running of the home farm, changing the dairy and moving the beehives, advising him as to the furnishing, and planting a private garden with her favourite flowers. He sounds flustered and pleased. She sounds as if she is revelling in being a country lady once more. Her girls are running wild, Sir John has given them ponies and they are galloping all over Wiltshire. The tone of Sir John's report is indulgent, as if he is enjoying having his house turned upside down by a beautiful woman and two energetic girls. Most importantly he reports that she attends chapel daily and that she receives no secret messages. I should be glad that she is neither plotting nor casting spells, but I cannot rid myself of the wish that she was still in sanctuary, or locked in the Tower like her sons, or disappeared altogether like them too. There is no doubt in my mind that I would be at peace, that England would be at peace, if she had died with her husband or disappeared with her boys.

The three oldest Rivers girls come to court with their heads held high, as if their mother were not guilty of treason against us. Richard tells me that they will pay their respects to me in the morning, after chapel and breakfast, and I am conscious of arranging myself in the beautiful rooms of Greenwich Palace with my back to the bright light from the windows, in a dark gown of red and a high headdress of deep ruby lace. My ladies sit around me and the faces that they turn to the slowly opening door are not friendly. No woman wants three pretty girls beside her for comparison, and these are Rivers girls looking for husbands, as Rivers girls always are. Besides, half the court has knelt to these girls, and the other half kissed their baby fists and swore they were the prettiest princesses that had ever been seen. Now they are maids in waiting to a new queen, and they will never wear a crown again. Everyone is anxious that they understand their dive from grandeur to pauperdom, and everyone secretly hopes that they will misunderstand, and make fools of themselves. It is a cruel court, as all courts are, and nobody in my rooms has any reason to love the daughters of Elizabeth Woodville who queened it over all of us.

The door opens and the three of them come in. At once I

understand why Richard forgave the mother and ordered the girls to court. It was for love of his brother. The oldest, Elizabeth, now eighteen years old, is the most complete combination of her mother's exquisite beauty and her father's warmth. I would know her anywhere for Edward's daughter. She has his easy grace: she smiles around the room as if she thinks she is greeting friends. She has his height: she is tall and slender like a sapling from the oak tree where he was bewitched. She has his colouring: her mother was so fair that her hair is almost silvery, but this Elizabeth is darker like her father, with hair like a wheatfield, gold and bronze, one curl escaping from her headdress and coiling in a ringlet falling to her shoulder. I imagine that when she lets down her hair it is a tumble of honey curls.

She is wearing a gown of green as if she is spring herself, coming into this court of world-worn adults. It is a simple gown with long deep sleeves, and instead of a gold chain she has a green leather belt knotted around her slim hips. I imagine there was no money left to buy the girls gold or jewels for them to come to court. Elizabeth Woodville may have robbed half the treasury, but rebellions are expensive affairs and she will have spent all her money arming men against us. Her daughter, Princess Elizabeth – or, as I must remember to say, Mistress Elizabeth Grey – wears a neat cap on her head, nothing ostentatious, nothing like the little coronet she used to wear as the favoured oldest princess of indulgent parents, and the promised bride of the heir of France. Behind her come her sisters. Cecily is another beauty, only this Rivers girl is dark-haired and dark-eyed. She flaunts a merry smile, full of confidence, and wears a dark red that suits her. Behind her comes little Anne, the youngest, in palest blue like the edges of a sea, fair like her eldest sister; but quiet with none of the strutting confidence of the other two.

They stand in a row before me as if they were sentries presenting their arms, and I wish to God that I could send them back to the guardroom. But they are here, and they are to be greeted not as nieces but as wards. I rise from my throne and my ladies rise too, though the rustle of a dozen costly gowns does not trouble Elizabeth. She looks from one to another as if she would price the material. I can feel myself flush. She was raised at court by a queen who was a famous beauty, and I don't need to see her scornful smile to know that she finds us drab. Even I, in my ruby gown, am a pale queen beside her memory of her mother. I know that for her, I will never be anything but a shadow.

'I welcome you three, Mistress Elizabeth, Cecily and Anne Grey, to my court,' I say. I see Elizabeth's eyes flash as I give her the name of her mother's first husband. She will have to get used to this. Parliament itself has declared her a bastard, and her parents' marriage a bigamous sham. She will have to get used to being called 'Mistress Grey' and not 'Your Grace'.

'You will find me an easy queen to serve,' I say pleasantly, as if we have never met before, as if I have not kissed their cool cheeks a dozen times. 'And this a happy court.' I sit down and extend my hand and the three of them, one after another, curtsey and kiss my cold fingers.

I think the welcome has been done well enough and is over as the door opens and my husband Richard chooses this moment to come in. Of course he knows that the girls are being presented this morning. So he has come to make sure that everything goes well. I conceal my irritation in my smile of welcome.

'And here is the king . . .'

Nobody is listening to me. As the doors opened Elizabeth turned and when she sees my husband she rises from her curtsey and goes light-footed towards him.

'Your Grace, my lord uncle!' she says.

Her sisters, quick as weasels, snake after her: 'My lord uncle,' they chorus.

He beams at them, draws Elizabeth to him and kisses her on both cheeks. 'Looking beautiful as I knew you would,' he assures her. The other two get a kiss on the forehead. 'And how is your mother?' he asks Elizabeth conversationally, as if he inquires after the health of a witch and a traitor every morning. 'Does she like Heytesbury?'

She simpers. 'She likes it well, my lord uncle!' she says. 'She writes to me that she is changing all the furniture and digging up the gardens. Sir John may find he has a difficult tenant.'

'Sir John may find his house improved beyond measure,' he assures her, as if bold-faced impertinence needs reassurance. He turns to me: 'You must be glad to have your nieces in your rooms,' he says, a tone in his voice that reminds me that I must agree.

'I am delighted,' I say coolly. 'I am so delighted.'

I cannot deny that they are pretty girls. Cecily is a ninny and a gossip, Anne barely out of the schoolroom, and I see that she has lessons in Greek and Latin every day in the morning. Elizabeth is a perfect piece of work. If you were to draw up the qualities of a Princess of England she would match the pattern. She is well read – her uncle Anthony Woodville and her mother took care of that, she had the new printed books made by their bookmaker Caxton dedicated to her when she was barely out of the cradle. She speaks three languages fluently and can read four. She plays musical instruments and sings with a sweet low voice of surprising quality. She can sew exquisite fine work and I believe she can turn out a shirt or hem a fine linen shift with confidence. I have not seen her in the kitchen since I – as the daughter of the greatest earl in England, and now queen of my country – never have much cause to go into the kitchen. But she, having been cooped up in sanctuary, and the daughter of a countrywoman, tells me that she can cook roasted meats and stewed cuts, and dainty dishes of fricassees and sweetmeats. When she dances no-one can take their eyes off her; she moves to the music as if it is inspiring her, half-closing her eyes and letting her body respond to the notes. Everyone always wants to dance with her because she makes any partner look graceful. When she is given a part in a play she throws herself into it and learns her lines and delivers them as if she believed them herself. She is a good sister to the two in her care, and sends little gifts to the ones who are in Wiltshire. She is a good daughter, writing weekly to her mother. Her service to me as a lady in waiting is immaculate; I cannot fault her.

Why then, given all these remarkable virtues, do I loathe her?

I can answer this. Firstly, because I am foolishly, sinfully, jealous of her. Of course I see how Richard watches her, as if she were his brother returned to him only as a young, hopeful, merry, beautiful girl. He never says a word that I could criticise, he never speaks of her except as his niece. But he looks at her – indeed the whole court looks at her – as if she were a delight to the eye that makes the heart glad.

Secondly, I think she has had an easy life, a life which makes it easy for her to laugh half a dozen times a day as if the day-to-day round is constantly amusing. A life which makes her pretty, for what has she experienced that could make her frown? What has ever happened to her, to draw lines of disappointment on her face and lay grief in her bones? I know, I know: she has lost a father and a beloved uncle, they have been driven from the throne, and she has lost two beloved young brothers. But I cannot remember this when I see her playing cat's cradle with a skein of wool, or running beside the river, or weaving daffodils into a crown for Anne as if these girls should not fear the very thought of a crown. Then she seems to me utterly carefree, and I am jealous of her joy in life that comes so easy to her.

And lastly, I would never love a daughter of Elizabeth Woodville. I never ever will. The woman has loomed like a baleful comet on my horizon for all my life, from the moment I first saw her, and thought her the most beautiful woman in the world at her coronation dinner, to the time that I realised that she was my inveterate enemy and the murderer of my sister and my brother-in-law. Whatever smiling means Elizabeth took, in order to get her daughters entry to our court, nothing has charmed me, nothing will ever charm me into forgetting that they are the daughters of our enemy; and – in the case of the Princess Elizabeth – they are the enemy themselves.

There is no doubt in my mind that she is here as a spy and a distraction. She is betrothed to Henry Tudor (her mother's widely announced change of heart means nothing to me, and nothing – I suspect – to him or to her). She is the daughter of our enemy and the betrothed of our enemy. Why would I not think of her as my enemy?

And so I do.

When the snow melts off the hills of the North and we can travel home again we leave London. I am so glad to go that I have to pretend reluctance for fear of offending the London merchants and the citizens who come to court to bid farewell and the people who line the streets to cheer as we go by. I think of London as a city that loves the Rivers, and I can hear the roar of applause as the three Woodville girls ride side by side behind me. London loves a beauty and Elizabeth's warm prettiness makes them cheer for the House of York. I smile and wave to take the compliment for myself but I know that for me there is the deference for a queen, but not the affection that a pretty princess can create.

On the road I set a brisk pace so my ladies in waiting are all left behind, so that I don't have to hear her and her sisters chattering. Her voice, which is musical and sweet, sets my teeth on edge. I ride ahead and my guards ride behind me and I don't have to hear her or see her.

When Richard comes back from the head of the procession he puts his horse beside mine and we ride companionably together as if she were not smiling and chattering behind us. I glance sideways at his stern profile and wonder if he is listening for her, if he will hold his horse steady and drop back to ride beside her. But then he speaks, and I realise that my jealousy is making me fearful and suspicious when I should be enjoying his company.

'We will stay at Nottingham Castle for the month,' he says. 'I plan to rebuild your rooms there, make them more comfortable for you. I shall continue Edward's building programme. And then you can go on to Middleham if you like. I will follow you. I know you will be in a hurry to see the children.'

'It has seemed such a long time,' I agree. 'But I heard only today from the physician that they are all well.' I speak of the health of all three children. We never like to admit that Teddy is as strong as a hound puppy – and with as much sense – and Margaret is never ill. Our son, our Edward, makes slow progress to manhood, small for his age, easily wearied.

'That's good,' Richard says. 'And after this summer we can bring them all to court and keep them with us. Queen Elizabeth always had her children with her, and the princess tells me that she had the happiest childhood at court.'

'Mistress Grey,' I correct him, smiling.

NOTTINGHAM CASTLE,
MARCH 1484

We arrive at Nottingham Castle in the evening just as the setting sun is making the towers black against a sky of peach and gold. There is a fanfare from the walls of the castle as we approach and the guard spills out of the guardhouse to line the path to the drawbridge. Richard and I ride side by side, acknowledging the cheers of the soldiers and the applause of the people.

I am happy as I dismount from my horse and make my way to the new queen's apartments. I can hear my ladies in waiting chattering as they follow me, but I cannot distinguish the voices of the Rivers girls. I think, not for the first time, that I must learn not to look for them, I must work to diminish their effect on me. If I could teach myself to care nothing about them, one way or another, then I would not look to see if Richard is noticing them, or if the oldest girl, Elizabeth, is smiling at him.

We have been at Nottingham for several days, hunting in the wonderful forests, eating the venison we kill, when a messenger comes to my rooms one evening. He looks so exhausted from his ride and so grave that I know that something terrible has happened. His hand, as he holds out the letter, trembles.

'What is it?' I ask him, but he shakes his head as if he cannot tell me in words. I glance around and find Elizabeth looking steadily at me, and for a cold moment I think of her and her mother cursing the line of whoever killed the princes in the tower. I try to smile at her, but I can feel my lips stretch over my teeth and know that I am grimacing.

At once she steps forwards, and I see that her young face is filled with pity. 'Can I help you?' is all she says.

'No, no, just a message from my home,' I say. I think, perhaps my mother has died and they have written to me. Perhaps one of the other children, Margaret or Teddy, has taken a tumble from their pony and broken an arm. I realise I am holding the letter and not opening it. The young woman is looking at me, waiting for me to do so. I have an odd fancy that she knows, she knows already what it is going to say, and I look round at the circle of my ladies who have one by one realised that I am clutching a letter from home, too afraid to open it, and they fall silent, and gather round.

'Probably nothing,' I say into the quietness of the room. The messenger lifts his head and looks at me as if he would say something, and then puts his hand over his eyes as if the spring sunshine is too bright, and drops his head again.

I can delay no longer. I put my finger under the sealing wax and it comes easily from the paper. I unfold it and see that it is signed by the physician. He has written only four lines.

Your Grace,
I deeply regret to tell you that your son, Prince Edward, has died
this night of a fever, which we could not cool. We did everything
we could do, and we are all deeply grieved. I will pray for you
and His Grace the king in your sorrow.
    Charles Rhymner

I look up but I can see nothing. I realise my eyes are filled with tears and I blink them away but am still blinded. 'Send for the king,' I say. Someone touches my hand as I grip the letter and I feel the warmth of Elizabeth's fingers. I cannot stop myself thinking that the heir to the throne now is Teddy, Isabel's funny little boy. And after him, this girl. I take my hand from hers so she cannot touch me.

In moments Richard is there before me, kneeling to me so that he can look into my face. 'What is it?' he whispers. 'They said you had a letter.'

'It is Edward,' I say. I can hear my grief about to burst out, but I take a breath and tell him the worst news in the world. 'He is dead of a fever. We have lost our son.'

The days go by but I cannot speak. I go to the chapel but I cannot pray. The court is dressed in blue so dark that it is almost black and nobody plays games, or goes hunting, or plays music, or laughs. We are a court that has fallen under an enchantment of grief, we are struck dumb. Richard appears ten years older; I have not looked in my own mirror to see the marks of sorrow on my face. I can't care. I can't find it in me to care how I look. They dress me in the morning as if I were a doll, and at night they drag the gowns off me so that I can go to bed and lie in silence and feel the tears seeping out from my closed eyelids to wet the linen pillow.

I feel so ashamed that I let him die, as if it were my fault or that I could have done something. I feel ashamed that I did not breed a strong boy, like Isabel did, or like the handsome Woodville boys who vanished from the Tower. I feel ashamed that I had only one boy, only one precious heir, only one to carry the great weight of Richard's triumph. We had only one prince, not two, and now he has gone.

We leave Nottingham for Middleham Castle in a rush, at once, as if by getting to our home we will find our son as we left him. When we get there we find the little body in the coffin in the chapel, and the two other children kneeling beside it, lost without their cousin, lost without the routine of the household. Margaret comes into my arms and whispers: 'I am so sorry, I am so sorry,' as if she, a little ten-year-old girl, should have saved him.

I cannot reassure her that I don't blame her. I have no re-assurance for anyone. I have no words for anyone. Richard rules that the children shall now go to live at Sheriff Hutton. Neither of us will ever want to come to Middleham, ever again. We have a small funeral and see the coffin go into the darkness of the vault. I feel no peace after we have prayed for his soul, and paid the priest to pray for him twice daily. We shall create a chantry for his little innocent soul. I feel no peace, I feel nothing. I think I will feel nothing forever.

We leave Middleham as soon as we can, and go to Durham, where I pray for my son in the great cathedral. It makes no dif-ference. We go to Scarborough and I look at the great waves on a stormy sea and think of Isabel losing her first baby and how losing a baby in childbirth is nothing – nothing – to losing a son grown. We go back to York. I don't care where we are. Everywhere people look at me as if they are puzzling about what they can say. They need not trouble. There is nothing to say. I have lost my father in battle, my sister to Elizabeth Woodville's spy, my brother-in-law to Elizabeth Woodville's executioner, my nephew to her poisoner, and now my son to her curse.

The days grow brighter and warmer and when they throw the gown over my head in the morning it is made of silk rather than wool. When they walk me into dinner and sit me like a puppet at the high table they bring me spring lamb and fresh fruits. It grows noisier at dinner, and one day the musicians play again, for the first time since the letter came. I see Richard glance sideways at me to see if I mind, and I see him recoil from the blankness of my face. I don't mind. I don't mind anything. They can play a hornpipe if they like; nothing matters to me any more.

That night he comes to my room. He does not speak to me, but folds me in his arms and holds me tightly to him, as if the pain of two people can be lessened by putting two broken hearts close to one another. It does not help. Now I feel that my bedroom is the centre of grief, as we lie side by side in our pain, instead of at either ends of the castle.

Early in the morning I wake as he tries to make love to me. I lie like a stone beneath him and say nothing and do nothing. I know he will be thinking that we have to conceive another child; but I cannot believe that such a blessing could be given. After ten years of barrenness? How should a son come to me now that I feel I am dead, when a second son did not come when I was filled with hope and love? No, we were given one son and now he has gone.

The Rivers girls have tactfully left court to visit their mother and I am glad that I don't have to see them – three of her five beautiful daughters. I cannot think about anything but the curse that Richard heard them make, mother and daughter, when they swore that whoever had taken their son and heir would lose his own. I wonder if this is proof that Robert Brackenbury took the hint I gave him, and crushed those two handsome healthy boys in their bedding, to give their title to my poor lost son. I wonder if this is proof that my husband has looked me in the face and lied to me with utter conviction and without shame. Can he have had them killed without telling me? Can he have had them killed and denied it to me? Would he have told such a lie to their mother? Can her power have seen through his lie and taken my son in revenge? Is not a witch's curse the only explanation for Edward's death – dead in springtime, dead just as he came through the dangerous years of childhood?

I think so. I think so. After long sleepless nights of puzzling away at it, I think so. Edward was frail, small-boned, delicate, but he was not prone to fever. I think her ill-will sought him out and enflamed his veins, his lungs, his poor, poor heart. I think Elizabeth Woodville and her daughter Elizabeth killed my boy to avenge themselves for the loss of theirs.

Richard comes to my rooms before dinner to escort us to the great hall, as if the world were still the same. I only have to look at him to see that everything is changed. His face, always strong, is now stern, even grim. From his nose to either side of his mouth are grooved two deep lines and his forehead has two hard lines at each eyebrow. He never smiles. When his grim face looks into my pale one, I think that neither of us will ever smile again.

In the heat of summer the Rivers girls come riding back to court, like a little cavalcade of confident beauty, and are greeted with joy by all the handsome young men of the king's service. Apparently they have been sadly missed. The three of them walk into my rooms and curtsey low to me and smile as if they think I can greet them kindly. I manage to ask after their journey and for the health of their mother, but even I can hear how thin and quiet is my voice. I don't care about their journey, or the health of their mother. I know that Elizabeth will write to her mother and tell her that I am pale and nearly dumb. I expect she will remark that her sorcery that killed my son has nearly stopped my own heart. And I no longer care. The Elizabeths, mother and daughter, can do no more against me. Everyone whom I have loved has been taken from me by the two of them; the only person left to me in the world is my husband, Richard. Will they take him too? For I am so swaddled in sorrow that I no longer care.

It seems that they will take him. Elizabeth walks with Richard in the garden in the cool of the evening. He likes to have her at his side and the courtiers, who always follow a favourite, are quick to praise the quiet wisdom of her conversation, and the grace of her walk.

I watch them from my chamber windows set high in the castle

wall so that they are far below, walking to the river, like a painting of a knight and his lady in a romance. She is tall, almost as tall as he, and they walk together head to head. I wonder idly what they talk about with such animation, what makes her laugh and stop and put her hand to her throat, and then makes her take his arm to walk on. At this distance, from my high window, they are a handsome couple: well-matched. They are not far from each other in age, after all. She is eighteen and he is only thirty-one. They both have the York charm that is now turned fully on each other. She is golden-haired like his brother and he is dark as his handsome father. I see Richard take her hand and draw her a little closer as he whispers in her ear. She turns her head with a little laugh, she is a coquette as most beauties of eighteen are bound to be. They walk away from the court and people follow them, at a little distance so that they can imagine themselves to be alone.

The last time I saw the court walking behind the king and carefully judging their paces was when Edward was walking arm in arm with his new lover Elizabeth Shore, and Elizabeth his queen was in confinement. The moment she came out the Shore whore disappeared from court and was never seen again by us – I smile at the memory of the king's bashful apologetic tenderness to his wife and her grey-eyed level gaze at him. Odd now for me to see the court taking slow strides once more; but this time it is my husband who is being given privacy, as he walks alone with his niece.

Why would they do that? I think idly, my forehead against the cold glass of the thick window. Why would the courtiers step back so courteously unless they think that she is to be his mistress? Unless they think that my husband is seducing his niece, on these evening strolls by the river, that he has forgotten everything he owes to his name, to his marriage vows, to the respect he owes to me as his wife, and the bereaved mother of his dead son.

Can it be that the court has seen so much more clearly than I that Richard has recovered from grief, recovered from heartbreak, can live again, can breathe again, can look about him and see the world again – and in this world sees a pretty girl who is all too ready to take his hand and listen to his words and laugh as if delighted at his speech? Does the court think that Richard is going to bed his brother's daughter? Does it really think he is so far gone in wickedness to deflower his niece?

I approach this thought, whispering the words 'deflower' and 'niece', but I really cannot make myself care about this, any more than I can make myself care about the hunting trip tomorrow or the dishes for tonight's dinner. Elizabeth's virginity and Elizabeth's happiness are alike of no interest to me at all. Everything seems as if it is happening a long way away, feels as if it is happening to someone else. I would not call myself unhappy, the word does not approach my state of mind; I would call myself dead to the world. I cannot find it in me to care whether Richard is seducing his niece or she is seducing him. I see, at any rate, that Elizabeth Woodville, having taken my son from me by a curse, will now take my husband from me by her daughter's seduction. But I see that there is nothing I can do to stop this. She will do – as she always does – as she wishes. All I can do is lean my hot forehead against the cold glass and wish that I did not see this. Or anything. Anything at all.

The court is not solely devoted to the hypocrisy of flirting with the king and mourning with me. Richard spends every morning with his councillors, appointing commissioners to raise the shires if there is an invasion from Henry Tudor in Brittany, preparing the fleet to make war with Scotland, harrying French shipping in the narrow seas. He speaks to me of this work and sometimes I can advise him, having spent my childhood at Calais, and since it is my father's policy of peace with the Scots and armed peace against the French that Richard follows.

He leaves for York in July to establish the Council of the

North, the recognition that the North of England is a country in many ways quite different from the southern parts, and Richard is, and will always be, a good lord to them. Before he leaves he comes to my room and sends my ladies away. Elizabeth goes out with a backward smile at him and for once he does not notice. He takes a stool so that he is seated at my feet.

'What is it?' I ask without a great deal of interest.

'I wanted to speak to you about your mother,' he says.

I am surprised but nothing can catch my interest. I complete the sewing I have in my hands, pierce the needle through the embroidery silks, and put it to one side. 'Yes?'

'I think she can be released from our care,' he says. 'We won't go back to Middleham—'

'No, never,' I say quickly.

'And so we could close the place down. She could have her own house, we could pay her an allowance. We don't need to keep a great castle to house her.'

'You don't think she might speak against us?' Never am I going to refer to the question of our marriage. He can think me now, as I was then, utterly trusting. Now I cannot bring myself to care.

He shrugs. 'We are King and Queen of England. There are laws against speaking against us. She knows that.'

'And you don't fear she will try to take her lands back?'

Again he smiles. 'I am King of England, she is unlikely to win a case against me. And if she were to get some estates back into her own keeping, I can afford to lose them. You will have them back again when she dies.'

I nod. And anyway, now there is no-one to inherit from me.

'I just wanted to make sure that you had no objection to her being freed. If you had a preference as to where she should live?'

I shrug. There were four of them at Middleham that winter, Margaret and her brother Teddy, my son Edward and her, my mother, their grandmother. How is it possible that death should have taken her grandson and not taken her? 'I have lost a son,' I say. 'How can I care about a mother?'

He turns his head away, so that I cannot see his grimace of pain. 'I know,' he says. 'The ways of God are mysterious to us.'

He rises to his feet and puts his hand out for me. I get up and stand beside him, smoothing the exquisite silk of my gown.

'That's a pretty colour,' he says, noticing it for the first time. 'Do you have more of that silk?'

'I think so,' I say, surprised. 'They bought a bolt of it from France, I believe. Do you want a jacket made from it?'

'It would suit our niece Elizabeth,' he says lightly.

'What?'

He smiles at my aghast face. 'It would suit Elizabeth's colouring, don't you think?'

'You want her to wear a matching gown to mine?'

'Now and then – if you agree that the colour is good on her too.'

The ridiculous concept stirs me from my lethargy. 'What are you thinking of? The whole court will think that she is your mistress if you dress her in silks as fine as mine. They will say worse. They will call her your whore. And they will call you a lecher.'

He nods, utterly unshocked by the hard words. 'Just so.'

'You want this? You want to shame her, and shame yourself, and dishonour me?'

He takes my hand. 'Anne, my dearest Anne. We are king and queen now, we have to put aside private preferences. We have to remember we are constantly observed, our acts have meanings that people try to read. We have to put on a show.'

'I don't understand,' I say flatly. 'What are we showing?'

'Is the girl not supposed to be betrothed?'

'Yes, to Henry Tudor, you know as well as I do that he publicly declared himself last Christmas.'

'And so who is the fool, when she is known to the world as my mistress?'

Slowly I understand. 'Why, he is.'

'And so all the people who would support this unknown Welshman, Margaret Beaufort's Welsh-born boy, because he is betrothed to marry the Princess Elizabeth – the beloved daughter of England's greatest king – think again. They say, if we rally for Tudor we are not putting the Princess of York on the throne. For the Princess of York is at her uncle's court, admiring him, supporting him, an ornament to his reign as she was an ornament to her father's reign.'

'But some people will say she is little better than a whore. She will be shamed.'

He shrugs. 'They said the same of her mother. We passed a law that said just that of her mother. And anyway, I would not have thought that would trouble you.'

He is right. Nothing troubles me. Certainly not the humiliation of the Rivers girl.

The threat from Henry Tudor in Brittany absorbs the whole court. He is only a young man, and any king less jealous than a York one might have disregarded his distant claim to the throne of England through his mother's line. But it is a York king on the throne and Richard knows that Tudor is planning an invasion, seeking support in Brittany from the duke who has protected him for so long, approaching France, the old inveterate enemy of England, for help.

Margaret Beaufort, his mother, my one-time friend, sulks in her country house, gaoled by her husband at Richard's instruction, and his bride-to-be Elizabeth of York is now all but the first lady of court, dancing every night in the palace which was her childhood home, her wrists bright with bracelets, her hair sparkling under a gold net. She seems to have gifts that arrive every morning as we sit in the chambers that overlook the grey wintry river. Every morning there is a knock at the door and a pageboy bringing something for the girl whom everyone now calls Princess Elizabeth, as if Richard had not passed a law to declare her a bastard and to give her the name of her mother's first husband. She giggles when she opens it, and she gives a quick guilty glance at me. Always, the gifts come without a note but we all know who is sending her priceless fairings. I remember last year when Richard gave me a present every day for the twelve days of Christmas. But I remember with indifference. I don't care for jewels now.

The Christmas feast is the pinnacle of her joy. Last year she was a disgraced object of our charity, named as a bastard and claimed as a bride by a traitor, but this year she has bobbed unstoppably upwards, like a cheap light cork in stormy water. We now go for dress fittings together as if we were mother and daughter, as if we were sisters. We stand in the great room of the wardrobe while they pin silks and cloth of gold and furs on us, and I look at the great silvered mirror and see my tired face and fading hair in the same bright colours as the smiling beauty beside me. She is ten years younger than me and it is never more obvious than when we are standing side by side and dressed alike.

Richard openly gives her jewels to match mine, she wears a headdress like a little gold coronet, she wears diamonds in her little ears and sapphires at her throat. The court is gorgeous for Christmas, everyone dressed in their best, and entertainments, sports and games every day. Elizabeth dances through it all, the queen of the revels, the champion of the games, the mistress of the feast. I sit on my great chair, the cloth of estate above me, the crown heavy on my forehead, and fix an indulgent smile on my face as my husband gets up to dance with the most beautiful girl in the palace, takes her hand and leads her away to talk, and then brings her back into the room flushed and tumbled. She glances towards me as if she would apologise – as if she hopes I don't mind that everyone in the court, and increasingly everyone in England, thinks that they are lovers and I have been set aside. She has the grace to be shame-faced, but I can see she is driven too hard by desire to step back. She cannot say no to him, she cannot deny herself. Perhaps she is in love.

I dance too. When it is a slow and stately dance I let Richard lead me out and the dancers follow us round the floor in the smooth paces. Richard keeps my steps in time; I can hardly be troubled with the beat of the music. It was only last Christmas when the court was in its pomp – a new king come to the throne, new wealth to disperse, new treasures to buy, new gowns to show – and then my son took a little fever and died of nothing more than a little fever, and I was not by his bed. I was not in the castle. I was celebrating our success, hunting in the forests of Nottingham. I cannot think now what there was to celebrate.

Christmas Day we keep as a holy day, attending church several times. Elizabeth is prettily devout, a scarf of green gauze over her fair hair, her eyes downcast. Richard walks back from chapel with me, my hand in his.

'You are tired,' he says.

I am tired of life itself. 'No,' I say. 'I am looking forward to the rest of the days of Christmas.'

'There are some unpleasant rumours. I don't want you to listen to them, there is nothing in them.'

I pause and the court halts behind us. 'Leave us,' I say over my shoulder to them all. They melt away, Elizabeth glancing at me as if she thinks she might disobey. Richard shakes his head at her and she drops a little curtsey in my direction, and goes.

'What rumours?'

'I said, I don't want you to listen to them.'

'Then I had better hear them from you so I don't listen to anyone else.'

He shrugs. 'There are those who say that I am planning to put you aside and marry Princess Elizabeth.'

'Your courtship charade has succeeded then,' I remark. 'Was it a courtship? Or was it a charade?'

'Both,' he says grimly. 'I had to discredit the betrothal between her and Tudor. He is certain to invade this spring. I had to cut away the York affinity from him.'

'You take care you don't cut away the Neville affinity,' I observe shrewdly. 'I am the kingmaker's daughter. There are many in the North who follow you only for love of me. Even now my name counts for more than anything there. They won't be loyal to you if they think you slight me.'

He kisses my hand. 'I don't forget it. I won't forget it. And I would never slight you. You are my heart. Even if you are a broken heart.'

'Is that the worst of it?'

He hesitates. 'There is talk of poison.'

At the mention of Elizabeth Woodville's weapon I freeze where I stand. 'Who is speaking of poison?'

'Some gossip from the kitchen. A dog died after a dish was spilled and he lapped it up. You know how much is made from little at court.'

'Whose was the dish?'

'Yours.'

I say nothing. I feel nothing. Not even surprise. For years Elizabeth Woodville has been my enemy and even now, with her released and living at peace in Wiltshire, I can feel her grey gaze on the nape of my neck. She will see me still as the daughter of the man who killed her beloved father and brother. Now she sees me also as the woman who stands in the way of her daughter. If I were dead then Richard would get a dispensation from the Pope and marry his niece Elizabeth. The House of York would be reunited, the Woodville woman would be dowager queen once more and grandmother to the next King of England.

'She never stops,' I say quietly to myself.

'Who?' Richard seems taken aback.

'Elizabeth Woodville. I take it that it is she who is suspected of trying to poison me?'

He laughs out loud, his former impulsive crack of laughter that I have not heard for so long. He takes my hand and kisses my fingers. 'No, they don't suspect her,' he says. 'But it doesn't matter. I will guard you. I shall make sure that you are safe. But you must rest, my dear. Everyone says you look tired.'

'I am well enough,' I say grimly, and to myself I promise: 'I am well enough to keep her daughter from my throne.'

It is the twelfth night, the feast of the epiphany, the last day of the long feast of Christmas, which this year seemed to last forever. I dress with particular care in my red and gold gown, and Elizabeth, matching in every detail in her red and gold gown, follows me into the throne room and stands beside my chair, as if to show the world the contrast between the old queen and the young mistress. There is a masquing, telling of the story of the Christmas feast and the epiphany, there is music and dancing. Richard and Elizabeth dance together, so practised now that their steps match. She has all the grace of her mother; nobody can keep their eyes off her. I see Richard's warmth towards her and I wonder again, what is courting and what is charade?

Twelfth night, of all the nights of the year, is one where shapes shift and identities flicker. Once I was the kingmaker's daughter, raised in the knowledge that I would be one of the great ladies of the kingdom. Now I am queen. This should satisfy my father and satisfy me, but when I think of the price we have paid, I think that we have been cheated by fate itself. I smile down the room so that everyone can know I am happy with my husband dancing hand-in-hand with his niece, his eyes on her blushing face. I have to show everyone that I am well and that the insidious drip of Elizabeth Woodville's poison in my food, in my wine, perhaps even in the perfume that scents my gloves, is not slowly killing me.

The dance ends and Richard comes back to sit beside me. Elizabeth goes to chatter with her sisters. Richard and I are wearing our crowns at this final feast of the season, to show everyone that we are King and Queen of England, to send the message out to the most distant shires that we are in our pomp. A door opens beside us and a messenger comes in and hands Richard a single sheet of paper. He reads it briefly and nods to me as if a gamble he has made has been confirmed.

'What is it?'

He speaks very quietly. 'News of Tudor. No Christmas announcement of his betrothal this year. I have won this round. He has lost the York princess and he has lost the support of the Rivers affinity.' He smiles at me. 'He knows he cannot claim her as his wife, everyone believes she is in my keeping, my whore. I have stolen her and her followers from him.'

I look down the long room to where Elizabeth is practising her steps with her sisters, impatiently waiting for the music to start again. A circle of young men stand around, hoping that she will dance with them.

'You have ruined her if she is known throughout the country as broken meats, the king's hackney.'

He shrugs. 'There is a price to pay if you venture near the throne. She knows that. Her mother, of all people, knows that. But there is more—'

'What more?'

'I have the date for the Tudor invasion. He is coming this year.'

'You know this? When is he coming?'

'This very summer.'

'How do you know?' I whisper.

Richard smiles. 'I have a spy at his ramshackle court.'

'Who?'

'Elizabeth Woodville's oldest son, Thomas Grey. He is in my keeping too. She is proving a very good friend to me.'

Richard prepares for invasion. I prepare for death. Elizabeth prepares for a wedding and a coronation, though there is nothing in her quiet respectful service that would reveal this to anyone but me. My senses are extreme, on the alert. Only I see the glow in her cheek when she comes back from walking in the garden, the way she pats her hair as if someone has pulled her towards him and knocked her headdress askew, only I see that the ribbons of her cloak are untied as if she has opened them to allow him to put his hands on her warm waist and pull her close.

I have someone to taste my wine, I have someone to test my food, but still I weaken steadily though the days grow lighter and the sun is warmer and outside my window a blackbird is building a nest in the apple tree and sings for joy every dawn. I cannot sleep, not at night nor in the day. I think of my girlhood when Richard came and saved me from poverty and humiliation, I think of my childhood when Isabel and I were little girls and played at being queens. It is incredible to me that I am twenty-eight years old, and there is no Isabel, and I no longer have any desire to be queen.

I watch Princess Elizabeth with a sort of shrewd sympathy. She thinks I am dying – I give her the credit to believe that it is not her hand that is sprinkling poison on my pillow – but she thinks I am dying of some wasting sickness and that when I have wasted quite away then Richard will make her queen for love, and every day will be a feast day, and every day she will have a new gown, and every day will be a celebration of her return to the palaces and castles of her childhood as her mother's heir: the next Queen of England.

She thinks that he does not love me, she probably thinks that he never loved me. She thinks that she is the first woman whom he has ever loved and that now he will love her forever and she will dance through her days, always adored, always beautiful, a queen of hearts just as her mother was.

This is so far from the reality of being Queen of England that it makes me laugh till I cough and have to hold my aching sides. In any case, I know Richard. He may be taken by her now, he may even have seduced her, he may have bedded her and enjoyed her gasping pleasure in his arms; but he is not such a fool as to risk his kingdom for her. He has taken her away from Henry Tudor – that was his ambition and he has succeeded. He would never be such a fool as to risk offending my kinsmen, my tenants and my people. He will not set me aside to marry her. He will not put the Rivers girl in my place. I doubt even her mother can bring that conclusion about.

I find I must prepare for my death. I don't fear it. Ever since I lost my son I have been weary to my soul, and I think, when it finally comes, it will be a lying down to sleep without fear of dreams, without fear of waking. I am ready to lie down to sleep. I am tired.

But first there is something I must do. I send for Sir Robert Brackenbury, Richard's good friend, and he comes to my rooms in the morning, while the court is out hunting. My maid in waiting lets him in and goes when I wave her away.

'I have to ask you something,' I say.

He is shocked at my appearance. 'Anything, Your Grace,' he says. I see from the quick flicker of doubt in his face that he will not tell me everything.

'You asked me once about the princes,' I say. I am too weary to mince my words. I want to know the truth. 'The Rivers boys who were in the Tower. I knew then that they should be put to death to make my husband safe on the throne. You said I was too kind-hearted to give the order.'

He kneels before me and takes my thin hands in his big ones. 'I remember.'

'I am dying, Sir Robert,' I say frankly. 'And I would know what I have to confess when I receive the last rites. You can tell me the truth. Did you act on my wishes? Did you act to save Richard from danger, as I know you will always do? Did you take my words for an order?'

There is a long moment of silence. Then he shakes his big head. 'I couldn't do it,' he says quietly. 'I wouldn't do it.'

I release him and sit back in my chair. He sits back on his heels. 'Are they alive or dead?' I ask.

He moves his big shoulders in a shrug. 'Your Grace, I don't know. But if I was looking for them I would not start in the Tower. They're not there.'

'Where would you start looking?'

His eyes are on the floor beneath his knees. 'I would start looking somewhere in Flanders,' he says. 'Somewhere near their aunt Margaret of York's houses. Somewhere that your husband's family always send their children when they fear for them. Richard and George were sent to Flanders when they were boys. George Duke of Clarence was sending his son overseas. It's what the Plantagenets always do when their children are in danger.'

'You think they got away?' I whisper.

'I know they're not in the Tower, and I know they were not killed on my watch.'

I put my hand to my throat where I can feel my pulse hammering. The poison is thick in my veins, filling my lungs so I can hardly breathe. If I could catch my breath I would laugh at the thought that Edward's sons live, though mine is dead. That perhaps when Richard looks for an heir, it will not be Elizabeth the princess but one of the Rivers boys who steps forwards.

'You are sure of it?'

'They are not buried in the Tower,' he says. 'I am sure of that. And I did not put them to death. I did not think it was your command, and anyway, I would not have obeyed such an order.'

I give a shuddering sigh. 'So, my conscience is clear?'

He bows. 'And mine too.'

I go to my bedchamber as I hear the hunting party return; I cannot bear the noise of their talking and seeing their bright faces. My maids help me into bed and then the door opens and Princess Elizabeth slips in quietly. 'I came to see if there is anything you want,' she says.

I shake my head on the richly embroidered pillow. 'Nothing,' I say. 'Nothing.'

She hesitates. 'Shall I leave you? Or shall I sit with you?'

'You can stay,' I say. 'I have something I should tell you.'

She waits, standing near the bed, her hands clasped, her young face alert but patient.

'It is about your brothers ...'

At once her face lights up. 'Yes?' she breathes.

Nobody could think for a moment that this is the face of grief. She knows something, I know that she does. Her mother has done something or managed something or saved them somehow. She may once have thought them dead, and cursed the man that killed them. But this is a girl who expects to hear good news of her brothers. This is not a girl crushed by loss, she knows they are safe.

'I think I know nothing more than you,' I say shrewdly. 'But I have been assured that they were not killed in the Tower, and they are not held in the Tower.'

She does not dare to do more than nod.

'I take it you are sworn to secrecy?'

Again, that infinitesimal movement of the head.

'Then perhaps you will see your Edward again in this life. And I will see mine in heaven.'

She sinks to her knees by my bed. 'Your Grace, I pray that you get well,' she says earnestly.

'At any rate, you can tell your mother that I had no part in the loss of her sons,' I say. 'You can tell her that our feud is over. My father killed hers, my sister is dead, her son and mine are buried, and I am going too.'

'I will give her this message, if you wish. But she has no enmity for you. I know that she does not.'

'She had an enamel box,' I say quietly. 'And in it a scrap of paper? And on that scrap of paper two names written in her blood?'

The girl meets my eyes. 'I don't know,' she says steadily.

'Were those names Isabel and Anne?' I ask. 'Has she been my enemy and the enemy of my sister? Have I rightly feared her for all these years?'

'George and Warwick were the names,' she says simply. 'The paper was from my grandfather's last letter. Her father wrote to her mother the night before he was beheaded. My mother swore she would be revenged upon George and your father who caused his death. Those were the names. None other. And she was revenged.'

I lean back on my pillow and I smile. Isabel did not die of the Woodville woman's curse. My father died on the battlefield, George she had executed. She does not hold me in thrall. She has probably known for years that her sons were safe. So perhaps my son did not die under her curse. I did not bring her curse down on him. I am free of that fear too. Perhaps I am not dying of her poison.

'These are mysteries,' I say to Princess Elizabeth. 'I was taught to be queen by Margaret of Anjou, and perhaps I have taught you how to be queen in turn. This is fortune's wheel indeed.'

With my forefinger I draw a circle in the air, the sign of fortune's wheel. 'You can go very high and you can sink very low, but you can rarely turn the wheel at your own bidding.'

The room starts to grow very dark. I wonder where the time has gone. 'Try and be a good queen,' I say to her, though the words are meaningless to me now. 'Is it night already?'

She gets up and goes to the window. 'No. It's not night. But something very strange is happening.'

'Tell me what you can see?'

'Shall I help you to the window?'

'No, no, I am too tired. Just tell me what you can see.'

'I can see the sun is being blotted out, as if someone were sliding a plate across it.' She shades her eyes. 'It is bright as ever but this dark sphere is moving across it.' She looks at the bed, blinking as she is dazzled. 'What can it mean?'

'A movement of the planets?' I suggest.

'The river has gone very still. The fishing boats are rowing for shore and the men are pulling up the boats as if they fear a high tide. It's very quiet.' She listens for a moment. 'All the birds have stopped singing, even the seagulls aren't crying. It is as if night has come in a moment.'

She looks down into the garden. 'The lads have come from the stables and the kitchens, they are all looking up at the sky, trying to see it. Is it a comet, do you think?'

'What is it like?'

'The sun is like a ring of gold, and the black plate hides it except for the rim which is blazing like a fire, too bright to look at. But everything else is black.'

She steps back from the window and I can see the small diamond-shaped panes are as black as night.

'I'll light the candles,' she says hastily. 'It's so dark. It could be midnight.'

She takes a taper from the fireplace and lights candles in the sconces either side of the fire and at the table beside my bed. Her face in the candlelight is pale. 'What can it mean?' she asks. 'Is it a sign that Henry Tudor is coming? Or that my lord will have victory? It cannot be – can it? – the end of days?'

I wonder if she is right and this is the end of the world, if Richard will be the last Plantagenet king that England ever has, and I will see my son Edward this very night.

'I don't know,' I say.

She goes back to her station at the window. 'It's so dark,' she says. 'As dark as it has ever been. The river is dark and all the fishermen are lighting their torches on the riverbank, and all of the ships have pulled in. The kitchen boys have gone back inside. It is as if everyone is afraid of the darkness.'

She pauses. 'I think it is getting a little lighter. I think it is growing light. It's not like dawn, it is a terrible light, a cold yellow light, like nothing I have seen before. As if yellow and grey were one.' She pauses. 'As if the sun were freezing cold. It's getting brighter, it's getting lighter, the sun is coming out from behind the darkness. I can see the trees and the other side of the river now.' She pauses to listen. 'And the birds are starting to sing.'

Outside my window the blackbird makes its penetrating questioning call.

'It is as if the world is reborn,' Elizabeth says wonderingly. 'How strange it has been. The disc is moving from the sun, the sun is blazing in the sky again and everything is warm and sunny and like spring once more.'

She comes back to the bed. 'Renewed,' she says. 'As if we can start all over again.'

I smile at her optimism, the hopefulness of the young and foolish. 'I think I will sleep now,' I say.

I dream. I dream that I am on the battlefield at Barnet, and my father is speaking to his men. He is high on his black horse, his helmet under his arm so everyone can see his bold brave face and his confidence. He is telling them that he will lead them to victory, that the true prince of England is waiting to set sail across the narrow seas, and that he will bring with him Anne, the new Queen of England, and that their reign will be a time of peace and prosperity, blessed by God, for the true prince and the true princess will come to their thrones. He says my name 'Anne' with such love and pride in his voice. He says that his daughter Anne will be Queen of England, and that she will be the best Queen of England that the world has ever seen.

I see him, as bright as life, laugh in his confidence and his power, as he promises them that the good times are coming, that they need only stand fast, be true, and they will win.

He swings his leg over his horse and he drops to the ground. He pats his horse's neck and the big dark head turns with trust as his hand goes up to pull gently the black moving ears that flicker forwards to listen to him. 'Other commanders will ask that you stand and fight, will ask that you fight to the death,' he tells them. 'I know that. I've heard that too. I have been in battles where commanders have asked their men to fight to the death but then ridden away and left them.'

There is a ripple of agreement from the men. They have known battles where their commanders have betrayed them, just like this.

'Other commanders will ask you to stand and fight to the death but when the battle goes against them they will send their pages for their horses and you will see them ride away. You will face the charge alone, you will go down, your comrades will go down, but they will be spurring their horses and riding away. I know that. I have seen it as well as you.'

There is a mutter of agreement from men who have been able to run away, who remember comrades who could not get away in time.

'Let this be my pledge to you.' He takes his great broadsword and carefully, feeling for the horse's ribs, puts the point of the sharp blade between the ribs, aimed at the heart. There is a low murmur of refusal from the men and in the dream I cry out, 'No, Father! No!'

'This is my pledge to you,' he says steadily. 'I will not ride away and leave you in danger for I shall have no horse,' and he thrusts the blade deep into the ribcage, and Midnight goes down on his forelegs and down on his backlegs. He turns and looks at my father with his dark beautiful eyes as if he understands, as if he knows, that this is a sacrifice my father has to make. That he is a pledge that my father will fight and die with his men.

Of course he died with them, that day on the battlefield of Barnet, he died with them to make me queen, and I had to learn alone later what a hollow crown it is. As I turn in my bed and close my eyes once more, I think that tonight I will see my beloved father, Warwick the kingmaker, and the prince who is my little boy, Edward, and perhaps, in fields greener than I can imagine, Midnight the horse is turned out to graze.

AUTHOR'S NOTE

This is an historical novel based on a character whose own biographer predicted that the life would be impossible to write because of the lack of information. Luckily for all of us, historian Michael Hicks found much valuable material about Anne Neville despite being hampered by the usual silences that surround women in history.

What we know from Hicks and from other historians is that she was related to most of the great players of the Cousins' War (only called the Wars of the Roses centuries later in the 1800s). What I suggest in this novel is that perhaps she was a player in her own right.

She was the daughter of the Earl of Warwick, known in his lifetime as 'the kingmaker' because of his extraordinary role as puppeteer to the claimants of royal power in England. First he supported Richard Duke of York, then his son and heir Edward, then the second son George, then their enemy Henry VI. Warwick died fighting for the House of Lancaster, having lived his life as the great supporter of the House of York.

Anne, although a young woman, moved with her father through these twists and turns of loyalty. She attended the coronation dinner of the new queen of the House of York and witnessed her father's gradual exclusion from the court, which became dominated by the Rivers family and adherents. As the

427

novel describes, Anne fled with her father into exile in France, returning to England as his new candidate for queen, at the head of a Lancaster army, married to their Prince of Wales, and in little more than a year was married into the house of her enemy: York. It is at this point that I suggest that the young woman, who had lost her father and her husband, and whose mother had abandoned her, took her life into her own hands. Nobody knows the true story of how Anne escaped from the protection or imprisonment of her sister and brother-in-law. We have no reliable account – but some wonderful versions – of her courtship and marriage to Richard. My version of these stories is to put Anne at the heart of things.

It was fascinating to me as a novelist to portray the York court as a centre of intrigue and a source of fear for the Warwick girls. Part of the joy of writing this series based on rivals and enemies is turning the page upside down (as it were) and seeing a totally different picture. As an historian the known facts looked very different when I changed my viewpoint from my favourite, Elizabeth Woodville, to my new heroine, Anne Neville. The confused conspiracy around the death of Isabel and the judicial murder of George suddenly becomes a far darker story with Elizabeth as the villain.

Another reputation which I have had to address in this story is that of Richard III. As I suggest here and in *The White Queen*, I don't subscribe to the Shakespearean parody that has blackened his reputation for centuries. But also I don't acquit him of usurpation. He might not have killed the princes but they would not have been in the Tower without the protection of their mother except for his actions. What I think might have happened to the two royal boys is the subject of my next book, the story of their sister and Richard's secret lover, Princess Elizabeth of York: *The White Princess*.

I list here the books which have been most useful to me in writing *The Kingmaker's Daughters*.

BIBLIOGRAPHY

Amt, Emilie, *Women's Lives in Medieval Europe* (New York, Routledge, 1993)

Baldwin, David, *Elizabeth Woodville: Mother of the Princes in the Tower* (Stroud, Sutton Publishing, 2002)

Baldwin, David, *The Lost Prince: The Survival of Richard of York* (Stroud, Sutton Publishing, 2007)

Baldwin, David, *The Kingmaker's Sisters* (Stroud, The History Press, 2009)

Barnhouse, Rebecca, *The Book of the Knight of the Tower: Manners for Young Medieval Women* (Basingstoke, Palgrave Macmillan, 2006)

Castor, Helen, *Blood & Roses: The Paston Family and the Wars of the Roses* (London, Faber and Faber, 2004)

Cheetham, Anthony, *The Life and Times of Richard III* (London, Weidenfeld & Nicolson, 1972)

Chrimes, S.B., *Lancastrians, Yorkists, and Henry VII* (London, Macmillan, 1964)

Cooper, Charles Henry, *Memoir of Margaret: Countess of Richmond and Derby* (Cambridge, Cambridge University Press, 1874)

Duggan, Anne J., *Queens and Queenship in Medieval Europe* (Woodbridge, Boydell Press, 1997)

Field, P.J.C., *The Life and Times of Sir Thomas Malory* (Cambridge, D.S. Brewer, 1993)

Fields, Bertram, *Royal Blood: King Richard III and the Mystery of the Princes* (New York, Regan Books, 1998)

Gairdner, James, 'Did Henry VII Murder the Princes?', *English Historical Review*, VI (1891)

Goodman, Anthony, *The Wars of the Roses: Military Activity and English Society 1452–97* (London, Routledge & Kegan Paul, 1981)

Goodman, Anthony, *The Wars of the Roses: The Soldiers' Experience* (Stroud, Tempus, 2006)

Gregory, P., Jones, M., and Baldwin, D., *The Women of the Cousins' War*

(London, Simon & Schuster, 2011)

Griffiths, Ralph A., *The Reign of King Henry VI* (Stroud, Sutton Publishing, 1998)

Grummitt, David, *The Calais Garrison, War and Military Service in England, 1436–1558* (Woodbridge, Boydell & Brewer, 2008)

Hammond, P.W., and Sutton, Anne F., *Richard III: The Road to Bosworth Field* (London, Constable, 1985)

Harvey, N.L., *Elizabeth of York: Tudor Queen* (London, Arthur Barker, 1973)

Haswell, Jock, *The Ardent Queen: Margaret of Anjou and the Lancastrian Heritage* (London, Peter Davies, 1976)

Hicks, Michael, *False, Fleeting, Perjur'd Clarence: George, Duke of Clarence, 1449–78* (Stroud, Sutton, 1980)

Hicks, Michael, *Warwick the Kingmaker* (London, Blackwell Publishing, 1998)

Hicks, Michael, *Richard III* (Stroud, Tempus, 2003)

Hicks, Michael, *Anne Neville: Queen to Richard III* (Stroud, Tempus, 2007)

Hicks, Michael, *The Prince in the Tower: The Short Life & Mysterious Disappearance of Edward V* (Stroud, Tempus, 2007)

Hipshon, David, *Richard III and the Death of Chivalry* (Stroud, The History Press, 2009)

Hughes, Jonathan, *Arthurian Myths and Alchemy: The Kingship of Edward IV* (Stroud, Sutton Publishing, 2002)

Hutchinson, Robert, *House of Treason: The Rise and Fall of a Tudor Dynasty* (London, Weidenfeld & Nicolson, 2009)

Jones, Michael K., and Underwood, Malcolm G., *The King's Mother: Lady Margaret Beaufort, Countess of Richmond and Derby* (Cambridge, Cambridge University Press, 1992)

Jones, Michael, K., *Bosworth 1485: Psychology of a Battle* (Stroud, The History Press, 2002)

Karras, Ruth Mazo, *Sexuality in Medieval Europe: Doing unto Others* (New York, Routledge, 2005)

Kendall, Paul Murray, *Richard the Third* (New York, Norton, 1955)

Laynesmith, J.L., *The Last Medieval Queens: English Queenship 1445–1503* (Oxford, Oxford University Press, 2004)

Lewis, Katherine J., Menuge, Noel James, Phillips, Kim M. (eds), *Young Medieval Women* (Basingstoke, Palgrave Macmillan) 1999

MacGibbon, David, *Elizabeth Woodville (1437–1492): Her Life and Times* (London, Arthur Barker, 1938)

Mancini, D., Cato, A., translated by Armstrong, C.A.J., *The Usurpation of Richard the Third: Dominicus Mancinus Ad Angelum Catonem De Occupatione Regni Anglie per Riccardum Tercium Libellus* (Oxford, Clarendon Press, 1969)

Markham, Clements R., 'Richard III: A Doubtful Verdict Reviewed', *English Historical Review*, VI (1891)

Maurer, Helen E., *Margaret of Anjou: Queenship and Power in Late Medieval England* (Woodbridge: The Boydell Press, 2003)

Mortimer, Ian, *The Time Traveller's Guide to Medieval England* (London, Vintage, 2009)

Neillands, Robin, *The Wars of the Roses* (London, Cassell, 1992)

Phillips, Kim M., *Medieval Maidens: Young Women and Gender in England, 1270–1540* (Manchester, Manchester University Press, 2003)

Plowden, Alison, *The House of Tudor* (New York, Weidenfeld & Nicolson, 1976)

Pollard, A.J., *Richard III and the Princes in the Tower* (Stroud, Sutton Publishing, 2002)

Prestwich, Michael, *Plantagenet England 1225–1360* (Oxford, Clarendon Press, 2005)

Reed, C., *The Tudors: Personalities & Practical Politics in 16th Century England* (Oxford, Oxford University Press, 1936)

Ross, Charles Derek, *Edward IV* (London, Eyre Methuen, 1974)

Ross, Charles Derek, *Richard III* (London, Eyre Methuen, 1981)

Royle, Trevor, *The Road to Bosworth Field: A New History of the Wars of the Roses* (London, Little Brown. 2009)

Rubin, Miri, *The Hollow Crown: A History of Britain in the Late Middle Ages* (London, Allen Lane, 2005)

St Aubyn, Giles, *The Year of Three Kings: 1483* (London, Collins, 1983)

Seward, Desmond, *Richard III: England's Black Legend* (London, Country Life Books, 1983)

Seward, Desmond, *The Last White Rose* (London, Constable, 2010)

Simon, Linda, *Of Virtue Rare: Margaret Beaufort: Matriarch of the House of Tudor* (Boston, Houghton Mifflin Company, 1982)

Storey, R.L., *The End of the House of Lancaster* (Stroud, Sutton Publishing, 1999)

Vergil, Polydore, and Ellis, Henry, *Three Books of Polydore Vergil's English History: Comprising the Reigns of Henry VI, Edward IV and Richard III* (Kessinger Publishing Legacy Reprint, 1971)

Ward, Jennifer, *Women in Medieval Europe 1200–1500* (Essex, Pearson Education, 2002)

Weinberg, S. Carole, 'Caxton, Anthony Woodville and the Prologue to the "Morte D'Arthur"', *Studies in Philology*, 102: no 1 (2005), 45–65

Weir, Alison, *The Princes in the Tower* (London, Bodley Head, 1992)

Weir, Alison, *Lancaster and York: The Wars of the Roses* (London, Cape, 1995)

Willamson, Audrey, *The Mystery of the Princes* (Stroud, Sutton Publishing, 1978)

Wilson, Derek, *The Plantagenets: The Kings That Made Britain* (London, Quercus, 2011)

Wolffe, Bertram, *Henry VI* (London, Eyre Methuen, 1981)

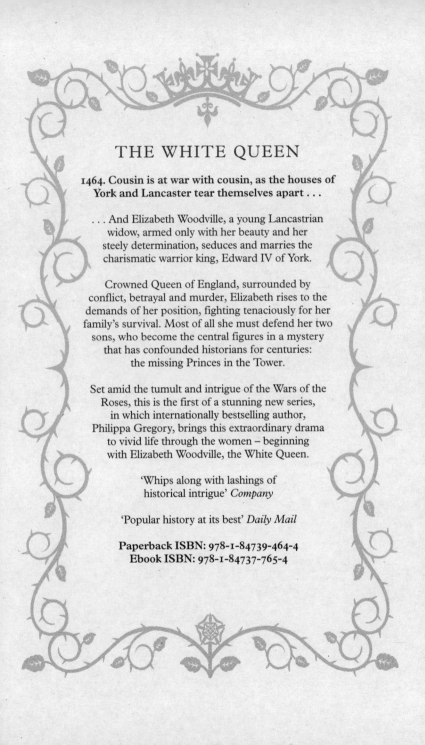

THE WHITE QUEEN

1464. Cousin is at war with cousin, as the houses of York and Lancaster tear themselves apart . . .

. . . And Elizabeth Woodville, a young Lancastrian widow, armed only with her beauty and her steely determination, seduces and marries the charismatic warrior king, Edward IV of York.

Crowned Queen of England, surrounded by conflict, betrayal and murder, Elizabeth rises to the demands of her position, fighting tenaciously for her family's survival. Most of all she must defend her two sons, who become the central figures in a mystery that has confounded historians for centuries: the missing Princes in the Tower.

Set amid the tumult and intrigue of the Wars of the Roses, this is the first of a stunning new series, in which internationally bestselling author, Philippa Gregory, brings this extraordinary drama to vivid life through the women – beginning with Elizabeth Woodville, the White Queen.

'Whips along with lashings of historical intrigue' *Company*

'Popular history at its best' *Daily Mail*

Paperback ISBN: 978-1-84739-464-4
Ebook ISBN: 978-1-84737-765-4

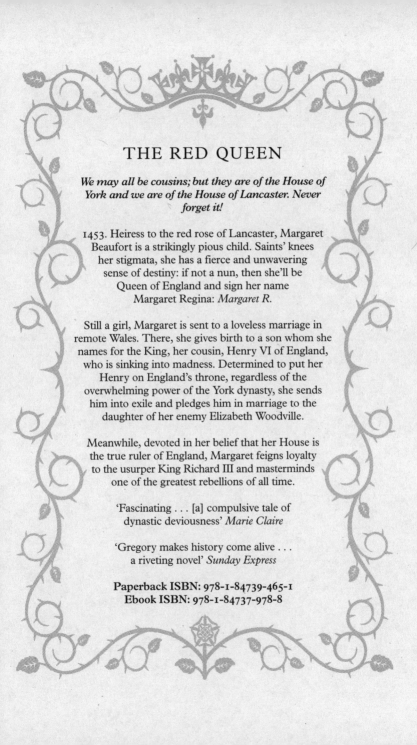

THE RED QUEEN

We may all be cousins; but they are of the House of York and we are of the House of Lancaster. Never forget it!

1453. Heiress to the red rose of Lancaster, Margaret Beaufort is a strikingly pious child. Saints' knees her stigmata, she has a fierce and unwavering sense of destiny: if not a nun, then she'll be Queen of England and sign her name Margaret Regina: *Margaret R.*

Still a girl, Margaret is sent to a loveless marriage in remote Wales. There, she gives birth to a son whom she names for the King, her cousin, Henry VI of England, who is sinking into madness. Determined to put her Henry on England's throne, regardless of the overwhelming power of the York dynasty, she sends him into exile and pledges him in marriage to the daughter of her enemy Elizabeth Woodville.

Meanwhile, devoted in her belief that her House is the true ruler of England, Margaret feigns loyalty to the usurper King Richard III and masterminds one of the greatest rebellions of all time.

'Fascinating . . . [a] compulsive tale of dynastic deviousness' *Marie Claire*

'Gregory makes history come alive . . . a riveting novel' *Sunday Express*

Paperback ISBN: 978-1-84739-465-1
Ebook ISBN: 978-1-84737-978-8

THE LADY OF THE RIVERS

*'This is a man's world, Jacquetta, and some women
cannot march to the beat of a man's drum.
Do you understand?'*

1435. Rouen. Jacquetta Luxembourg is left a wealthy
young widow when her husband, the Duke of Bedford,
dies. Her only friend in the great household is Richard
Woodville, the Duke's squire, and it is not long before
the two become lovers and marry in secret.

The Woodvilles return to England and to the Lancaster
court, where Jacquetta becomes close friends with young
King Henry VI's new queen. But Jacquetta can sense the
growing threat from the people of England, and the danger
of royal rivals. The king slides into a mysterious sleep;
Margaret, his queen, turns to untrustworthy favourites for
help; and Richard, Duke of York, threatens to overturn the
whole kingdom for his rival dynasty, the House of York.

Jacquetta fights for her king, her queen, and for her
daughter Elizabeth Woodville, for whom she senses an
extraordinary and unexpected future. A sweeping, powerful
novel rich in passion and legend, *The Lady of the Rivers* tells
the story of the real-life mother to the White Queen.

'Popular historical fiction at its finest, immaculately
researched and superbly told; Kate Saunders, *The Times*

'Jacquetta is a memorable addition to the author's portrait
gallery of women who endeavoured to make history rather
than merely become its victims' *Sunday Times*

Paperback ISBN: 978-1-84739-466-8
Ebook ISBN: 978-0-85720-430-1

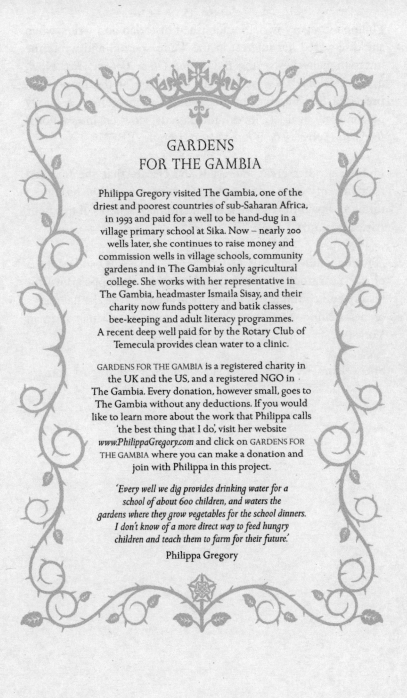

GARDENS
FOR THE GAMBIA

Philippa Gregory visited The Gambia, one of the
driest and poorest countries of sub-Saharan Africa,
in 1993 and paid for a well to be hand-dug in a
village primary school at Sika. Now – nearly 200
wells later, she continues to raise money and
commission wells in village schools, community
gardens and in The Gambia's only agricultural
college. She works with her representative in
The Gambia, headmaster Ismaila Sisay, and their
charity now funds pottery and batik classes,
bee-keeping and adult literacy programmes.
A recent deep well paid for by the Rotary Club of
Temecula provides clean water to a clinic.

GARDENS FOR THE GAMBIA is a registered charity in
the UK and the US, and a registered NGO in
The Gambia. Every donation, however small, goes to
The Gambia without any deductions. If you would
like to learn more about the work that Philippa calls
'the best thing that I do', visit her website
www.PhilippaGregory.com and click on GARDENS FOR
THE GAMBIA where you can make a donation and
join with Philippa in this project.

*'Every well we dig provides drinking water for a
school of about 600 children, and waters the
gardens where they grow vegetables for the school dinners.
I don't know of a more direct way to feed hungry
children and teach them to farm for their future.'*

Philippa Gregory

Philippa Gregory was an established historian and writer when she discovered her interest in the Tudor period and wrote the internationally bestselling novel *The Other Boleyn Girl*. Now, in *The Cousins' War* series, she is looking at the family that preceded the Tudors: the magnificent Plantagenets, a family of complex rivalries, loves and hatreds, now an international television series, *The White Queen*, from the BBC.

Philippa's other great interest is the charity that she founded nearly twenty years ago: Gardens for the Gambia. She has raised funds and paid for 180 wells for the primary schools of this poor African country.

A former student of Sussex University, and a PhD and Alumna of the Year 2009 of Edinburgh University, Philippa's love for history and commitment to historical accuracy are the hallmarks of her writing. She lives with her family on a small farm in Yorkshire.

She welcomes visitors to her site www.PhilippaGregory.com